THE LORD OF FREEDOM

BOOK ONE

The Lord of Freedom

Book One

The Bell Tolling

Amena Jamali

NEW DEGREE PRESS
COPYRIGHT © 2021 AMENA JAMALI

The Lord of Freedom
Book One - The Bell Tolling

ISBN

978-1-63730-646-8   *Paperback*
978-1-63730-729-8   *Kindle Ebook*
978-1-63730-920-9   *Digital Ebook*

The story of the Quest of Freedom's Ascension
is lovingly dedicated
to the Lord whose favor transforms dust into gold
and
to the Prince whose affection reveals the glory
of the ones he nurtures.

CONTENTS

AUTHOR'S NOTE

Dear Readers:

My thanks for opening this book and perusing its contents. Your consideration means much to me, for the publication of this story is itself an act of gratitude.

I first dreamt of Icilia when I was ten years old, scribbling in metallic green and blue gel pen of a girl who saved her land and her people. Two years later, while drowning in a crisis of depression, that first conception of the Quest Leader became my saving grace. And in the years since, my hero, my hope, and my guide in my own quest for meaning, faith, and virtue.

Though this story draws from that childhood spark, the inspiration for this particular book comes from something far more immediate: the upheaval of my life in March 2020. Like many of you, the declaration of the pandemic marked the moment all my plans for the future shattered. I was completing graduate work in Cybersecurity, a field esteemed for its necessity to every organization and its employment opportunities, yet I could not find work. The usual routines of my life, from prayer at the mosque to visiting friends and professors, had vanished. My uncle had passed away, yet I could not travel to offer my final respects. On top of everything, I still had to graduate. If only to maintain some level of self-worth.

Amid that sense of suffocation came an odd—and ill-timed—spark of inspiration. I waited a few days, consumed as I was by final projects, and then could not resist the lure of relief any longer. What came out of my pen that late March evening became the first chapters of *The Bell Tolling*. A character I had never known by more than name was born full-formed on the lined page: Lucian.

As you will find in the coming pages, that character is unlike any other. Lucian does not follow the customary archetypes of heroes—he does not refuse the call of his position or flee his destiny. Unlike the leaders we tend to respect within literature, he is comfortable with the reverence shown to him and does not hesitate in command. Moreover, when he is given absolute power, he is not corrupted. Not in the slightest degree.

Political power in literature, and in the world, is believed to be something that inevitably corrupts the person who wields it, no matter how virtuous initially. That belief inescapably leads to the conclusion that only those who do not seek such ascendancy are worthy of it. Yet, that conclusion ignores the reality that someone who does not want something may never fully accept and adjust to having it, if indeed that person is even capable of rendering an adequate performance.

Considering the importance of political rule in determining the fate of a people, while humility is always a desired virtue, there is not much margin for error. Thus, Lucian's story establishes a different narrative: political rule is a tool, and the factor that leads to corruption is inherent in a person's soul. What such power does is amplify what is already there. In Lucian's case, dominion only reveals the dazzling majesty of who he is. He holds absolute power, and he is absolutely good. Favored by the divine.

In the light of the magnificence of his character, I found myself challenged by who his enemy should be. With our flawed vision, we only understand light by looking into darkness. A villain who followed the usual custom of literature, resorting to villainy out of a misunderstanding or mistreatment or a passion gone wrong, would be no challenge for Lucian. So I came upon the Blood-soaked Sorcerer... who is absolutely evil. I must admit that writing him has terrified me like few other things have. I give you a warning, dear readers: his actions are neither for the faint of heart nor the young. Be wary.

The plot of this story also gives rise to several other themes. Chief among them is an exploration of feminism and the empowerment of women (a topic dear to my heart). Because of the violence inflicted by the Blood-soaked Sorcerer on the people of Icilia, such upliftment is absolutely necessary—and Lucian provides it. On large occasions and small, he teaches his companions and his people their value and reminds them of the value of free choice. In the model of my own father, he is a truly empowering male figure and a father to his people despite his youth. Though this story is a fantasy, its themes are not.

As you might have noticed, I have the musing style of a philosopher—indeed, this story is an expression of my own philosophy, political and otherwise. It is shaped by the fruit of whatever years I have of contemplation and study, both in religion and in university, and is in many ways, the summary document of the experiences of my life. The story is Lucian's, but the careful reader might also find me lurking in the shadows.

For shadows, of both good and evil, abound in Icilia. And though Lucian has unparalleled might and unmatched magic, his enemy has tricks and secrets of his own.

The reader who desires the mystic quality of epics and high fantasy with the perfume of spirituality is in for quite a tale. Alongside enjoyment, I pray you receive hope from Lucian's story as I did. Though his world convulses under the dark fist of the Blood-soaked Sorcerer, Lucian shows the path to true freedom.

What follows hereafter is translated from *a'Laètaqqe é a'Raah-é-Fazze*, the first volume of the annals compiled by the Archivist under the wishes of the Lady of Icilia and the guidance of the Guardian of Names.

With Gratitude,
Amena Jamali
September 2021

MAP

THE BEGINNING

In the beginning, nothing stirred. The divine cleansing of the land had left none who dared to move, for the memory of the purge haunted each breath. But with time, those who survived the purge believed themselves to be spared and then immune to any form of accounting. So, before many years had passed, the land devolved into chaos. Iniquity abounded, and no conscience whispered the truth. There was only darkness.

But then, amid the disorder, came Light. The Light entered the morass in the figure of a man, one who shone. Folding his sleeves up, he gathered a people, a few who were just a little less unruly than their neighbors. He brought them together, he healed them, he nurtured them. Dazzled by his light, they knelt at his feet and pledged to follow him and through him his Master the Almighty always.

The Shining Guide, as they revered him, pleased with this pledge, gave them civilization. He taught them the arts of government and writing, the sciences of farming and metal-working, and the sanctities of family and community. Eagerly they learned, and he smiled and called them Muthaarim, those who shone. He then showed them the treasure that blossomed in their country, the trees which bore athar, the most blessed substance ever known. He taught them new disciplines, the ways of benefiting from athar and forming their natural magic. Thus, the people flourished.

Yet then came the day on which the Shining Guide bid them farewell. He had completed his task, so his Master called him to another land, and he would answer. The Muthaarim, his heart's children, cried and begged for him to not leave them amid the chaos. The Shining Guide, seeing their misery, smiled and promised them that they would not be abandoned. For one day, the land would unite with them, and, whenever troubles overwhelmed them, saviors would come. And with that assurance, he departed.

Much time passed, and the Mutharrim lost the fervency of their devotion. Thus was the first trouble that broke upon them.

But the Shining Guide's promise was not hollow. Four generations after he had first chosen the Muthaarim to be his people, the Quest of Light arose and fulfilled his promise and prophecy. With the dedication and effort of their lifetimes, three of the Muthaarim, Aalia, Manara, and Naret, spread the blessings of civilization to all the land, which they named Icilia.

So connected, the Mutharrim found companionship with the Areteen, the Ezulal, the Nasimih, and the Sholanar. Seven mighty nations formed, and peace reigned. And the land revered the names of Lady Queen Aalia the Ideal of Light, Graced Queen Manara the Exemplar of Truth, and Honored King Naret the Exemplar of Love only beneath the name of the Shining Guide.

But, as is the way of things, prosperity did not last...

THE PROMISE

From the writings of Lady Queen Aalia the Ideal of Light, supreme ruler and Mother of Icilia:

Deliverance shall come when the skies grow dark
The Almighty does not abandon any to slavery
The contrast between the faithful and the faithless is stark
Only amid sorrow shall the people of Icilia learn the
    meaning of liberty

*(Prophesied on Eyyélab, the twentieth day of the tenth moon,
Thekharre, of the year 219 amid the Civilization of the Quests, C.Q.)*

Though my Lady Queen Aalia the Ideal of Light sent these words to every household, none understood them until the massacres of the Blood-soaked Sorcerer drowned every house in sorrow. Then, the people of Icilia, both in hiding and in captivity, prayed desperately that the prophecy of legend given by the Shining Guide, would not go unfulfilled.

The enclosed is the first volume of seven which present the story of the Quest of Freedom as drawn from their personal journals and memoranda.

So writes the Archivist.

PART 1

BONDED

From the writings of Lady Queen Aalia the Ideal of Light addressed to the second Quest Leader:

"The Quest Leader has power untold and unrivaled, power that reigns supreme over all that Icilia is and will be. But remember, my Heir, that your greatest power is in your companions. They are the Almighty's blessing unto you. Do all that you can to nurture and protect them, for only with them can you fulfill your purpose. Cherish them in every moment with all your heart."

FIRST READ BY LORD LUCIAN AJ-SHEHATHAR

AT THE AGE OF SEVEN

CHAPTER 1

CIRCLING ENDLESSLY

Perspective: Malika
Date: Eyyéqan, the ninth day of the fifth moon, Marberre, of the year 499, C.Q.

Gratitude to the Almighty. I dared to breathe again as the soldier turned back to his comrades, dismissing the shuffle of a pebble on sand that had almost stolen my hard-earned freedom.

I waited a moment, then crept forward through the shadows cast by the last of the tents.

A few steps more... I chanted within my mind.

The soldiers' encampment stretched to the north and the south in a limitless ocean to rival the desert itself. Erected overnight, it was intended for a single goal: my recapture. For what else could explain the presence of a contingent of Ezulal soldiers, who required copious amounts of water to live, in the deserts of Zahacim? Routine patrols were composed of women and men of the Areteen; these Ezulal troops, once members of my own loyal forces, were here to torment me.

How many times I had been forced to watch the Blood-soaked Sorcerer overthrow their free will by pouring water mixed with black spells down their throats. How many times they had subsequently aided the Blood in committing unimaginable violence against me.

The memories brought caustic bile to my mouth, further searing my achingly dry throat. Sharpening the quintessentially Ezulal longing for water to an almost unbearable degree. Far greater, though, was the ever unquenched desire to care for my people.

If only I could free some of them...

But, after those many years of abuse, I could not be certain whether breaking their contrived loyalty was at all possible. And, if I chanced an attempt, and it failed, I would never have another... I needed to disappear. Until he next found me.

After nearly seven years in the desert, I had abandoned trying to understand how the Blood repeatedly calculated precisely the direction in which I would travel next and sent soldiers after me. He had never relented in his pursuit. I would never be rid of him, never escape this endless dash for survival.

Despite my thirst, tears welled in my eyes as I disappeared behind a pair of sand dunes. My memories were the grounds of nightmares...

I had been the Blood's most closely guarded prisoner, for I was his prize, the Heir to Koroma, the nation whose fall marked the death rattle of Icilia's resistance. He had stolen me from where I had knelt sobbing in the blood pooling around my parents' desecrated corpses. As he dragged me from the throne room, he had laughed at my pleas for pity and mercy. Though I was a child of only six years, all alone, my parents dead and my baby brother missing.

In the months that followed, he crushed every wisp of my spirit, suppressing my magic (whatever it had been), tearing away my dignity, and shattering my mind. There had been little at all left of me. And yet he continued to endlessly torment me, relishing in my pain for nine years. I had lost all thought of escape.

Somehow the thought returned to me when he casually mentioned that I was near the age of majority. Trapped for so many years in a nightmare, I had immediately known that he had designs on my womanhood, a torture he had delayed in inflicting so that he might better savor it.

Somehow, a fire ignited in my heart: I would not suffer this one torture, though I had not saved myself from so many others.

With that spark providing animation to my movements, I gathered strands of my hair, day after day. When I had enough strands, I used the dirt and grease from my own person to stick them together into a lock-pick. With much struggle, in quiet moments between patrols and his visits, I unlocked my manacles. With the heavy chains I overpowered the next guard, who had come with the trickle of sustenance that was the Blood's only attempt to stave off starvation, and crept out of the fortress.

My pale skin had been so filthy that the shadows easily concealed me. With hunger and pain weakening my every movement, my escape was the Almighty's blessing, and my survival thereafter even more so.

Stumbling over mountains and neglected fields, I had fled northwest at first, desperate to simply leave the Blood's capital territory behind, even if that meant never returning to my own nation. But, as his soldiers pursued me, I realized that the old border between Koroma and Bhalasa, though defunct because the Blood tyrannized all of Icilia, was too heavily guarded. Despite the vast distance and thick forests, I had a better chance of passing into Zahacim, the eastern border of which with Koroma had sparser patrols, if I was desperate enough to brave the desert. And I had been certainly so desperate.

I was still no less desperate seven years later.

How low the noble are brought, I thought grimly as I slipped down another dune toward an Areteen caravan. I was the last Heir to Koroma, raised from birth to rule with a pure, kind heart and all virtue, but the Blood had turned me into a thief and a fugitive. I had only a filched dagger, a poorly constructed bow, and a pair of dull arrows, and I had not been raised to hunt in Zahacim. To survive, I had to steal from people who had little more food and security than I did.

Since the Blood had a military presence with even tiny, settled caravans, I could not shelter in the same area for more than a few days at a time. Because a terrifying number of soldiers guarded the northern and western borders and no passage south out of Icilia existed, I could not leave Zahacim. So I circled endlessly.

I, Malika tej-Shehenkorom, was going to die on these dunes. My life, my promise, was wasted.

CHAPTER 2

EMPOWER THE BEATEN

Perspective: Crown Princess Malika tej-Shehenkorom, Heir-apparent to Koroma
Date: Eyyéfaz, the nineteenth day of the ninth moon, Alkharre, of the year 499 C.Q.

The harsh winds snuffed out the tiny fire and, with it, my heart.

I had toiled for hours to kindle that one lonely flame, and it had burnt the last of the bush stems I had collected in its desperate attempt to survive. Then, regardless of its efforts, it had died.

The parallel to my own desperate plight was uncanny.

Without that flame, there was no light to be had, for the waning moon overhead was shrouded in smog.

I shuddered and tried to draw my legs closer to my chest. I tightened my arms over my chest and buried my numb fingers in my armpits. I pressed further back into the sand of the dune. But nothing helped. Autumn had arrived on the blustery winds, and winter would soon follow.

A winter that I would not survive. I had managed to gather fewer provisions this year than in any of the seven previous. My clothes were nearly tatters, and my weapons were almost too blunt to cut. And I could not renew any of my supplies, for, as I had discovered during the summer, caravans across the desert were better patrolled than in years past.

I might have escaped the Blood's prisons, but this whole desert was a prison. That I could not escape.

Tears welled in my dulled eyes and rolled down the dry gray skin of my sunken cheeks. I tasted salt on my lips, but I could not muster the energy to lick them, much less to wipe my face. The wind nearly tore away the worn rag protecting my head, but I had not the strength to secure it. My breath stuttered in my choking throat, a suffocation inflicted with the sharpest of weapons—unalleviated despair.

I am beaten, I admitted to myself, as though the thought was something new. *And there is no one to care, save the Almighty.* I closed my eyes. *May at least my last moments have mercy.*

A bright light dazzled my vision, turning everything as white as sunlight.

Bemused, I quickly blinked open my eyes.

Before me was a pair of clasped hands, cream with a distinct silver glow like the moon, silhouetted against a dark midnight blue.

Anticipation overcame me, as though the moment I had always awaited had finally come.

I looked up.

An unthinking prayer of gratitude came to my lips.

For the face I beheld was... It seemed to hold all the beauty and grace that had ever filled the land. Smooth silvery cream skin curved into the harmonious angles and arches of high cheekbones, a firm and straight nose, full pale lips, gently sloping mustache, long golden lashes, and slanted brows. Locks of white-gold hair that gleamed like sunlight itself twisted into the perfect waves of his hair and spiraled into the thick curls of his beard. The jewel-like gold-flecked violet eyes that crowned his ethereally handsome face pierced my own.

His presence swirled over me like he was a cloud of rain and I the parched earth. Authority wreathed him, though it was like no authority I had ever felt: his aura commanded absolute obedience, yet it did so in a tender, cajoling manner, like a mother coaxing her child toward something good and wholesome. Alongside that power, he emanated a sense of fulfilled yearning, of wonder and possibility. He glowed with his own light even as moonlight pierced the parting clouds and sheathed him in a column of incandescence.

My chest expanded with the first free breath I had ever taken.

A conviction swept over my heart, inundating the very depths of my soul. An unfamiliar warmth flared fathoms beneath layers of scars.

I fell forward onto my knees, and, without pause or hesitation, I raised my hands to him, palms up and touching, in the symbol of allegiance.

For, whoever he was, he merited my devotion. He was radiant with a light that had the perfume of the divine.

My gesture of fealty seemed to please him, for he smiled. The expression, framing his lips and mustache with deep creases, turned his already beautiful face into perhaps the closest approximation to an image of ideal, eternal goodness that Icilia would ever see. His smile lit up the black night like the brightest of lanterns.

Then he spoke, in a baritone voice so perfectly melodious that it rivaled the sounds of rain and rivers, "May the Almighty bless you, Malika."

I gasped in shock at this shining man's knowledge of my lowly name.

"I am Lord Lucian the Ideal of Freedom, Heir to the Quest of Light and supreme ruler of Icilia. And I am blessed to meet you, Crown Princess Malika tej-Shehenkorom."

My mind whirled, barely able to understand his words. He knew my name, the name that everyone had forgotten… but what would ordinarily be shocking was eclipsed by—*I am in the presence of the Quest Leader! The prophesied savior of Icilia! Our highest liege! And, and, he knows my name! He is my one chance at redeeming myself… If he would have me, I would do anything for him.*

I opened my mouth to beg for a chance to serve him.

No sound left my lips.

I winced, and if I had not been transfixed, I would have looked away in shame. I was no one's image of a worthy vassal, much less his.

Those vivid violet eyes flashed with something odd as my Lord the Quest Leader chuckled softly. "I know, Malika. Do not worry; I am a mindlinker, and, if you would allow, I can listen to you speak without need of a voice."

My breath rushed from my lips as I stared up at him. The staring was starting to border on uncouth, but I could not help it. To speak again… after over a decade of voicelessness… 'Please,' I attempted to mouth.

My Lord's violet eyes actually glowed brighter as a second feeling, one of deep sympathy, underlay the sense of freedom in his aura. Then he bent forward and lightly kissed my forehead.

The soft touch lasted no more than a second, but it was the first touch in sixteen years that did not pain me. Indeed, alongside the cool touch of his magic, like ice water on a dry throat, it brought me a kind of contentment that I had never imagined I could merit. I treasured it. I wanted another.

My Lord straightened and said, smiling that dazzling smile again, *Speak, Malika, as your heart wishes.*

I drew in a shaky breath. *My Lord...* I whispered the first words that I had spoken since the Blood had stolen my voice. As my Lord had promised, his magic allowed me to speak directly from my mind to his. Tears welled in my eyes, but these were cool, happy ones. *Thank you.* My throat bobbed as I swallowed. *How may I serve you?* A distant corner of my mind marveled at the sound of my voice, no longer shrill as it had been as a child, when I had last heard it, but instead deep and smooth, almost musical. Like his.

His smile became brighter, if that were possible. *Malika... your words are the sweetest that have ever been spoken to me. I cannot tell you in any short period of time of how happy I am... Malika tej-Shehenkorom, you are my Second-in-command, my champion, my support, my voice and hands, my sister, my heart. I have traveled far in search of you.*

My mouth dropped open in star-struck wonder. What he was saying about me was...

The few memories I had of a life before endless survival adamantly stated that the Quest Leader was Icilia's closest link to the divine. His companions, his highest vassals and deputies, would join his sacred purpose.

And he was offering me the place of Second at his side? To go from Heir to only one nation to Second of the supreme ruler... I would fail in that role just as disastrously as I had in my birthright.

Doubt curdled my wonder as I whispered, though I did not want to say it, *My Lord... is this really true?* My cheeks heated in shame. *I have nothing to offer you. My throne is gone, my soldiers are murdered, scattered, or stolen, and my magic is buried far too deeply for me to touch. I cannot even speak. I-I do not deserve even a glimpse of you.* I thought that would be the end of his presence and mourned his leaving.

But, contrary to all my fears, he responded firmly, *I am not mistaken, my Second. Neither are my dreams lies, nor is the Almighty's sign tainted by falsity. Though our enemy sought to destroy you, he could not rob you of your foretold ascension.* He smiled reassuringly. *Have faith, and see beyond your circumstances. You are great, and you are indeed worthy. You have the Almighty's blessing and favor.*

The conviction in his words, coupled with how confidently he had taken the Almighty's name, somehow soothed my fears. Hope sparked in my heart, even as tears slid down my cheeks.

He is my only chance, I thought within my own mind, outside of the link. *If I refuse him, I have nothing.* My heart quailed at the thought of returning to my cold, empty life. *Now that I have seen him, I could not live without him. And with him, my life and purpose would not be wasted... May he have mercy upon me.*

My own conviction solidifying, I dipped my head and lifted my hands again toward him. Seamlessly, with but an indication of my will, his magic let me say, *Thank you, my Lord, for believing in me when I am nothing.*

You have never been nothing, he stated firmly. Then he smiled again, his face softening. *Let me teach you the words of the pledge.*

Unable to express what his words and his belief meant to me, I hoped that he could read the gratitude in my eyes.

I had never dreamt I could have this chance of redemption, but, now that I had it, I would not squander it, like I had everything else.

My Lord smiled down at me and recited several sentences, which he told me were the hallowed words that my Lady Queen Aalia the Ideal of Light had designed for her own Second.

Though I had not asked, indeed not wondered, he clarified that, by offering this pledge, I would forfeit my surname and previous rank of crown princess. The Quests' laws ordained that, since the Quests sat above the monarchs, no Potentate could also be heir to a throne. Choosing Lucian's side would void my birthright.

It was a sacrifice I was glad to make. I understood the wisdom of the law, yes, but far more important was the sense that choosing Lucian's name and title was being born anew, free of the Blood's taint. And if surrendering my royal name and title was the offering necessary to cement my place at Lucian's side, I was all the more eager for it.

Seeming pleased, Lucian completed his description of the sacred ritual.

When I had memorized the words and the steps, I murmured, *I am ready, my Lord.* Sitting straight like the princess I had once been, I lowered my hands and placed them on my knees. Holding my breath in anticipation, I waited for him to begin.

A dazzling smile, bright like sunlight, caressed my Lord's lips. His person began to glow, radiating such overwhelming waves of wonder and authority that I could soar on the wind simply from drinking in his presence.

Then he spoke, "In the name of the Almighty and the Shining Guide sent unto us, I am Lord Lucian the Ideal of

Freedom, Leader of the Quest of Freedom, Heir to the Quest of Light, and supreme ruler of Icilia. My thoughts, my words, and my acts are dedicated to the love and glory of the Almighty and intended for the happiness and betterment of Icilia. In the light of your faith, swear your loyalty to me and speak the truth of your heart."

Those words were no ordinary words... Both by the virtue of the voice that intoned them and by their own, those words reverberated like the sound of a great bell across the whole of Icilia, invoking something far beyond my understanding...

The air thrummed with a powerful energy.

My Lord held out his hands, palms facing downward, fingers slightly spread, and thumbs lightly touching, toward me.

Knowing my cue, I spoke through the only medium I had, *By the Light of the Almighty and the Shining Guide sent unto us, I promise my love and swear my allegiance to you, my Lord Lucian the Ideal of Freedom. I will uphold your commands and proffer my best service to you on every day of my life. I will follow your example and be your champion in your every wish. With your happiness shall I breathe, with your blessing shall I speak, with your authority shall I act. May all that I am please the Almighty.*

I held out my hands, palms facing upward, fingers tightly pressed together, and small fingers and sides of my palms touching, toward him.

His face shining, my Lord placed his hands on mine—his soul touched mine, so profound was the connection...

He spoke, "For freedom by the Almighty, I accept your allegiance and promise my love and my heart to you in return. May the Almighty bless you, Graced Malika the Exemplar of Wisdom, Second of the Quest of Freedom. May our partnership remain forever indivisible under the Almighty's favor. And may the Almighty be pleased with all that we are. Praised be the Almighty."

A burst of energy passed from him to me... and I felt like a part of him. My connection to him was one that would never fade, never disappear, never ebb, and it brought me a glimpse into the vastness of who he was. He was goodness incarnate, his nature as blessedly divine as it was mortal incé, his very self the clean, clear breath of one beyond the trap of vice... the awesome power of his magic, absolute authority, empathy entire, and utter holiness... the depth and steadfastness of his conviction and purpose. My knowledge of him extended to his heart and soul, and I knew, in a flash of epiphany, that he was, in essence, my Lady Queen Aalia the Ideal of Light reborn.

As I peered into the profoundness of his being, the experience left its mark upon me: my own heart and soul changed, somehow, substantially shifting and stretching for my new identity. Warmth filled my numbed heart, clarity sharpened my dulled mind, and energy vibrated throughout my enervated body. And, at the core of who I was, there was... an expansion, a stirring in a place long forgotten.

Love sparked as my eyes gazed into his.

I gasped, my spine arching, as the connection settled in place. In its wake, my heartbeat pulsed with an echo—his heartbeat. As our hearts became synced, I knew, with a certainty unlike any, that he was my brother and I his sister. He would be my peace and my hope if only I would not impede myself.

I had a family again.

An adoring smile quirked his lips as the intensity of the moment subsided. He knelt in the sand.

Then, tugging me forward, he drew me into the first embrace I had ever received since my mother had hugged me on the day on which Koroma fell. Relishing his touch, I melted into his arms even as I cringed at the thought of his unsullied clothes touching my filthy person.

My Lord, your beautiful clothes... the objection spilled from an unwilling mind.

Lucian, he corrected, evoking another star-struck stare. *And I will not lose this moment for anything, least of all dirt.*

I squirmed as his face touched my greasy and undoubtedly foul-smelling hair. But then I relaxed, unable to resist the contentment and warmth radiating from his person, and rested my head on his shoulder.

I savored his comfort.

When he drew back, I almost did not let him go. But I wanted to see his eyes, which twinkled as he said, *I am overjoyed to have met you.*

My lips curved up into my first smile in sixteen years. A faint blush heated my cheeks as I replied, *I am, too. I-I did not think that I would ever have a purpose again, or anyone to care for me.*

His smile softened, though his eyes flashed with a different emotion. *You have always had this purpose. You were born for the Quest just as much I was.* He leaned closer to me and pressed another brotherly kiss to my forehead.

I closed my eyes and sighed contentedly. He was cradling me in his arms, and I did not ever want to leave...

What are your plans for your next movement? he asked.

I suppressed a wince as the words reminded me that eventually I would have to stand. But I kept my eyes on his, not wanting to look away for as long as I still had with him, while I answered, *I was intending to go further west. His armies still pursue me.* I could not say the name, but he seemed to understand.

My Lord—no, *Lucian*, for he had offered me his name, and refusing would sound ungrateful—tilted his head in thought. *I would like to travel to the nearest oasis first, which is a few hours' walk toward the northwest. But then I wish to journey north, past the banks of the Anharat and into Bhalasa. If my calculation is correct, I will meet my second companion two days' walk to the north of the river and my third and fourth companions three and seven days' walk to the northwest of that location. Will you come with me?*

Yes, of course, I quickly answered as a fear that I had not even acknowledged gave way to eagerness. *I have long wanted to leave Zahacim, and I would go anywhere with you regardless.* I remembered something he had said… Blinking, I asked, *Other companions?* I immediately blushed. *Yes, of course you have others.* Obviously his attention would not be mine alone… I glanced at him with interest. *Three others?*

He chuckled, the sound warm and delightful. *I am the first Quest Leader to have four. One of the Sholanar from southwestern Bhalasa, one of the Areteen from Zahacim, and one of the Nasimih from Khuduren. You of the Ezulal from Koroma, and me, representing in a way the Mutharrim, complete the representation of the kinds.*

What are their names? I breathed. If what remained of my memories from before were accurate… these three people would become my family!

A longing and wistfulness tinted his smile that, oddly enough, did not provoke my jealousy. *Elian, Arista, and Kyros*, he murmured, sounding as though he already loved them, though he had not met them.

Yet I, too, was feeling the first inkling of connection. *I would be surprised, but it now feels natural to want to meet them*, I whispered, amazed and delighted.

They will be yours. Of course it does, he said simply. Leaning back, he turned slightly and swung a pack (half as tall as he was) over his shoulder. *Let us eat. You deserve a feast, such as I can provide, and I am famished.*

With those words, delivered as though the thought of sharing food was actually commonplace, he rummaged in his pack and removed some strips of salted meat, a few pieces of bread, and two small red fruit from several cloth packages. He assembled a sandwich, all while I sat halfway on his lap, and offered it to me along with one of the fruit and an ornately carved flask.

In celebration of your ascension, he said. Observing a tradition that I had long forgotten, he intoned a quick prayer of thanks to the Almighty for the food and the peace in which we ate it.

Trying to suppress another shameful blush, I received the food. Yet all I could do was stare at it, unwilling to eat despite the eviscerating pain in my belly, until he gave me an encouraging smile. With his reassurance, I placed the fruit in my mouth and broke the red surface with my teeth.

The tender, juicy flesh was sweeter than my faint memory of sugar. It tasted like sunshine, almost reminding me of him.

My Lord smiled and ate the other fruit. He nodded to the flask and the sandwich.

I smiled myself at the lingering taste. Then hesitated. *I do not want to eat your provisions and drink your water.*

My Lord—*Lucian*, I needed to remember—bit into his own sandwich, elegant even in that. *It is my duty and honor to arrange a feast for you. As for the provisions, remember that we are two hunters now. But most importantly, Malika, you have not eaten, and you are thirsty.*

Still I hesitated, wondering how he had known about my thirst and hunger. But, at a pointed look from him, I drank and ate. I tried to savor the bread and the meat, better than anything I had tasted in years, but it was too quickly devoured, a dream of wondrous relief amid my starvation. My pleasantly full belly, neither achingly empty nor uncomfortably distended (the portion he had given was the exact size I could accept), remained, however, to attest to the wonder. The water I gulped from his flask wet the dried crevices of my throat such that I could swallow without pain.

Contented, my eyes fluttered closed as soon as the sandwich had disappeared. Lucian chuckled and cocooned me in smooth and silky blankets that kept the sand from prickling against my skin and the chill from stabbing it. He lay down beside me and brushed my head, the motion soothing.

For the first time in years, I fell asleep easily. And when the colder winds of the deep night woke me, I had someone whose side I could cuddle for comfort and warmth—instead of refusing me, Lucian threaded his arm beneath my head and stroked my cheek.

For the first time in years, I had no nightmares.

CHAPTER 3

REDEEM THE DISGRACED

Perspective: Graced Malika the Exemplar of Wisdom
Date: Eyyéfaz, the nineteenth day of the ninth moon, Alkharre,
of the year 499 C.Q.

Reveling in the cool taste of the water, I dipped my flask into the pool for another filling and whispered shyly, *Thank you, Lucian.* How marvelous it was to speak and know that someone listened! How wonderful to savor as much water as I needed without the fear of the flask being torn from my fingertips.

A compassionate smile on his lips, Lucian responded, *For your happiness, Malika... Would you wish to bathe? I would stand guard for you.*

I almost choked on the precious mouthful of water and turned to stare at him.

No matter the years that had passed since I had been stolen from my home, I was one of the Ezulal. I dearly loved water, from its taste to its sparkles under the sun, to the feel of it enveloping me. Yet, alone as I was—as I had been—in the desert,

I could not chance a bath, for soldiers could come upon me at any time. As I had experienced once in my first days. Even years later, their grotesque leers still burned my bare skin...

Out of wariness and precaution, I had since denied myself more than cursory washes. Layer upon layer of dirt blanketed my skin, sand and filth and blood... stripping away more of my worth, branding my soul with dishonor and effacing any claim I had to the ranks of the civilized.

Lucian was offering to restore my dignity as incé, as a mortal child of Icilia. As he had with my voice.

Please, I whispered.

Though sorrow gleamed in his eyes, Lucian smiled gently as he removed a large bundle of cloth and a small wrapped block from his large pack. Then, placing his back to the oasis, he said, *As you bathe, allow me to wash your outer garments and provide you with soap.*

Thank you, I whispered again, though the words seemed inadequate to express the depth of my gratitude.

Of course, Sister, he replied, holding a square cake of soap over his shoulder.

How sweet it smelled... like the soaps my mother would select for my baths...

Face flushed by my delay, I undressed and stepped into the blue pool, concealed from the sand by a ring of palm trees. I relished the soft waves even as I timidly reached for the soap.

Though I normally struggled to withstand the cold, the chill of this water, cool and clean, refreshed my senses. The well of magic that comprised the characteristics of my kind, the Ezulal, rippled to life and soothed away some of the weakness and despair that plagued my limbs.

Reveling in the rare luxury and the new strength, I soaked in the feel of the water, warming slightly as the sun dipped behind the smog toward the western horizon. Rocked by the swells, my eyes drifted closed, lulled to sleep, confident in the power of the one who protected me...

The cool of the water turned into an icy cold.

Startling awake, I splashed upright and looked for Lucian—who leaned back on his palms as he gazed up at the darkening smog overhead. He would have seemed to be at his leisure if not for the alert posture of his head. A posture he had maintained for hours.

L-Lucian, I stammered, *I-I am sorry.*

There is no cause for apology, Malika, he said lightly. *The journey ahead will be difficult, and you needed this time.*

Despite his understanding, my cheeks flushed again. He had been kind to me from the very moment I had woken, preparing my breakfast and letting me cling to his arm, caring for me in countless tiny ways. Instead of leaving me to flounder or walk in silence, he conversed with me despite my lack of education. Indeed, as my discomfort vanished in his presence, he indulged my long-buried questions about the sciences, the history of Icilia, magic, and politics. In everything, he treated me as though I were worthy of respect.

Yet this leisure he had granted me was more unbelievable than anything else.

Taking it was still a mistake.

How could I make the Liege of Icilia wait for me! I fretted to myself as I leaned forward to retrieve my dried rags.

Malika, Lucian said, calling my attention back to his shining face, *I have something for you.* He gestured to a pile of dark blue fabric that lay to his right. *I brought a set of robes similar to mine for you. They will provide you with more warmth... Wear them if you so choose.* Compassion rang in his voice.

Despite my anxiety, I could not help but smile. After so many years deprived of another's care, how the Almighty had blessed me with his attention...

Gladly I accepted the clothes and spread them out over the grass. Murmuring words of gratitude, I marveled over the gift—appreciation which it indeed deserved, for the garments were cut from the same soft, silky, yet thick and durable fabric as his own. I had forgotten the name of the cloth, but certainly it was rare, the dress of monarchs. And moreover, the color and style were the same as his: midnight blue robes, well chosen for travel at night. When I wore them, I would look like him.

How blessed I was! He was the prophecy of legend in incé form, the true heir to Icilia herself, yet he cared for me. Sixteen years had passed since anyone had cared for me, since even I had cared for myself... I could barely comprehend that he was doing so.

Still smiling, I quickly dressed and twisted to examine myself.

Delicately embroidered in pale blue thread, the tunic folded smoothly into the waistband of the trousers, the long sleeves of one reaching my wrists and the other my ankles. The loose folds of the coat fell to my knees, rippling out like a cape, while the slit in the middle left the material draped open over my front. Ties lined that slit above the waist, which I had fastened for additional warmth. Openings for numerous thin and thick pockets dotted the sides of all three garments (I wondered what weapons Lucian kept in his). A weapons belt, gloves, and boots, so deeply blue as to be nearly black, accompanied the ensemble. As did a cap to cover my head and a ribbon to tie back my hair. And undergarments and socks. Everything was well tailored to the six feet of my height, though loose around my current figure. So clearly intended for me.

Warm, soft, and resplendent with his protection—had I ever worn better clothes?

Almost humming with delight, I folded my old rags and tucked them into the tiny sack in which I carried my supplies.

Then, whispering I was dressed, I waited for Lucian to turn.

He faced me with a smile ready on his lips.

His eyes widened. His face blanched. And, for a moment, he seemed completely and utterly speechless.

Unable to read the odd emotion in his eyes, I shifted uneasily and dropped my gaze to the soothing water.

Out of the clear water peered a face I did not recognize, yet was eerily familiar...

Looking closer, I startled. For the face was my own: though I had before resembled a filthy skeleton, the elegant cut of the robes transformed my person into an image of strength, even majesty. The rich color flattered the angular lines of my face and the blueness of my eyes. It complemented the gleaming red-gold of my newly washed and untangled braid. With the dark offset, my hair gleamed like honey and strawberries... and the gold, I now realized, bore some similarity to the gold shade of Lucian's own hair.

My cheeks warm, I glanced up at Lucian, who seemed to have recovered from whatever had shocked him. That strange emotion, which could not possibly have been fright, had faded into an untroubled serenity, profound yet enigmatic. But my incipient questions vanished as he smiled gently, affectionately, and commented lightly, *How beautiful you are, Malika.*

The praise was offered in a brotherly manner, but it was the first compliment that I could ever remember receiving. The warm sincerity of it jolted a spark of animation into the ruins of my confidence even as it further heated my face.

I answered bashfully, *You are beautiful, too.* And truly he was, though I felt only the dismissive appreciation that a sister had for her brother's handsome appearance. There was not even the faintest hint of romance, for he was truly and utterly my brother, though we did not share parentage or heritage.

Lucian laughed. *How would I otherwise inspire anyone?* The silver glow of his face sparkled but did not intensify (as it would in his kind's equivalent to an Ezulal blush). Though perhaps another would have said those words with arrogance, only a playful, casual humility tinged his voice.

I actually laughed a little, for the first time in sixteen years, and could not help but add, *You look like sunlight.* The white-gold of his hair and the silver-cream of his skin created that effect, and his natural majesty and aura of authority only emphasized it.

Lucian cupped his hand over his heart, his cheeks only now silvering. Then stated, smoothly changing the subject, *I have a gift to offer you.*

Another gift? I did not deserve even these robes.

Indeed, Malika, he answered, chuckling, *one of the five symbols of your new office, the one you might like most. Would you wish to see it?*

Though I dreaded receiving another gift, I dipped my head and answered, *As you wish.*

Lucian chuckled again as he held out his hand. *You do not need to observe the rules of etiquette with me, Malika. I taught you the Quest's etiquette earlier so that you would know what deference to expect from others, not what to give me.*

Easily accepting his touch, I mumbled, eyes on my knees, too diffident to meet his gaze, *I asked to learn it for you.* What remained of my childhood memories clearly illuminated the importance of etiquette and protocol in establishing and reinforcing order, discipline, and authority. As his Second, as well as a former princess, I most of all needed to maintain the dignity of his office. I could only hope that my attempts to do so would not end in miserable failure like everything else I did.

Lucian tugged me to my feet and revealed what his other hand had concealed behind his back.

A sword. Magnificent. Radiant.

About the length of my entire extended arm, the sword was shining silver steel. Dark wood wrapped in soft choc-olate-colored leather comprised the hilt. An elegant curve of gold formed the cross-guard. The pommel bore a deep green emerald set in gold and carved with an elegantly ornate flower-like crown, the etchings of which were painted silver. Even my untrained eyes could see how the blade, when I nudged it out of its sheath of dark blue metal, glittered with multiple sharp facets and edges, threaded with veins of green light. Runes in the sacred tongue Alimàzahre, which I had long since forgotten how to read, glimmered in gold down the length of the blade.

The gift was a symbol of office, yes, but he seemed to have chosen it just for me.

When I was a child, I whispered, transfixed, *I loved weap-ons. Few of my memories remain, but I do remember that. I had begged to be allowed to train...* Fumbling slightly, I wrapped the thick cords hanging from my belt around the upper portion of the sheath and knotted the ends (exactly as Lucian had secured his own sword). The blade fell perfectly against my leg, and I spun in a circle as I enjoyed its weight on my hips. *Thank you, Lucian!*

I am happy that you are so excited. Lucian nodded to the gift that was so much more than a possession to me. *That is no ordinary weapon: it was designed for you in accordance with the specifications given by my Grace Manara of Light. The flower-like crown is the insignia of the Quests; that symbol and the green of the emerald form my emblem. The sword is one of the marks of your position as my Second.*

Though he did not intend so, the knowledge about its special design ruined my excitement. The inclusion of this weapon as a symbol of office meant that I actually needed to know how to use it, to be able to demonstrate martial prowess. But I knew nothing.

My face burned with shame. I wanted to disappear.

But Lucian was waiting for my response, and I did not want to try his patience twice in one day. So I swallowed, the movement harsh on my throat, and admitted what I dearly wanted to omit: *Lucian, I do not know how to use it.*

One side of his mouth quirked upward. *Malika, my Sister,* he said softly, *do you truly think that I would choose you and then abandon you without the means to fulfill your duty?*

I stared, speechless again. Not voiceless now because of my curse but from the inability to express what he meant to me.

A ruler, as the Quest of Light had guided, was supposed to be a scion of civilization, a student of every art and science and a master of politics. Yet I had had little time to learn anything before Koroma's fall, and the years since had erased much of what I did study. Indeed I knew little more than the basics of survival, my grasp of even that flawed. My lack of education should have precluded ever regaining my birthright, much more becoming a Potentate of the Quest. I was a poor choice.

But Lucian... he seemed prepared to teach me what I lacked. Why would he ever make such an effort? Surely there were others who were far more learned! I was so unworthy.

Lucian raised a brow and stated, each word slow, measured, and firm, *Malika, knowledge can be gained by anyone. Your capacity for faith, love, and reason are the marks of your position. You are worthy because you were chosen.*

Twisting my fingers together, I tried to accept his words. But I doubted that I could. My scars ran to the core of my being.

Lucian sighed and cupped my cheek. *We will journey far together*, he proclaimed in the tone of a promise. Then he winked and added, *We start training with the sword this evening.* At the surprised delight on my face, he chuckled and kissed my forehead, before turning and beginning preparations for our supper.

As I watched him, I could not believe how blessed I was.

I had long ago given up any hope for a promise and a future. What about my utterly and shamefully unworthy self had possibly pleased the Almighty so much that I was given this second chance at life?

I was still reeling from the shock of his appearance and his declaration of my position behind him.

The road ahead would not be easy: Lucian was not here to rescue me and whisk me away to some hidden castle far from the Blood's reach. Rather his coming and my pledge meant that I would join him in freeing Icilia. I did not know how that would even be possible—how the Blood could possibly be dethroned and how I could contribute anything to that worthy effort.

But, somehow, the sunshine glowing on Lucian's sunlight hair and his easy laughter gave me hope I did not deserve yet had been given all the same. For only Lucian had the compassion and patience to empower one so beaten as me. And if he could care to uplift someone as worthless as me, then surely there could be salvation for Icilia.

My heart blazed with the love that I was meant to have for him.

CHAPTER 4

DRAGGING USELESSLY

Perspective: Elian
Date: Eyyéqan, the ninth day of the fifth moon, Marberre, of the year 499, C.Q.

My wings dragged uselessly behind me as I struggled up the steep incline. The mountain, like all the mountains of Bhalasa, was meant for a proper child of the Sholanar, not a defective reject like me, but, if I wanted to offer my respects to my late parents, I had to toil for it. Nothing was easy for me, for I deserved nothing, but my parents had a claim to my veneration. Thus, I climbed.

I crawled over the edge of the small, flat meadow at the top of the slope, halfway up the mountain, and collapsed. Thirteen years I had lived on my own, without working wings, yet I was still so weak, so useless.

Recollecting my breath, I shakily stood and tottered to the gravestones, simple gray granite slabs with only a line of inscription each and fell to my knees.

THE BELL TOLLING · 43

Tears immediately filled my eyes as the last time I had seen my parents rose to the forefront of my mind. As I was dragged away from their corpses, I had managed to take one last look over my shoulder. Then I had been pushed down the slope, tossed from the cliff I had just climbed.

Winded from the fall, my eight-year-old body fragile and racked with pain, I had lain at the base in shock for too long. By the time I had snuck up the cliff, the burial was over, my parents tossed unceremoniously into the holes dug for them, and the aerie residents had flown away. Leaving me alone, alone to somehow find and shape two gravestones, alone to grieve, and alone to survive.

I had never expected any better. My mother was of the Mutharrim, the kind associated with the glorious first Quest, the Mothers and Father of Icilia, the Quest of Light. But she had dishonored her kind, in the eyes of anyone who knew her, by marrying a brother of the Blood. The relationship might have been forgiven, for her at least, but she had been too clear about having fallen in love and trying to redeem her husband's reputation.

Indeed, she had been in love—requited love, for my father had genuinely loved her with all of himself, even if he fumbled with showing it. The purity of their love was clear in my early memories, as were the ways in which my father had changed for her, abandoning the cruelty of the Blood so that he could become a man worthy of her respect. And I, born of that love, had been dearly adored and cherished by my parents.

But they could not escape ridicule and hatred, not even with concealing spells and frequent relocation from place to place in Koroma and Bhalasa. They were banished from Asfiya, not welcome in Nademan, Etheqa, and Khuduren upon pain of death, and even treasonous Zahacim reviled them. For the twelve years of their marriage, they lived like fugitives and traitors. In the last four, after the Blood's seizure of Koroma, they could not leave Bhalasa but changed locations almost monthly within its borders. Magic and tactful moves were all that saved us from the aeries and the crown. Yet nothing could protect us when the Blood tired of his brother's waywardness and came for us. He had taken their lives and my wings. How I wished that he had taken my life also.

For the Blood was crafty and cruel in his torments. After completing his goal, my parents and I left lying in the bloody snow in front of our humble, temporary dwelling, he had summoned the local aerie residents. Then he had disappeared—and for a few minutes, I had thought help would come.

Yet the villagers, come in fear of the Blood, then and ever filled with disdainful indignation and outrage, had sneered at my pleas. They had carried my parents away, burying them only because the Almighty's laws forbid leaving a body unburied, and had beaten and tossed me away as I had attempted to follow. And in the years since, they had made my life a misery with torment after torment, insult after insult, abuse after abuse.

The health that I had once received from my parents' love was long lost. I survived, but my heart was in shards and my mind in tatters. My magic, healing and wizardry of the gale, although great in magnitude, struggled and lashed back at me whenever I attempted to truly practice with it according to my mother's teaching. My wings were cursed to never fly or even fold closed, so I could not practice the exercises with which my father had trained me. And most of all, each movement pained me; the shifting of each feather burned like searing fire against my skin. It would have been less painful if they had been cut from my back.

Living as I did amid such pain, death called to me more than life. I lived only because my faith in the Almighty burned in the dregs of my soul, and that faith dictated that my life was not mine to take.

A wind stirred in the clearing by the cliffside, rustling through the pine trees that now shrouded the shattered stones of my parents' last home on the other side of the glade from the graves. The sweep of air called to me, tugging at my magical senses and urging me to fly, but, as ever, I forced myself to turn away.

Taking a deep, shaking breath, I placed my hands on the crude letters spelling my parents' names, Elima and Janen Izzetís. Though Asfiyan and Koromic tradition dictated that every person's gravestone bear the surname that had been theirs as children, my parents bore the same name, for my father had entirely abandoned his old one when he took my mother's as his own. He had even accepted a new given name of my mother's choosing. That choice had, more than anything, reassured me that he had truly loved her. And it had, more than anything, angered the Blood.

I rubbed the letters that I had lovingly carved. "May the Almighty give peace to you," I prayed and then added, as I always did, "I hope that you are not worrying about me, Ammi, Abbi. I will survive." *Somehow, though I do not know why I try.*

Then I stood and made my way back down the treacherous cliff. I was desperately hungry, and I carried some food with me in case of an emergency, as was my habit, but my stomach roiled at eating in that clearing, amid the memory of the violence tainting that ground. It was my parents' resting place, but it brought little comfort to me.

I hiked to the base of the mountain, the descent only slightly less arduous than the climb, and walked to the wooden hut that I had painstakingly built and maintained with my own hands. I could not live in my parents' old hut, and I could not leave, for the mountains around this place were no place for a wingless child of the Sholanar. So I stayed and suffered silently.

Sooner or later, I, Elian ben-Janen Izzetís, would die here, my life sentenced to death by my birth. I had never had a future or a promise.

CHAPTER 5

DEFEND THE BROKEN

Perspective: Elian ben-Janen Izzetís, citizen of Bhalasa
Date: Eyyélab, the twelfth day of the tenth moon, Thekharre,
of the year 499, C.Q.

Dry soil flaked off the precious vegetables cradled in my arms. I frowned at the pitiful bundle. Every year my vegetable and herb garden was yielding less and less, no matter the amount of water and fertilizer I used nor the size of the patch itself. What was already arid land was becoming ever more so… Soon enough, I would be forced to rely solely on meat gleaned from hunting. Which meant smaller and smaller meals loomed in the future, for my crippled wings impeded every attempt to pursue more than the meekest of prey. Well, unless I devised something new…

My gaze grew unfocused as plans flashed through my mind. *A more elaborate trap might catch those elusive hares…*

Lost in thought as I was, I did not notice the telltale whoosh that accompanied diving wings. Not until a brutal kick landed on my back and shoved me forward.

A shriek tore from my lips as I sprawled on the ground. My weight broke the squash, carrots, and potatoes, but I hardly noticed, frozen by the sight of the figures circling overhead like vultures. The chips of light reflecting off the iridescent scales of their wings looked more like spots of blood than anything beautiful.

"Oh Blood-spawn!" one of the aerie residents called, his voice singsong. "How does the food you're stealing from us taste?"

I was too panicked to think.

"How does the water you steal taste?" another called.

They pelted several more jeers at me.

Then swooped.

I crawled away as fast as I could, but I covered no more than a few feet before the first of them dipped down and yanked out a feather.

I screamed as the curse turned a bare pinprick into what felt like the twisting stab of a knife.

A second resident yanked out a feather. Then another. And another.

Wild with pain and terror, I scrambled for my little shack. Though even there I would not find safety.

Jeering laughter filled the air as my tormentors plucked feather after feather. All the while I screamed.

"Today is the day we strip the Blood-spawn of those wings!" a woman taunted, and several took up her words as a rallying cry.

Just as I reached close enough to touch the wall of my house, another brutal kick hit my bottom.

I flew through the air and landed jarringly, upside down, against the wall. The air rushed from my lungs, and my head spun with the force. My wings shrieked at the abuse of my body crushing them.

I flopped to the ground and lay stunned.

Footsteps crunched on the dying grass and further crushed the already mangled vegetables. More laughter and cruder taunts beat in time with those footsteps.

Knowing how vulnerable I was, I hauled my aching body around to face them. The tiny scales dotting my skin, just like theirs, turned a brown ochre at the look in their eyes: black murderous intent.

Too terrified to squeak, I cowered against the wall of my hut, as if it would protect me.

Two middle-aged women leading the villagers stalked a few steps forward.

A navy streak flashed across my vision.

I blinked.

My mouth fell open as a midnight-blue figure stood before me, his back facing me. From what little I could see of his front, he held a sword. It was pointed at the villagers.

The man spoke in a cold yet rich, musical voice, "Leave this place." Light, pure and white and peaceful, glittered off his form. Authority radiated from him in the way that fog unfurled off of the rapidly heating mountains following the rain.

The residents stood dazed, their jaws hanging as they stared at him.

One of the women in front spoke, "Who are you? You would protect that piece of filth?"

I flinched at the insult.

The shining man answered, "One whose name you do not deserve to learn. As he is no piece of filth. And, yes, I will protect him."

I started, my heart skipping beats. I could not have heard what I thought I had.

"Who you are is a fool," the woman sneered. "He deserves all scorn. He deserves all abuse for his parentage."

I closed my mouth and swallowed. She was right.

But the shining man disagreed: "One's ancestry does not determine one's worth," he proclaimed.

Disbelief widened my eyes. No one could possibly mean that—parentage determined magic, kind, and rank, all the things that established a person's identity and place in life. Parentage was everything.

Another resident scoffed. "His does. How could he be anything other than evil? He deserves to suffer endlessly."

He is right... The shining man defends me now, I thought, resigned, *but the moment that he learns what they know, he will treat me the same. Still, it was nice to see someone defend me just this once...*

More voices cried from the mob, and I quivered. Cries of "A waste of space!" "A blight on Bhalasa!" "An eyesore!" "A monstrosity!" reverberated in my ears, audible even over the pounding of my pulse.

Clear sunshine brightened the meadow around my hut, while my hands and knees shook with the need to obey. But amid my cowering, I could barely pick apart the sensations from my terror.

One resident, an older man, shouted in a voice that pierced both the fog in my mind and all the other sounds, "He does not deserve the Almighty's mercy, much less yours!"

Despite the hurtful poison of those words, my attention snapped to the shining man.

He had frozen in place.

Then, before anything else was shouted, the light and command of his presence... changed. It became the cause of fear. Pure, utter, strangling fear. His fury prowled through the air as the sunlight itself became hard and sharp, like shards of glass.

I was terrified. But my body did not cringe or shake. In the recesses of my heart, I knew, somehow, with utter certainty that the anger was for me, on my behalf, not against me.

The residents, however, seemed too frightened to move or speak.

The shining man said, his voice cold, even, and quiet, "Leave."

The residents spread their wings and jumped into the air before the syllable was even complete. They flapped their wings in haste and quickly disappeared into the distance, between the sides of the mountains to the north.

The shining man's battle-ready stance relaxed some, and he sheathed his sword. He tilted his head back and seethed silently.

Utter silence filled the glade, not even a bird daring to squawk nor a rabbit daring to rustle.

The fear and sense of unyielding command faded, slowly retreating back to the man until the peace and light that had originally radiated from him returned.

The man took a deep breath and then turned to face me.

My scales were still a burnt brown with fright, but what ruled my emotions was awe. For, as much as he had scared me, he had defended me... No one *ever* defended me.

Red and gold flashed in the corner of my vision, and I hazily registered the presence of another person. But my focus was on the shining man's beautiful silver-cream face. His hair and beard shone like sunlight streaming through rain-heavy clouds, mirroring the light piercing the smog above. Kindness and peace cloaked him like the coat of his robes. His very presence reminded me of the crisp winds that had once lifted my fledgling wings.

The man's beautiful eyes dimmed.

I cringed slightly, for I knew what he saw: an abused wreck of a man. My whole person was crushed by hardship. My clothes were torn and encrusted with dirt and trampled vegetables. My forest-green eyes, once the same jewel-bright color as my mother's, had dulled. The once-rich dark umber of my hair and beard had lost all luster and was caked with dust. The tiny golden scales that dotted my chocolate skin in clusters of five, like little crowns, did not glow or glitter. And worst of all were my wings.

The golden feathers, the sign of a child of both the Mutharrim and the Sholanar, had grown discolored, bent, and twisted. The supple scales and central shaft that comprised each feather barely remained attached as they should. The brown skin beneath was blackened with unhealing bruises. Though my wings had grown to a full span of twenty-one feet, the top swells above my shoulders and the tapered points below my knees, they were shriveled. Atrophied. I had stopped cleaning them.

I was ashamed of how I appeared before him.

But the shining man smiled and spoke, "May the Almighty bless you, Elian ben-Janen Izzetís. How are your hurts?"

My eyes widened as he spoke my name. He actually knew my name! He actually asked after me! No one *ever* cared about how I felt.

My scales flaring with the same wonder that brightened my gaze, I whispered, "You defended me." I almost flinched—the resonant, clear tenor of my own voice, remarkably like the high roll of a bell, sounded strange and alien amid my usually endless silence. Well, silence save for screams.

The shining man's smile gained a steely edge. "I will always defend you. Not only today but every day hereafter."

His words rendered me speechless and star-struck. In that moment, as my gaze fixated on his, my world became those violet eyes.

He took a step closer.

I quickly arranged myself so that I knelt and held out my hands to him. "I know little," I whispered, "but I know that I should give you my loyalty, as unworthy as it is, if you would but deign to receive it. In what way may I serve you?"

That smile, already shining like warm sunlight, brightened so that looking at him felt like staring at the sun.

"Those words, the ones about loyalty," he answered, "are the fulfillment of a dream." He chuckled at the amazed disbelief on my face. "But know my name first: I am Lord Lucian the Ideal of Freedom, Heir to the Quest of Light and supreme ruler of Icilia." Affection sparkled in his glowing eyes. "And you are the third Potentate of my Quest."

I was too shocked to speak, my mind as blank as though all the thoughts had emptied out through my ears.

And in the emptiness the residents taunted, *"You are nothing, Blood-spawn! Nothing. You deserve nothing. Even the Almighty doesn't want you!"*

My eyes and scales dimmed at the reminder, though I did not look away. "I am so unworthy. I am nothing," I muttered.

A nephew of the Blood just could not be a Potentate of the Quest and a companion of the Quest Leader. Simply being in my Lord's presence was a dishonor on the Shining Guide's promise. If I were to accept, my very breathing would ruin everything for my Lord. How would he not refuse me once he learned whose child I was?

My Lord's smile gentled to one of reassurance. "You are worthy because you were chosen. The faith and piety at your core are too great to be broken, and greater than anyone else's in Icilia. You have borne your suffering with gratitude and honor, and you hold within you unmatched potential. But, most of all, you are worthy because you were chosen. The rest is… more like personality quirks." He turned his head slightly and winked at the person standing beside him. He turned back to me and added, "You do not yet see your greatness, but have faith that I do."

I could not believe his words, yet how desperately I longed for them to be true! Tears misting my vision, I pled, "Why would anyone choose me? What greatness could I possibly have? My wings are crippled! Even my magic is useless!" *And my blood is poison*, I added within my mind.

My Lord's smile did not waver. "Because you never lost your faith in the Almighty. Because your heart is pure and good. Because you love your parents and do not hate your abusers." His smile faded as the awesome power in his gaze intensified. "Neither blood nor rank nor kind interest me as much as the Almighty's blessing and favor do. That is what you have." He glanced briefly at the person standing at his side.

My breath hitched in my throat. Though I myself had never realized it, his words indeed captured the truth of my heart… But, moreover, they indicated that he knew about my ancestry. And—even more amazing, so amazing as to be unbelievable—he accepted me regardless!

His eyes intent upon mine, my Lord spoke more firmly, "With knowledge of the Almighty's choice, I choose you, Elian. If you swear allegiance to me, trust me to know well enough to choose properly." The words made clear what decision was before me.

I swallowed, a tear born of fear and pain trickling down my cheek. Yet my choice was apparent: I had been willing to swear allegiance without knowing his name; I was all the more willing after learning that he was the savior of Icilia. If I wanted to serve him, to grasp my one chance at having a life more meaningful than uneasy survival, I needed to accept his words completely and utterly without reservation. I needed to trust him even if I could not trust myself. I needed to rise and accept the hope that he offered.

Hope I so desperately needed.

I nodded to myself and again held out my hands to him. "Thank you," I whispered and prayed he understood how much this opportunity meant. I did not deserve the boon that he was bestowing upon me. How I hoped that someday my actions would be worthy of his confidence.

My Lord gave that dazzling smile again. "Would you rather wash and dress first?"

No matter the pain that racked my person, I could not delay a moment, fearing he was a dream that would disappear the moment I turned. Unable to accept his kindness, I shook my head.

He chuckled softly. "Very well." He motioned to the person at his side. "Elian, I present you to her Grace Malika the Exemplar of Wisdom, my Second-in-command."

Only now noticing her presence as more than a form at my Lord's side, I glanced shyly up at her.

I froze, transfixed. She was beautiful... her azure eyes, the color of the cloudless sky but far more brilliant, sparkled with kindness and intelligence, and her red-gold hair shone like the rose gold sight of the setting sun... my Lord's declaration of her as his Second seemed only right for one so regal. The loveliness of her features and more so of the spirit within was only second to the ethereal majesty of our Lord's. If he was the divine-blessed sunlight, then she was the exalted sky lit by the glory of the sun.

With such affection sparking in my heart, the gray pallor of her skin, the dark depressions beneath her haunted eyes, the wrinkles on her young face, and the gauntness of her frame sparked the first protective instinct that I had ever felt for anyone.

I hastened to bow as best as I could from my kneeling position.

Dipping her head, my Grace smiled hesitantly. If I dared to say so, there might have even been wonder in her eyes...

"Elian," my Lord spoke, and most of my attention returned to him, "would you allow me to connect you to my links? I am a mindlinker, as well as an athar magician by birthright, and her Grace only speaks through links. She should teach you the words of the pledge."

I nodded without question. I loathed what the requirement indicated about her voice, but, like the torment afflicting her appearance, I could not think it a detractor from her majesty.

My Lord smiled and lightly kissed my forehead—which sent a wave of comfort all throughout my person, relieving my pain, as well as the stream of his cool, contenting magic.

He straightened and nodded to my Grace, whose cheeks were a sweet pink. But despite her obvious embarrassment, she regally bowed her head and delivered the recitation, the musical contralto of her voice confident and sure. She instructed me on the steps of the ceremony.

I listened and then said respectfully, "Thank you, my Grace." I had dredged my mind for the history my mother had once taught me for the correct address while she spoke.

At her nod, I sat as straight as I could with my pain-filled, crippled wings rumpled behind me. I placed my palms on my knees.

"Ready?" my Lord asked.

I inhaled deeply and nodded again. My hands were shaking and clammy, but my scales warmed with anticipation and excitement.

My Lord beamed, dazzling like the long distant summer days spent in my parents' arms, and spoke his part of the ceremony. A great power made itself known around him.

I answered without hesitation, savoring each beautiful word, "By the Light of the Almighty and the Shining Guide sent unto us, I promise my love and swear my allegiance to you, my Lord Lucian the Ideal of Freedom. I will uphold your commands and proffer my best service to you on every day of my life. I will serve your example and support your Second in fulfilling your every wish. With your happiness shall I breathe, with your blessing shall I speak, with your authority shall I act. May all that I am please the Almighty."

Passion and devotion kept my voice firm and unwavering. As I concluded my portion, I held out my hands. I hoped that he could see the plea in my eyes and would not turn me away, would not refuse me when I was so close to gaining the beginnings of a purpose.

My Lord's smile glowed even brighter as he placed his hands on mine.

I held back a gasp at the immensity of the power that vibrated between us.

He intoned, his rich voice suffused with happiness, "For freedom by the Almighty, I accepted your allegiance and promise my love and my heart to you in return. May the Almighty bless you, Honored Elian the Exemplar of Esteem, companion in the Quest of Freedom. May our bond remain forever unbreakable under the Almighty's favor. And may the Almighty be pleased with all that we are. Praised be the Almighty."

Energy exploded between his palms and mine... reverberating throughout my heart, mind, and body, changing me so that I resonated with him, as though I were an extension of him. The transformation flung me onto the slopes of his identity. For an eternal moment, I breathed in the perfection of his virtue, the sanctity of his nature... embodying his title, he was freedom itself. And his power, his mindlinking and his athar magic and a strange magic unlike anything I had ever heard described... it was beyond my comprehension. So deeply immersed as I was in his very self, the truth of his devotion and destiny was manifest.

The immersion imbued a brightness unto my heart and soul, a fortitude that I had thought myself incapable of having. The very foundation of my mind gained a strength that I had long lost. Energy tingled throughout my whole body, from my face to the tips of my ruined feathers. And something in the nature of my magic changed, as though a barrier had fallen...

For the first time in years, my scales and feathers glowed golden like the morning light, unmarred by smog and darkness.

My forest-green eyes on his violet ones, I knew him to be my brother. A conviction settled into my soul that he would forever treasure me. He would be my family and would give me a family again. If only I kept my faith in him.

Besides him, my Grace's blue eyes shone with a wonder and delight that warmed my heart yet further.

My Lord, still smiling, kneeled and pulled me into his embrace. It was a draught of pure comfort, soothing away my pain, the first gentle touch I had known in thirteen years. Overcome with emotion, I did not hesitate to return the gesture, though I winced at how his person was touching the filth on mine.

Rather like how his exaltedness was associating with my lowliness.

I opened my mouth to protest, but my Lord spoke then, his voice thoughtful, "Now that is indeed strange." He tilted his head back to glance at my Grace and narrowed his eyes. Nodded to himself and pressed his lips together. Then said, "You both must promise me something, Malika, Elian."

My Grace and I immediately dipped our heads.

His lips formed a straight line. "You must promise me that both of you, specifically, will never remain alone together or touch each other in any way unless entirely necessary per the demands of emergency." His brow furrowed. "The connection between you both is… unexpected."

My Grace's face creased with anxiety, and my own scales dimmed.

My Lord's mouth curved into the hint of a reassuring smile. "There is no defect in your relationship nor in that of the Quest as a whole. But you are not siblings as you are each with me, and you must remain aware of this." The words were delivered in the tone of a command, though not with the weight of one.

But I took them as an order, as did my Grace. We both murmured the proper response, 'As you wish,' in our various ways and did not ask questions. Indeed, the mandate made sense: the sort of burgeoning sibling love I was feeling for my Lord did not match what I felt for my Grace. My Lord's concern for propriety was reasonable.

My Lord smiled fully and rose. He extended a hand to me as he said, "Come, Elian, let us medicate your wounds, clean your feathers, and array you in fresh clothes. Then let us eat."

Unable to refuse, I took his hand. But his words had inadvertently reminded me of the humiliation I had just suffered and how pathetic I appeared before him. That alone would have dimmed whatever fire lit my scales. But, as I nearly collapsed against him in my struggle to stand, my embarrassment further leeched light and warmth from my scales until they were again a dull ochre. My wings, released from being pinned against the wall and the ground, tumbled down so that they dragged in the dirt.

When I was finally standing, my Lord wrapped his arm around my waist and mine around his shoulder. "To your house?" he asked lightly, though some strange emotion flashed in his eyes at the same time.

I nodded. "Yes, my Lord," I whispered, forcing my tongue to unstick itself from the roof of my mouth.

"Lucian," he said gently. "I will teach you the etiquette for our office, but we do not observe it in our privacy." He nodded to my Grace. "When I offer you my name, I offer all of the Potentates'."

Malika smiled shyly.

As honored as I felt to be able to call them by their names alone, my attention was consumed by trying not to fall again. His touch and presence kept the worst of my pain at bay, but I was losing my balance, slowly leaning further and further into him.

He shifted slightly, letting the whole of my weight fall against his side and chest. Then, step by step, with Malika walking behind us, he helped me inside the simple wooden walls of my house.

We paused in the doorway as Lucian and Malika (he did say I could address them so familiarly!) surveyed the tiny space, barely twelve feet by twelve. Only a few furnishings alleviated the stark barrenness of the space: a cot made of some scraps of fabric and dried moss, a small table atop which lay three worn knives and a blunt dagger, and an uncomfortable straight-backed wooden chair. A rectangular door-like cutout, barely taller than my frame of six-and-a-quarter feet, on the left wall marked the opening into the outhouse, which itself featured a framework of wooden slats over a collection of misshapen clay pots.

In one wall, another opening revealed a shallow, aboveground pit built of smoothened pebbles, an external fireplace which could be covered with a wooden board during rain and snowfall. A pot with too humble a stew, now that my vegetables were gone, simmered atop the coals. My only other possessions, a few tattered books on magic and history, an open chest of tattered clothes, and six flasks of varying sizes, sat by my bed.

Admiration flashed in Malika's eyes, and even Lucian seemed amazed.

I tried to see it as he and Malika saw it but could not. Though it was my shelter, though I had built it with my own hands and lavished all my leisure on innovations for it, I did not consider it my home. Even if it had not been my desperate replacement for a life without my parents, the aerie residents had pursued me inside enough times to inspire my revulsion.

If my Lord Lucian had allowed me to follow him, I would have been more than happy to leave this place behind. It was not home. I had not had a home in thirteen years.

But that was perhaps no longer true. For I was quickly associating Lucian, as he helped me clean and dress myself in the outhouse and then gave me both medicine and new clothes, with the sense of caring and comfort that came with a home. As I was with Malika, who hurried to arrange a meal for all of us, from fetching water to the very last of the vegetables in my garden.

In their presence, I relaxed fully for the first time since my parents' embraces so long ago.

CHAPTER 6

BENEFIT THE PERSECUTED

Perspective: Honored Elian the Exemplar of Esteem
Date: Eyyéqan, the thirteenth day of the tenth moon, Thekharre,
of the year 499, C.Q.

Gripping the rope with one hand, I shaded my face with the other. About ten feet above me, Lucian was surmounting the edge of the cliff. Once he had risen to his feet, he smiled and walked backward, tugging the rope knotted around his waist. The rope grew taut around Malika, and she scrambled forward, bracing herself on boulders. Before it could pinch my own middle, I copied her. Grasping at hand- and footholds, we climbed up… though our efforts contributed far less to the task than Lucian's strength. Through the rope that connected the three of us, Lucian was essentially dragging us up the slope.

It was the easiest climb I had ever made, and the experience seemed to be but a taste of what traveling with Lucian would be like.

After he had explained his plans for travel yesterday, I had seized upon the offer to accompany him. With his and Malika's support, I threw all of my possessions, particularly my flasks and cooking implements, into a sack, dismantled my snares and traps, and finally closed up my shack this morning. Only then did I realize I was actually leaving—and only then did I think to ask, suppressing some chagrin, when we would depart.

Lucian had suggested that we visit my parents' graves first.

No one else had ever visited them.

Lucian's graciousness truly defied all cynicism. He not only cared for my wounds and relieved the pain that would have taken weeks to fade of its own accord, but he also gave me new clothes and a sword of my very own, and with them a sense of connection to the stories my mother had once told me of her birth-nation. Then, kindness atop kindness, he promised to train me in weaponry and in all the subjects I had missed, from magic to politics. As he spoke, accompanied by Malika's shy mentions of what they had already studied, I marveled at how he was remedying all the injustices that had broken me.

The greatest of those remedies, in my view at least, was his binding of my wings. The request, which I had tearfully made while watching him connect us with a length of rope, was one that no child of the Sholanar should ever have had to make. But, because my wingspan was so great that I could not tie them closed myself, I had no choice but to ask. With my wings loose I would never be able to walk with him.

I had expected him to refuse.

Yet, despite his discomfort, he had torn a strip from his own blankets (though they were made of invaluable athar) and strapped them to my back.

As contradictory as it sounded, his doing so had restored much of the mobility and speed, at least on the ground, that I had lost. The binding kept my wings from dragging, which in turn prevented my feathers from twisting in my flesh.

Thus, I could follow him without burdening him.

Tilting my head back, I waited patiently for Malika to climb over the edge. Though she was light, Lucian had wanted to keep her between his strong person and my heavy one. Like all of the Mutharrim and the Nasimih, he weighed less than his mass; that, along with his balance and strong hold, meant he would not slip. My weight on the other side would anchor her to the slope if she fell. She would not be left dangling.

The planning was a sign of his protective instinct for her, which I was quickly beginning to share.

Malika disappeared over the top. Then, reappearing, she wordlessly beckoned me to follow.

The rope pinched my waist, and I began to climb again. But part of my attention remained on her face as I examined it for any indication that the gray tinge had lessened.

She needs to drink more water, I thought, frowning.

In a private link, Lucian had explained that the grayness indicated long-term dehydration among the Ezulal. As long as that effect lingered, she would not be able to reach her full strength or access her kind's natural magic.

I had immediately, silently, vowed to help her recover. Even if that meant scrounging for water or giving up my own share. I knew well what losing the magic of one's kind felt like, and I loathed that she bore this pain atop the curses on her magic and her voice.

Perhaps the commitment sounded hasty, but, as she had mumbled something of her history last night, I sensed that she would be my dearest friend if only I would dare to earn her affection. I certainly admired her—even as the knowledge that she had once been Heir to Koroma and a prisoner of the Blood made my comparative inferiority and the shame of my parentage all too clear.

Still, even such shame could not dampen my wish to share my parents' gravesites with Lucian and Malika.

I swallowed dryly as I pushed myself over the cliff. No longer able to distract myself, tears overflowed and spilled down my cheeks. My scales dimmed to a near-black as I ran to the gravestones.

Collapsing to my knees, I sobbed and threw my arms over them. "Ammi, Abbi, forgive me for leaving!" I cried.

Cloth brushed on cloth, and Lucian's commanding presence permeated the air.

I turned my head against the stone to see that both of them had followed me and knelt on either side.

Malika's blue eyes glittered with tears as she whispered, *May the Almighty bless you, Elian's parents.*

His face grave and solemn, Lucian pressed his hands to both stones and bowed his head. He whispered a prayer, which carried the tones of the funereal dirge that had never been sung for my parents, and said, smiling faintly, "Mother Elima, Father Janen, I thank you for loving Elian and for giving your lives for him. You did not know he would become a Potentate of the Quest, but you had glimpsed the first signs of his future office and so raised him with all the faith and knowledge that you possessed. Thus I proffer my gratitude and my reverence to you, and Icilia will one day give no less. May the Almighty bless you."

I stared in awe, almost unable to believe the veneration with which he, the Quest Leader, treated my parents—my parents who had never before been respected by any but me.

Lucian removed a late-blooming wild rose from a pocket of his robes. Sorrow creased his face as he plucked its petals and scattered them atop the memorials.

So this is the mourning custom of Asfiya... I thought, sniffling, to myself. *If only I had known before...*

Malika pressed her hands to the stones and whispered a prayer. *Thank you for giving Elian to us, Auntie, Uncle.* Though unable to read, she kissed the carvings that formed their names, then stood and retreated a few steps.

Lucian kissed both stones as well, then rose and bowed slightly, before stepping back.

My eyes burned with more tears as I turned back to my parents. Again I remembered how no one had ever respected them while they lived... how dearly they had cherished me... They had been torn from me.

I blinked rapidly as grief overwhelmed me. Sobs burst from my throat.

Lucian swiftly knelt beside me.

I flung my arms around him. "You and Malika are the first to ever mourn them," I choked through my sobs. "Why did they leave me!"

Lucian sighed and returned the embrace. Not speaking, he stroked my back as I cried as if I had never mourned—though I most certainly had over the many long years I had spent alone. But no one had ever comforted me, ever cared for me, not after their deaths and not over the many years since.

He was remedying that.

And that made me cry all the more.

When my sobs finally subsided, I voiced my deepest fear, unwilling but knowing I needed to tell him, "I do not know if I have the strength to serve you." I shuddered as I clung to him. "I am... I am in pieces."

Lucian smoothed my hair beneath my cap and answered, to my wonder amid my misery, "I will put you back together." There was unshakeable confidence in his voice. "I will give you strength, and I will make you whole. I am here for you, and I love you, Brother."

I clung more tightly to him as I desperately tried to believe his words, to have faith in the hand that he held out to me. But I was drowning amid my despair, my grief, the pain born of years of torment and loneliness, and the hatred for myself that contaminated my every thought. So long had I been deprived of even the most basic consideration that any incé merited under the Almighty's laws... I did not know how to have faith.

Lucian continued, his voice warming with conviction, "I am born with the patience to guide you until you see your worth. Just as I restore you, I will revitalize Icilia, the purpose for which we breathe."

I trembled in his arms, too shattered to hope.

His embrace lasted for many more minutes. Then I stirred and drew back. Turning, I held my hands to my parents' names, lightly tracing the rough edges, memorizing the curves and angles, as I prayed. Kissing them, I bid them farewell.

I did not know if I would ever see their gravestones again. Lucian seemed adamant that his success was guaranteed in the Almighty's name, and it surely was, but long life was not. So I savored my last moments, pained though they were, by the graves I had faithfully tended for much of my life. I hoped they would understand why I had to leave.

Once the edge of my grief receded, I stood and rejoined Lucian and Malika, the new family who had respected my lost one. The reassurance on Lucian's face was the only reason I could walk forwards.

If anyone could breathe life into the remains of my esteem for myself, the Quest Leader could. For he possessed the wish and the patience to care for a broken land that did not deserve him.

Perhaps I, too, would find myself restored at his hands.

CHAPTER 7

WATCHING HELPLESSLY

Perspective: Arista
Date: Eyyéqan, the ninth day of the fifth moon, Marberre, of the year 499, C.Q.

I counted the number of guards around the corner: eight, less than the full squad of ten I had feared. Only a small edge, but I needed every advantage possible in my escape.

In obeying the Almighty's laws there is salvation. As that hymn echoed through my mind, I called on my gift of sorcery of the inferno and muttered in the sacred language of Alimàzahre, "Sholit ai sholeh, ashoneret é enerel, sholorim, shosholitorim, shosholehrim! Treperim zidilëm!" Simultaneously, I used the magic that flowed in my blood to catalyze a few drops of my physical strength into power and streamed it through the diamond that adorned my thin circlet (really, a hairband), which amplified the flow. I then imbued that power and my words into the flames, which would trigger the spell in accordance with my intention.

Although I had enough magic to cast spells that were quite abstracted from my element itself, directly manipulating fire would obscure my passage. Every magician in the city would know upon the slightest glimpse of the magic's residue that an abstract spell was my work, for I was the only one in the city with that great a level of magic, but several of the royals and nobles could cast a simpler direct fire spell. Only a deep examination could reveal my identity, and I doubted anyone would perform it as long as I moved with stealth.

How imperative that stealth was.

I released the spell, and the flames of the hallway's torches increased in size, threatening an uncontrolled blaze.

The guards took the bait and dashed toward the possible fire.

Footsteps silent, I darted to the great doors, strained to push one ajar, and slipped out. Closing it behind me, I rushed across the courtyard, through the open gate, and into the nearest alleyway. With my detailed memory of the city's design, I crept through the back lanes and streets unnoticed and quickly reached the last line of houses. Sprinting past them, I left the soil of the capital oasis for the sand dunes beyond.

Only when I was over a thousand feet from the edge of the city did I look back. The creamy sandstone walls of the Zahacit royal palace, pale amid the smog-darkened twilight, were just barely visible over the dunes. Though I left much behind, I would not miss my life there.

The vitality and vibrancy of Rushada, the capital of Zahacim, and its heart the palace, would have shaped a wonderful childhood in any age but this one. In this age, to be a member of the queen's family was to be marked for exploitation.

To the chagrin and anger of Icilia, my house, the royal family of Zahacim, had defected to the Blood-soaked Sorcerer five years after he had first begun his bid for power in 468 C.Q. Led by the family's best commanders, Zahacit soldiers had comprised the bulk of his armies and carried his conquest far from the southern fringes of Koroma.

At first, in return for supporting him when he had not ruled even a single province, the Blood had given my grandmother, the high chieftain, the advantage she sought: control over lands and trade beyond the borders of Zahacim and the resources to greatly expand and enrich every Zahacit caravan, both wandering and settled. Her wars and initiatives brought power and prestige to every clan, and amid that glorious explosion Icilia's ruin had been easy to ignore. Blinded by their prosperity, no one, from chief to general to royal, objected.

Save my parents. But, unsupported as their voices were, their efforts were confined to the upbringing of their daughters, whom they raised in the virtuous, honorable, and devout ways of our ancestors even as those ways were abandoned by the rest of the nation.

I was five years old when everything changed.

With the fall of Koroma and the capture of Asfiya in 483 C.Q., the Blood dropped all of his pretenses and firmed his control over Zahacim into total slavery. My grandmother perished in her attempt to reason with him, and her heir, my eldest aunt, cowered in fear. She did not have the courage to resist when the Blood and his governor turned the proud warrior princesses of the royal family into entertainment and objects of pleasure and decoration.

No one lifted a finger in our defense. Though once our loyal followers, the caravans did nothing for fear of the Zahacit military, long since swindled into willing allegiance to the Blood. Thus, the nation of Zahacim, who had idiotically trusted the charm and illusion of a man who held no loyalty for the blessing of the Quests' civilization, came to regret the decision she had so foolishly made.

Amid this horror, my parents and my two sisters gave everything to protect me. Despite the torment burdening his spirit, my father devoted his every day and night to train me in weaponry and magic in secret. While my mother and my sisters... once the Blood's governor, a cruel man known as the Choker, began to send for me, my mother and my sisters took my place in his bed, bearing the violence he wreaked so that I would not be forced to suffer it.

When I objected, hating how they sacrificed themselves for me, my parents reminded me of their belief that I was born for something great, something that would save Icilia.

"Arista, my blossom," my mother, Serama, often said, "you are our nation's only hope of ending this degradation. Like any flower, you will only be able to spread your scent if your petals are not crushed as they bloom."

My father, Atres, always continued, "Brave girl, a sacrifice freely given must be honored. Honor them by training hard. You will need that knowledge when you become the ruler whom you were born to be."

My mother then concluded, "You are the Almighty's blessing unto us, and a little sacrifice is the best way for us to ensure you fulfill your destiny." My father and sisters would nod in vehement agreement with her.

My twin sister Areta, nearly identical in appearance, would usually add, grumbling, "I am four minutes older than you, Baby Sister. That means I get to protect you. Now just accept it!" She would roll her eyes. "Better me than you."

Thus, the four of them had shielded me from the plagues that crushed the royal family.

But, still, their shielding could only go so far. We watched helplessly as my warrior aunts and their heirs, my warrior cousins, along with the brave and proud men they had married, were slowly demeaned until they began to speak well of the Blood and the Choker. They praised our humiliation and our cowardice in capitulating to the Blood without much more resistance than a few skirmishes. The nobles and the citizens spoke much of the same, and the soldiers actually admired their violent masters.

We were surrounded by people who were cheerfully resigning themselves to slavery.

How I feared being so destroyed in spirit.

My parents, my sisters, and I were horrified, but we could do nothing without risking my safety. Though I longed to rebel and defy the Choker for the sake of Zahacim, my parents and sisters emphasized my wellbeing over everything.

My sister, Henata, rebuked, "You keep your head down until it is time to raise it."

What right did I have to object when they were the ones who suffered? I could only obey, burying my guilt and fear in my training.

Until, again, everything changed.

Four months ago, but days after my twenty-first birthday, my aunt the queen began to publicly note my absence in every event, large and small, involving the Choker. My mother at first succeeded in brushing away the accusations of my disloyalty, but as her attempts grew less and less persuasive, my family and I began to plan our escape. Gathering weapons, supplies, and information, we readied ourselves to flee.

Then, this morning, but a day before our departure, my aunt commanded me outright to attend the Choker.

If we all left, our absence would be unmistakable, and the soldiers would capture us within hours.

So my family ordered me to leave them behind. Areta would take my place, and my parents would prevent any discovery of my absence.

As I bid them farewell, I was certain I would never see them again. But all I could do was respect their wishes and obey.

Gathering the discreet pack filled with my books, weapons, and provisions, I had donned the sand-colored combat armor my sisters had stolen from the old armory for my nineteenth birthday. At my mother's and my elder sister's insistence, I wore the circlet that marked me as a possible heir to the throne. Then I had snuck through the palace and waited for twilight.

Though fondness had relaxed my posture as I had gazed at the palace, I now scowled at it. It was a death-trap, the probable tomb of my parents and sisters, and it reeked of cowardice.

The plates on my cheeks vibrated with my tumultuous emotions as I turned and fortified myself with a deep breath of the free air.

My parents had advised me to travel north, toward Bhalasa, and I prayed to the Almighty that I would find my destiny there, beyond Zahacim's borders and the reach of the soldiers who would pursue me.

If I did not, I, Arista sej-Shehenzahak, would die trapped in the halls of the place that should have been my home. I had to have a future, a promise, so that my parents' and my sisters' sacrifices would not be worthless.

CHAPTER 8

RAISE THE CRUMBLED

Perspective: Princess Arista sej-Shehenzahak, auxiliary heir to the throne of Zahacim
Date: Eyyéala, the sixteenth day of the tenth moon, Thekharre, of the year 499, C.Q.

My fingers trembled on the hilts of my swords. I clenched my teeth and tightened my grip.

I had come so far; I could not falter now.

Pebbles skittered several yards behind me.

I quickened my pace down the steep slope.

A loud snap echoed off the foothills as a branch broke underfoot.

I increased my speed until I was running. Only the sure-footedness characteristic of the Areteen, my kind, enhanced by my training, saved me from falling.

My swords at the ready, I dashed across the valley and climbed up another tall hill. My breath wheezed, and my legs and abdomen cramped painfully, but I did not dare slow.

Though I wondered if the effort was at all worthwhile.

After escaping the palace, I had fled north across the desert toward Zahacim's border with Bhalasa. For two-and-a-half months I slept little and ate sparingly as I strove to maintain my lead on the soldiers surely sent to retrieve me. Pushing my body to the upper limits of its strength, I had succeeded, my pursuers so far behind as to be entirely out of sight.

Until I reached the border, the great scarlet and burgundy canyon formed over uncounted ages by the frothy white waters of the mighty river Anharat, which crossed Icilia in a jagged line.

That border, contrary to the reports my parents had collected, was heavily guarded. A wall lined the canyon's edge, and multiple shifts of guards patrolled the area. Those precautions only exacerbated the near impossibility of crossing the canyon at all without powerful magic. Magic that I could perform, but which required more finesse than I could muster to retain any appreciable degree of stealth.

I fumbled the crossing.

It brought the soldiers down on my head.

I only just barely avoided an attack on the Bhalaseh shore and managed to slip into the foothills of the mountainous nation. However, between the soldiers' familiarity with the terrain and my decided lack thereof, I could not shake their pursuit.

The past six weeks had been filled with battle after battle, ambush after narrowly escaped ambush.

I cannot keep this pace much longer, I thought, despairing, as I crested the hill and sped down its other side. *My swords are losing their edge, my armor is damaged, and my body is failing.* How I wished to scream these thoughts, but there was no one to hear me besides my enemies.

I had never been so alone in all my life.

As much as I hated Rushada, there I had always had my parents and my sisters for company. Now, though I escaped that life of degradation, I had no one. No one to care what happened to me.

If my body does not collapse, my mind might, I thought grimly, my plates stilled like coarse, cracked earth. With each passing day, my mind grew less clear, fogged by exhaustion and deafened by shrieking loneliness. My spirit, which had never been truly whole, was crumbling.

I ran across the valley to the base of the next hill.

Something whooshed passed me—an arrow. Even as it flashed by me, I recognized the make: the slender shaft was constructed from the hard branches of desert scrub and capped by a large thorn rather than flint or stone. Only one people used its like—the Areteen soldiers of Zahacim. Once my defenders, now my pursuers. My people, once loyal to the queen's daughters and now subservient to the Choker. Regardless of my horror at spilling blood, even after so many skirmishes, I would have to take their lives if I wanted to escape.

Bracing my feet, I skidded to a stop and slid smoothly around to face them. Bending my knees and widening my stance, I brought my swords up to the ready position.

Fourteen soldiers charged, the remains of the original three squads who had followed me from the border. Their eyes, dark like my own, gleamed with murder and the sickly sweet desire for vengeance. Their swords, machetes, and scythes flashed wickedly in the meager sunlight passing through the smog.

I shuffled my feet, checking that the ground was smooth, and then sprang forwards. Simultaneously I cast a basic spell that set both my blades on fire, compensating for the dulling edges.

The spell would leave residue, but my pursuers had already found me. I needed every advantage

Propelling my body into the air, I slashed down with both blades and cleaved the necks of two soldiers beneath their helmets. My feet only momentarily lit upon the ground before I spun and impaled a soldier who was lifting his axe overhead.

In a fight with soldiers who matched my own height, height was my best advantage. Alongside my training.

Sparking fire beneath my feet, I propelled myself higher and curled my knees to my chest to dodge another blow. Somersaulting forward, I landed behind the next set of opponents and dispatched them before they could turn.

I turned to repeat a version of the same move but found myself hemmed in on all sides. I spun both blades, simultaneously parrying and landing glancing but stinging blows, as well as cuts wherever their armor had shifted. Bouncing on my feet, I kept myself from being forced to the ground.

But with their superior numbers, the soldiers hammered me from every direction. Their blows caught the fraying edges of my bracers, the rents left in the leather covering my shoulders and legs, and the weakened links in the chainmail draped around my torso. Each wound further sapped my strength.

No matter how I twisted and dodged, they tore apart my defenses. Silently—all Zahacit warriors, from princesses to infantry, were trained to fight in complete silence—but the mockery and cruelty on their faces were all too apparent.

The hard thwack of a blade landed on my shoulder, nearly dislocating the joint. The hilt of one sword slipped from my fingers, the blade's fire flickering out as it fell.

Another blade pierced my bracer on the other arm just above my wrist. I managed to wrench my hand away, preventing a more serious injury, but the pain loosened my fingers enough that they dropped my other sword. The fall extinguished its flames as well.

I fisted both hands and raised them to my chest. Though hand-to-hand moves were of little use against sharp blades in such close combat. But I refused to surrender.

The commander of the squads, a stocky man with a sneer of a grin, raised his sword with both hands for a blow I would not be able to deflect.

I tensed my muscles anyway and prepared to combat it.

The blow never landed.

A blade of silver steel and green light appeared, blocking the swing.

The commander stared, wide-eyed, at the blade, which had come from behind him. The soldiers gawked.

I immediately ducked for my swords. Bracing myself on my fists, the hilts clenched by my fingers, I kicked my legs out and knocked down the soldier behind me. Then I pushed myself to my feet, skipped back over him so that my back would be clear, and slit his throat before he could rise.

I glanced back up, only to freeze.

A figure of midnight blue—who left an impression of light and authority on my heart and all five of my senses even in the middle of a battle—swirled through the enemy. His heavy two-handed sword decimated soldier after soldier. He had barely to land a blow to destroy his opponent.

His shining figure poured strength into my limbs.

Revitalized, I fell upon another soldier, parrying three thrusts before slipping beneath his guard and impaling him.

The body fell at my feet, and I spun, only to find that the battle was over.

All of the soldiers, who had chased me for weeks, were dead. Lowering my blades, I tilted my head back...

And looked into the face of true power. And utter kindness.

He was the sunlight molded into incé form, from his hair and beard to the gleam of his jewel-bright eyes. He radiated power, but, like the sun's, it was a power that seemed to buoy me up, as though I had been suffocating and was just granted free breath. Indeed, the light and authority that wreathed him felt like that restorative breath, the breath that calmed one's person after the exertion of running for one's life. As I had just done, as he had just saved me.

For his timely intervention alone, my Honor dictated that I owed him a great debt. But that light and authority...

Without hesitation, I knelt on the bloody battlefield and offered up my hands in the pledge of allegiance. In this at least, I would not be foolish: such power could belong to only one person. Only one person shone with such light. Though my mind reeled at the thought that I could actually be meeting him.

At the corners of my vision, red-gold and golden gleamed. But I kept my gaze on him, as was respectful. It was the moment to do credit to all of my royal training, though I certainly did not deserve to be called royal.

Amusement and (if I dared to say) pleasure sparkling in his eyes, my Lord smiled. "May the Almighty bless you, Princess Arista sej-Shehenzahak. I presume that you have guessed my identity?"

My breath stuttered. Between that bright smile and his knowledge of my name... oh yes, I was certain. Though how could I possibly be so blessed to encounter him myself!

I tried to unstick my tongue to speak, but all I could do was mutely nod in answer to his question. Though I hoped he could read the plea on my face for the knowledge of his name.

My Lord's laughter echoed lightly in the valley like a cool breeze. "My name is Lord Lucian the Ideal of Freedom, Heir to the Quest of Light and supreme ruler of Icilia." His smile softened, becoming less overwhelming but all the more sweet. "I am delighted by your offer of allegiance, but let us first address the remains of this battle. If it would please you, rise. Would you like some salve or bandages for your wounds?"

Shaking my head, I stood, still mute, even as I marveled at the quality of his manners.

But apparently that was the least thing about him to admire. For, before I could turn, my Lord turned and said to the two others standing nearby, "Malika, Elian, would you help me with the burial of these soldiers? And, Malika, would you collect your bolts?"

I startled, almost tipping forward onto my face. *He wants to bury the bodies of his enemies!*

Malika and Elian—referring to them by their names was probably disrespectful, but I could only guess at their titles—both dipped their heads. Malika dismantled a small, lightweight crossbow—there were, I noticed, bolts embedded in a few of the soldiers felled by my Lord—and tucked it into a belt-quiver. She and Elian retrieved their sheathed swords—both large enough to be two-handed and copies of my Lord's, save in size. Indeed, even their dress matched his.

They were most likely his companions, and the more marked similarity of the woman's aura to his suggested that she was his Second.

My Lord glanced around, lips pursed, and pointed to an area bare of brush to the side of the battlefield. "Let us begin there." Sheathing his sword, he untied the knots securing his scabbard and strode to the patch of earth.

My eyes bulged. Then, too frantic to evaluate whether I was breaching the Quest's etiquette, I ran over to him and pleaded, stumbling over my words, "My Lord, I can dig the grave!" The words echoed through the staccato vibration of my plates, those discrete pieces of my skin, riven by narrow grooves, that marked me as a child of the Areteen (unlike Sholanar scales in that they were part of my skin rather dotted atop it).

He glanced at me over his shoulder and smiled. "If you would, please." Retying his sword to his belt, he walked to the side of one of the corpses. Without hesitation he lifted it.

Taking deep breaths to steady my nerves, I turned and examined the exposed clay. Recalling my lessons, I muttered, "Fire does not have direct control over the earth. But hot air... yes, it could blow the soil. But how to prevent a dust plume... Perhaps a controlled stream of heated air?" I nodded to myself. "That is exactly what I need."

Invoking my conviction about the Almighty's laws, I composed a spell in the sacred tongue Alimàzahre, the language best suited for magic, and chanted it as I sparked catalysis of my physical energy. I streamed the power through the jewels adorning my swords and then imbued it into the faint warmth in the autumn air.

The air heated, drawing warmth from both the earth and my own catalyzed energy. Once it was warm enough, I coalesced the heated air into a precise, pressurized stream. Wielding it like a pickaxe, I pierced the earth and used the flow of the current to move the soil to a pile off to the side. With the concentrated quality of the heated air, only the soil I indicated moved to the place I had designated. No dust flew into the air. And, better yet, the efficiency of each movement preserved my strength far better than a huge gust would have.

The spell required about twenty minutes to clear a deep pit big enough to serve as a mass grave for so many soldiers. But, considering the number of corpses, it was ready just as my Lord and his companions finished piling the bodies.

Joining them, I helped roll the corpses into the grave.

The whole experience was odd: I had killed several of these soldiers, for they would have willingly killed me, or delivered me to a fate worse than death, if they had been allowed the chance. They were my enemies. And yet, I was burying them.

The act healed something that had torn when I shed their blood, something I only realized was broken when it was healed.

I wished I had not fled before burying the other soldiers who perished on my blades.

Once all the corpses were interred, I recast my spell for the heated air but in reverse. Instead of moving soil out, the air pushed all that I had removed back into the pit and smoothed the top.

As soon as the earth settled, my Lord knelt by the grave. Touching the churned earth, he whispered, "May the Almighty be merciful unto you, wayward children of Zahacim." There was actual sorrow on his face.

My staring was bordering on disrespectful, but I could not help it.

At my Lord's nod, my Honor Elian emptied a flask of water atop the grave.

My Lord murmured another prayer and stood. "If it would please you, Arista, would you accompany me as I clean my sword and armor?"

I remembered to bow this time.

Acknowledging the reverence with a smile, he strode to a stream that cut across a corner of the valley. Kneeling again, he did… something to his robes and removed the coat. Dunking it in the river, he rubbed the fabric, tinting the water pink. At some unspoken cue, he gave his scabbard to my Grace Malika, who removed the blade and scrubbed it alongside her crossbow bolts. My Honor Elian refilled a pair of water flasks, one of which bore gilded etchings.

Giving myself a shake, I scrubbed the blood splatter on my armor. But only the freshest drops would come out, and the washing made little difference, for much of the once-supple sand-colored leather was stained brown with blood. Even a spell, particularly with my element, would not help.

I shoved the worry to the side, though, as my Lord rose to his feet.

He smiled yet again at me. "If it pleases you, let us speak at some distance."

A huge grin split my face. "It would be my honor!" Only a lifetime of royal training prevented an excited whoop from leaving my lips.

He chuckled, seeming pleased, and led his companions and me over a couple of hills to a cave. Within it lay three packs and a couple of blankets—probably their possessions, considering that one of the packs and the blankets were made of the same material as their clothes.

My Lord knelt on the stone floor, and we quickly copied him.

Directing a dazzling smile at me, my Lord spoke, "Arista sej-Shehenzahak, you are the fourth Potentate of my Quest."

I blinked rapidly, unable to make sense of what he was saying. "How can that be?" The words fell from numb lips. Distress stilled even the faint, ever-present murmur of my plates. "You know who I am; I could not possibly be so honored." My family had assured me that I possessed a grand destiny, but this seemed like too much. At absolute best, one of my treasonous ancestry could only beg to be a foot-soldier in his army.

Do their sins not mark me? I did not dare to whisper the words aloud. *No traitor to Icilia could be blessed so.*

My Lord pressed his lips together. "Arista," he said, "you do not bear the stain of their actions. You have the power to choose your own path. The Almighty has bestowed choice unto everyone."

Those words... my trembling lips stretched in a grimace, and tears slipped down my cheeks. Those words were what I had always longed to hear... to hear them from his lips, the lips of the Quest Leader...

Desperation choking my throat, I frantically searched his violet eyes for what he truly believed.

Untainted truth sparkled in those jewel eyes. In them, I found what I needed.

Inhaling a deep breath, I bowed my head. "I will not waver behind you." Serving him would give me the dignity I had never been able to retain. I did not deserve such an opportunity to prove myself, but I would acquit myself well. Somehow. With all the intelligence and education and magic I possessed.

Somehow actually pleased by my words, his face glowed as he immediately introduced me to his companions, both of whose positions I had guessed correctly. His Second, my Grace, seemed a shy yet kind woman, though haunted and obviously undernourished, but there was steel buried deep in her soul, if the resolute cast of her lovely face was any indication. Her red-gold hair was an unusual color.

My Honor, in contrast, was sweet and gentle to his core, from the compassionate gleam of his forest-green eyes to the understanding set of his full lips. The soft, tight umber curls of his unevenly shorn hair and his thick, springy beard enhanced that endearing sweetness. The rounded features of his chocolate face matched my Lord's and my Grace's in beauty, as though he was the solid steadfastness of the mountains and they the stars and sky.

I gritted my teeth at the sight of the discolored golden wings bound shut behind his shoulders.

As soon as he introduced us, my Lord kindly asked me if I would consent to be joined to his links for my Grace's sake... as though he needed to ask.

I clenched my fists as I realized her voice had been stolen.

Once my Lord kissed my forehead (the action suffused with affection though it was what mindlinkers generally did to establish powerful links), my Grace explained the ceremony. I listened intently, though I had known of all of it save the words I needed to speak.

"Good riddance!" I exclaimed when my Lord explained the annulment of my birthright. "Can I throw my circlet away?"

My Lord laughed, a faint tension easing from his beautiful features. "Keep it for Mother Serama's sake, Arista."

I grumbled playfully, already at ease around him, then grinned and indicated I was ready.

His smile brightening, my Lord began the ceremony of my ascension. Around him swirled a power that was surely the same as that which formed the foundations of our land.

Adrift as I was in the blessed sense of that power, each second was both a fleeting instance and an eternity.

Giving me the name Honored Arista the Exemplar of Bravery, my Lord touched his hands to mine.

Magic unlike anything I had ever experienced or even imagined crackled between us. It ignited, like the first spark of an inferno, and the radiance of its heat burst through the whole of who I was, changing me from my heart to my body, bestowing a potency beyond my comprehension. Indeed, my magic flourished, flaming brighter as though a portion of the sun had been imbued unto my soul.

As this transformation occurred, elevating me beyond all I could hope of achieving, the brilliance of his power seared through my soul with the truth of who he was… I basked in the light of his virtue and divine-blessed nature and the warmth of his magic. Particularly the magic fueling this connection, the ardor of obeying authority that was worth obedience.

The blaze burned a confidence into my heart that he would forever respect me. He was my brother, the foundation of a new family, and his power would never suppress my voice. He would build up my spirit, which had never been given a chance to soar. He would always encourage me, if only I would listen.

In him I found the confidence for which I searched.

And with him came a new sister and another brother, whose hearts pounded in my chest alongside my own.

I smiled contentedly up at him as the intensity of the moment faded yet the connection remained. My whole body buzzed with the soothing vibration of the plates that comprised various areas of my skin.

His smile dazzling, my Lord knelt and swiftly embraced me. I relaxed, welcoming the touch that felt like home but better.

Then I stiffened.

My Lord drew back and, his brow furrowing, asked, "What troubles you, Arista?"

Though I hated to prompt that crease between his brows, I could not answer and dropped my gaze.

How I must have appeared before him! My leather armor and the clothes beneath were in tatters, in areas to the point of immodesty, unevenly covering the four feet and ten inches of my frame. My ragged helmet was misshapen beyond repair. My weapons were nearly destroyed. From the sallow tint to my warm olive-bronze skin and the snarled mess of my mahogany hair, the golden and red strands within my bun too greasy to shine, to the deterioration of my muscle mass, I presented a shameful image. Nothing like the warrior politician whose service he deserved. Nothing like I was trained to be. A disappointment.

"Arista," my Lord said.

I could not raise my eyes even at the kindness in his voice.

"Arista," he repeated, "if it would earn your happiness, I have brought a gift: robes made of athar cloth like my own, Malika's, and Elian's. They harden to armor upon command."

My gaze shot up to meet his. "Truly?"

His smile was tender. "Indeed." He offered me a bundle of dark blue cloth.

Numbly accepting, I caressed the light and silky but serviceable cloth. When I wore these clothes, I would fit the image of warrior royalty and, better yet, match my Lord, my Grace, and my Honor like I belonged with them. It was a perfect gift, such that my pride could not muster a single objection.

My plates stilled. *What value is there in armor when my swords are too ruined for battle?*

"Arista," my Lord said again.

I miserably glanced up... and beheld a sword, the scabbard midnight blue like the robes, the hilt chocolate, the pommel inlaid with an emerald. Identical to my Lord's, my Grace's, and my Honor's. Breathtakingly so.

My Lord's smile had gained an odd, hesitant edge. "I know your swords are gifts from your parents, but if it would please you, I would ask that you accept this blade as well, as a symbol of your office. It is designed for you—it can split into two thinner blades at your pleasure."

My mouth dropped open, and my eyes widened.

A beat of silence passed.

My lips split in a grin so wide that my cheeks ached. "Gratitude to the Almighty! I would be honored, my Lord!" I exclaimed. Seizing it from his hands in my excitement, I unsheathed it so that I could marvel at the green lights and golden symbols on the shining metal. A thin line traced around the sword, dividing it neatly from pommel to point.

Their faces shining, sharing my joy, my new family turned around for my privacy, and I hurried to wear the robes and buckle on the sword.

As much as I once loved the leather armor and steel dual swords, I would love these gifts so much more. They were untainted, the sign of a new life. The life I had always wanted yet never dared to imagine.

My parents and my sisters would have been pleased.

CHAPTER 9

DIGNIFY THE
BESMIRCHED

Perspective: Honored Arista the Exemplar of Bravery
Date: Eyyéfaz, the seventeenth day of the tenth moon, Thek-harre, of the year 499, C.Q.

The tips of my fingers hovered just above the enameled surface of the painting. The tiny image was made so long ago that it depicted my twin sister and me as infants, but it was the only portrait I had of my family. My only way to remind myself of their faces so that I did not forget.

"Mammy, Pappy, Hannys," I whispered, "you would be proud of me. I met the Quest Leader, not six months out of Rushada, and I swore allegiance to him." I swallowed. "Serving him will make my escape worthwhile. Or at least I hope you would agree..." I angrily brushed away a tear. "Since you are the ones who paid for my escape." The words prompted more tears.

I closed the locket and let it drop onto my curled knees. I covered my face, trying to muffle my sobs. Malika and Elian were still sleeping, and I did not want to wake them.

But somehow the thought of controlling my tears only made me cry harder.

Escape was not so sweet all by myself.

Clenching my knees, I pressed my face into my thighs. How I longed for my father's gentle embrace and Areta's insistence on finding my favorite fruit. My mother's stiff yet loving pats and Henata's awkward assurances.

Lost amid my tears, I almost jumped at a hand touching my shoulder but did not draw a dagger—even with less than a day of acquaintance, I recognized the touch.

The hand and the arm connected to it curled around my shoulders, then lightly drew me into a warm embrace.

Straightening my legs, I turned and pressed myself into Lucian's chest. Muffling my face in his robes, I cried, too miserable in that moment to care about my royal bearing.

He lightly kissed my head and stroked my back. He did not speak, but the pure comfort of his touch and the sweet richness of his scent eased my pain, drop by drop. I felt safe and at peace with him.

When my tears had dried, Lucian spoke in our private link (separate from the one that connected all four of us), *I will pray every day for your reunion, Arista.*

My lips curved into a tremulous smile. *The Almighty surely listens to your prayers. My gratitude, Lucian.*

He kissed my head again and tightened his embrace. Then he commented, his tone light, *I hope I did not wake or disturb you when I left the cave. I have a habit of waking at first light and thinking in solitude before the sun rises.*

Understanding what he was doing, I responded similarly, *You did not, for I also wake at first light. My father instilled the habit.* Speaking of Pappy was somehow easier with Lucian than remembering him alone.

It is a good habit, he replied and laughed quietly. *So long as one actually slept the night before.*

Fond memories flashing through my mind, I laughed as well. *There were nights on which my father would push training until the middle of the night and then still demand that I wake at the same time the next morning.*

Lucian's answering chuckle had a rueful tinge. *My guardians—those who raised me—certainly had that expectation. Perhaps I could have prevailed on them to let me sleep further, but I slept little as a child anyway. Regardless of the time I slept the night before, I almost always woke at first light.*

Thoroughly captivated now, I tried to imagine the childhood self of the Quest Leader. *You must have been a spirited child, too full of energy to ever sit still.*

Oh I was, he said. *I had an ever-present need to learn and study and simply do more. That has not changed.* His tone remained light, but his words were no longer quite so.

My breath caught as I understood why. He was speaking lightly with me to ease my misery, but he had certainly been no ordinary child, the office of the Quest Leader his from birth. Not that I was in any danger of forgetting that—his person emanated waves of power even in so casual a moment.

Silence existed between us for a moment, permeated only by the soft sounds of the others' breathing.

Lucian kissed my head again and rose to his feet. *The sun will be rising soon. Let me go wake Malika and Elian for weapons practice.*

Weapons practice? I asked, interested.

He nodded. *All of us need to master many disciplines. It is my duty to prepare my companions.*

I stared at him, as I constantly seemed to be doing.

My parents had placed such emphasis on my receipt of a full royal education, no matter the sacrifice required, because the laws established by the Quest of Light placed paramount importance on the necessity of intensive education for rule. Regardless of peace or war, a fault in education and training prompted (not 'possibly' but 'always') a forfeiture of the rank of heir, even for those first in line, and sometimes even a loss of royal name and privilege entirely. No extenuation mattered. No remediation counted. An heir (and in some nations, like Zahacim before her betrayal, all royal family members) simply could not lack education. Only education allowed heirs to achieve maturity, the moment their magical connection to their nation was formed. And that had to occur by her or his twentieth birthday.

Malika and Elian were both beyond twenty and far behind in education.

Thus, for Lucian to bother to prepare his companions… to redeem instead of censure them… my mind could barely grasp the idea.

I was too stunned to move as Lucian roused Malika and Elian, who jolted out of their sleep at merely their names in his voice. They both collected flasks of water and their swords and rushed outside, Lucian strolling out after them.

Shaking myself, I scrambled to his side. *May I join you?* I asked breathlessly.

Lucian glanced back with a welcoming smile. *Of course.*

Slipping my locket beneath the collar of my new robes, I grabbed my sword and joined him as he began a set of stretches.

A few minutes later, Malika and Elian stumbled out of a nearby grove, seeming more awake now that their needs had been attended, and copied Lucian and me.

Silence filled the air among us, but it was one of warmth and the awkward comfort of new friendship—a far cry from the madness I had faced for the last five months.

Finishing the last stretch, an exercise of the neck, I said, seizing my chance, "Lucian, if you wish, would you honor me with a practice duel?"

Lucian raised an eyebrow but seemed pleased (the reaction I wanted). "I would be the one honored. Malika, Elian, would you practice blocks and parries?"

Malika and Elian murmured their agreement and gave us room. They raised their swords for their exercise but repeatedly glanced back at us.

I drew my new sword. Deciding to try the qualities Lucian had described last night, I raised it with both hands on the hilt and squared my stance.

Lucian, however, stood casually, his sword loose at his side.

A moment passed.

I sprang forward, leaping into the air, and attacked his shoulder. The sword's heft decreased smoothly as I swung it up.

His arm blurred as he raised his blade to block.

At the last moment, I changed the arc of my swing and struck at his knee. The sword's weight increased to lend force to the blow.

Lucian jumped back to dodge the attack. "Nice," he breathed, sounding impressed. Then, placing both hands on his hilt, he feinted toward my waist and swung at my shoulder.

I blocked the blow and clenched my teeth at the jarring force he had used. But I maintained my stance and thrust downward at his legs. The sword's weight further increased with each inch of the swing.

Lucian skipped backward and simultaneously cut toward my head.

I leaned back to dodge, straightened, and jumped into a kick aimed at his stomach while also swinging toward his shoulder.

He blocked my kick with one arm and my blow with his sword.

Landing lightly on the soles of my feet, I disengaged and struck again.

Thus we continued.

Though our faces were hard with focus, enjoyment lit both our gazes. Lucian was unquestionably the best swordsman I had ever seen—and I had been raised by the warrior princesses of Zahacim. He did not soften his blows or simplify his movements, just as I reached ever deeper into my repertoire of combinations and sequences. Flowing from pose to pose, he seemed to enjoy the challenge as much as I did.

From this small sampling of his skill, there was much I could learn from him. For all my study, he had trained more and had a greater affinity with the sword than I had. I welcomed the thought.

Many minutes passed uncounted as we dueled.

Ending an intricate series of movements, Lucian twisted his sword and arm around mine and tapped the center of my chest, over my heart. "Yield," he breathed. Only a few drops of sweat rolled down the silver-cream skin of his forehead, and his breathing was almost steady.

I was only slightly more visibly wearied. "Yielded," I answered.

Lucian lowered his sword and drew back. The early morning light glimmered on his sunlight hair and seemed to match the brightness of his smile. "Well done, Arista. You are a true master!" he exclaimed, laughing.

I grinned, enjoying both the experience of the duel and the pleasure on his face. "On the contrary, there is much that I can learn from both your skill and experience." My plates thrummed in delight.

The faint silver glow of Lucian's cream cheeks intensified in his kind's version of blushes, flaring scales, and vibrating plates. He touched his chest in acknowledgment of my praise (a traditional gesture my father had told me was an indication of greatest humility) and then turned to supervise Malika's and Elian's practice.

I idly flexed my fingers on the hilt of my sword. In addition to Lucian's skill, I had been observing the sword's magic, which adjusted the blade's weight depending on what would be most effective for each movement. Downward swings gained more force from an increase in weight while upward swings had the reverse, rendering the sword easier to lift. The sword consequently had the advantages of both light and heavy weaponry. In practical use, the magic had made my blows, strikes, and blocks in this duel my best ever.

It really will become my favorite weapon, I thought, smiling. Then jolted forward and exclaimed, "And not least because of that!"

Elian's hand had slipped down the hilt onto the sharp edge... and remained free of injury. But a moment later, Elian misjudged his swing such that the blade, edge first, hit Malika's wrist. The skin did not even redden.

Exactly as Lucian had promised, these enchanted swords could not cut us. Any of us.

I grinned, caressing the elegant curve of the pommel. The possibilities for training were endless. Unlike my childhood self, Malika and Elian could afford to make mistakes while still learning the weight of a real blade.

At that thought, my attention snapped to Lucian as he demonstrated the proper motions for a parry. From what I had observed so far, Malika knew little of sword-craft, despite her enthusiasm, and Elian knew nothing at all. And Lucian planned to teach them everything a ruler needed to know? That encompassed far more disciplines than merely wielding weapons.

Helping him would make sense... I mused. *It would be efficient... and I am starting to care for Malika and Elian... But...* my brow furrowed. *Why has he not commanded me? He does not need to ask.*

I realized then that he had so far not commanded a single thing of me. Not before I had pledged, not even after. In everything he had only asked me, in the tone of true requests, contingent upon my pleasure and happiness. Everything had been a polite question. Though he was my liege.

Without thinking, I asked, *Lucian, why have you not you given any orders to me?*

Sidestepping Elian's messy strike, Lucian glanced at me. His cheeks tinted silver, but the violet of his eyes glittered like steel. *I will never ask you to do anything against your own choice, Arista.*

But one does not choose to follow orders, I mumbled, my mind reeling again.

Lucian sent an impression of the shake of his head through the link. *I will not command anything of you until you feel that I have earned your trust. Even then, I will always listen to you speak. You will always have a choice with me, Arista.* He returned his attention to Malika's swing.

I was too dazzled to look away. Those words... they were what I had always wanted to hear, though I had not known it.

My family's degradation had stripped us of our choice.

And now the Quest Leader restored mine. As he would for all of Icilia.

He is everything, I whispered to myself. *I would do anything for him.* He did not need to wait for my trust, for he already had it.

Stepping forward, I declared, "Lucian, I beg your permission to help you teach. In every subject."

Lucian actually startled, and Malika and Elian nearly dropped their swords in shock.

A brilliant smile curved Lucian's pale lips. "My gratitude would be unending, Arista."

I grinned, warmed by his happiness. "The Quest Leader's unending gratitude is exactly what I want," I quipped and strode to join them. "Now, Malika, you need to start the thrust from this position…" I demonstrated the move.

She smiled shyly and copied my form, her mimicry not quite exact. *Thank you, Arista*, she whispered.

"For your happiness, Sister," I replied. "Now angle your sword this way…"

As I guided her through the motions and corrected her mistakes, I felt at peace for the first time in my life. I had finally started on the path worth my family's sacrifice. If only I did not ruin it.

CHAPTER 10

SUFFERING CEASELESSLY

Perspective: Kyros
Date: Eyyéqan, the ninth day of the fifth moon, Marberre, of the year 499, C.Q.

Kneeling, I pressed a kiss to my young sister's forehead. She slept soundly, despite the tear marks on her cheeks, clutching the doll I had made for her fourth birthday.

My lips moving silently, I recited a formal father's prayer, "Oh Almighty, hear the prayer of this father! May my child delight my eyes with the acts that earn Your happiness. Free her with Your beloved virtues. May all my efforts ensure her success. Bless my child!"

I kissed her forehead again and sighed, the sight of her sleeping figure both a balm and a knife to my heart, and stood. I had made every arrangement for Kalyca to live in the home of our aunt, our father's sister, who would keep her as safe as any child could be in this age. As much as I worried, I could stay no longer, for my visions grew ever more troubling. If I did not act, then what had happened to our parents and siblings would befall her as well.

How that thought terrified me.

Though eight years had passed, the night in which my dear parents, my beloved older sister, and my treasured younger brother were massacred haunted my every dream and tainted my every joy. I had to protect Kalyca from such a fate, no matter how my aunt or the mayor argued the irrelevance of my visions and the irresponsibility of my intentions. No matter what taunts I heard from the rest of the village.

My visions were not wrong. For this was no age of peace. And how could I continue to cower when the land itself trembled under the smoke-wreathed sky?

Since the day on which the Blood had established unchallenged dominion over Icilia, the day on which the last country to stand, Khuduren, had fallen after months of siege and resistance, three years after the fall of Koroma, the skies had grown hazy with smoke. Smoke that first spread from the fires lit in unholy celebration by the Blood's armies and then remained because of the taint of his black magic. The sun shone, but the caress of its light was only dimly felt, and the moon seemed to exist only in stories. Thus, the Blood's conquest ruined even the crops and fields that his forces had never touched. Every year the harvests grew smaller and the pickings in the forest leaner. Though the land still held a little vitality, the day would come soon on which the people of Icilia would starve because all else had been choked to death.

Amid such abject terror, how could I do nothing? How could I live as though this were any other age, farming the fields of the village, constructing new buildings, and hunting to provide some extra meat? How could I walk by the Blood's soldiers, who tormented any who crossed their path, and not shudder at what their tyrannical presence could mean for my sister? Not remember the role of their peers in my family's murders? The land that flashed in my farsight and the future that flickered in my foresight revealed only death and suffering.

I did not have a clear plan, yes, as my sister accused, and my magic was untrained, as my aunt and the mayor charged, but I could not ignore the stirrings of duty. Duty to Icilia as a whole and, even more so, to my sister.

I left for her sake.

Firming my resolve, I walked downstairs on silent feet to the front door. There I slid on the slim pack I had placed by the shoe rack, secured my dull sword and dagger to my belt, affixed my worn longbow to my back, and slung my half-empty quiver over my right shoulder. Kneeling, I donned a mismatched pair of boots, the sturdiest shoes I had, before I straightened and turned to face the cottage.

I blinked back tears at the sight of the empty room. My sister had argued with me until she had fallen asleep; my aunt, my uncle, and my cousins so disapproved of my decision that they would care for Kalyca but refused to bid me farewell. No one would see me off.

Quietly I left, closing the door with nary a sound, and walked to the small clearing behind my cottage, neighbor to my aunt's house. Removing flowers from my pocket, I knelt at the four gravestones there. As I kissed the names and left a blossom in front of each stone, tears trickled down my coarsening cheeks. For, though I tried to avoid it, I could not help but remember that night. And why it had happened.

Khuduren had fallen only so long after Etheqa, Koroma, Asfiya, and Nademan because the Blood had toyed with it. His forces swelled by each country that he conquered or that submitted to him, he had more than enough soldiers to grind Khuduren to dust. But, as was well publicized by his lieutenants, the Blood had cackled and stated after the penultimate survivor, Nademan, had fallen that he wanted some entertainment.

For a year, he taunted Khuduren, giving respite and punishment in turns, until he launched a devastating blow amid the autumn months of 486 C.Q. My parents, soldiers in the Khudurel military, barely survived the final battle. Terrified of the cruelty they had witnessed, they escaped with my aunt's family to a tiny Ezulal village, called Tresilt, in southeastern Khuduren. My family was of the Nasimih, a different kind, but the village grudgingly accepted us as supplements to the ranks of their farmers, many of whom had perished in the war.

But the Blood's torments did not end with the war. From the great forests and plains of Khuduren and the mighty mountains of Etheqa, he seized young boys and girls for various forms of entertainment, most infamously gladiator matches fought on the western plains of Khuduren. Many had been taken from Tresilt.

I had escaped the notice of his soldiers only because my parents had taught me to carefully disguise my strength with ragged clothes and my handsome face with dirt and soot. My aunt and I did the same with Kalyca and our cousins, who often looked like vagrants instead of the treasured daughters and sons they were. For the same reason, my mother had trained me in suppressing my magic instead of using it (another lesson I shared with Kalyca). Though my farsight and foresight left little residue to be traced, despite their great strength, my powerful gift of teleportation could have easily drawn attention if I had ever succumbed to instinct. I had to resist my own nature to remain safe.

But, even with such precautions, we did not escape the Blood's cruelty. For, beyond the atrocities wreaked upon our whole nation, he and his governor, a man known only as the Slicer, every so often chose a village and a family. Then massacred that family in the most brutal way possible as a public spectacle that the village had no choice but to attend. Eight years ago, not seven months after Kalyca was born, their target was Tresilt and my family. We had no warning.

Earlier that fateful day, with the delight of a fascinated older brother, I had snuck out with Kalyca to the fields. Hours of play later, when I had returned at twilight, troubled by the scent of blood and smoke and the cruel figures flickering in both my farsight and foresight, I had found myself a spectator to my family's torture and murders. Standing at the edge of the crowd, my arms holding my infant sister, I could do nothing. I could only watch. I could only pray.

Monstrous fires glowed beneath the moonless sky on cruel blades, on thunderclouds of black conjury, on my family's screaming faces, on the rivers of blood staining their flesh.

Once the Blood and his governor left, their lust for destruction temporarily sated, the village stirred from where they had frozen and watched. Most, including my parents' friends, fled to their homes, but my aunt's family and the mayor's stayed by my side. And, at the tender age of thirteen, I lowered the four corpses of my parents and siblings into graves, reciting the funeral dirges which entreated the Almighty to favor their souls.

How I had longed to join them beneath the rising soil and the gleaming gravestones.

But I could not.

For, though I lamented my own survival, I had inadvertently saved my baby sister. I had no time to grieve, for I needed to make a life anew for her.

I could not let any from the village adopt us, for I was already seeing the hatred and hostility on their faces: they blamed us for the Blood's cursed attention having turned to Tresilt, atop the difference in kind, and spoke without shame of how they would leave us to fend for ourselves, defying all responsibility.

Not considering my own fate, I feared that another family might neglect, even abuse, my sister—perhaps even cast her to the soldiers. At the same time, for fear of the stigma affecting my aunt's family, I could not accept her offer to take us into her household. The villagers loathed her family's presence but tolerated them because of my uncle's skill with construction; that forbearance would have changed had they adopted my sister and me. And, despite the terrible prejudice, I could not leave, for the roads grew increasingly unsafe and the soldiers increasingly stricter about travel. I would have left our family's graves for my sister, but there was nowhere to go.

So I took all responsibility for her. I submitted myself to unceasing abuse, from mockery to unfair demands of labor, all so I could raise her. And, from the age of thirteen, I became not only doting older brother but mother and father and sister to Kalyca. I gave my life to her.

And for her I now left.

My visions, mere glimpses though they were, signaled that I was at a crossroads: if I did not leave, on this day, I would not be able to save her again from our family's fate.

Filth protected her now, yes, but she would soon become too beautiful to escape the soldiers' notice.

But even if that were not so, this world was not the one I wanted for her future: there was no equilibrium under the Blood's control, no uneasy balance, no wary happiness. His unbearable cruelty accumulated day by day; with every day, we grew less safe in our own homes. At any moment, he could seize our food, our children, all of our lives. There was no living under his tyranny.

If my actions could do anything to change that future, for both Kalyca and Icilia herself, I had to try. If my visions were correct in their prediction that I would find the right path to hope should I leave, I could not ignore that call.

"May the Almighty give you peace, my mother Meriel, my father Nikos, my sister Zabraka, my brother Terros," I murmured the names of my family one last time.

Then I rose, shouldered my pack, and oriented myself toward the southeast, toward Bhalasa, the direction to which I felt called.

Taking the first steps of the journey, I prayed to the Almighty for success, for the chance to do something to protect my family, my country, and Icilia herself.

I had to find the way free of this nightmare, or I, Kyros Dinasiett, would die in my own home, smothered by guilt and regret. I would have no future or promise to share with my sister if I did nothing.

CHAPTER 11

SUPPORT THE CRUSHED

Perspective: Kyros Dinasiett, citizen of Khuduren
Date: Eyyéqan, the twentieth day of the tenth moon, Thekharre,
of the year 499, C.Q.

Pain roared in my ears, spreading across my skull in a wave of agonizing sound.

Oh Almighty! I screamed wordlessly. *A few minutes more! Please!* My jaw ached from how tightly I held it shut, and my limbs spasmed from how squeezed they were against my torso, but I simply had to endure. I could not let my teeth chatter or my body shake. I hardly dared to breathe.

Since I had left Tresilt, the combination of my sights, teleportation, and incredible speed saved me from dozens of patrols and countless enemies. Although not fully reliable due to a lack of training, these natural gifts had protected me so well that my weapons remained unused, except for hunting. Though the journey was still perilous, I had wondered if I had been wrong to leave Kalyca behind.

Until the crossing into Bhalasa.

Though the Nasimih could run like the wind on flat earth, both plains and forests, my kind became as awkward as newborn foals in the mountains. Such imbalance, coupled with our natural sensitivity to the cold, was enough reason for none of the Nasimih to ever risk traveling alone through even the foothills of Etheqa and Bhalasa.

But the terrain and the temperature became the least of my worries. For, some weeks after I had entered the mountains, a lone soldier, one of the Sholanar, had caught sight of me.

At first, I had believed that overpowering a singular soldier would be easy. The thought of spilling blood churned my stomach, but I would steel myself to ensure I had the chance to fulfill my purpose here.

Then, as the man drew closer and closer, I saw the smoke well from his fingertips and knew he was a wielder of conjury. The slightest brush of that magic produced a fear so potent that it destroyed all semblance of free will.

Choking on terror, I ran as fast as I could, nearly tumbling into ravines and falling off cliffs, not even death scaring me as much as my pursuer.

He had chased me for the last four weeks.

I could not escape. I was trapped in a game, a torment, of his design, for his pleasure, my fear the result of both his magic and his sadistic scheme.

I was only clinging to survival, my only motivation to continue searching for the path my visions had promised. Which I still had not found.

Perhaps Kalyca, my aunt, and the mayor had been right. Perhaps I should not have trusted my magic so much. Perhaps I should have stayed where I knew the evils than go where I did not.

Even amid the crippling pain and fear, I flinched at those thoughts.

The magic of Icilia, of both categories as well as that unique to each kind, was considered a blessing of the Almighty. Wish magic, the category that included all three of my gifts, had been bestowed by the Shining Guide Himself unto the Muthaarim, and the Quest of Light had subsequently led the other kinds to discover it in themselves. All six types of wish magic—athar magic, mindlinking, healing, foresight, farsight, and teleportation—were considered the marks of civilization.

And similarly esteemed was the element-based category of arms magic, which was comprised of wizardry, sorcery, and warrior magic. Though they were not entirely born of Icilia, they were the mark of true civilization's generosity and supremacy. Gifts of the Almighty, regardless of their mixed origin.

Thus, to doubt my magic reeked of doubt in the Almighty.

Not that the use of magic led to infallible conclusions and results... but the visions I had had were not the normal flickering of possibilities that foresight was supposed to produce. They had been certainties, and my future had been split into two paths at my feet.

Doubting my magic was what was truly foolish.

But this conjuror's torment atop so many months alone and lost eroded the last of my strength.

I pray this is a test of my conviction. In desperation, I sent my farsight beyond the tiny confines of the hole in which I hid, though I knew my sights were blind to the approach of conjurors. *I could not bear it if all of this were a waste.*

The thuds of wings drew closer.

I bit my tongue, stifling a whimper.

The sound receded.

I breathed and let go of my head.

A hand thrust into the hole. "What a clever hiding spot, *dear* little boy." Black smoke blew directly into my face.

Panicking, I chose the first place I saw in my farsight and used the dregs of my energy to teleport. Then scrambled to my feet and prepared to run.

Only to find that I stood on the edge of a sheer bluff, a fall I could not survive.

I spun around, desperate for another path.

The conjuror landed in front of me, his scales as black as smog and his grin as cruel as the Blood's. Smoke wound its way through the air toward me.

Paralysis stiffened my spine and my lungs. Black dots began to consume my vision as my head spun from the lack of air. Unadulterated fear clawed at my sanity.

There was nowhere else to run.

The evil parting of his mouth widening, he stepped closer and closer, until his chest brushed mine. He reached for a sensitive, private part of my body, then seemed to decide on another course. With a quick dart of his smoking hand, he pushed me off the mountain.

I tumbled backward, my arms suddenly unfreezing enough to grasp the edge, curling my fingers over it.

My body slammed against the bare rock, wrenching and nearly dislocating both arms.

Pebbles bounced down the cliff-face, stinging my legs and torso, hurting all the more because of the cold. The dust released showered over my face. Though I coughed, I could not clear my mouth.

"Beg for mercy, little boy," the conjuror jeered. "Beg me to save you."

My fingers were slipping, too stiff from the cold to cling for long. *Kalyca, forgive me for not returning! Oh Almighty, save me!*

"Beg!" More smoke wafted toward my face.

My mouth slackened, my will weakening as my fingers were...

A bright light flashed at the top of the cliff.

The conjuror screamed, shrill voice agonizing to the delicate organs of my ears.

Then the smoke vanished.

And I slipped.

Still reaching for the cliff-face, I fell.

Save me, oh Almighty! Kalyca's face flashed before my eyes.

Something grasped my hands.

My body jerked to a stop.

This time my shoulders did not throb with pain, and whatever was folded around my hands felt incredibly soothing, cool yet comfortingly warm at the same time... driving out every vestige of the taste of conjury...

Are those hands? I squinted. *Yes, definitely hands. But whose?*

I had barely time to wonder before the hands began to pull me up.

The cliff-side collapsed beneath my weight, my body sinking into the falling pebbles. But the upward movement remained smooth.

My head poked up over the edge. Dust erupted in my face.

I immediately closed my eyes.

My chest, then my middle, then my legs were dragged over the edge.

I lay too stunned to move, save for shaking lips whispering prayers of gratitude.

The pair of hands shifted from mine to my shoulders.

At the gentle nudge, some of my will returned, and I folded my legs beneath me, rising into a seated position. I tried to wipe the dust from my face so I could thank my rescuer but only succeeded in further smearing it.

I noted distantly that my shoulders and the various places at which my body had collided with the rock did not ache. Even the chilly breeze did not affect me.

The hands left my shoulders—I could not suppress a whimper as the relief and the warmth disappeared. Then a soft cloth touched my face and proceeded to wipe it.

Stunned—no one had done anything like this for me in eight years—I savored the caring touch. My cheeks moistened with gloss, like an Ezulal blush, as a sweet pleasure lightened my spirit.

As the cloth retreated, I opened my eyes.

My visions clicked into place.

He was the one for whom I had been searching.

The white-gold sunlight that had dazzled my eyes on more than one occasion was his person… the glinting violet jewels his eyes… the play of silver light his skin… the pillar providing support for my broken back and a haven from hostility was his authority… His presence was the first full breath after suffocating under the burden of tears. Merely looking upon him eased the chokehold of grief and abuse that had so long darkened my vision.

Every vision of the future in which Kalyca was safe revolved around him.

Only one person shone with such light.

Without hesitation I raised my hands.

A smile lit that blessed face yet further, the sight the substance of divine-gifted visions. "May the Almighty bless you, Kyros Dinasiett. I presume you know who I am?"

His knowledge of my name did not surprise me. Delighted me, yes, but did not astound me. My fumbled grasp of magic had allowed me to glimpse him; surely the magnitude of his power had shown him far more.

My Lord chuckled softly, the sound prompting my cheeks to again gloss just as surely as the wind did. "My name is Lord Lucian the Ideal of Freedom, Heir to the Quest of Light and supreme ruler of Icilia." His smile faded slightly as his gaze flickered over my person. "As overjoyed as I am by your fealty, Kyros, should we not first care for your injuries and clothes?"

I pressed my lips together and considered the thoughtful question. Then I shook my head. "I do not want to waste a single moment." Indeed, pledging while covered in dust so soon after such torment seemed fitting for it reflected who I was.

My Lord's brow creased momentarily, but his smile returned in full. "Then I will speak of the true gravity of your pledge: Kyros Dinasiett, you are the fifth Potentate of my Quest."

My mouth dropped open in the most uncouth manner. "Me?" I squeaked.

"Indeed, yes," my Lord replied.

"But I am a peasant! An orphan!" My rumbling bass voice was embarrassingly high-pitched.

He raised an eyebrow. "Is such a choice truly so hard to believe, Kyros?"

I sputtered but could not find the words to refute his argument. Taking responsibility for my baby sister as I had done was no common choice.

"You saw the face that few have seen, Kyros," he said quietly. "That is itself divine blessing. And this is the path for which you prayed."

I blinked rapidly. *This is what those visions foretold.* The thought rang true and certain, filling my heart with a peace

I had rarely tasted. And along with it came a realization that my Lord knew of my visions. If that was not a validation of them, then I did not know what was. And… for the first time in eight years, someone other than Kalyca was choosing me.

Wetting my lips, I answered, "Then I choose this path." I prayed I would be able to honor this welcome into his inner circle and confidence. Somehow, I would become what he wanted me to be.

His sudden smile sealed my choice, such was the affirmation it provided. Affirmation that no one had given any of my choices before.

Turning, my Lord introduced me to his companions, who, though I had not noticed their presence before, immediately captivated me. My Lord's Second, my Grace, wore an open, curious look on her beautiful yet tormented face. The gentleness of her gaze promised her kindness, even as the way she did not hesitate to meet mine revealed her strength.

Beside her, my Honor Elian radiated compassion and sweetness, despite the bitter sight of his bound wings. His shy nature was evident in how his eyes only met mine in uncertain flickers.

My Honor Arista, however, standing on his left, presented an entirely different image: though of lesser height, she stood straight and proud, her carriage marking her as both warrior and royal (the impression was truly unmistakable, though I had never seen royalty before). The determined gleam of her dark amber eyes, the austere bun in which her mahogany hair was twisted beneath her cap, and the controlled thrum of the plates etched against her olive-bronze skin contributed to that image of disciplined poise. The confidence in her bearing complemented my Lord's air of pious self-assuredness; the only reason she did not appear more like the Second than my Grace was her lack of the sense of inherent power that hummed around my Grace like a swarm of bees.

As I examined their faces, I considered my own, viewing it with the magical vision of my farsight: gently curved features, from arched brows to broad, rounded nose, hairless light beige skin which often gleamed like polished glass, ash-blond hair and beard that glistened like metal in places. A fatherly care creased the skin around my glowing steel-gray eyes and full lips, as Kalyca often said. Tall as I was for one of the Nasimih, I had the same height as my Honor Elian, who was an inch taller, physically, to my Lord and three inches to my Grace.

My physical and magical visions presented these sights together in a sort of double-vision, which my brain processed as an overlay of the magical atop what my eyes saw.

And with that magic came certainty that, despite my insecurity, I belonged with them. The beauty and splendor of our faces complemented each other, a harmony enhanced, not detracted, by the difference of kind amongst us. My Lord and my Grace as the sun rising in the bright blue sky, my Honor Elian, my Honor Arista, and I the vast expanses of land beneath steadfast mountains, fertile soils, and uplifting winds. The essence of Icilia at her greatest promise, incarnated in the five of us.

My farsight dissipated as my hold on the magic wavered. I blinked, still dazzled, and returned my attention to my Lord as I agreed to join his links. From the sparkle in his eyes, he knew of my distraction, but he did not mention it as he bent to place a brotherly kiss on my forehead. Then he directed me to my Grace, who taught me the sacred words and acts.

How I hated the cruelty that had stolen her voice.

Thus came the moments I would cherish forever: the ceremony that forever bound me to the Quest and to the

Almighty's will, the bestowal of my new name, Honored Kyros the Exemplar of Strength.' Power built in the air, shocking my magical awareness... culminating when my Lord touched his hands to mine.

Magic inundated all of my senses, pouring from him into me... all that it touched it transformed, molding my heart, my mind, my spirit, and my body so that it matched something of the contours of who he was. His virtue, his strength, his selfless ambition... the magic afforded me a glimpse of the magnificence of his identity and then pressed a portion of that glory unto me. For a moment worthy of my lifetime, I witnessed the grandeur of his divine-blessed nature and magic and the rightness of his authority... bestowing unto my tortured spirit a contentment I could never have hoped to attain.

As these changes occurred in the fabric of who I was, my magic transformed—my visions gained clarity, a discernment of the details of the distance and the shades of the future they had not had before, and my reach for teleportation extended and stabilized. A whirlwind of color passed before my eyes: impressions of the future, my own and Icilia's.

Every perception inscribed into my being the certainty that he would always support me. I would never need to doubt his steadfastness, for he would never place his own advantage above mine. He would aid me whenever I asked for it and stand by me whenever I wanted to act on my own. He would always succor me, if only I would trust in him.

How long I had been deprived of such assurance.

But with him I was not alone. And with him were two sisters and a brother, swelling the ranks of my family as I had long desired. They were the anchors of my senses, assuring me I would never feel lost again.

My face glossed, smoothening the creases of sorrow and stress, as the first smile since I had left Kalyca curved my lips. "Thank you," I whispered.

Chuckling, my Lord knelt and folded his arms around me—the first embrace that I had received in eight years that sought to give comfort rather than take. I relished the feeling, the warmth I received far beyond the physical...

My Lord drew back. "Meet my eyes," he commanded.

Curious, I obeyed.

A pulse of energy exploded from his person, and the accompanying light brightened my vision to white.

Then an image coalesced in my farsight...

Kalyca.

Her pink lips parted in laughter as she smoothed a lock of metallic hair behind her ear. She raised both hands, a cookie in one and a wooden stylus in the other. Nibbling on the treat, she lowered the pencil to a clay tablet. She wrote something and glanced up, a mischievous look on her sweet, soot-streaked face.

I caught my breath, my heart pounding, as the vision faded. "Was that really her?" I whispered, numbed by my overwhelming emotions.

My Lord dipped his head and answered in the private link between us, *Yes. With my magic, I extended your farsight for a glimpse of her at this very moment.*

She was happy then. The arrangements I had made for her—our aunt's family quietly taking custody of her to avoid the stigma, the saved currency I had set aside to compensate for the loss of my labor—they were keeping her safe and fed. My departure had not been the disaster I feared.

I hoped my face expressed the depth of the gratitude in my heart as I met my Lord's gaze.

He smiled, the expression gentle, and offered me a handkerchief, its edges embroidered in gold.

Realizing that my glossed cheeks were wet, I accepted it and wiped my face.

Once my tears had stemmed, my Lord lifted me to my feet and turned slightly to address all of us.

While he spoke, my Grace's and my Honors' gazes repeatedly returned to my dust- and tear-stained features.

At first, my mind focused on my Lord's words and the task of disposing of the conjuror's body, I did not comprehend what seemed odd about their expressions.

Then, as my Lord directed us northwest, I realized: instead of the anger I was accustomed to seeing from those of another kind, the diametric opposite shone on their faces—affection. With barely a few words, they cared for me. Though they were more than me.

Marveling at this blessing, I prayed for the day on which I could introduce them to Kalyca. For, finally, we had a family again.

CHAPTER 12

WELCOME THE REJECTED

Perspective: Honored Kyros the Exemplar of Strength
Date: Eyyédal, the twenty-second day of the tenth moon, Thek-
harre, of the year 499, C.Q.

The deep breath of freezing air did not steady my nerves. I considered taking another, but more moments of hesitation and chilling wheezes would not make this any easier.

Clinging to what courage I had, I approached the portion of riverbank where Malika, Elian, and Arista knelt. All three were filling empty flasks, Elian clutching twice as many as the others. From the words that drifted to my ears on the glacial wind, Arista was explaining the precepts of wizardry to Elian, who was deeply interested. Malika, from her questions in the links, was also listening. Their heads were bent together, their attention upon each other.

The sight intimidated me. But, if I wanted to try to forge a relationship with them, beyond wearing the same style of clothes, I simply had to approach them and speak. Though I did not know what to say—I did not know much at all about arms magic, as I did not possess it, and regardless they seemed too at ease with each other for me to interject myself. They had not even given me flasks to fill, instead taking on that task themselves.

But I had to try. And hope my attempts at friendship would not hurt as much as all the rejected overtures to my Tresilt peers.

Reaching Arista's side, I stood awkwardly and scoured my mind for something to say. *No, that is not it... no, not that... That is what I would say to Kalyca, not to anyone who is not eight—sorry, nine...* The thought of my sister depressed my spirits, but I tried not to dwell on my absence.

A little desperate, I glanced at Lucian, who stood turned away from us with his hand on his sword's hilt, but stuck to my resolve. If I asked him to help me, I would not ever have a relationship with them on my own merit. And I needed one: I was about to live and travel with these three for the rest of my life. If I wanted to actually be part of the Quest's future endeavors, I needed them to trust me. That could not happen without a relationship.

Good goal; poor execution. As usual.

Wringing my hands, I focused on Arista's voice in the hope of finding something to say.

But, lured by the sound of her clear, melodious alto voice, I quickly became too interested by her description of an arms magician's process of catalysis and imbuement to scheme up an interruption.

"...quite right, Elian—all the steps do not need to be done together," Arista said, putting aside her last flask. "The hymn, catalysis and the recitation of your spell can all be done separately. So can the optional step of amplifying power with jewels, for those with sufficient control. But you must imbue your command, your spell or intention, into the catalyzed power at the same time as into your element. You and I, Elian, cannot use magic with our will alone as wish magicians and warrior-mages can. Without our elements, we do not have any connection to the land around us; without the power, the element cannot fulfill our command."

"Why can they not be done separately?" Elian asked curiously. Sounding bashful, he added in a mutter, "That is the most difficult part for me."

Arista gave him a warm smile. "You will learn with practice." She shuffled back a few paces and angled herself such that her face was tilted equally toward Elian and me. But her gaze remained upon him. "Yes, theoretically, we could imbue the power and then the element, or vice versa. But this is unsafe. On one side, power given a command will immediately act to fulfill its task, and our spell will rebound upon us without the effectuating connection to the land provided by our element. On the other side, the elements are too vast to be grasped for long. Grasping the elements is like clutching a fistful of the silky cloth of a large tapestry: it quickly escapes our grip and returns to its natural, inert state. Our power is mere thread that we are sewing into the tapestry. We have to act quickly before our fingers lose their grip. Otherwise… you know as well as I do that rebounding spells, particularly those that did not finish the casting process, often cause injury and harm to their caster."

Malika shifted so that she sat at a right-angle to Elian.

Uncapping his last flask, Elian winced. "That is why magicians are supposed to learn as children." He turned slightly, his face becoming more clearly visible to me.

Arista nodded. "Yes. Catalysis and imbuement are complex tasks. As children, building the reflexes for them is like learning to move a limb. As adults..." She winced herself. "There is a reason that most untrained magicians do not attempt training after adolescence, regardless of how stifled they feel."

Lucian's willingness, Malika observed, *to use his Quest Leader's magic to dispel those consequences is quite a mercy.*

Elian and Arista emphatically murmured their agreement.

Malika then asked, *What about the warrior magic? I know it is element-based, but not how.*

Arista traced the edge of the plates on her bronze cheeks. "The warrior magic, the rarest, really, of all forms of both wish and arms magic... it is considered elemental because it manipulates energy in a way that no other type of magic does, with its focus on the magician's own body. From what I have studied, though, using it in any way that does not directly concern weapons is the province of the most powerful." She smiled apologetically. "I know little more than that, Malika. You might consider asking Lucian."

Malika dipped her head. *Thank you for your indulgence, Arista.* At Elian's gentle tug on the flask she held, she pressed it into his hands.

"Of course," Arista replied. Then she turned to me and asked, nonchalant, "How does your experience with catalysis and imbuement contrast with Elian's and mine, Kyros? I have always wanted to ask a true wish magician."

I startled. The curious, relaxed expressions on their faces... and her question... Had they already known I was listening? But I had not said anything to draw their attention! So how had they...

Examining their postures, I understood, with a jolt, that they had indeed acknowledged me: all three of them had moved to face me.

They had included me of their own accord.

Dazed, I somehow managed to stammer, "W-well, as Elian must know… W-wish mag-magic requires that catalysis occurs simul-simultaneously with the ex-expression of intention and convic-viction. Con-conviction for us instead-instead of hymns. It t-takes ef-effect immediately. That- it is why- well, once we start catalysis, it does not, um, take more concentration to keep going."

"What is the flow of energy like then?" Arista asked, sounding sincerely interested. "As in, how much energy do you use to start, and how much do you use to continue?"

I rubbed my hands together, both delighted and overwhelmed. "Umm… well, farsight, and I suppose mindlinking, only use a burst of energy to start and then con-continue with t-trickles. Foresight, teleportation, healing…" I remembered to nod to Elian, who had mentioned yesterday that he possessed healing, "those require bursts of energy with every use and are- are easier to- to amplify with jewels."

"There is that much similarity!" Elian breathed, scales glowing golden. "How do you change between your types, Kyros?" He filled the last flask, not recoiling at the bone-chilling water, and gathered all of them in his arms.

My cheeks glossed. "Umm… I was hoping to learn. The only other magician I know can do it naturally, but I tend to mix up my sights. And I was always taught to not use teleportation."

Malika, Elian, and Arista nodded, wearing commiserating smiles, and Arista seemed about to ask another question when Lucian called out, "Malika, Elian, Arista, Kyros, come. I do not wish to linger."

We—there was a 'we'!—obeyed, rising to our feet, and huddled behind him, Arista and Malika at my sides and Elian on Arista's. Their closeness banished nearly all of the chill that clung to my limbs.

Once we had climbed another foothill (which were becoming progressively less steep), Arista turned to me. "So," she said, curious, "who is the other magician, the one whose experience you referenced?"

"My sister Kalyca," I answered immediately, her dear face filling my vision.

"You have a sister?" Arista exclaimed. "What magic does she have? What is she like?"

"Well, she has foresight and a hint of teleportation, much like I do. And… she is my world." The words prompted a sudden effusion, so much did I miss her. Today was her birthday… and I was missing it. The first birthday I had ever missed. How desperately was I worried that no one would remember and celebrate.

So, to somehow compensate for my absence, I told the Quest-Potentates about her. Her favorite foods, games, and lessons. Her scrapes and pranks. Her favorite birthday treats. I told them about what I would have done for her birthday if I had been present. She was reaching the great big age of nine, and I had been making plans since last year. Plans now trampled in the dust by my own feet. Drowning my sorrow, I spoke yet more of her.

When I paused to blink back my tears, I realized, with another jolt, that the expressions on their faces were ones of interest. They were really listening. Actually, truly, giving their attention to me as I waxed poetic about my sister. All of them—Malika, Elian, Arista, and even Lucian. They were all facing me or tilting their heads in my direction.

But I had dominated too much of the conversation. Hoping to turn it back to them, I asked awkwardly, "Do you have siblings?"

No one commented on the abrupt change in subject.

Instead, Arista replied, "Yes, I do! I have two sisters: one is older, Henata, by six years, and the other, Areta, is my twin. She is older than me by four minutes, and she looks exactly like me." Despite the affection in her voice, she sounded sorrowful, almost melancholic, even perhaps guilt-stricken.

Elian shrugged. "I have none."

Malika pressed her lips together, rubbed her eyes, and answered, *Once I had a baby brother. But I lost him long ago, when I was a child.* Grief emanated from her presence in the links.

I flinched, wishing I had not asked. As usual, I brought others pain and ruined the moment. *Of all the questions to ask—*

Lucian said, his voice quiet, "I have an older brother: Darian."

Malika, Elian, Arista, and I reacted the same way: almost tripping over our own feet as we turned to stare at him.

"You have a brother?" Arista exclaimed.

Lucian nodded with a slight smile.

She exhaled and kneaded the vibrating plates on her forehead with one hand. "Of course you do. Because none of us have actually asked about you." Dropping her hand, she ruefully grinned. "If it would be in accordance with your wishes, would you tell us your history?"

Please do, I begged within my own thoughts. My desire to know him eclipsed, for the moment at least, even my deep yearning to be with Kalyca. How I wanted to be trusted so.

Lucian's smile widened. "Of course. I have been waiting for the full Quest to assemble. Now that we are together, and unlikely to be interrupted by patrols, I am pleased to confide my history."

Malika, Elian, Arista, and I shuffled closer to him as he began his story.

CHAPTER 13

RESTLESSLY WAITING

Perspective: Lord Lucian aj-Shehathar, Heir to the Quest of Light
Date: Eyyésal, the tenth day of the fifth moon, Marberre, of the year 499, C.Q.

Sheathing my sword, I reached for the first branch. I swung myself onto it and extended my hand for the next. My grip sure and confident, I did not pause as I pulled myself upward and reached for the third. With the smooth, graceful motions that came so naturally to me, I effortlessly climbed the tallest tree in the province, as I did every three days.

The climb thankfully passed quickly, and within moments I seated myself on a branch near the very top. My head peeking above the canopy, I oriented myself toward the southwest and the early morning sun.

The sight of the hallowed peak of Mount Atharras, visible over the other mountains of Asfiya and the giant trees of northwestern Nademan, immediately calmed me. The wind ruffling my hair and blowing strands of my beard brought comfort now, instead of irritation. And I could see the value again in my extensive training and education. The peace that I knew in that moment was ephemeral and illusory, but it was the most I had attained since the day on which I had achieved maturity. Without regular visits to this place, where the magic of Icilia brought me glimpses of the sacred mountain, I could not have withstood the restlessness that tormented my patience.

A patience that only now required discipline to maintain.

From the very day on which I was born, my parents had begun to prepare me for what I would one day become. As auxiliary heirs to the throne of Asfiya, my parents, Diyana and Beres sej-Shehasfiyi, had the grasp of lore necessary to know the meaning of the drops of athar in liquid form that had coated my newborn face. Terrified, they immediately demanded an audience with my grandfather the king, and, together, they designed a plan which they prayed would save Icilia. It would require great sacrifice.

My parents and my grandfather understood that my birth signaled the fulfillment of the Shining Guide's prophecy for our age: a blessed champion come to bestow salvation in a time of deepest anguish and strife. Which meant that, in contradiction to their previous assessment, the Blood-soaked Sorcerer possessed the power and motivation to permanently destroy Icilia, and with her all of the Shining Guide's blessings and the Quest of Light's boons.

The Blood was their destruction, and they could not escape even if they wished, for the Shining Guide had entrusted the athar orchards to their ancestors. There was regardless nowhere to go, no passage out of Icilia. And, to counter the Blood's power, for any chance at a future, I, a newborn child, was their only hope. A hope that would materialize only in the distant future, for I had to live long enough and be prepared enough to fulfill that promise.

Thus, my family invested everything in me: from the very day of my birth, my parents embarked on an ambitious program to provide me with every form of education and training that might possibly be of benefit to me. Fearing that they might not live out the year, much less see me to maturity, for Asfiya's coming loss seemed imminent, they resolved not to waste a single moment even as they mourned and regretted the deprivation of my childhood.

In devotion to me, they cast aside everything: their royal duties, their own studies, and, most importantly, the attentive care of my elder brother, Darian. Though he was an heir of Asfiya, he was overlooked, save for when he was of use to me. He was but a year-old infant, yet he already had begun to taste abandonment even as he was raised alongside me. For both he and I were erased from the royal records of Asfiya and sequestered from all but the most trusted family members and officials, so that the Blood might never learn of my existence.

Raised so, my earliest memories were of holding a book and a sword and reading as I practiced form and stance, rather than playing with my brother. Yet, though I wanted to spend time with him and ease the pain he bore even as a small child, I happily undertook all the studies placed before me. Possessing as I did a precocious awareness of the world around me, I returned my parents' love and devotion by absorbing as much as I could of what I was taught. Indeed, I found enjoyment and contentment, for it was my task at the time.

One year passed into six, and the royal family prayed in gratitude for the time they had been granted and hoped for yet more.

Then the news came of Koroma's fall and the Blood's abduction of her crown princess, rocking my entire world.

In terrified response, my parents and my grandfather selected for my care twelve of the most powerful warriors and the most learned scholar-magicians, the most trusted and pious members of the court. These women and men smuggled me, along with my brother, from the capital at Azsefer to safety amid the giant trees of northwestern Nademan. With this act, heeding the seers' visions, the king prioritized my safety over the hope of his own success against the Blood and instead set about devising protections for the athar orchards.

His preparation was prescient, for, by the time the Blood reached Asfiya's borders, my brother and I were already safe, ensconced in heavily warded cabins far above the forest floor. But my parents had accepted one last royal duty in remaining behind to defend Asfiya. Amid the smoke rising on the night of the final battle, like so many of the Mutharrim, my mother offered the sacrifice of her life in the defense of Mount Atharras. My father was the only one who escaped, fulfilling his vow to her by living for my sake. His arrival was marked by heartbreaking grief. How much I had tried to comfort him, my brother, and my caretakers despite the sorrow nearly crushing my pure heart.

In the isolated years that followed, the warriors and the scholars became far more than teachers. My father was ruined by his grief and guilt, and my elder brother was more a child than I was. So, in devotion, my teachers became the ones who raised me, lavishing that same love and care I had once known from my parents. I named them my guardians, my family, and they taught me everything, from politics and history to science and magic, to the way of the warrior, to what it meant to be royal and to be pious.

The most important study, however, was one I completed alone: the lore of the Quest. Though many had perused the volumes written by my predecessors and ancestors, the Quest of Light, the books contained various passages that made sense only to me and a multitude of sections that only I could open. It was this study that shaped who I was. It was this study that told me of my destiny.

Always the holy words shone before my eyes: "My son, shaped of sunlight, violet and silver, you are the first Heir to the Quest of Light, the love of the Shining Guide incarnated for the salvation of Icilia. Amid the evil besieging our people, may the Almighty reveal through your hands the path to true freedom."

Armed with the lore's arguments, Darian and I confronted our father and my guardians on my fifteenth birthday. Though with much reluctance, worried that I would reject my place, they confirmed what we had long suspected.

In answer, I said, "Father, Safirile, I do not ask because I wish to give credence to your fears. By the Almighty's name, my heart long ago accepted my duty. If it pleases the Almighty for this lowly servant to become the Lord of Icilia, then I submit myself for the sacrifice. I have asked for your acknowledgment because I wish for you to listen to my plan."

Insisting that I would never be able to succeed if all I knew was the motions of mere practice and the confines of utter seclusion, I turned my guardians into agents of intelligence and covert warfare. Using their various skills, as well as a heavy dose of athar magic to neutralize magical residue, the younger scholars spread throughout Nademan and ventured into Asfiya, Bhalasa, and even Khuduren to gain the information I sought. The elders secured and prepared abandoned mansions and fortresses in Nademan and Khuduren. And the warriors accompanied me to battle: at my demand, we found circumstances in which I could fight against the soldiers who tormented the western and central provinces of Nademan. Using clandestine maneuvers, we ended all manner of abuse, from the torture of townsfolk to the theft of supplies. Thus, I sowed the seeds for my future reconquest.

My studies and these preparations consumed my days, sating my deep desire to act, until the day on which I achieved maturity. By my nineteenth birthday, I had mastered my personal gift of powerful mindlinking and my birthright gift of powerful athar magic, as well as every discipline and weapon of which my guardians could conceive. My character was full-formed, arrived at an unrivaled height of conscious devotion and piety. All that my guardians could teach, I had learned. So, as happened for every royal heir upon reaching the magically set standard of maturity (a standard set nearly impossibly higher for me because of my office), I perceived a sense of clicking, as though my connection to Icilia were snapping into place.

Confident and assured, I had smiled at my family.

Then collapsed.

The magic of my destiny swept through me with the force of the Anharat in spring flood.

It altered the very structure of my heart, my mind, my soul, and my body.

Amid its rushing currents, it bestowed upon me an aura of authority and command unlike any other, enough to bow the proudest monarch's head, as well as an intelligence and magical ability beyond what any other could dream. And, at the same time, it had given me an awareness.

An awareness of every person in Icilia.

An awareness so poignant that I felt, as though it were my own, every trouble that befell every one of my people.

What had before deeply grieved and troubled me now tore at my heart and mind, nearly ripping my sanity to pieces. Only the fortification given by my new magic enabled me to survive the torment.

Reeling, I had cried myself to sleep... only to find my dreams devoured by the horrors haunting my companions and plaguing my people. Even my waking hours were consumed, for, if anything distressful occurred to my companions, I would see the events as though I walked in their shoes. Between the nightmares of their history in my dreams and the brutal waking visions of their daily trials, I came to know my companions as I knew myself.

There was no respite. The dreams came almost every other night, sometimes every night.

I could not continue. I had before known that Icilia suffered. But now that my understanding was so deeply intimate... trapped in the throes of nightmares that were not truly dreams... I could not help but chafe at the security of my shelter and the routine of my studies when I was meant to have the power to turn the tide. My inability to leave on further missions, debilitated as I was by my nightmares, only exacerbated my frustration. My family worried, but their words of comfort rang hollow.

For, no matter how much I wished to bring succor to my people, no matter the blood-drenched horror of my dreams, I could not act. My sign had not yet come. And without the sign of the Almighty's favor and blessing I would not ascend. Only at my ascension would I receive the rest of my magic—the torrent of magic that had given me this awareness was but a wave in comparison to the sea that the lore said I would receive. Without that magic I was not capable of defeating the Blood-soaked Sorcerer and healing the destruction he had wrought.

I had to be patient just as I forgot the meaning of patience.

Crossing my legs on the branch, no longer able to sit straight, I rested my head against the trunk. Tears welled in my eyes and slid down my cheeks as I remembered my latest dreams of my companions. They so desperately yearned for a future and a promise, yet the hands that could fulfill their wishes were tied.

And until my coming, who will remind Malika of the grandeur of her purpose? I lamented silently. *Or defend Elian? Or assure Arista of her dignity? Or support Kyros as he needs while he gives all of himself to Kalyca? Malika and Elian languish in their endless struggles, and Arista and Kyros leave their families, yet where am I to receive them?*

What good is all my power, all my knowledge, all my virtue, if I cannot serve the Almighty and save the people of Icilia? Of what value is the mark of the Quest Leader, the first Heir to the Quest of Light and a true son of the Muthaarim, if I am not fulfilling my purpose? Why was I born if I am meant to waste my days?

"Oh Almighty! Source of Light and highest Lord, Father and Mother both, for Whom the Shining Guide was Messenger, Liege of my soul—I beg of You the favor of my sign," the prayer tore from my lips, "for my people need what Your Guide has promised, the foretold Quest Leader, suffering as they do under my enemy, who grows ever more cruel, vicious, and powerful as he feeds on my people's misery. Give us Light as You have before amid our darkness. I beg of You: do not forsake us!"

More tears spilled from my eyes and wet my bread. I closed my eyes and sobbed.

Sometime amid my misery… something changed.

I opened my eyes as the air grew weighty, as though a momentous undertaking was about to commence.

And then I beheld the light: the sunbeam which reached down from the sky, through the smog, and sheathed me in its warm and gentle embrace. Far away the peak of Mount Atharras, where resided the great orchards of the athar trees, glowed, sparkling like the sunlit faces of a white jewel.

I smiled, fully for the first time in three years, as true contentment suffused me. Sure of my balance, I uncrossed my legs and folded them beneath me. Straightening and kneeling, I held my hands, palms up and the right over the left, toward Mount Atharras.

With the greatest happiness I had ever known, I declared, "Praised be the Almighty! I pledge all that I am to the service of the Almighty. I am Lucian, Leader of the Quest, and I hold love and loyalty entire for the Almighty, who frees the enslaved. I am a true and devout follower of the Shining Guide, and I will forever and always seek the holiness of walking in the ways that he bestowed upon the Muthaarim. By the Almighty's blessing, may I fulfill the promise of my birth."

A wind rustled the treetops with the sweet musical sound of pleased laughter. And the sunlight and the light of Mount Atharras poured into me, like rain unto rich soul, until I brimmed with power. I came into the fullness of my gifts, my heart rising to an even greater pinnacle of piety and compassion, my mind soaring to an even loftier summit of intelligence, my body climbing to an even higher level of strength, my magic reaching its full potential. The magic and command of the Quest radiated in full throughout my soul. My prayers had been answered, for I had ascended.

As the light slowly became veiled from my sight, five names came to me: Lord Lucian the Ideal of Freedom… Graced Malika the Exemplar of Wisdom… Honored Elian the Exemplar of Esteem… Honored Arista the Exemplar of Bravery… Honored Kyros the Exemplar of Strength…

A fierce smile curving my lips, I stood easily on the branch, facing toward the southwest and the base and capital of my enemy. My voice reverberating throughout the foundations of Icilia, I vowed, "I am Lord Lucian the Ideal of Freedom, Heir to the Quest of Light and the supreme ruler of Icilia, and the praised Almighty favors me with divine choice. I will free Icilia even if it costs me all of the breath in my person."

Bowing my head toward Mount Atharras, I crouched and swung myself onto the branches below. I would gather supplies, maps, and the weapons and gifts set aside for this day, the swords, rings, and pendants that were three of the five symbols of the Quests' office, as well as the clothes made for each of them. I would meet with my father, my brother, and my guardians one last time. Then, charting my course, I would travel to where my Second-in-command would be amid her dash for survival and subsequently to where each of my other three companions would be found, in the order their names had been given to me. With my union with each of them, I would finally show them their future and promise and ask for their allegiance.

My age dawned. And I, Lucian aj-Shehathar, was ready to die to free Icilia, for I had dedicated my future to the Almighty and accepted my promise of saving all of my people. By the Almighty's grace, regardless of the sacrifice required, I would succeed. Unto my hands the Almighty had given freedom.

CHAPTER 14

KNOW THE PATH

Perspective: Lord Lucian the Ideal of Freedom
Date: Eyyédal, the twenty-second day of the tenth moon, Thek-
harre, of the year 499, C.Q.

" . . . then I traveled south through Khuduren and, in the middle of the summer, crossed the border into Etheqa. I traversed those mountains and then entered Zahacim. Along the way, I took some occasion to act. With my dreams and visions as guides, I predicted where you, Malika, might next travel so that our paths would meet. And since that blessed night, I have not parted from you," I concluded. A smile curved my lips, despite my unease, as I waited for the questions that would follow.

Their gazes fixed on my face, my companions still considered all I had told them.

Patiently expectant, I guided us away from a rather sheer slope toward a more manageable one. With the senses that had come with my ascension, I watched the area within three miles of my position for the telltale signs of troops. Unless

I used my full abilities, my connection to the land's magic provided only this limited glimpse, minuscule compared to the potential of Kyros' farsight, but the range had saved me from many perils on my solitary journey south.

A journey that had ended only for the great one of my life to begin.

My Lady Aalia of Light chose well for the name of her divine-gifted family and her divine-blessed task, I thought. *Indeed, it is a path to follow, for me, for my companions, and for Icilia.*

Troubled as I was by the disheartened states in which I had found my companions, those words did not bring the usual surge of hopeful anticipation. My dreams had revealed the full reality, but upon meeting them I loved them so much more than I had through the lens of magic. Their pain thus anguished me all the more.

The pattern was one which every interaction on my journey south had followed—though, of course, all the more poignant with my own companions.

From all I have heard and seen, there is much I must do. I can only pray that my life extends long enough for me to accomplish all of it... May the Almighty grant me enough life.

I held back a wry chuckle at the irony of the thought. Though I meant the number of days granted on this earth, the words could also address the one aspect of my current circumstance I had not entirely predicted: my copious need for the magic of the Quest Leader.

The magic of my destiny was unlike any other.

Both wish magic (the magic of prayer and principle) and arms magic (the magic of privilege and practicality) drew upon physical energy for catalysis. The magic exhausted one as physical exertion did, and food and rest similarly provided restoration. Excessive use usually resulted in exhausted unconsciousness, with coma as the worst consequence, and a proper use of jewels might deflect such cost through amplification. Physical energy was precious, with true students of magic pouring years into building their stamina, but not too precious to spend. What was too precious was life energy, the energy of one's soul, which could not be amplified and without which death was certain.

For you, I thought, drinking in the sight of my companions as they continued to stare at me, *I would gladly give all of my life.*

It was no idle promise.

Life energy was what the magic of the Quest required to perform its numerous wonders, and indeed it was wondrous: the magic of the Quest had the ability to command anything of anyone at anytime in anyplace for any reason. Unlike wish and arms magic, which were limited to their specific purposes and allowed for only a certain degree of abstraction, the Quest-given magic could be used to cast any spell I wished.

Absolute discretion, granted only because of my purity. Fueled by my life. For only the life of the Quest Leader could cast such wonders. And only the life of the Quest Leader was so bountiful, so capable of quick, easy, and natural regeneration, as to sustain this magic.

Even so, there were limitations I needed to follow for the sake of my health.

As my Lady Aalia of Light had written, my companions' pledges, more than any other, required a massive toll of life energy to seal. So much so that I had felt precariously balanced on the verge of death for a few moments after each pledge—a sacrifice which matched theirs of faith and trust. That should have been all I used.

But my companions were mostly untrained and unable to support me. I had consequently found myself catalyzing again and again: to ease the edge of Malika's malnourishment, to teleport us both across the guarded river-border between Zahacim and Bhalasa, to eliminate the rebound of Elian's failed practice spells, to heal Elian's, Arista's, and Kyros' wounds… With such excessive use, I dreaded the day on which I would teach them the portion of the lore dedicated to the explanation of this magic. I did not wish to contribute to their burdens of guilt and shame.

As we crested the next hill, guilt and shame were exactly what I saw emerging on their faces.

Frowning, I probed the circle of sacred bonds that formed the Quest and the web of my links. "What troubles you?"

They seemed unwilling to speak.

Then Arista wet her lips and answered quietly, "The thought that you were forced to see everything I did. No one should have to see such degradation."

Her words evoked an outpouring of lamentation from Malika, Elian, and Kyros.

"I did not want anyone to share my suffering!" Elian exclaimed.

"No one should have to feel the humiliation I did," Kyros whispered, "particularly not you."

I wish you had remained protected from all evil! Malika cried. *Just as your parents intended when they heard of what happened to me.*

"You deserve to be sheltered," Elian agreed, shuddering. "I wish I had not ever felt upset so you would not have to experience it."

"If only all of Icilia's troubles could be brought to your feet while you remain guarded at home," Arista emphatically stated. "As long as you are safe, all of us may hope."

"Your protection is everything," Kyros agreed. He paused, pursed his lips, and added, in a quieter voice, "Do you still suffer the same intensity of dreams? Now that you are with us and we no longer feel distressed?"

For all my power and understanding, I, the foretold Quest Leader, was stunned. I had expected dissatisfaction, discomfort, suspicion... I had just admitted to knowing the most personal moments of their lives, which they had suffered while I lived in nearly perfect shelter... and yet they were worried for me. For *me*.

My heart swelled, brimming with love and utter happiness, such warmth rising within my soul that I did not know whether I walked on the earth or flew through the sky. A huge, rare grin spread my lips as I proclaimed, "Gratitude to the Almighty for your love, Malika, Elian, Arista, Kyros."

Though embarrassed pleasure tinted their expressions, my family remained silent, demanding an answer.

Laughing, I said, "In answer to your question, Kyros, I do, but the dreams have shifted from your histories to portions from those of others. But regardless, I am not overwhelmed: the magic I received at my ascension has turned my heart and mind into a veritable fortress. And I am better now that I act."

My awareness of every person had also shifted, from endless clamoring to a faint buzz. I was still aware of and grieved every trouble and injustice, and I could at any moment choose to focus on particular persons or people, but the sensations no longer wielded a hammer against my mind. Only my companions were always prominent to my magical senses, like limbs unattached to my person yet still my own. Their hearts beat in harmony with mine.

Arista examined my face, as though to ascertain whether I understated, and Malika, Elian, and Kyros wore unhappy looks. But then, with sighs, they let go of the matter.

You spoke of much, Malika said, a bit hesitant, the words in the links like the cool brushes of rain on my head, *but not the plans you said you had made...*

"Excellent question," I responded, pleased. Tilting my head, I considered the hills and found the nearest cave, only a few feet from us behind a low, scraggly brown bush. I ducked inside, and my companions followed.

Settling on the floor, I pulled my pack over my shoulder and searched inside for a cylindrical leather case. Retrieving it, I uncapped the leather and unfurled the scroll within on my lap.

"Is that a map!" Kyros gasped as my family sat in a semicircle in front of me. "I thought what few that had ever been made were destroyed by the Blood."

Arista laughed. "Of course you would have such a treasure."

I chuckled. "A treasure truly, for it is a copy of my Lady Aalia of Light's own, from the handwriting to the national borders."

My companions gasped, and Arista exclaimed, "Her maps still exist?"

I nodded. "My guardians carried the Quest of Light's original works when they fled with my brother and me. One of their tasks has been to remake the copies lost in Asfiya's capture. The crown of Asfiya refused to make the same oversight that led centuries ago to the destruction of the Shining Guide's own writings." I smiled wryly, days of holding a quill and etching tiny drawings flashing before my eyes. "I learned how to write by helping make those copies." I gestured to the elegant script that marked every city and country, as well as where the members of each kind tended to live.

That is wise, Malika murmured, amazed.

"One more thing," Kyros murmured, his gaze on me, "that the Blood has not been able to take from us."

"Gratitude to the Almighty," Elian whispered.

A playful smirk twitched Arista's lips. "Those must have been quite the penmanship lessons."

Elian clapped a hand to his mouth, muffling his giggles, while Malika and Kyros smiled in amusement, although not without hesitation, glancing at me as though seeking permission.

I laughed, enjoying her mischief myself. "Oh indeed. Particularly because my guardians had an unspoken expectation about my handwriting becoming an exact replication of my Lady Aalia of Light's script." Removing a journal, I opened it to a page of mundane entries and laid it next to the map. "Well? How successful was I?"

Relaxing further in my presence, my companions peered at the samples of script.

"It is a perfect match," Kyros breathed. With one finger, he lightly traced the places where the letters began and where they connected.

"Not anywhere near as ornate as what I was taught," Arista muttered, "really so austere, but that only makes it more beautiful, neat, elegant... Like the straight perfection of printed basics... I do not think just anyone could write like this... no one other than you, her Heir..." The words cooled my cheeks, surely bringing a silver glow.

Elian was similarly impressed, but Malika's face fell, black despair contorting her joyful features. She covered her face with her hands.

Selecting our private link, I said to her, *Malika, do not worry.*

She snuck a glance at me. *I cannot read, Lucian. I cannot read!* The words were a silent shriek.

I will teach you, I calmly replied. *And you will learn quickly.*

My solid confidence reassured her enough that the gloom and anguish receded. She dropped her hands.

I winked, startling her. Then, letting my lightheartedness fade, I spoke in the collective link, *I must ask something of you: do you understand what it is that I am born to do?"*

All four of my companions nodded, eyes wide and filling with terror.

There is no question, Arista whispered. *Defeating the Blood-soaked Sorcerer is certainly the reason.*

Grimly pleased, I dipped my head. *A task for which you are born as well.*

The doubt creasing their faces was painful to witness.

But I continued, *This is my plan, in its current form.* I waited for nods. *Let us first be clear in our strategic goals: the Blood has enslaved the people of Icilia and has consumed their dignity through fear and vice. To restore the Icilia founded by the Quest of Light, we must not only destroy the Blood and his subordinates but also revive each of the old governments and the customs of our ancestors.*

We must reveal to Icilia, as the Quest of Light did, the correct way. As my Lady Aalia of Light often stated, it is all too easy to return to the darkness and all too difficult to come to the light. I arched an eyebrow. *Our task is to free Icilia. Understand that our journey will be years long.*

Malika, Elian, and Arista bowed their heads immediately, but an apprehension flashed in Kyros' eyes.

Though I noted it, I did not pause. *I have developed this strategy since I learned of my destiny.* Bending over the map, I tapped the southwestern region of Bhalasa. *We are currently here.* I moved my hand and tapped the nation who had sheltered me. *I wish to start in Nademan.*

PART 2

COMPOSED

From the writings of Lady Queen Aalia the Ideal of Light addressed to the second Quest Leader:

"Remember, my Heir, that you bear responsibility unlike any other; you were born for the service you must accomplish. Do not treat your mission lightly or leave its unfolding to chance. Plan well, and prepare thoroughly. Maintain margins for unexpected occurrences, both the helpful and the harmful. But be patient. Be patient with your companions, be patient with the people of Icilia, and do be patient with yourself. Though you may wish it, despite your power, all will not fall ready at your feet. Plan, act, and trust that the Almighty will bring your efforts to fruition."

READ BY LORD LUCIAN AJ-SHEHATHAR

AT THE AGE OF FOURTEEN

CHAPTER 15

EVADE
THE UNRELENTING

Perspective: Honored Elian the Exemplar of Esteem
Date: Eyyélab, the third day of the eleventh moon, Mirkharre,
of the year 499, C.Q.

Arista grabbed ahold of the lower edge of my wing and yanked me against the hillside. I stifled a shriek and pressed my back to the yellowed grass and rock, trying to ignore how the motion worsened the pain.

Sorry, Arista breathed, *but your wing was all I could reach.*

I forced myself to nod. Though we had spent much of the last ten days sharing our histories at Lucian's encouragement, I had not mentioned the extent of my wings' curse or the full reason behind the Blood's vengeance to anyone. I knew I did not need to fear their knowledge, of my curse at least, but, though they seemed to truly care for me, I could not help the secrecy with Malika, Arista, and Kyros. As for Lucian himself... if he knew, he certainly had not spoken of it. As he had not spoken of my parentage.

I did not understand why, despite his explanation, but I was grateful. His silence allowed me the chance to earn respect on my own merit. Even if I would never be able to retain it.

Kyros tensed slightly, drawing my attention, as Lucian raised one hand. His lips pressed together, he searched the sky. Then he beckoned to us and darted out from the shadow of the hill, into the open.

We followed, sprinting behind him to the lee of the next hill.

Malika reached the shelter.

Then Kyros.

A few more feet. I was almost there...

My wings shifted against my robes.

The weight pulled me sideways.

Pain sliced through my back.

I stumbled and tipped forward, the ground rising alarmingly fast.

Arista caught ahold of my hand and pulled me behind her, saving me for the second time in five minutes.

Just as we reached the shade, a swarm of shadows drifted over the snow but a few feet ahead of us.

I held my breath and clutched Arista's hand.

The shadows disappeared.

I exhaled slowly, trying not to make noise. *Thank you, Arista.* I tried to smile, despite the swelling wave of revulsion for how dearly my mistake had almost cost us.

Tilting her head back, she flashed a smile. *Of course, Elian.* Her eyes flicked behind me and widened, and her plates quavered. *Apologies, Elian—my tug loosened the binding on your wings.*

The nauseating taste of disgust sharpened. A little pull, and my wings ruined everything. As they always did—though bound, they made it impossible to balance during Lucian's lessons on weapons. Even before the tug, Lucian and Arista had had to catch me twice today. My wings were worse than useless; they were a liability. As I was.

Perhaps cutting them off would make me at least somewhat useful.

I can tighten the binding.

The quiet words, Kyros', only weakly penetrated through the fog of disdain. But I still startled. Kyros, more than even Lucian, seemed unable to bear the sight of my wings. Yet he offered…

Do so now, Lucian ordered, words crisp, his expression one of utter focus. *The patrols are doing another sweep. In one minute, we move for the next hill.*

Stepping behind me, Kyros untied the cloth holding the useless limbs to my waist. Before they could fall limp, he caught one and Lucian the other. They gently folded the stiff membranes shut along the delicate bones.

I gritted my teeth, stifling a scream. Lucian's touch caused me not the slightest hint of pain, even despite the curse… but Kyros' gave me enough agony to knock me unconscious.

Can you estimate why they came upon us? Arista asked. *Could they have been informed by the Zahacits?*

The slight huskiness of her usually clear voice jolted me from the cage of my pain and loathing. I squeezed her hand, the dainty yet callused fingers still wrapped in my unwieldy ones.

Lucian shook his head. *The Blood's governors despise each other. It is why any and every patrol is composed of one kind only. Why the soldiers on the borders guard against each other as much as they do against us. The governors do not work together, unless the Blood demands it. And even then...* a wry smile quirked his lips. *They obey only reluctantly. They are loyal only because they must be.*

Kyros knotted the binding on my wings, securing them to my back.

I blinked. *How do you know that?*

Because of– Arista started.

Now. Lucian ran to the next hill.

We followed—Arista's grip the only reason I did not trip a fifth time.

The moment we reached the patch of shadow, Lucian signaled again.

We darted to the next hill. Then the next. And the next.

Weighed down by my wings, my breath unrelenting wheezes, I could barely match the others' pace. But the shadows drifting across the ground and the accompanying cacophonous thuds spurred me forwards.

For those minutes, my world narrowed to the midnight blue of Kyros' back as Arista and I brought up the rear. Flashes of gold ahead were the only reminders of Lucian's and Malika's presences. The prickly hillsides and the rock-strewn dips between them blurred into streaks of granite and umber. Pain thrummed through my wings with every movement.

I prayed I would not be the reason we were caught.

Finally, when I wondered if my lungs might collapse from the headlong run, Lucian relaxed against a boulder instead of urging us to the next hill. Donning a weary smile, he said, *Most of the flock has passed overhead.*

Arista let go of my hand and collapsed onto the ground with a groan. *How many miles was that?*

Blinking like he might fall asleep, Kyros lay down beside her and covered his face with the edge of his coat.

I, however, dithered, unsure what to do with myself. Sitting down would hurt so much...

Six, maybe? Malika offered, coughing as she approached Lucian.

Lucian shifted so she could lean against the same boulder. *Seven, actually,* he answered, raising and resettling his cap over his head—though it was not necessary, for the locks remained in perfect, neat curls, all the miles and brutal pace not having mussed a single strand of either hair or beard.

They really spread out so far? Arista grumbled. *For a mere patrol?*

I removed a flask from my pack and offered it to Malika. Then, making up my mind, I fell to my knees and let myself collapse onto my belly. I groaned, the bottoms of my feet throbbing like giant bruises in spite of the cushioned soles of my sturdy athar boots. *They do it because they can,* I answered Arista. *They dominate the air and so move with impunity, because flying is the only way to travel here.* A shudder shifted my pain-riddled wings. *Even though they never fly above the mountains' tree-lines, the miles-wide patrol ensures that no one ever leaves their aerie.*

Arista sighed aloud. *Much like the patrols who scour Zahacim. The small units are relentless. Finding the holes in their movements is nearly impossible.*

The Koromic are just as bad, Malika whispered. *I was always only ever just ahead of them.*

The Khudurel ones are no better, Kyros said, his voice shaking even in the link. *They move across the plains like slicing knives. Unpredictable and fast.*

The soldiers in Nademan travel through the treetops, Lucian said, the note of anguish in his voice a blow to my own heart. *Because of the vast difference in tree heights across the nation, they each have limited ranges. But their tendency to swoop down without warning makes any travel fraught with tension. They may not be... diligent... but they delight in unexpected brutality.*

I raised my head in time to join my new friends in a strangely accordant exchange of glances.

We are oddly unified in our suffering. Arista's smile held more mockery than mirth. *Even as it carves us into pieces. We choose to succumb to the cruelty and call it inescapable. We let his evil succeed in its endless pursuit.*

Kyros' expression was too pained to be anything other than a grimace. *We waste our lives quarreling over whose suffering is worse and what was the cause and why we suffer at all. Instead of realizing that we need each other. That only together can we find salvation.*

We need to understand that before we can avail ourselves of the Almighty's mercy. Malika did not even attempt a smile as she nodded to Lucian.

Mercy which we do not at all deserve, I muttered. A bitter frown contorted my lips, though I did not avert my eyes from Lucian's face.

Contrary to what I expected, yet so true to his own character, he beamed, warm and bright. *But mercy which the Almighty bestows on us regardless.* Before any of us could react, he added, searching the sky again, *The patrol is sweeping back in this direction. And there is a storm building.*

I jerked upright and examined the sky.

Lucian was right: the smog, which muted all sunlight (save his), seemed thicker than usual. A telltale sign of storm clouds. It was barely midday, still hours from sunset, but the sky wore the gloom of evening. The western sky was nearly black.

It will be a bad storm, I breathed.

We will look for shelter once we pass out of the patrol's range, Lucian said, his expression returning to the earlier one of honed focus. *Come.*

Arista, Kyros, and I scrambled to our feet, and Malika tucked the flask still in her hand into her pocket.

Lucian beckoned to us, and we sprinted northwest.

All the while the mix of storm and smog overhead thickened.

CHAPTER 16

ENDURE THE ENRAGED

Perspective: Honored Elian the Exemplar of Esteem
Date: Eyyélab, the third day of the eleventh moon, Mirkharre,
of the year 499, C.Q.

Breathing in with my nose and exhaling with my mouth as instructed, I tried to center my focus on my wavering magical senses and reached as far out as I could, grasping for information… Sweat beaded my forehead, itching my scales, and my teeth clenched.

"Peace, Elian," Lucian murmured. One finger touched a feather… and the pain that usually tormented me faded, fleeing that blessed hand.

With the relief, my focus finally sharpened, my broken senses brightening enough to read the disturbances in the air currents…

The wind's speed is not decreasing, Lucian, I whispered. *In some places, it is even swirling in the beginnings of twisters. At its speed… The fringe might be twelve miles away, but it will not take long to reach us. Maybe ten or fifteen minutes.*

The temperature is dropping rapidly, Arista added. *The rain could turn to sleet. Or freeze as it falls.*

I caught my breath. An early winter Bhalaseh storm was perilous, especially now, but one with sleet... in the foothills, without the mountains' shelter... Survival itself was at stake. For all of us, not just Malika and Kyros. Though their states were markedly worse, their kinds far more sensitive to the cold than Lucian's, Arista's, or mine, we were all vulnerable to such frigid temperatures...

What are we going to do, Lucian? I asked frantically.

Lucian pressed his lips together, his expression grave. He tightened his arms around Malika, who, teeth chattering, clung to him for warmth. *We need to build a shelter. It is our only option now.*

I winced—no hastily constructed shelter would be as effective as a cave. But we were somehow in the only section of foothills that were devoid of all but the shallowest indents. And the last cave we *had* passed, twelve miles southeast, had been the home of a massive bear and her cubs. They were deeply asleep, but they were almost as undesired company as the soldiers.

At least the skies would remain empty of patrols.

But the storm was not much better.

A particularly chilling gust of the harshening wind crashed into us, its strength barely abated by the tall foothill in the shadow of which we stood. Kyros shivered and reflexively leaned into the arm I had placed around him. His skin glossed, but with a frosty sheen rather than its usual glass-like polish.

Where would we construct a shelter? And out of what? Arista asked. She shuffled closer to Kyros and folded her arms around his waist. The plates on her cheeks were abnormally still, but she bore the cold far better than he did.

Based on every examination I have done of our surroundings, Lucian replied, *our only options are to use tree branches or to dig a hole. Your opinions, please.*

Another burst of wind assailed us. Kyros flung both arms around me, desperate for the natural warmth emanating from my skin and wings.

White-hot agony scalded my back, but I quashed the sensation as much as I could. Returning the embrace, I frowned at the amount of chill seeping through his athar robes… though he was not as cold as he could have been, his skin bore the first signs of frostbite…

I do not think we could dig a hole fast enough for Malika and Kyros, I said, anxiety overcoming my usual hesitance. *But I could work with tree branches. If we–*

Come. Lucian swung Malika up into his arms, easily cradling her tall form. He turned and hiked up the hill, long strides rapidly covering huge amounts of slope.

I tried to smile at Kyros. *I cannot cradle you, so stay close,* I said, hoping to bring some cheer to his miserable face.

His lips, tinged blue, barely quirked.

I cast a concerned glance at Arista, who responded with a grimace. She grasped Kyros' arms and maneuvered him, despite his heartrending whines, so that he faced forward, squeezed between us.

We timed our steps together and followed Lucian up the hill. But, though we supported him as best as we could, Kyros stumbled more than walked.

How I despised my weakness. *What is the point of one of the Sholanar being part of the Quest if he can provide neither physical strength nor aerial advantage?*

The wind's force nearly doubled in the time it took to reach the crest, with us fighting the gusts at every step. Kyros' beige skin took on a distinctly blue cast, exposed as we were to more of the wind. Even Arista's form shivered. Even my teeth chattered.

The cold was such that it numbed my mounting pain, even as the wind yanked my feathers against the scaled skin and wrenched my wings against their binding.

By the time we reached the top, Lucian was disappearing into a grove of thick, scraggly trees at the hill's base.

Arista, Kyros, and I almost tumbled down the slope in our hurry.

The first spatters of rain struck my face. Lightning flashed, forking through the charcoal sky. Thunder crashed in its wake.

We entered the trees.

Arista and I dropped Kyros by where Lucian had placed Malika (who crawled over to hug Kyros) along with his pack. Leaving aside our own sacks, we muttered only the tersest apologies before rushing to Lucian's side.

Copying him, I set to hewing branches from the trees' trunks with the sharp edge of my enchanted sword. A faint glow illuminated the area, but I did not stop to investigate its origin.

Arista pulled out a dagger and, with some direction from me, began sharpening the ends of the branches and splitting apart any longer than four feet.

As soon as Lucian and I had collected enough branches, I paced off a section of clear ground amid the trees, a large enough rectangle for all five of us to recline side by side. Following my footprints, I began to dig holes, evenly spaced, grinding the hilt of my sword into the mud.

How grateful I was that the blade would not cut me!

With but a few words of coordination, Lucian started on the other side.

Arista followed behind both of us with the branches, jamming their ends into the holes. The sticks were close enough together to form solid walls.

I finished and found that Malika had managed to pull out Lucian's two blankets, made of athar cloth the same color and thickness as our clothes. Effective for both warmth and camouflage.

Thanking her, I grabbed the first blanket and spread it over the top of the shelter.

Circling the walls, Lucian traced the blanket's edges and murmured spell after spell, the words a soothing lilt as the rain turned from a stinging drizzle into a pelting downpour.

Arista ushered Malika and Kyros inside and dropped in Lucian's pack. Then, walking behind Lucian, she pressed the blanket against the sharpened tips until the material parted and sealed around the wood, forming an impenetrable ceiling that would not blow away in the wind.

I spread the second blanket.

Go inside, Elian, Lucian ordered. *Arista and I will finish.*

Though the drops of water streaming over my feathers hurt, I hesitated. *I want to support you.*

You have, Arista assured me, impressing a smile into the link. *You designed the shelter, did you not? Let us now do our share.*

Despite the cold, my scales flared hot as I crawled through the one opening Arista had left.

Kyros nearly flattened me as he threw himself into my chest and slipped his hands between my wings and back. I ignored the way my wings shrieked, crumpled beneath my bottom and touched by his fingers, and wrapped my arms around him. Malika clung to Kyros—careful even in this circumstance to not touch me.

The haunting sound of the howling winds lessened, indicating the second blanket was fully sealed, and I turned to see Arista duck inside. Behind her, Lucian entered and fitted the last four branches in place.

Raising his hand, he lightly touched the athar cloth. Light flashed around his fingers.

The interior warmed noticeably. And barely a drop of rain passed through the wooden walls.

Just in time—only moments later, shards of ice thrummed against the cloth ceiling. Yet the blankets held—bouncing slightly, throwing shadows through the pale light illuminating our faces, but strong and steady.

I bowed my head. *Gratitude to the Almighty.*

Malika, Arista, and Kyros repeated the prayer—Kyros' thoughts barely more coherent than a mumble.

Praised be the Almighty, Lucian murmured, turning toward us.

Only then did I realize the source of the white glow.

His face.

"You are actually shining!" I breathed, forgetting to speak in the link.

Malika, Arista, and even Kyros shifted so they could stare, wide-eyed, at him.

Lucian's creamy cheeks silvered, the pulse of color spreading through the luminescence as well. He exhaled a chuckle and cupped a hand over his heart—the pious response to a compliment, an old tradition few followed. Then he tugged Malika into his embrace, kissing her head, and asked, *Are we all warm? Should we risk asking you for a spell, Arista?*

Malika shuddered but answered, *N-no. I will be all right soon.*

Sh-should b-be f-fine, Kyros whispered, trembling against me.

Arista quickly pressed herself against his back. Pursing her lips, she tilted her head back and forth, tapped her fingers together, and said, *The patrols might be grounded, but, judging from your last mention of their presence half an hour ago, they are probably still nearby. Since the residue of sorcery is so easily traced and pinpointed, I would not risk it. Unless you command otherwise.*

Lucian contemplated the blankets. Then sighed and shook his head. *If only I had pure athar to cast stable masking... Arista, I must ask you for a spell.* He gestured at our clothes. *We are quite soaked.*

Preoccupied as I was in pulling my wings out with one hand from underneath my bottom, I did not comprehend his words... until I felt the wetness of the feathers and gasped. *Please, Arista!*

P-please, Lucian! Kyros cried.

She dipped her head and chanted a spell. Across the shelter, Lucian did the same, his face momentarily flashing brighter.

"H-have you ev-ever c-contract-tracted it?" Kyros spoke in my ear. His ice-cold fingers burrowed into the thick, warm, cursed skin that connected my wings to my back.

"Yes. Twice." I quavered from both the memories and the pain. "I nearly died both times."

"Kalyca n-nearly d-died twice as- as well," he said grimly.

I murmured words of sympathy. Over the last two weeks, I had heard enough about his little sister to know something of his intense, fatherly love for her, and I could only wonder at how much more painful her illness must have been for him. How much more painful the very thought of the storms must be.

The storms, heralds of misery and illness.

My parents had often told me of the days in which storms were regarded with happy caution. In many parts of the seven nations, they wet the ground before the first plow, nurtured the blooms and saplings of spring, beckoned prey from their burrows, replenished ponds and streams, nourished the harvests just before they ripened... rain was life.

Until the Blood's conquest. The noxious fumes that arose from his celebratory bonfires had not dissipated. Instead, they had lingered and spread and covered the whole of Icilia, blocking much of the sun's light from warming our faces and the parched earth. Breathing it, especially in large amounts, was almost instant death—even the Blood's own Sholanar troops no longer flew at great heights, and normally the fumes' direct ill effects could be escaped by remaining on the ground. But that smoke did not always remain in the sky.

Though rain was becoming increasingly rarer, when it did come, it came in the form of huge, destructive storms... in which the smog had melded with the raindrops... and so brought sickness to those directly exposed. Drinking the rainwater once it had already entered rivers and lakes or eating plants nourished by it did not seem to cause that same harm, but... what once had been celebrated was now feared. No matter the time of year, no matter the type of storm.

Among the storms, however, the worst were those of autumn and winter, like the one screaming above. The cold they brought, far beyond its own deadly power, weakened one's defenses to the disease in the rain, and it so easily permeated all but the thickest layers of wood and stone... The enchanted athar cloth strung above my head, shielding us from chunks of ice and bitter drops of water, was a true miracle.

Yet how effective could even that be when our hair—and my wings—dripped water? The rain had not soaked our robes to the skin, nor the chill settled in our bones, but even the limited exposure we had could be fatal.

The imminence of such death burned the scales on my forehead and neck, which cooled unnaturally, and my wings crackled with this pain atop the curse…

Then Arista's spell took effect.

A pleasant warmth caressed my head and limbs, leaving dryness behind.

Malika and I breathed sighs of utter relief, and Kyros relaxed enough to withdraw slightly from my chest.

Exchanging a few words, Lucian and Arista arranged our satchels in a corner and switched positions, Malika cradled in her arms while he shifted to my side. A gentle smile on his lips, he carefully tugged out the rest of my wings and arranged them so that my weight no longer crushed them. His blessed fingers were cold but refreshing, soothing away the pain and malignant chill.

Once I was more at ease, Lucian threaded an arm around my back and gathered Malika and Arista on his other side. Tipping his shining face back, he said, *You may sleep, if it pleases you. The storm will rage for a while. I will wake you for supper.*

Drawing Kyros closer, I removed my cap and leaned my head into the curve of Lucian's neck, snuggling as close as I could. Light, sweet scents of incense, musk, and roses filled my nose—the perfume of my family.

So welcomed into their embrace, the thirteen years of turmoil in my soul calmed, I could almost believe I belonged with them. That I was worthy of their love.

As peace filled my heart, my eyes closed, trusting that Lucian would protect me.

Resting his chin on my shoulder, Kyros whispered, again in my ear, "Th-Thank you, Elian. I know this is n-not physical touch you w-would otherwise give."

My scales flared with warmth and golden light.

But before I could answer him, a shrill, keening scream pierced the air.

CHAPTER 17

SHELTER THE FROZEN

Perspective: Honored Elian the Exemplar of Esteem
Date: Eyyélab, the third day of the eleventh moon, Mirkharre,
of the year 499, C.Q.

The terror, misery, and hopelessness in that scream pierced straight to my soul. Resonating deep within the caverns of my heart.

"Can we not act?" the words exploded from my mouth, with an odd echo.

I blinked, then a reluctant smile tugged at my lips: Malika, Arista, Kyros, and I had all exclaimed the same words.

But that smile quickly faded as I brought my hands together over Kyros' back and cupped them, as though about to collect a mouthful of water, in the old traditional gesture of entreaty my mother had taught me.

Arista and Kyros made the same gesture, while Malika stared up at Lucian, her hands on his arms. *Surely concealment is not that important?* she whispered.

Lucian tilted his head, as he often did whenever he used his sense. *Two squads of Sholanar troops landed half a mile to the east of our location. They hold captive a child of the Sholanar, a boy of purple scales...* Anger flashed in and then froze his violet eyes. *From their taunts and laughter, they plan some greater act of ill intent. They are fixated enough on such malice to ignore the dangers of the storm.*

My heart skipped beats as I realized what such ill intent probably was, and, from their expressions, my family undoubtedly shared my horror.

Can we act? I pled.

Lucian's eyes held a terrifying cast, but the wan smile he gave in response was still kind. "Malika, Elian, Arista, Kyros, as long as we act with strategy and caution, the time for concealing the name of the Quest has ended. What is our purpose but to succor the fearful?"

Arista smirked in answer, and the rest of us exchanged glances of hope.

Lucian pressed his lips together. *We must move; he cannot wait.* He gently drew back Malika, Arista, and me and removed a cloth case from a pocket.

Malika twisted to retrieve his crossbow.

She cannot possibly intend to go! Even as the thought formed in my mind, I blurted, "Malika and Kyros will stay behind, will they not?"

Malika and Kyros cast irritated looks in my direction.

But Arista nodded. *You will stay behind.*

They glanced at Lucian, whose stern expression gained a hint of apology. *This endeavor will be dangerous enough for Elian, Arista, and me, who have the advantage of kind. I do not wish to unnecessarily risk your health.*

Both were dissatisfied but did not object, only murmuring their obedience.

Acknowledging them with a nod, Lucian shifted to the opposite side of the shelter, slid his fingers beneath the bottom edge of several branches, and levered the pieces of wood from their spots.

The wind immediately invaded our shelter, blowing rain, sleet, and ice inside.

His face creasing in that characteristic grim focus, Lucian exited. Arista crawled over Malika's legs and followed him.

Replacing my cap on my head, I disentangled myself from Kyros—who immediately hugged Malika—and scooted outside.

The pellets of ice slammed against my wings like the rocks the villagers had once thrown at me. Upon contact with my skin and wings, the sleet and freezing rain sizzled—and then immediately refroze.

Within moments, I wore a cloak of ice.

Like the night two years ago on which the villagers had abducted me and dropped me two valleys away just before a storm broke. The sleet had nearly broken off my fingers, toes, and feathers...

"Come, Elian," Lucian said, his voice somehow clearly audible over the wails of the wind.

I glanced up, brushing ice from my lashes, and took the hand he offered, standing with his aid.

Arista replaced the last of the branches and snatched up my other hand.

Lucian gave my fingers a tug. *Come.* He marched forward, as did Arista, their steps matched to the same beat.

I stumbled between them, their support the only reason I did not fall behind on the slippery slopes.

Alert and tense, we traversed hill after foothill. Though the sun had not yet set, the sky was black, as though night had fallen without even the least glimmer of any stars or the moon to offer comfort amid the terrifying dark. The hills loomed like the jagged black teeth of a monster. Only the white light from Lucian's face and the pale pastel green light from a pendant centered on his chest illuminated our way, revealing the land for what it really was.

I clung to my new family's hands.

As we surmounted the third hill, the glows orbiting Lucian faded.

Lucian, the light– I began, frightened.

He indicated with a thought in the link the yellow lamps flickering in the valley at the base of the next hill.

A flash of lightning lit the leering faces of the soldiers who crowded around a patch of open ground. In that tiny opening, a figure cowered, curled into a ball.

Are they tainted, Lucian, according to their magical signatures? Arista asked, letting go of my hand and loading her small crossbow. She uttered the command Lucian had taught us, the sacred word, "Pisterim," and the material of her robes smoothed and hardened. Armor without either the gleam and weight of metal or the weakness of leather.

No, Lucian said. *They act of their own will, not because of magical manipulation.* He balanced several daggers among his fingers as his own robes became armor. *We will aim to sow confusion first. Climb down to the right flank of the hill. On my mark, release at will. Once they are sufficiently distracted, climb the other hill and attack from that side.*

Arista saluted with one hand and slid down the slope.

Lucian glanced at me and said, briefly affectionate, *When you see an opening, rescue the boy. Arista and I will shield you.*

Indeed, yes, Arista said. *Keep your sword ready, but do not seek engagement.*

I swallowed but clumsily rendered my own salute and whispered the command for my robes. At a gesture from him, I staggered down the hill to its rocky base.

A soldier yelled several foul words and yanked at one of the boy's wings. Eliciting another scream.

The soldiers laughed.

Lucian ordered, *Mark.*

The soldiers, too focused on their evil to notice the threat, began to collapse. Bolts and daggers sprouted in necks, backs, and chests. Spurts of blood gleamed vermilion in the dingy lantern glow.

Shouting outrage, the soldiers raised their weapons and spun in the direction of the attacks. But the dim light of their lanterns did little to pinpoint our locations, robed as we were in midnight blue.

At Lucian's order, I edged south over the lower swells of the hills.

More soldiers fell. Lamps flickered out.

A pair of soldiers roared and, rallying clumps of their fellows, charged toward Lucian's and Arista's positions.

Leaving only three soldiers behind.

I crept toward them, sword in hand.

Something dark flashed against the black hill.

Steel rang against steel.

Soldiers fell like boulders—one cluster attacked from the west by a short figure and the other from the south by a tall one.

Two of the remaining enemies screamed challenges and ran toward the fights.

Only a single soldier stood by the boy, claws hooked into his wing.

She did not seem inclined to move.

Indeed, her attention was fixated on the boy. Who tried desperately to crawl away.

I had tried to flee from the Blood as he strangled my wings with his grip and chanted words in a twisted tongue, his magic drenching me in mind-breaking terror...

No, Elian, focus! I shook my head to clear it and stepped forward.

The soldier pressed a knife to the top curve of the boy's wing. Blood bubbled around the blade.

The boy shrieked.

I charged.

The soldier raised the knife and chopped down.

Just before the blade hit its mark, I rammed my shoulder into the soldier's chest-plate.

She stumbled back, dropping the weapon and the wing.

"Run!" I cried to the boy.

He was curling back into a ball, too petrified to flee.

The soldier snarled and drew a sword. She thrust it at me, and I barely managed a block.

Lucian! I screamed.

Spitting foul words, the soldier reared back and struck at my head.

I nearly fell over as I tried to dodge.

She swiped again. The blade passed with a hair of my torso.

Jeering, she raised the sword for a cleaving blow.

A dagger, Lucian's dagger, buried itself in her chest. Piercing the armor with ease. Squirting blood.

She fell to her knees and then to her side, lifeless.

Bile rose in my throat, but I turned to the boy.

His wide eyes were trained on the soldier.

No child needs to see such a thing. He was not really a child, nearly my height and weight, appearing to be about halfway through adolescence, but, with my own memories so fresh, I could not help my protective instinct.

I crouched in front of him, blocking his view.

He immediately cowered away from me.

Ignoring the pain striking my heart, the throb in my shoulder, and the ever-present blaze of my wings, I directed all my attention toward the boy. Clearing my throat, I tried to mimic Lucian's soothing tone. "Blessings, Bhalo." I used the formal demonym for a male citizen of Bhalasa.

The boy froze and stared.

I continued, trying not to discourage myself, "If it would please you, perhaps you might come with my siblings and me. We have a shelter in which we can wait out the storm in warmth and dryness."

He did not react. No indication of whether he had heard me.

I repeated the words.

Same reaction.

I squirmed, aware that the storm was only increasing in intensity. Coats of thickening ice encrusted both of us, and the wind shrieked ominously around the summit of the hill to the north. My magical senses screamed with the stomach-churning feel of a tornado's gathering force.

A warm presence brushed my side. The boy's mouth dropped open, his eyes bulging in his thin face.

Lucian, I sighed. He would be able to help.

His face shining again, he crouched beside me and extended his hand to the boy. "We can protect you, little brother, if you would allow."

The rich melody of his voice visibly melted the tension in the boy's shoulders. Not a moment passed before he grasped Lucian's hand with both of his own.

Lucian chuckled, the sound resonant in spite of the fierce winds, and helped the boy to his feet. He smiled at me as I stood beside them. *Excellent performance, Brother.*

I almost fell back down at the endearment and praise.

Lucian chuckled again and led us both to where Arista stood.

Feet braced in a wide stance, she cast the same spell she had on the day I met her, the one which managed to use fire sorcery to scoop soil.

"Bhalo, if you would, I ask that you might go ahead with my brother," Lucian addressed the wide-eyed boy. "My sister and I will follow as soon as we bury these soldiers."

Is that prudent? As soon as the words left my thoughts, I began stuttering an apology.

Perhaps a burial seems more than a bit imprudent, Lucian acknowledged, *despite preserving our adherence to principle. But only if we bury them now can we hide their disappearance long enough to stave off concentrated pursuit. I am masking Arista's efforts; we will follow shortly.* He tapped the jewel on the pommel of my sword, which began to glow with the same sweet green light as his pendant.

Sheathing my sword, I nodded and held out my hand to the boy. Hopefully, he would finally take it, for he especially could not remain exposed a moment longer.

The boy's gaze flickered from Lucian's to mine. But this time, instead of flinching, a small smile curved his lips. Letting go of Lucian's fingers, he grasped mine and drew close enough to me that I could see the trust brimming in his hazel eyes.

I returned his smile and bowed my head to Lucian before pulling us both up the hill.

Barely an ice-slicked slope passed before we wrapped our arms around each other's shoulders.

"We need to run," the boy breathed. "And be careful of that boulder."

"That black mass is ice," I warned, "and that tree looks like it might fall."

A blinding bolt of lightning struck a nearby hilltop. The bitter bite of the sleet began to bruise instead of sting.

"Hurry," I panted, directing us toward where my bond with Malika and Kyros tugged.

"Careful!" The boy yanked me away from an ominous puddle, which gleamed maliciously in my sword's light. Then he spread his wings, clutched me to him, and jumped, gliding over a much larger pool of water collecting in a dip in the ground. He whimpered but spread his iced, wounded wings and leaped again.

Breathing heavily, I tried not to panic. Being flown in this way, coupled with the brutal wind's freer access to my wings, reminded me too much of how the villagers had thrown me in the air...

"Which way?" the boy asked.

I managed to point.

He landed and leaped again. And again. And again.

Until he glided down to the exposed roots of a tree.

At the last moment, a branch swaying in the storm whipped my back.

Screaming, we tumbled head over heels until we crashed into the ground.

He groaned, but I jumped up and pulled him into the cover of the grove. Tripping over my feet, I shouted, "Malika! Kyros!"

Four of the branches jiggled before the wall opened.

I dropped to my knees and pushed the boy into the shelter. I crawled in myself, replaced the branches, then turned around and slumped against the wall. *Finally, warmth and safety...*

Turning to check on Malika and Kyros, I blinked at the green light illuminating the interior. It came from all three of our swords.

Lucian instructed me in our private link on the spell, Malika said, following my gaze. *He and Arista are half-way here.*

I nodded. *Did you eat?*

Yes, Kyros replied, holding out two athar cloth packages, which contained strips of meat from yesterday's hunt.

As I took them, I noticed both Malika and he seemed far more relaxed, despite the occasional shiver. Which meant the shelter fulfilled its purpose. Evident in how the ice was starting to thaw on my numbed wings.

A bit pleased with myself, I turned to the boy, whose stomach rumbled as he gazed mournfully at the packets. I flipped open the cloth cover of the fuller of the two and handed it to him.

His mouth dropped open again, though he accepted the offering. As soon as Kyros repeated Lucian's usual prayer, the boy crammed several strips into his mouth.

Smiling slightly, I chewed my own portion. Soaked and frosted though I was, I easily relaxed into a daydream of how I might next flavor the meat with herbs, or perhaps prepare a proper stew…

Lost amid my thoughts, I nearly spit out a mouthful when the boy spoke, "My name is Elacir bi-Dekecer." His hands trembled as he folded the cloth of his packet into a tiny square, but his voice was calm as he stated, "I owe you and your friends my life and my wings. How may I honor you?"

Malika, Kyros, and I stared, but blessedly we were saved from answering as the branches shifted again and Lucian and Arista entered.

A flurry of movement passed as Arista cast drying spells, Kyros served their supper, and I replaced the branches.

Once we had all finished the meal, Elacir inhaled deeply and looked to Lucian. "What do you plan to do with me?" This time his voice shook.

Lucian clasped his hands together on his lap. Narrowing his eyes, he directed a terrifying, soul-piercing gaze at Elacir.

The boy squirmed but exclaimed in a rush, "Can I come with you? My parents passed into the Almighty's reward last year, and my cousin turned my village against me before I was stolen." The sober reddish plum of his scales, patterned in clusters of four-pointed stars, dimmed against the cocoa of his skin and the burgundy of his hair and patchy beard. "I would serve you, cook for you, carry your possessions. But, please, do not leave me."

That is a plea to which I cannot say 'no', Lucian observed, his voice brimming with compassion as he spoke in the link. *What do you say, my companions?*

After all that effort to save him, Arista commented, wryly amused, *I certainly do not want to leave him to the soldiers.*

If we do not take him with us, Malika stated, staring at her hands, *he would be forced to flee from the soldiers for the rest of his life.*

He is too young to be on his own, Kyros insisted.

My new family turned to me.

I bit my lower lip. Elacir was both brave and noble—he risked flying with torn and frozen wings to protect both of us, and he sought to honor those who had helped him. He was sure to be loyal to Lucian as soon as he realized with whom he spoke. And his loyalty would be an advantage: as one of the Sholanar, with his wings and strength, perhaps he could remedy my lack... As inferior as that thought made me feel, such an arrangement would be best for Lucian and the Quest.

So I whispered, hunching my shoulders, *I want to say 'yes.'*

"Please, Bhalo," Elacir begged desperately, catching ahold of my hand.

"Elacir," Lucian said gently, drawing his gaze, "welcome to the circle of the Quest."

CHAPTER 18

REVIVE THE INCURABLE

Perspective: Honored Arista the Exemplar of Bravery
Date: Eyyéthar, the ninth day of the eleventh moon, Mirkharre
of the year 499, C.Q.

My leg broke through the brittle crust of ice and sank knee-deep into the snow.

I sighed, the breath swirling around my face like white mist. *Well,* I thought, *that settles it: even after three explanations from Elian and another two from Kyros, I still cannot judge which patch of ice obscures a drift of snow deep enough to swallow me and which covers only a faint blanket over flat ground.* The slight exhale turned into a wheezing cough.

I lifted the other foot and tested another patch. Only for that leg to be swallowed as well.

My fists clenched around the flasks, the knuckles straining beneath my athar cloth gloves. *No matter what it takes.*

Steeling myself, I lifted one foot and shoved it forwards. The raw strength of my muscles gained me a few inches even as the same limb flared with a brutal, gnawing ache. Not enough as a regular step, but still progress.

I nodded grimly to myself and forced another step. Then another. And another. And yet more.

My goal, the hard white glint of a frosted river on the other side of the hill, glittered tantalizingly under the little winter morning sunlight that struggled to filter through the smog. Normally, reaching the water and returning would be barely five minutes' work. But with the snow I could not promise Lucian any time shorter than an hour.

Such delay was shameful, but, in this one instance, it was not unjustified: I did not know how to traverse snow-covered terrain (I had not even seen snow before this week), I had no support, and I was gravely ill. But those perfectly valid reasons did not blot out my shame.

I had to retrieve that water.

My new family's lives could very well depend on it.

Another hacking cough erupted from my lips, shaking my entire person. I pressed my wrist against my mouth but did not halt my slow forward movement. Even when the cough felt like it might turn to vomit as my stomach churned.

Lucian woke me and asked me to go, I reminded myself, *because I fare the best out of everyone save him, and he needs to remain to prepare the remedy.*

I slogged a few more steps forward, but the river seemed just as far away as before while the drifts were rising toward my waist. With each contraction of muscle, my legs felt like they were splintering, about to shatter into pieces.

I filled my mind with the faces of my new family: Malika, who could barely breathe for the congestion clogging her nasal passages and the soreness bruising her throat, the gray tinge of her face starker than usual. Elian, who groaned that his wings were disintegrating. Kyros, who could barely sit up for the aches plaguing his head, chest, abdomen, and limbs. Elacir, whose fever burned so hot that he was beginning to hallucinate, screaming until his throat was raw at phantom enemies and tormentors. And Lucian, whose shining face was crumpled with stress and anxiety as he labored over a remedy for an illness that should not exist.

Though I had hoped dearly that we would, we had not escaped the ill effects of exposure to the storm. As Lucian had anticipated, the symptoms began to emerge the day after.

The moment the storm had ended with its finale of snow, late at night on the fourth of the moon of Mirkharre, Lucian had roused us, ordered us to dismantle the shelter and hide all traces of our presence, and bid us follow him.

In the darkness he led us northwest, almost without break to eat or care for our personal needs. Even at dawn, he did not halt for more than an hour of sleep. Before we could truly rest, he urged us onward again over the lower slopes of the foothills. So the pattern had continued for the next four days, fueled by swallows of food and snatches of sleep.

Well, Malika, Elian, Kyros, and Elacir slept the hours he gave them. I had been awake for half of those breaks. *I doubt Lucian has slept more than a few minutes since the storm.*

Yet the grueling, taxing pace had been necessary.

Halfway through that unending run, the shadows of the patrols had appeared again. But this time, the troops dove and examined every valley and cave. Only Lucian's ingenuity in creeping through thorn-filled bushes while wearing hardened athar (robes for the Potentates, blankets for Elacir) saved us.

To be captured was a fate worse than death.

And is that not proved in this situation? By not tending to our health immediately—depending on Lucian's prediction that we could leave behind the patrols before the disease truly took effect—we let the illness spread. The athar tears Lucian fed us before leaving the shelter staved off the symptoms for only so long.

Which, upon consideration, is... more than concerning. Athar tears are panaceas for physical illness and weakness of every kind. Sometimes, if the heart is pure, even for mental and emotional ones. The illness not being eradicated by the athar tear is... troubling.

Yet, at the same time, there is something rather unusual about all of this: Malika, Elian, Kyros, and I should be much sicker than we are. My brow furrowed, while I coughed into my sleeve. *We should be like Elacir—cooked alive by fever and tormented by reenactments of our worst memories. Even with the difference in levels of exposure. But, ill though we are, the four of us have no more than mild fevers... rather like Lucian himself. Which is... if my head were clearer, the implications would cause me to topple face-first into this snow.*

I wrinkled my nose. *Suppose that is a mercy, then. As enamored as I was to see it that first morning, even while scrambling over these brutal slopes, I am nowhere near as fond now. It is worse than sand at swallowing someone up.*

Wait! Worse than sand... That means...

I shoved the flasks inside the pockets of my coat, unbuckled my sheathed sword from my belt, jammed it into the snow in front of my leg, and shoved forward. The powdery snow compacted just enough for me to take a step. A much less hindered step.

Yes! I cheered, careful not to voice my exuberance aloud.

Repeating the process with the other leg, I began making much more progress. So much so that, despite the pauses needed to break or avoid the slabs of hardened snow my compressions formed, I reached the stream in nearly half the time predicted.

I grinned, despite the coughs and aches.

Then I looked at the stream.

Much of the surface of the water was crusted with ice.

Ugh. More snow. How does anyone choose to live in these places? There certainly is a reason that my ancestors chose the desert and the caverns beneath the Etheqor mountains.

Kneeling on the bank, I examined the ice, searching for the most bumpy, translucent part, as Lucian had instructed, and slammed the hilt of my sword into it.

The patch crumbled, and I immediately stuck my flasks into the water with both hands.

I nearly yelped at the spatter of cold water that shocked my skin even through the athar cloth gloves.

Do not let go! He said he needed both!

Gritting my teeth, I watched until the water bubbled over the mouths of the flasks, then yanked them out and quickly sealed them. Carefully placing them in pockets, I rose to my feet and began the trek back.

Enough of my earlier path remained that within twenty minutes I was slipping into our cave.

I stopped short.

The way Elian was crouched over Elacir's shaking form... tears gushing down his cheeks...

"No," I whispered, refusing to acknowledge the possibility.

"Arista." My name in Lucian's slightly hoarse, yet still musical, voice snapped my attention to his weary face.

His creamy skin had lost even more silver glow over the scant hour I was away. I had been alarmed when he had woken me; now I was almost lightheaded in my panic.

Not him too!

"Arista," he repeated.

I hurried forward and proffered the flasks.

His smile was a faded mockery of his usual dazzling beam as he thanked me. Uncapping both, he poured the water into the small iron pot Elian had carried from his dwelling.

Buckling my sword onto my belt out of habit, I sank to the floor and stared at Lucian. I barely managed a greeting for Malika and Kyros, who sat leaning against the cave wall and anxiously watched Elian and Elacir.

Lucian's focus, however, was entirely on his task: not twitching at Elacir's cries and Elian's sobs, he placed both hands on the rim of the pot and whispered sentence upon sentence in the sacred tongue Alimàzahre. Bright white light spilled from his fingers into the lusterless interior, and his violet eyes repeatedly flickered between turning entirely silver, from the whites to the irises and pupils, to glowing so brilliantly that I could not keep my gaze upon him. In time with the glow of his eyes, his face emanated pulses of light before fading back to a dull silver sheen.

He had been doing the same before I left. All night long. Since my eyes fell shut yesterday evening.

I could only imagine how much energy he was expending.

Elacir screamed, sweeping his hand across his body and nearly smacking it into the stone before Elian caught it.

How much longer, Lucian? Kyros begged, gray eyes lit by the telltale glimmer of foresight.

Lucian did not answer him in words but indicated with a sweep of expression in the link that he needed ten more minutes.

Devastation coarsened Kyros' face. *He does not have ten more minutes!*

Elian twisted to face Lucian, cupping his hands in entreaty. *We cannot lose him!* he cried. *We promised to protect him when we saved him! When he pledged to you that night!*

Lucian's eyes narrowed even as he continued to chant. Beneath his fingers, the red gleam of the five athar tears seemed to float in a vat of light rather than water. And yet more light poured from his fingers.

I did not know how he could further rush his efforts.

Over the past four days, Lucian had explained the remedy his guardians used to prepare after any significant exposure to the rain: a handful of the athar tears (which they had smuggled from Asfiya before her capture), globes of pure, unenchanted athar (smuggled at the same time), and fresh river water all mixed together in a brew which required at least five days of enchantment with athar magic to heal both the short- and long-term effects of the disease. Entirely effective, unlike anything else in Icilia, yet so costly as to be impossible. Even for us, though we had the athar tears and the most powerful athar magician living in the form of Lucian himself—the guardians' own supply of pure athar had long since been exhausted, so even Lucian did not carry any.

Yet, when I had mentioned our lack of time and one of the ingredients, Lucian responded that he would find a way to compensate. That was what he did now, draining his own energy into the remedy, forming it with magic beyond my understanding.

His effort would still not be enough for Elacir.

How could he be asked to do more? His face was losing its glow, depleted far more by his efforts on our behalf than by his own illness.

I stood and opened my mouth to ask him to stop. As much as I was growing to care for Elacir, as dear as Elian's happiness was, Lucian's life was itself salvation, too precious to spend for anyone.

Before I could speak, an idea sparked in Lucian's dimming eyes. He lifted both hands off the black rim. Then, the movements almost too fast to perceive, he drew a dagger, rolled back his sleeve, and sliced his forearm.

Blood trickled from the wound and fell into the pot.

Midair the ruby flashed and transformed into a radiant white. As though a fraction of the Almighty's Light, veiled within the ruby, had burst through, burning away its concealment. Changing the drops into a substance other than blood.

The drops hit the swirl of light, athar tears, and water.

Light exploded from the remedy.

Dazzling.

Too much to perceive.

White blinded my vision.

I blinked frantically.

Color slowly seeped through the haze. As did thought.

What did you do, Lucian! I screamed, tossing my head as I tried to find him. *What did you just sacrifice!*

The others echoed my words with shrieks and demands of their own.

The world began to resolve into silhouettes of white amid shadows of gray and midnight blue.

What was necessary, Lucian said. As though the matter were really that simple.

A blazing retort on my lips, I swiveled to face him the moment my vision cleared, only to freeze as he lifted Elacir's head and raised a cup brimming with the light to the boy's death-stricken face.

His lips were parting on the wheeze of a rattle.

Lucian tilted the cup and, as he moved it down over Elacir's supine form, let the light trickle onto the bruised skin. Glowing as it seeped through the cracked scales of his wings. Soaked into his stilled chest and the lungs beneath. Drenched the belly emptied by desperate retches.

Honed battle-focus stern on his features, Lucian carefully watched the boy's face as the whole cupful disappeared.

I did not dare to breathe. Malika, Elian, and Kyros were equally still. As though our breath had been robbed alongside Elacir's.

Lucian lowered the cup and murmured something, his voice too quiet to hear.

Elacir's chest remained unmoving.

Please, Almighty, Elian begged.

The boy did not stir.

Elian's face crumpled.

I took a step to comfort him over yet another loss.

A gasp burst from Elacir's bluing lips... then another... and another...

Lucian sat back on his heels, weary satisfaction brightening his face.

My family and I startled, barely believing what we were seeing.

Elacir's eyes flickered open, bloodshot yet vibrant. "Elian..."

A sob tore from Elian's chest. "Little Brother! You live!" Weeping, he flung his arms around Elacir.

Shuffling forward on his knees, Kyros did the same.

"My Honors, you are squeezing the life back out of me," Elacir grumbled but returned the hugs.

Unable to hold back a grin, I wiped the tears trickling between my plates with my sleeve. Then I turned to Lucian, who scooped another cupful of the light. Injecting every bit of my furious concern and terror into my voice, I spoke, "What. Was. That?"

Elian's and Kyros' frantic questions, Elacir's adorable gripes, and Malika's whispered prayers of gratitude faded.

Straightening, Lucian raised an eyebrow the color of sunlight as he met my gaze. "I protected my companions and my first vassal from the Blood's evil with all the resources at my disposal," he said coolly. Kneeling in front of Kyros, he held out the cup.

Kyros did not move. "I do not want to benefit from your sacrifice," he whispered, his gaze on the blood still oozing from Lucian's arm.

Nor do I, Lucian, Malika objected. *We are not worth it.*

Elacir scowled, curving down those lips that were still not quite clear of blue. "My Lord, what did you do?" he demanded with astonishing daring.

"What was that?" I repeated, ignoring the rasp in my voice that heralded a hacking cough. "Your magic brought back Elacir from the brink of death. What cost did you sustain?"

Green eyes flashing with unusual boldness, Elian echoed my question.

Lucian pressed his lips together, evidently unwilling to answer.

Despite the coughs rasping from our throats, Malika, Elian, Kyros, and I did not yield. Elacir jutted his lower lip out in a clear, if childish, indication of stubborn refusal.

The tension mounting in the air was too thick to cut with a sword.

Then Lucian sighed and, gesturing to himself, said, "As you can see, I did not expend more than what I am capable of bearing."

He is right... I admitted reluctantly to myself. *His face has lost much of its glow, but even now it returns... And he* is talking and moving, steady as always, as though he really did not weaken himself... Even that cut is quickly clotting.

The contemplation on my family's faces mirrored my own. As did Elacir's.

"Also," Lucian added in a quieter yet deeply passionate voice, "would you truly deny me an act of devotion in service to the ones whom I love? What value has my office and power if I do not choose to use it for those who are entrusted to my care? Tell me, my Sisters and my Brothers."

Our faces, softened by his words of love, now burst ablaze in the expressions of emotion characteristic to our various kinds; my plates actually hummed against my skin. No one knew how to answer him.

Instead, his face polished like glass, Kyros accepted the cup and sprinkled its contents over his body. He then offered it to Elian, who scooped servings for Malika and me.

I did not protest but instead poured onto myself the light... which smelled (impossibly) like sunshine, love, and holiness given form. With every inch it slid over my skin, it healed me: banishing the haze of fever, the wet rasp of coughs, and the sharp throb of aches. Ridding my body of every vestige of exhaustion and the illness born of the Blood's magic.

Too overwhelmed to speak, I gave back the cup, and Elian scraped the bottom of the pot in his own share. The athar tears, I noted, had entirely dissolved in the liquid when Lucian completed his spell.

Turning to thank him, I froze.

The smile that curved Lucian's pale lips was dazzling like the glimpse of divine Light revealed through his blood. And the answering sense of contentment which arose in my heart at earning his happiness resolved the matter.

Yet, as I watched him laughingly accept Kyros' offer to care for his arm, I wondered whether I was too easily letting go of the questions I should ask.

That thought quickly slipped from my grip as Malika reminded us that we needed to keep moving.

CHAPTER 19

CHEER THE MELANCHOLY

Perspective: Honored Arista the Exemplar of Bravery
Date: Eyyéthar, the sixteenth day of the eleventh moon, Mirkharre, of the year 499, C.Q.

I peered at the map and then squinted at the hills stretching into the horizon. *Are they really flattening out?*

Yes, Lucian answered, amused despite the number of times I had asked, *but very slowly. The transition to the plains will only be clear when we are closer to the border.*

And that is still a long way away, I muttered, examining the map. My mother had once stolen into the queen's study for the one remaining map possessed by the royal family, and my father had then spent a week explaining the geography of Icilia to my twin sister and me. If I remembered how to read maps correctly… My eyes widened. *We have quite a distance left to travel.*

Around seven hundred miles to the border, Lucian said, *and approximately three weeks, should our pace not falter.*

Lightly tugging with the hand wrapped around my elbow, he directed me around a patch of snow.

Elian, however, cracked through the crust and slogged directly though the drift, his legs sinking to only the middle of his shins.

Seven hundred miles? Kyros squeaked.

And another four hundred miles beyond the border to Tresilt, Lucian replied, sympathy sweetening his smile.

Kyros seemed stunned. Then his gray eyes dimmed, and his face fell. *That is so far away.*

Malika patted his arm, which was twined with hers. *But we* are *going there,* she said quietly.

Yes, that is true. Kyros sighed and smiled faintly. *Thank you, Lucian.*

Lucian chuckled. *This is nothing for which to thank me. As I explained when I first showed you the map, we cannot travel directly north to the base in Nademan where my brother and my guardians will await us. The mountains are too steep in central Bhalasa for all but those who fly—and too dangerous in general for us, as Bhalasa's crown was a defector. Since we must pass through Khuduren, visiting your village, Kyros, will not be too long a detour. Also*—his smile widened—*I have always wanted to meet your sister.*

Kyros' lips twitched into a broader grin. *You are the image of her heroic ideal.*

Lucian cupped his hand over his heart as his cheeks tinted a gentle silver.

Kyros' face brightened but did not entirely lose its edge of anguish.

As are you, I countered, wanting to ease that pain, for I understood it all too well. *You certainly seem the image of our Honored King Naret the Exemplar of Love to me.*

As I had hoped, Kyros dropped his gaze as his face glossed, the skin gleaming like polished glass under the noon sun.

Satisfied, I grinned as I rolled up the map. Before I could turn to stow it, Elian plucked the scroll from my fingers and slid it into Lucian's pack. He buckled the flap closed, then wrapped his hand again around my other elbow.

Ahead of us, Kyros' footsteps left a slightly deeper imprint than usual in the brittle crust that covered the snow. The same snow spread out in ripples from where Malika's legs sank into it, yet her pace did not slow. She moved as though she waded through the waters of a shallow stream.

As we approached that same drift, Lucian and Elian lifted me by my elbows. Lucian's feet sank to his ankles, and Elian's sank to his knees, while the tips of my boots barely skimmed the surface.

Suppressing a groan, I waited until they set me down on the other side of the dip in the bare rock of the hilltop. I then immediately resumed walking, determined to do as much as I could with my own strength. Though I had managed to survive months alone in these mountains, the moment winter had come, all my surefootedness had vanished and I had to be carried.

Still, being carried this way, as much as it irked me, was better than being dug out of deep, snow-filled cracks—an embarrassing experience I absolutely did not want to repeat. Besides, as Mammy often said, "practicality before pride." Snow was treacherous for one of my height, and that danger was only compounded by the recent melting and refreezing the foothills had undergone after the storm.

Lucian tilted his head back, considering whatever he perceived in his so-very-useful sense. *I would like to continue our lesson from yesterday. Elacir?*

He chirped back, *Yes, my Lord?*

Fondness sparkled in Lucian's vibrant violet eyes. *Would you return?*

As you wiiiiish! The spot of purple drifting overhead dove toward us, rapidly expanding into Elacir's plum wings and brown clothes (Elian's gift). The boy laughed unreservedly, his shrill voice bouncing between soprano and tenor.

I could not resist a broad grin as I teased, "He is quite taking advantage of your presence."

Lucian chuckled. "He did ask to fly, and I did say 'yes'."

"And," Elian added, "he *was* practicing the wing-strengthening exercises Lucian set him until we took out the map." He beamed up at Elacir, pure delight glittering on his chocolate-framed golden scales. "He flies beautifully, does he not? He could become a credit to your name, Lucian."

I raised an eyebrow at those last words and wondered to myself, *Is this just my thought or... is Elian trying to persuade Lucian of the value of Elacir's service to the Quest? I am certainly relieved that Elian does not appear jealous of Elacir's working wings, but... his comments are* quite *odd.*

If he noted anything strange, Lucian did not mention it, calling out, *Slow down, Little Brother!* Even he had started to use Elian's endearment, first given in a burst of affection after Lucian saved his life.

At the light command, Elacir snapped his wings open, finally changing his headlong plummet to a proper glide.

I smirked at how well he balanced my newly sharpened old swords. *That boy is a brother after my own heart.*

Thank you, my Honor! he trilled as he landed, skipping only a step forward before he transitioned to a walk at Elian's side.

Arista, Malika corrected, smiling at him over her shoulder. *Lucian already offered our names to you, Little Brother.*

Elacir rolled his eyes—singularly impolite but daring in a way I doubted many would ever be in front of the Quest. *I pledged to you; I am your vassal. Your* first *vassal.*

His grin was as mischievous as my own—yet, unlike mine, bore no sign of the scarring trauma he had experienced. Though I doubted it was entirely gone. But Elacir seemed to have wholeheartedly embraced the chance for an entirely new life: in his completely unexpected pledge not hours after his rescue, he had wholly dedicated himself to the Quest.

How in Icilia did Lucian think you were mature enough to pledge, Little Brother? Kyros lightly teased, for once not awkward.

You ought to ask your heroic ideal that! Elacir retorted.

We burst out laughing, and even Lucian chuckled heartily, elegantly covering his mouth.

Elacir strutted for a few paces, immensely pleased with himself—which prompted a second round of mirth.

The laughter, still an odd moment for us, lasted until we had descended that hill and begun climbing another.

Finally Lucian said, amusement still visible on his shining face, *If it would please you, Arista?*

I swallowed a final guffaw and said, in a far calmer voice, *Malika, Elian, Kyros, Elacir, focus.* How unfamiliar it was to be the teacher rather than the student!

My siblings indicated they were listening. Elacir shuffled his feet a bit, still hesitant about Lucian's decision after his recovery to include him in our lessons, but turned an attentive gaze to me.

I gave him an encouraging smile and then began one of my least favorite topics: the political history of Nademan.

The five provinces of Nademan lived quite harmoniously together, the people more focused on pursuing innovation and novelty in every part of their lives than engaging in political intrigue and war. The Nademani were known for frequently changing the locations of their villages, devising new forms of art and literature, and designing new inventions in magic and weaponry. In many ways, the broad spectrum of their interests and characteristics matched the wide variations of height among the trees of their great forest, the Dasenákder. A beautiful, colorful people, far different from the rigid warriors of my own nation yet accomplished in their own ways.

All of which had fallen apart because of their last king, Nirio, who deserved his royal name as little as my grandmother, the traitor queen. Flouting his ancestors' teachings and ignoring the plights of Koroma, Asfiya, and Etheqa, Nirio had done nothing when the Blood had marched on his borders. Nothing. Whatever he had accomplished in his reign, his name was synonymous with the consequences of a ruler's neglect.

Immersed in describing all this history, I dismissed a creeping tendril of nausea that threatened to waste my luncheon. I expected such discomfort in this part of the month.

Lucian and Elian lifted me over another drift packed into a jagged gap in the hillside.

A second burst of nausea caused me to choke for a moment. *That is unusual.*

We climbed to the top of the hill.

The nausea attacked with such force that I staggered out of Lucian's and Elian's hold and retched to the side.

For a moment, as I washed my mouth with sips from a flask, I was embarrassed.

Until I turned to see Malika, Elian, and Kyros doing the same, kneeling in drifts of varying heights. Elacir held back Elian's bound wings from tilting into the mess.

Lucian, however, had paled—the silvery sheen of his skin so dimmed that it resembled the gray pallor of illness. Like Malika's tinge of dehydration. He had not been so affected by the sickness from the storm or even by his sacrifice in crafting a remedy.

Arista... he whispered. *What do your magical senses tell you?*

I focused on my magic.

And reeled as Bhalasa's magic rang with discord, the warmth of community and of hands held together in service to the Almighty torn apart by the bitter anger of parent against child, spouse against spouse, sibling against sibling... The very elements seemed to be recoiling, chaotic and diseased in ways far deeper than the perpetual taint of the smog...

Squinting, I tried to make sense of all the perceptions crashing into my senses...

Then I saw it.

The burnt village on the horizon. The source of this magical disturbance. Around which even the snow glittered like frozen tears.

"*Lucian!*" I shrieked.

Malika, Elian, and Kyros jerked upright at my cry. They, too, screamed his name.

Following our gazes, Elacir whimpered.

Lucian audibly drew in a breath and then tripped forward into a run. Snow firmed beneath his feet, and shards of rock rolled aside for him.

We scrambled behind him, down the hill and across the valley.

Elacir jumped into the sky and flapped frantically to reach Lucian's side.

With a glance at me, Kyros increased his speed, streaking forwards, a blur on Lucian's heels.

Malika and Elian shifted so that Malika ran ahead of me and Elian behind—our pace only possible because of the remnants of Lucian's trail of ice.

We climbed another hill, smaller than the last one, and sped across the next valley.

Odors reached my nose: the coppery tang of old blood. The caustic odor of smoke. An odd corrosive scent that evoked rage and suffering and sorrow. The distinctive scent of death.

Drawing his sword without breaking his stride, Lucian led the way up the final hillside and into the village.

Passing first one ring of ruins, then the second, he stepped onto the central sward.

Then he fell to his knees, his sword flung to the ground beside him. A tormented cry ripped from his throat.

Kyros shrieked and collapsed.

Elacir plummeted from the air, impacting the ground with a brutal thud. Shaking, he picked himself up and huddled behind Kyros' back.

Malika, Elian, and I crossed the circles of broken buildings and crumpled to our knees. Clutching each other, we cried.

In front of us was the remains of a village. And the white that streaked through its grounds was not wholly snow, not shards of ice as we had thought from a distance, but bones.

Bones.

The skeletons of men, women, children, of babies.

They gleamed a whitish gray under the dimmed sunlight and were tossed every which way throughout the streets and on the central sward. Broken, from all manner of injury, and bearing the look of sticks shattered to bits under the hooves of horses. So old that the flesh that once coated them had rotted away or been picked clean by birds of carrion. Only the flecks of dried blood dotting them were reminders that they had once composed the frames of living people.

A people who had been brutally murdered.

And never buried.

Never mourned.

Abandoned.

In the center of the carnage loomed the flag of the Blood-soaked Sorcerer, a carmine skull centered on a black pennant. While the bones had been worn away by the elements, some to nubs, the pennant flapped in the screeching wind with nary a tear or hole, perfectly preserved. Another injustice.

Tears streaming down my face, my plates like dry, cracked stone, I bared my teeth at that hated banner. Every place its shadow touched it ruined.

As it had ruined Rushada. As it had ruined this village.

It deserved to burn. As its master did.

May I burn it? I snarled.

Lucian glanced over his slumped shoulder at me.

The heartbreak searing his violet eyes stoked my anger into a raging inferno.

The moment he nodded, I spat out a spell.

Flames ignited at the base of the pole. The tongues of fire quickly slithered up the wood and began to gnaw on the black cloth.

The pennant crumbled into ash.

Amid the roar of fury, a strange magic stirred in my blood.

And I looked upon a face come from the deepest abyss, blacker than night and blemished by the charcoal of soot.

CHAPTER 20

LAMENT THE ABANDONED

Perspective: Honored Arista the Exemplar of Bravery
Date: Eyyéthar, the sixteenth day of the eleventh moon,
Mirkharre, of the year 499, C.Q.

I panicked. My mouth inhaled air, yet I choked on my own breath. My limbs seized, my head spun in a dizzying swirl of vertigo...

Fingers, Malika's, tightening around my wrist restored sense to me.

Then I narrowed my eyes, thinking, *That is not the Choker. The Slicer does not have wings or that particular pattern... The Gouge never dresses in leathers... That is the Clawed! That means—*

The specter of the Clawed sneered at the groveling man who knelt just behind me and spun on his heel to face the ruins—or rather circles of spacious houses.

The people bustling about the sward froze as they noticed him.

A woman screamed.

Villagers scattered, some running toward the far side of the circle and others leaping into the air, desperate to get away.

The Clawed sniggered, his face twisted with glee. "Stand still, or your fields burn!" he barked.

Sholanar soldiers appeared above the houses, in the paths of the terrified villagers. Swinging spears, they herded the men and women back toward where the Clawed stood. Others broke open the doors of the houses and dragged out children and the bedridden, elders and the sickly. Pregnant women and their babies were tossed at the Clawed's feet.

At the sight of such vulnerability, the Clawed's leer promised the unrestrained malevolence which haunted my earliest memories...

The Choker had once assembled the queen and her family before the Blood. He, my grandmother's ally, had come on an unannounced visit and had insisted on an audience with the whole court. My mother protested, citing my sister's and my fifth birthday celebrations as a reason to refuse. But my grandmother indulgently agreed to the request, thinking she controlled the reins of the alliance.

Only to drown us in the bitter poison of conjury.

As the Blood's abyssal black skin had shimmered that day, so did the Clawed's.

Before the villagers could move, before I could react, the all-too-familiar shadowy cloud poured off the Clawed's body. Sensing eager prey, it swept over us.

My heart stopped. Then pounded so hard, fluttering so fast, that every throb beat my chest, as though it was trying to smash itself against my ribs. The pain stole my breath—and then I could not breathe. No inhale drew air. My lungs cramped with pain.

The aches spread across my chest and seeped up my throat, drying my mouth, into my head. Besieging my mind. Then the pain trickled, sadistic in its creep, down my spine. Sweat dripped from beneath my hair, down my neck, and soaked my back. Nausea unfurled in my stomach.

I trembled, unable to move of my own will. Unable to think. Unable to feel anything but the terror penetrating deep into my bones. The fear, black and potent, was all I knew. All I believed. My world.

I screamed as the villagers did.

A squeeze around my wrist restored something of my mind, and I remembered that I was nowhere near the Blood, the Choker, the Clawed, or anyone else who wielded conjury. Indeed, the presences around me emanated light akin to the sun itself. All I perceived was a vision—a brutal, horrifying vision—but only a vision.

I was so familiar with the virulence of conjury that only an image was enough to trigger the fear.

Tears spilled down my cheeks as I watched the villagers scream and cry and writhe on the ground as I so often had. In the very place we were supposed to be safe.

The Clawed laughed in utter delight as the Blood had and released some of the pressure.

The villagers pressed their faces to the earth and cried. Relief glossed their skin and brightened their scales.

I wept and covered my mouth with both hands.

The Clawed spread his arms. "Have your pick, troops!" The words of his master on that first day.

The Sholanar soldiers, mostly men, jeered and descended on the villagers. Seizing women, men, children, anyone they pleased. They tore off clothes and wreaked violence then and there.

The Clawed howled in laughter and picked his own victims, one hand wielding conjury and the other inflicting violence. Like his master.

The reddened sun slid down in the sky as the torture raged. The screams and sobs and shouted taunts spread on the wind. But no matter how the villagers begged for mercy, there was none. None for them, none for my family.

Shaking, wailing, I forced my eyes to bear witness. As I had for my family, ever only just snatched from suffering such a fate myself.

The Clawed abruptly let his victims go.

At the unspoken cue, so did the soldiers.

The Clawed, his wild, mad grin growing yet more deranged, unsheathed his swords. The bloodthirsty blades plunged into cowering bodies.

What followed was slaughter.

Chasing some, grouping others by family, sorting yet more by age—slaughter. Blood misted the air, rising in scarlet clouds over what was no battlefield.

Each breath I took seemed laden with blood.

Man, woman, child, infant—none were spared.

"Bring the torches!" the Clawed ordered.

Retrieving stacks of wood from a wagon parked outside the village, the soldiers poured oil and sparked flames.

The Clawed seized the first branch. With it he lit the mauled body of a child aflame.

Then the soldiers set each body individually on fire.

Screeching in pleasure, they swerved and swung through the greedy fires. Relished in the acrid smoke as the burning spread to the once-beautiful now-bloody houses. Laughed at the flesh melting from seared bones.

Days passed in the vision.

Only when the initial splatters of rain began to douse the flames did the Clawed summon horses. In their departure they crushed what remained of their victims, mere bones, beneath the hooves of the horses they had brought specifically for this purpose.

The vision held steady for a moment more, showing the flickering of the sun rising and setting, day after day after day. The seasons passed in the fall of rain and snow. But nothing grew. And two years elapsed.

Until the vision dissolved on Lucian's tear-streaked face, turned to me.

"You saw it?" he asked, his melodious voice hoarse.

I nodded, barely able to breathe.

"What did you see?" Elian's voice filtered through the pulse thrashing in my ears.

Was it the destruction of this place? Malika asked.

Lucian and I dipped our heads. In his gaze alone I found the shared agony of what I had seen.

"How could you bear such a vision?" Kyros whispered, horrified. His skin was so coarse it resembled tree bark.

"The magic of the Quest," Lucian answered. His gaze returned to mine, and a pained smile drew up his lips. "I have never shared a vision before. How I wish you were not yet capable of receiving them, Arista. A few weeks more together would have granted you the fortitude to withstand them."

I had no words to speak.

Lucian closed his eyes and exhaled a deep sigh. Then he rose to his feet and offered his hand to me. "Come, my sisters and brothers. We cannot erase this injustice, but let us at least honor them with burial."

I slid my fingers into his, but he had to pull for me to muster the strength to stand.

My plates spasmed against my cheeks as warm tears wound through the channels between them.

Lucian stroked one of those plates. "We will succor them, Arista," he said—but for once the words sounded a bit hollow.

Fresh tears spilled from my eyes. He was trying to comfort me even while his eyes were dull and his face gray with heartbreak.

Lucian pressed his lips together, controlling a wince. Then turned to Malika, Elian, and Kyros—whose sorrow and tears only deepened my own pain.

Elian and Kyros whimpered, and Malika pressed her hands to her heart as her mouth spread in a scowl of pain. But all three bowed their heads and knelt, gathering armfuls of bones.

I wet my cracking lips. "I will dig the grave."

"And I will help," Elacir volunteered from where he stood behind Lucian. Though grief marked his face as it did ours, a strange curiosity dominated all his other emotions.

Letting go of my hand, Lucian sheathed his sword and bent to gently cradle the skeleton of a child.

I inhaled deeply and reminded myself of my mother's words, "Rulers do not have time to collapse. But if they must, they do on the Almighty's mercy."

The Almighty will heal all of this, I told myself, my eyes on Lucian's form, the light in this darkness.

Tossing aside my pack, I searched the ruins. Amid the unusual combination of stone and wood, bones of the once living almost as much as the bones themselves, I found a pair of rusted shovels. Handing one to Elacir, I chose a flat patch of earth on the northern edge of the village.

Scraping away the crust of snow, I struck the earth.

Elacir silently joined me.

I widened the grave, and he deepened it.

Clods of red clay flew in the air as the metal dipped and rose, removing chunks of earth in a rhythmic motion that would have been calming if not for its purpose.

Steadily we worked until the tomb was twelve feet long, six feet wide, and eight feet deep. Unlike the mass graves I had made recently for enemy soldiers, I took care to neaten the corners and pack the base.

Elacir lifted me out of the burial pit. Lucian, who had returned with several skeletons of tiny bones, lowered himself into it. Then Elacir began to pass him the bones. Lucian prayed over each and pressed them into the safekeeping of the earth. I covered them by dropping some of the earth we had placed to the side. Malika, Elian, and Kyros brought back armful after armful.

Hours passed, and the sun neared the western horizon. Yet we continued, grimly wiping sweat, pausing only for sips of water.

When at last Lucian confirmed that all the bones were buried, Elian and Kyros helped him out.

Then he took the first handful of soil and sprinkled it into the grave.

We followed his lead with our shovels and hands, filling the villagers' final resting place with the soil of their worldly home.

As the earth rose to the surface, the nausea that coiled through the elements eased, the chaos in Bhalasa's magic fading, as though the land itself felt soothed.

Elian smoothed the last shovelful atop the mound, and I spilled a flask of water, darkening the red clay.

Lucian knelt then and pressed his hands into the loam. His voice a low hymn, he intoned, "May the Almighty bestow peace upon you, children of Icilia. May the Almighty enact justice upon those who harmed you. May the Almighty regard you with mercy and kindness. May the Almighty free you from your sorrows and griefs and endow you with the honor of martyrdom. May the Almighty bless you. Praised be the Almighty."

Rivers of tears spilled down his cheeks onto the freshly turned earth, giving peace that only the divine could, raising the villagers in the gaze of the Almighty.

The words, uttered in that blessed voice, and the tears, given from those blessed eyes, calmed the last of the convulsions shaking the land's magic.

Lucian raised his voice and chanted first the prayer and then the funeral dirge in the old custom of the Mutharrim. Malika and Elian sang alongside him, and Kyros, Elacir, and I murmured the funeral chants of our own nations, as was custom.

A faint whisper, like a sigh of heartfelt relief, reached my ears.

Then Lucian spoke, "May the Almighty bless you with peace, villagers of Temerilt. Of both the Sholanar and the Nasimih, you forged a life on the hinterlands of Bhalasa, courageously living together though the crowns of your birthplaces had begun to frown on such intermingling. Nineteen years you lived, if not happily then with contentment, and prayed in gratitude to the Almighty. You did not forsake those prayers even when our enemy tore apart all that you had made. May the peace you sought be yours in the hereafter given to you by the Almighty."

He sighed and lowered his head, closing his eyes, still more tears wetting the soil. "This should not have happened to you. We cannot undo it, but we will bring about a day after which the same will not befall another." A smile, pained yet dazzling with that divine blessing that so often transfixed me, curved his lips. "Know that the attendants of your funeral are the Potentates of the Quest of Freedom, who will exact justice for your suffering. Unto our hands the Almighty has given freedom."

His words echoed in the warming air, which swirled with faint tinkles of delight, the gentle hum of bitter despair mellowing into the warm acceptance of resilient grief. A freedom itself.

Lucian pressed a kiss to the grave drenched with his tears.

Malika, Elian, and Kyros, kneeling on his right, whispered their own addresses to the souls of the villagers and left their own kisses.

I, however, did not know what to say. I had seen their suffering and knew its feeling from my own. Lucian had experienced the same. But, crumbled as I was, I did not have Lucian's confidence to make any assurance.

But to honor them, I needed to speak, even if I could not summon the poetry such prayers deserved. So I spoke the truth: "The Quest Leader bore witness to your suffering. He will not forget you. And neither will I. May the Almighty bless you." After making my own kiss, I rose and stood back. Listening to the buzz of prayers, I let my emotions flow in a wave of tears.

When the sun stamped the underside of the smog with brushes of red and gold, Lucian rose. Turning, he strode into the rubble. Before any of us could offer our service, he retrieved a piece of wood unstained by blood and smoke. With a dagger, he carved the name of the village and the date of the massacre, a day nearly two years prior. Below it, he added a blessing and his own name.

At a brief order, I cast a spell that would preserve both the sign and the carving.

Lucian stepped back and said, "Come."

We dipped our heads and fetched our packs, yet more tears falling.

"Wait! My Lord, wait!"

At Elacir's voice, all five of us turned. Lucian, Malika, and Elian attempted smiles, which were more grimaces than any expression of warmth. Kyros raised an eyebrow. I did not have the strength left to react, even for the boy I was adopting as a younger brother. But all of us were listening.

Determination bright in his hazel eyes, plum scales gleaming against cocoa skin, Elacir took a step toward us and said, cracking voice uncharacteristically firm, "My Lord, my Grace, my Honors, you are Icilia's salvation. You are our only chance for freedom. I say this because, in your divine humility, you do not speak of the mercy you alone have." He gestured to the village and the grave. "No one else would have buried them, my Rulers. No one else would have dared in fear of the mere thought of the Blood's troops, even long gone. No one else might have even grieved, because such sights are not uncommon. And no one else would have dared to interfere on behalf of a captive, much less thought to feed, clothe, and heal him. No one shares anything they have, whether food, power, or emotion, coveting it as though it will save them. But you, my Rulers, share—though none of us deserve a share of your salvation."

He paused to draw a breath. "Many of your people have not remained entirely loyal to you; we do not deserve you. Your saving us is a boon, a favor, a mercy. These villagers must be, I am sure, honored to have been buried, mourned, and prayed for by no less than the Quest, by the Quest Leader himself. Only you could have relieved their suffering."

He took another deep breath and then said, seeming to plunge forward, "My Rulers, please, never think that your coming is late. You came when you were meant to come, and you will arrive in each country when they most need you. Just as you came for me when I most needed you." Desperation rendered his hazel eyes fever-bright. "Please do not allow doubt to ever taint that certainty."

Despite all my pain, I could not help a true smile. Neither could Malika, Elian, nor Kyros.

"Our gratitude to the Almighty for the purity and sweetness of your devotion, my vassal," Lucian whispered, finally smiling.

"So wise for a boy of sixteen," I added in praise.

Elacir breathed a sigh of relief and beamed, his plum scales flashing so brightly that they looked almost violet.

With a final prayer for blessing, we then left Temerilt to seek shelter for the night.

But I could not help a glance back.

I would never forget this place, for I had understood here, for the first time, unlike the vestiges I had known before, how much Lucian cared for his people. And how much his other companions and I truly partook of the depth of duty that animated his soul.

Because unlike anything had before, the tragedy of Temerilt had broken my own bones. And the agony of my Leader and his companions trampled them into dust.

CHAPTER 21

ELATE THE YEARNING

Perspective: Honored Kyros the Exemplar of Strength
Date: Eyyéala, the nineteenth day of the twelfth moon, Alshatte,
of the year 499, C.Q.

With a deep inhale, I filled my mind with thoughts of how the Almighty had given everything meaning and purpose, that no part of creation was superfluous or valueless... I dwelt on the role of grass, the benefits given by even the most irritating insects, the beneficence of the clouds... When such ideas consumed almost all of my attention, I reached for the cool magic mingled with my blood.

At my invocation, some of it pooled readily beneath the plane of my concentration. I gathered some of my physical energy and streamed it through the catalyst. As I balanced between the belief and the magic, power ignited, white-hot like the unfiltered, intense sunlight I remembered from my childhood.

My vision split in two, the magical an overlay over the physical; the same image formed in both sights of Elacir's intensely curious face.

Still carefully catalyzing, I directed the magical sight away, toward the north, pushing further and further. In the physical, I was watching Elacir make faces, while the magical revealed the familiar, empty fields that lay south of Tresilt. As jarring as the double vision was, especially in so sustained an effort, I somehow flickered naturally back and forth between the overlay and the underlay, processing both.

"Your catalysis is far smoother than before," Lucian praised.

My cheeks moistened with gloss even as sweat beaded my forehead, despite the chilly air. "I do not know how I am supposed to do anything else while using it though," I muttered. "I cannot understand how you can catalyze for our links and still teach, lead, and wield a weapon."

Lucian chuckled. "Practice, Brother. As you practice, you will rapidly improve. Your skill has already greatly increased since we met. Indeed, I am confident that you will soon master the entirety of your magic."

His words brought a contented smile to my lips, easing the intense strain furrowing my brow and relaxing my shoulders. "Thank you, Lucian."

"For your happiness," he replied, according to his custom.

Our conversation lapsed as I continued to catalyze. A few feet behind me, Arista guided Elian through another attempt at casting a spell of wizardry, with Malika's diffident encouragement. Besides me, after a few minutes, Lucian beckoned Elacir and quietly instructed him in using his own farsight—after Elacir had shyly mentioned last week that he had the gift, though in far lesser degree than mine, Lucian decided to train him as well.

The soothing sounds of my new family's voices filled my ears, but so did those of the wind roughly tossing loose snow in the air, like a child kicking rocks, more than ten miles away. Leafless trees rustled their branches, small hares hopped across the fields, thick-coated bison pushed aside refrozen, congealed heaps of snow to graze on the dried grass beneath, and wolves and coyotes prowled through thick drifts. A thousand different glimpses of life beyond the grasp of the incé of the five kinds.

Even they bore the signs of the Blood's tyranny: tree branches cracked and groaned, dried by endless drought. Grasses crumbled at barely a touch. Hares, coyotes—predator and prey both were so thin that their ribs and spine protruded, each bone visually countable.

The ruler's consequence affects everything, Kyros, Lucian spoke quietly in our private link.

I startled at his voice but did not look away from the sickly smelling bison and the starved gleam in the eyes of the wolves.

They do not deserve to suffer for the people's betrayal, I murmured.

Yet they do all the same, Lucian said. *The soldiers waste their lives as well, discarding grain as though it is not the product of months of determined growth and trashing meat as though it did not once live. But because they cannot speak, even fewer care for their suffering.* The sorrow in his voice had the ring of ancientness, a sharp contrast with the youth of his shining face.

My magical vision focused on a wolf that took another shuddering step, then collapsed, too weak to continue.

I swallowed. *It really is true, is it not? That the ineptitude and neglect of a poor ruler complicate the lives of every plant, animal, and incé in the bounds of her territory?*

Yes, Lucian answered. *And the cruelty of an evil ruler spreads across the land in an inescapable wave of poison.*

A brittle tree toppled in the distance, its trunk too dry for firewood. Another fell closer to Tresilt. The crunch of the breaking wood resembled how the bones of Temerilt had fallen to pieces in my very hands...

I may have left for Kalyca, I whispered, both to Lucian and myself, *but my responsibility is to so much beyond even my sister. Thank you, Lucian, for this opportunity to serve you.*

My Lord and brother clasped my shoulder with the pained smile I so hated to see on his beautiful face. Then, with a nod, he returned his attention to Elacir, who was grumbling about an inability to catalyze.

Behind me, Arista shushed Elian's despondent mumbles about his own magic and set him a new exercise.

I breathed a chuckle and continued to catalyze for my farsight, determined to exceed my last attempt.

So the last miles to Tresilt passed. The sun, reaching the peak of its eternal arc, began its smog-shrouded descent toward the western horizon, its rays stretching toward the land like the desperate fingers of a mother.

With every hour that passed, I grew more and more apprehensive, until I could no longer sustain my magic. Only Lucian and Malika, who had moved to walk at my sides, gave me the courage to continue placing one foot in front of the other.

The sun set, leaving us an hour away.

Lucian activated the enchantment on his pendant. The emerald glowed, but only enough to illuminate a few feet of our surroundings.

All too soon, the dark snow-covered shapes of Tresilt's buildings loomed ahead of us.

I exhaled a shuddering breath and, driven by a need for comfort, grasped Malika's hand. *I am afraid*, I admitted.

Malika squeezed my hand. *I think she will be happy to see you.*

But what if she is not? I asked, almost in tears. *I left her alone… I missed her birthday—and no one else remembers it!*

Malika shyly ducked her head. *Because I would be too happy to not forgive you, if I were in her place.*

The muttered words drew my attention to her even amid my rising anxiety and panic.

She smiled uncertainly. *You are my brother, Kyros.*

That affirmation lent me enough strength to not falter as Lucian directed us around the edge of the village. Dodging the few patrols, he brought us (without directions) to the door of the two-story cottage my uncle had built upon our arrival here.

He turned to me. *The patrols are on the far side of the village. Ready, Brother?*

I nodded, drawing comfort from his shining face and Malika's warm hand.

Lucian knocked on the door and stepped aside. As did Malika.

Footsteps pattered behind the door.

Then it flew open.

The face I had so longed to see stared up at me with wide eyes and a disbelieving look.

Wild ash-blonde hair, a hint more metallic than mine, curled around a heart-shaped face, heavily coated in soot. Steel-gray eyes a few shades lighter than my own, which usually gleamed with mischief, seemed dull and sad. A button nose and pink rosebud lips parted to reveal a gap between her two front teeth. A bundle of strength, beauty, and vivacity though short at four-and-a-half feet for a girl of the Nasimih. My dearest Kalyca.

Smiling hesitantly, I knelt in front of her so that my eyes were below the level of hers. "Blessings, Kalyca," I whispered, even as I noted how she had grown two inches without me present to celebrate.

"K-Kyros?" she whispered.

"Yes, it is me, your brother Kyros," I answered, holding my arms out. "I will understand if you do not want a hug—"

She flung herself into my arms, which folded around her, and buried her face into my neck. "Kyros!" she cried, half-sobbing even as her cheeks glossed, squeezing me in her endearing way. "Kyros! You're finally back!" Then she paused, drew back, and scowled. "You idiot! Why did you leave! And miss my birthday! You are such a big, fat, dumb idiot!"

Despite how the sweetness of her scent beneath the soot contented me, I winced. She had evidently been spending too much time with Periel, Ciella, and Donel, our cousins, who tended to use less polite words. But then, I had indeed left her with them… left her alone…

Screeching the impolite words, she beat at my chest. Then tears welled in her eyes, her cheeks wavering between gloss and coarseness, and she threw herself back onto me. Clutching my collar, she cried as I stroked her back.

The sight and feel of her tears burned my heart and seared my every nerve. But I said nothing so she could express all of her frustration. Even as I noted how no one had bothered to extend the hem of her dirt-streaked trousers, patch the rips in her cap, or properly trim her hair. At least she had not become any thinner since I had left.

A scowl adorably curving her lips, Kalyca tilted her head back for another tirade.

Her eyes caught sight of the five figures behind me—especially Lucian's shining face and his dazzling smile of sweet brotherly affection. Eyes wide and lips parted, Kalyca seemed to soak in his presence as though he were a beam of sunlight in human form, hope amid the endless night. Which he was.

I savored the moment.

"You are so beautiful," she finally said, her high-pitched voice dreamy and her face glossy. "Like the stars... Like-like sunlight..."

Malika, Elian, Arista, and Elacir grinned, eyes sparkling with mirthful agreement. Lucian's cheeks just barely tinted silver.

Kalyca stared at him a moment longer, then glanced sharply at me. "What is someone like him doing here with *you*?"

I pressed my lips together to hide a smile. How right she was! Even if those words were not polite or respectful. "It is a story I would love to tell you." *That I need to tell you, though I do not know how.*

Kalyca rolled her eyes, another indecent habit of our cousins, before noticing the others. "Wow!" she gasped. "They are beautiful, too!"

Our new family wore expressions of embarrassed delight.

The smile I had been hiding spread across my face. "They are our new family, my darling," I said, easily (though perhaps prematurely) returning to the comfort of our relationship.

"What?" she asked, narrowing her eyes. "What do you mean by that? And where did you meet them?" She gasped again. "Kyros, you have not even told me their names!"

My smile turned fatherly, as it often did—Kalyca's favorite smile. "Invite us inside first, my darling!"

She froze and gave me a so-very-familiar sheepish look at the subtle reminder for manners—and safety procedure. Then she nodded briskly and clambered off of my lap. Holding open the door, she said, in an attempt to imitate me, "I welcome you to my home."

Unable to stop smiling, I rose to my feet. Brushing snow and scraping soot off my skin and robes, I bowed my head to Lucian and ushered my new family inside. Only once they had entered did I do the same, removing my boots and setting them beside Malika's on the rack.

Kalyca politely closed the door behind me.

My new family looked around the main room: the meal area in the furthest corner, with its dining table and doors leading to my aunt's prized kitchen; the staircase on the opposite side; the curtained glass windows on the other walls, which were my uncle's much-lauded achievement; the shelves beneath that contained my cousins' extensive collection of natural curiosities; the lamps, all dark but one, placed in sconces around the room; the door on the far wall that led outside, to the outhouse; the four upholstered benches in the middle.

The homely space, though once the center of childhood adventures, now reminded me only of the bitterness of quarrels. Countless times had my eldest cousin, Solios, cornered me here and berated me over my stubbornness in caring for my sister. Innumerable times had my aunt and my uncle lectured me over some way I had fallen short in meeting the village's demands. Unlike its twin in my own cottage next door, the place evoked only misery.

But the presence of my new family soothed those memories. As long as they stood with me, I would not be alone. No matter what this visit to Tresilt brought.

CHAPTER 22

INCLUDE THE SHUNNED

Perspective: Honored Kyros the Exemplar of Strength
Date: Eyyéala, the nineteenth day of the twelfth moon, Alshatte,
of the year 499, C.Q.

Before I could open my mouth to give the introductions Kalyca wanted, a woman's contralto voice called down the stairs, "Kalyca! You know that no one is supposed to see you!"

"Aunt Cyanna!" Kalyca called back, her cheeks now smoothing to a glass-like polish. "Look who is here!"

Aunt Cyanna sighed loudly and pattered down the stairs, audibly grumbling as she came into view. Then she froze, her gaze upon me. "Kyros!" she gasped.

My smile did not disappear, but I stiffened. "Blessings, Aunt Cyanna," I warily greeted her. This confrontation was unavoidable, but that did not mean I was pleased to have it.

She swallowed, disbelief flashing in her dark gray eyes, so like my father's. Then she dashed across the room and launched herself at me. "Kyros, you have returned to us! We thought you had perished!"

I accepted the hug but loosely, while quickly donning the cautious façade I wore in front of all but Kalyca, and now my new family.

A second pair of footsteps thumped down the stairs, and the stunned blue eyes and glossed copper skin of my uncle's face appeared. He stared for a moment before limping across the room and throwing his arms around me.

I coolly greeted Uncle Leos. Though I had once esteemed him as a second father after the loss of my own, I remembered all too well how he increasingly let his wife and his son rip my heart to shreds without a murmur of protest.

Not defending me in front of the village to avoid drawing their ire was one thing, but to leave me defenseless even at home? I trusted them, yes, to care for my innocent sister, but I could not help but doubt their love for me. With every passing year, I seemed to become less and less a treasured family member and more and more a construction assistant and fieldhand who did not merit considerate treatment because he could never be driven away. I loved them, but the passion of that love had dimmed.

Aunt Cyanna and Uncle Leos squeezed me and then, finally, drew back, smiling widely, blind to my unease. Aunt Cyanna asked, "How are you, Son?"

I suppressed a flinch at the address. *How do I answer that? I do not want her to think I will respond to it...*

More perceptive than I wanted in this matter, Kalyca saved me from having to answer: "Of course he is well, Auntie. Now, the important thing: the names of Kyros' friends."

Aunt Cyanna and Uncle Leos jerked back, alarmed, and turned—only for their mouths to drop open at the sight of my new family.

My new family who were concernedly examining every aspect of my behavior. As well as how Kalyca was gently tugging me out from between my aunt and my uncle and holding my hand.

I tried to keep my smile—this moment was important for Kalyca, and I did not want to taint it. So, ignoring the realizations sparking on my new family's faces, I said, "Kalyca, my darling, do you remember the stories I like to tell you about the saviors of Icilia?"

Kalyca nodded, eyes huge.

My smile turned genuine. "Kalyca, my darling, the shining man who stands before us is the Leader of the Quest, my Lord Lucian the Ideal of Freedom, and he is more amazing than I could ever describe." I proceeded to introduce each of the Potentates and their vassal—much more informally than etiquette demanded, but, then, we were family.

By the time I finished with Elacir (to whom Lucian had given the honorific of Inase, trusted confidant), Kalyca was almost incandescent with excitement.

"Kyros!" she exclaimed. "How did you get such honor?"

I did not know how to answer.

Saving me as always, Lucian spoke, "Blessings, Kalyca Dinasietta."

She whirled around to face him.

He smiled, as warm and gentle as he was for me. "Your brother, Kyros, is the fifth member of my Quest, his Honor the Exemplar of Strength."

My aunt and my uncle, silent so far, made choking noises. But Kalyca froze.

I held my breath. *This is the moment that matters.*

She blinked rapidly. Tilted her head to consider Lucian. Rubbed her chin. Then said the last thing I had expected:

"Does that mean you really care about my brother? Do you think he is special?"

Now I was the one choking. "Kalyca!" I hissed.

She was bold, yes, and I loved the quality, but he was the Quest Leader!

Lucian's smile did not waver. "Yes, I do. He is the Almighty's blessing unto me, and he has the Almighty's favor. His piety is like that of my Honor Naret of Light—" he used an address only the Quest was entitled to use— "and his virtue will someday match my own. My faith in his devotion, intelligence, and capacity to uphold his office is as firm as the foundations of sacred Mount Atharras. I am the one who is honored by his presence at my side. My gratitude to the Almighty for his place in my Quest overwhelms my heart with every glimpse of his beloved face."

My whole face moistened as he spoke, for I had never thought to hear such praise. Indeed, I was so embarrassed in my delight that I could not meet his gaze but instead watched Kalyca.

Whose lips were curling with a broad satisfied grin. "Now that is what I wanted to hear," she proclaimed and stepped forward.

Then she flung her arms around Lucian's waist!

I jolted and hissed again, "Kalyca!" He let her challenge him, yes, but this was disrespect on an entirely different level!

Malika, Elian, Arista, and Elacir, who had been grinning like Kalyca while Lucian spoke, looked just as alarmed.

But Lucian laughed. And then returned the embrace! Not a single flicker of discomfort crossed his features as my sister's touch spread black soot all over his athar cloth robes (which had seemed pristine even after more than half a year of travel).

"Kalyca, my darling," he addressed her, using the same endearment as I did, "I have long wished to meet you, since the day I first learned of Kyros' place in my Quest. The Almighty has blessed me with this opportunity."

"Really?" Kalyca asked, voice muffled by his robes.

"Indeed, yes," he answered, his expression nearly blinding with affection, "for you are my sister as your brother is mine."

Even Kalyca seemed too amazed to speak.

Lucian chuckled softly, gently tipped her chin up so she met his gaze, and said, voice warm, "Sister, I have a gift for you."

Kalyca's grin was the brightest I had ever seen. But the words she spoke rang with an odd maturity, "Choosing my brother is the best gift you could ever give me. The best blessing ever."

"That blessing will come with pain," Lucian replied, his smile fading as he lowered himself into a crouch. "This gift will alleviate it." Then, from a pocket of his coat, he drew forth a necklace. Breathtaking, exquisite beyond belief.

The chain that dangled from Lucian's fingers was silver, and the emerald pendant was the size of my thumbnail. Yet as valuable as those were, what was truly precious were the beads which adorned the chain: interspersed with amethyst was a substance I recognized from its smooth shine to be hardened athar. The jewelry of royalty.

"The emerald holds a communication spell," Lucian explained, his gaze intent on hers, "that will allow you to contact Kyros at any time. The spell does not leave residue, but it does require much energy, from both you and him at every invocation, so I advise you to be cautious in its use. Additionally, these athar beads contain a masking spell attuned specifically to you."

Her face as grave as his, Kalyca nodded. "What is that spell for?"

"Before we leave, I intend to teach you enough about your magic that you may practice on your own. The jewel will amplify your power, and the beads will let you practice without fear of residue." A deep sadness flashed in his eyes. "Learn well, my darling. You will need your magic someday."

The expression Kalyca wore in response held a grim determination I had never seen before. Sounding much older than nine, she said, "I will not waste your gift, my Lord."

Lucian's smile returned as he slipped the jewelry around her neck and closed its clasp. "Lucian, Sister," he corrected. "Your receipt of our names is presumed."

She smiled back and threw her arms around his neck.

And he returned that embrace as well.

My mouth had probably fallen too far open to ever close again.

This kindness, this love and care... I had not expected such even from Lucian's divine-blessed hands. Yet he had planned this? Intended to honor my sister in this way? And include her among the ranks of his own family? Treat her as his own blood?

And alongside the wonder of Lucian's love was the way Malika, Elian, and Arista watched Kalyca with their hearts in their eyes, as though she meant the world to them as she did to me.

Even Elacir wore a look of affection.

The Almighty truly did bless me when I met him, I thought, almost lightheaded with joy. *Lucian really did give me a new family when I pledged to him. Indeed, 'our family'.*

Alight with as much joy as I was, I jumped when a throat cleared—and shocked me into the remembrance of my aunt's and my uncle's presences. As much as I wanted otherwise, I could not shirk from conversation with them. Turning, I said, pasting on a smile, "Yes, Aunt Cyanna, Uncle Leos?"

The middle-aged couple blinked.

Then threw themselves at Lucian's feet.

I started forward and then just stared, fingers flexing at my sides.

So they did understand what you were saying, Lucian, Arista observed.

I shook my head. *What?*

Lucian tapped Kalyca's shoulder, and she stepped to his side.

Malika answered, *His answer to Kalyca's question was also a subtle pronouncement of your worth to your aunt and your uncle. A way to ensure that they protect her after we leave.*

Truly? I gasped.

Of course, Lucian replied, amused. But aloud he spoke with a sort of warm formality, "Blessings, Khudurile Dinasiette." The address was the plural of the formal demonym for the citizens of Khuduren, coupled with the family surname.

Aunt Cyanna stuttered, "W-we want to- to pledge-edge our alli-allegiance."

Lucian smiled in response—but that smile was far different from his usual ones: it was dazzling, yes, full of light and warmth, as every expression on his face was, yet its charm was distinct...

"We w-want to," Uncle Leos added, "n-not on-on-ly b-because y-you s-saved Kyros. You- you are hope."

"If your heart is truly willing and committed to the Quest," Lucian stated, "then I will welcome your pledge."

It is not that the smile is not affectionate or compassionate, I thought, *because it is. His eyes sparkle with warmth as they almost always do. It is rather... authoritative. Yes, that is it: authoritative. It carries the assurance of his authority in a way his usual smiles—the ones he uses with his family—do not. It is rather… well, regal, but he is so much more than a monarch… it is* lordly. *Yes, lordly, for his title. Though, from the consideration Malika, Elian, Arista, Elacir, even Kalyca wear, only we can tell it is a different smile…*

Consumed in these thoughts, I only partially listened to Aunt Cyanna's and Uncle Leos' pledge. But I snapped back to attentiveness when Kalyca took a confident step forward and hugged Malika.

I startled, but Malika grinned and returned the hug, minding the soot as little as I did.

Further emboldened, Kalyca turned and hugged Elian. Then Arista. Then Elacir.

None of them refused her. And they were all as gentle as I would be.

Grinning, Kalyca ran back to me. Slipping her hand into mine, she tipped her head back and teased, "Kyie, if you do not close your mouth, you will dine on bugs!"

I exhaled an uneasy chuckle and rubbed my chest. *Her boldness will cause my heart to fail someday,* I muttered in the link.

She is a sister after my own heart, Arista proclaimed. *Sorry, Elacir—that designation is no longer exclusive to you!*

Elacir impressed a laugh into the link. *She is adorable.*

I hope we can someday bring her with us, Malika murmured, wistfully expressing my own wish.

If it would please you, Kyros… Elian shyly raised his gaze to mine before dropping it. *Could you show me what games she likes to play?*

My glossed cheeks ached with the broadness of my grin as I spoke of her favorites: hide-and-seek, tag-and-chase, and re-enactments of the stories I told of the first Quest.

Amid my descriptions, Lucian requested, his tone apologetic, *Kyros, if it would please you, wait a few moments.*

I quickly agreed.

Calling for our attention in the link, Lucian said, "Khudurile Dinasiette, I thank you for your willingness to provide us with supper. If it would be possible, I would prefer to take the meal in his Honor Kyros of Light's house. Along with that request, I give you a command: conceal our presence with every means at your disposal. I do not wish for any other to know of our visit."

My aunt and my uncle nodded eagerly.

"Whatever you wish, my Lord," Aunt Cyanna assured him.

Lucian inclined his head. "My gratitude." To our family he urged, "Come—the patrols have left this part of the village."

But a few minutes later, we stood in the main room of my cottage, the place that still echoed with the sights, sounds, and scents of my parents and siblings, which now mingled with the presences of my new family.

My past and my future collided.

And the desolate grief that had so long plagued me melted from my heart.

Contented, I relished the moment.

So far, a much better visit than I expected. Now, if only no one discovers our presence, these will be some of the best days of my life...

CHAPTER 23

ASSURE THE UNHEEDING

Perspective: Honored Kyros the Exemplar of Strength
Date: Eyyéfaz, the twentieth day of the twelfth moon, Alshatte,
of the year 499, C.Q.

I jerked forward and dropped my sword when a pair of
arms squeezed my waist. The sword sliced through the air
mere inches from the matching pair of dainty feet. Reacting
on instinct, I kicked the sharp blade away. Only when it
clattered to the floor across the room did my heart resume
its normal rhythm.

Closing my eyes, I took a deep breath. But my tone
betrayed nothing of my panic and frustration as I said gently,
"Kalyca, my darling, you cannot just appear like that when I
am practicing. I might lose control of the sword, and, though
the edge is not dangerous to me, it certainly is to you."

"Sorry, Kyie!" she replied—although she did not
sound sorry.

I began to elaborate, but, with a wink, she disappeared in a flash of turquoise light.

I blew out an exasperated breath but was thankful all the same. At least she had not stood in *front* of me—progress from some of her previous pranks. Such as the time she had sat on the inner edge of a well and leaned over to peer *inside*... Bile rose in my throat like a noxious fume at the memory.

At least she does these things only once—and only around me. If the elders, Countess Pistiem, or even Aunt Cyanna and Uncle Leos knew about them, we would be torn apart by the next morning. May the Almighty grant a switch to less dangerous pranks as she matures...

I hoped I would be around to see that.

Shaking my head, as though the motion could wipe clean that thought, I picked up my sword and restarted catalysis for my farsight. Once my vision had properly split, I returned to the exercise Lucian had set me: a sequence of blocks, parries, slices, and thrusts coupled with a continuous scan of our surroundings in my magical vision.

The first place I sent my vision was upstairs, to my parents' old bedroom, where Lucian was instructing Elian, Elacir, and Kalyca in their various forms of wish magic. As I watched, Kalyca reappeared. She bounced on her feet—until Lucian raised an eyebrow at her. Though he said nothing, she quailed and muttered an apology. Then, upon Lucian's instruction, she repeated it in the collective link: *Kyie, I am sorry for scaring you and not using my magic safely.*

I smiled, the last of my terror fading. *I forgive you. Please know better in the future, Kallie darling.* As she used the nickname she had given me, the one she considered exclusive to the two of us, so did I use hers—an indication of how comfortable we both felt with our new family.

Kalyca seemed ashamed—until she noticed Lucian was smiling again. Her own grin returned, and she leapt into his lap and demanded the next exercise.

Only Kallie, I thought to myself, amused amid my ever-present sorrow. *At least the patches I finished yesterday evening over the holes on this set of trousers are still holding. They may even hold after I leave.*

Reassured by that thought, I turned my magical vision to the common room, where Malika and Arista dueled and I practiced. Coming closer than I would ever dare physically, I observed the angles of their blades and the liquid quality of their moves.

Malika, you are quite beginning to rival Arista, I exclaimed in delighted surprise, *in only three months!* Though that terrible gray tinge still clung to her face and her hair remained dull and lusterless, she was excelling in her studies far more rapidly than Elian and I were. Proof, which I did not need, of why she was the Second and not either of us.

Crimson painted Malika's pale cheeks, but her swing toward Arista's shoulder curved in a perfect arc.

Arista barely avoided the blow, the tight braid of her mahogany hair swinging out below her cap, and laughed unreservedly. *I must agree, Malika! That is the third nearly successful blow this morning!*

Malika smiled shyly. *My gratitude for your teaching, Arista. And yours, Lucian.*

The teaching may be mine, Lucian responded, *but the potential is yours, Sister!*

I chuckled at the bashful pleasure on her face and then pushed my vision outside the walls of my cottage.

Dim sunlight, still brighter than the sparsely lit interior, met my magical vision, but without the shock my eyes would have experienced.

So I did not miss Countess Aniela Pistiem slipping inside my aunt's cottage and closing the door behind her.

A tingle of foreboding shot down my spine.

Acting on instinct, I directed my farsight into the common room of Aunt Cyanna's cottage.

Just in time to hear Countess Pistiem, the Ezulal noble who was the mayor of Tresilt, remark loudly, "Cyanna, you are positively glowing! I have not seen you so- so- *happy* in months!"

Aunt Cyanna startled mid-curtsy. "H-happy?" she squeaked. I winced.

The mayor's pale blue eyes narrowed, sharpening the thin wrinkles framing them. "Yes, happy," she replied, oozing suspicion. "You have barely smiled since little Kyros disappeared."

Aunt Cyanna tried to recover by saying, "Aniela, you know I have as much to celebrate as you do."

Countess Pistiem tossed aside her usual decorum and snorted. "As much as you love your son, you do not approve of his betrothal with Enthella *that* much."

I raised an eyebrow, momentarily distracted. *Solios is* betrothed? I exclaimed to Kalyca in the collective link. *And with the mayor's daughter? Did she not rebuke him for condescension at the spring festival?*

You are no more startled than I was, she said dryly. *But how did you hear of that?*

I jolted, reminded of what I needed to do, and answered wryly, *I am listening to Aunt Aniela ensnare our usually indomitable Aunt Cyanna. And, Lucian, I do not think she will manage to keep our secret. Aunt Aniela is too skilled at swindling a confession.*

My opinion is the same, Lucian said—who, I remembered with another jolt, perceived far more with his sense than I did with my farsight at such quarters. Not least because, while I had to direct my vision, he was aware of everything within his range. My training's strategic value, as he had explained, lay in my ability to far exceed three miles.

Before embarrassment could moisten my cheeks though, Lucian ordered, *Conceal our belongings, Elian, Elacir. Arista, can you cast a spell of concealment? Muffling sounds and eliminating the heat of our presence?*

Next door, Countess Pistiem, as suave and shrewd as ever, asked, "So, Cyanna, where is Kalyca? I have brought her favorite biscuits."

Thrown by the change in subject, Aunt Cyanna stammered incoherently.

"I thought so," Countess Pistiem proclaimed. "The only reason you would be so happy is if Kyros had returned." Her eyes narrowed again, dangerously this time. "And neither of you thought to tell me? Are the years of stalwart friendship I have given to your family so unimportant?"

Aunt Cyanna choked, well and truly cornered.

She will be here in moments, I reported as I rushed to store the drying dishes. Malika pushed the common room's benches back to their usual places. Arista stood in the center of the room and chanted under her breath.

Our packs are hidden in the chest in your parents' closet, Elian reported.

Arista, is that spell ready? Lucian asked. *I have catalyzed for masking. Kyros, bring our boots upstairs.*

I grabbed most of them, and Malika gathered the rest.

Lucian, Kalyca said quietly, *maybe... maybe you should not conceal yourselves.*

I stumbled. *Kallie, you cannot question his orders!*

No, Lucian said, *let her speak. What is your opinion, Kalyca?*

Well... She hesitated for a moment. *Aunt Aniela—Countess Pistiem—has missed Kyros a lot. Like she misses her son. If you just disappear, she will never have any peace about what happened to him. Also... she has supported us for years.*

I blinked, surprised, though I should not have been, at the depth of her perception. I switched my vision from Countess Pistiem's sparking anger to Lucian's thoughtful violet eyes.

For a moment, the cottage was utterly silent.

Then he said, *We will take the risk of meeting Countess Pistiem. Easing her worry and concern is the honorable act.*

Arista bit her lip. *Are you... are you sure, Lucian? You were quite clear in your wish for secrecy.*

Lucian beckoned to Elian, Elacir, and Kalyca and led the way downstairs. *I do wish for secrecy, but not because I do not wish to spread the Quest's name. As I said before our rescue of Elacir, the time to conceal it has ended. My desire for secrecy comes from our position of relative vulnerability in Khuduren, so far from a secure base.*

Then why will you take this risk? Malika asked.

Honor, and my knowledge of Countess Pistiem's character, Lucian answered, reaching the center of the common room. He added aloud, "She merits my consideration for her genuine welcome of Kyros' family twelve years prior and her support ever since."

From the sober look in his eyes, he did know that her advocacy had wavered much as my aunt's and my uncle's had and that she had not wholly protected me from the village's whims. Yet, without what assistance she had given me, in honor of my parents, Kalyca and I would have long ago been forced to flee Tresilt.

So I stood without protest at his side. Kalyca slid her hand into mine, and I clutched her fingers for comfort.

In my magical vision, Countess Pistiem squared her shoulders and banged her fist upon my door.

Lucian nodded to Elacir, who opened the door.

Marching inside, the mayor's plump figure more closely resembled the furor of a thundercloud than her usual cheerful self.

Until her eyes beheld the Quest Leader.

Countess Pistiem fell to her knees. She did not flinch when Elacir shut the door behind her.

Lucian curved his lips into that lordly smile I had noted yesterday. "Blessings, Countess Aniela Pistiem."

She started at the sound of her name intoned in that rich musical voice. But did not speak.

Lucian glanced at Arista, who at the cue, recited our names, ending with particular emphasis on mine.

Countess Pistiem's eyes widened further, if that were possible. Wetting her lips, she spoke, "The Almighty has blessed us with your presence, my Rulers."

Is that address not essentially a declaration of her loyalty? I asked, trying to remember Lucian's lessons on etiquette.

Yes, Arista said. *More importantly, in this circumstance, an acknowledgment of your new rank above hers.*

I blinked. *Truly?*

As though guessing what I was thinking, the mayor bowed her head specifically to me. "So this is why you left, my Honor." A faint, almost wry smile curved her lips.

Startled, I barely managed to keep my voice steady as I answered, "Indeed, yes."

Countess Pistiem winced then, a dim horror flickering in her eyes. "My apologies for all that I said before you left. And all that I have ever said about you."

I froze, too shocked to answer, for I had never imagined anyone in Tresilt, even she, ever apologizing to me.

Beside me, Kalyca shuffled her feet. Then, squeezing my hand, she mumbled, sounding subdued, *I am sorry, too, Kyie.*

My heart wrenched at the pain in her voice, my shock thawing into a gentle smile. *No apologies necessary, my darling,* I assured her in the link, before echoing the words aloud, "I offer my forgiveness, Countess Pistiem."

Kalyca and the mayor both sighed with what sounded strangely like relief.

Countess Pistiem then said, shifting her gaze to Lucian, "My Lord, how may I serve you? What would you ask of Tresilt?"

Lucian, whose weighty gaze had been on my face, now returned his attention to her. "Your reverence to the Quest pleases us, yet I ask only for your secrecy, Countess Pistiem. My companions and I will remain here in Tresilt for but three days before we continue our journey to Nademan, the nation where we will begin our reconquest."

"The news of your reconquest is itself the first drop of hope we have tasted in years," she responded. The flowery language she used should have tasted unctuous, yet the eagerness flashing in her eyes flavored her words with the sweetness of sincerity.

Her genuineness released some of the tension stiffening my posture, and my family relaxed as well.

Then Countess Pistiem furrowed her brow and said, "Respectfully, my Lord, Tresilt would be honored to welcome you properly, with a festival in your name. And certainly we would be honored to pledge our allegiance."

"We do not yet intend to reveal our presence," Lucian answered, "much less publicly receive pledges, Countess Pistiem." Though his lordly smile remained in place, the edges of his lips had slightly flattened—though I doubted the mayor could distinguish the difference.

"Please, my Lord," Countess Pistiem begged— actually *begged*, completely unlike her usual method of forcing agreement from whoever disagreed with her— "at least meet with our families. We would be honored to serve you."

"Revealing our presence," Lucian spoke slightly more firmly, "beyond this favor to you, does not suit my wishes, Countess."

She really is not acquiescing, Arista observed, impressing a raised eyebrow into the link. *She might sound like she is pleading, but those are the words of a bargainer.*

Her insistence is impolite, Elian muttered. *Disrespectful.*

I suppressed a scowl. *But she is still not going to let this go.*

I understand why, Elian commented, *but still, she should know better.*

All of us save Lucian indicated agreement, but what was so obvious to us did not seem to be to the countess. For she pushed one more time, "Please, my Lord, such a boon would bring us hope."

And that appeal is one I cannot refuse, Lucian said, displeased.

Arista impressed a frown. *She cannot force you to do anything you do not wish.*

Our reputation is still too new, Lucian said ruefully. *Yet... We might find the experience instructive. Are we in agreement?*

None of us had any arguments of use.

So Lucian stated aloud, "Countess Pistiem, I will allow only one meeting, with the heads of your families, in the secrecy and privacy of your home tomorrow night. But until then, I expect not to be disturbed."

The displeasure on his face was clear, but Countess Pistiem exclaimed, "You will not regret this favor, my Lord!" Receiving his permission, she jumped up and hurried out of my cottage, eager to begin arrangements.

We five Potentates, Kalyca, and Elacir exchanged looks.

Then Kalyca uttered what we all thought: "This will not end well."

Lucian sighed. "Let us arrange for our departure. Elian, what provisions do we need?"

Elian closed his eyes and began to recite a lengthy list, which everyone moved to fulfill, and the rest of the day passed in menial tasks.

Not a day, I thought, despairing, *and the village has already ruined what peace I could have had here.*

How I wished I could leave with Kalyca and never return.

CHAPTER 24

EXALT THE UNKNOWN

Perspective: Graced Malika the Exemplar of Wisdom
Date: Eyyéthar, the twenty-first day of the twelfth moon,
Alshatte, of the year 499, C.Q.

A single raise of Lucian's eyebrows quieted the entire room. Even the most vitriolic of the villagers cowered before the obvious disapproval in his eyes.

Lucian let the silence continue a moment longer. Then he said, in an even, quiet voice I had heard only once before, "What is the meaning of this?"

No one dared to answer. Or move.

Except Kyros.

He quickly crossed the common room from where he had been cornered by his own kitchen to Lucian's side. Slipping between Lucian and me, he swung my hand behind the folds of our robes and gripped my fingers as though they were all that held him upright. Indeed, from the coarseness of his cheeks and the despair of his expression, they very well seemed to be.

Do not worry, Kyros, I soothed. *Lucian will set everything right.*

The crush of his fingers loosened just a little.

"I ask again," Lucian said in that terrifyingly calm voice, "what is the meaning of this?"

No response.

His eyes blades of violet ice, Lucian turned to Kyros. "Your Honor Kyros, Exemplar of Strength, would you inform me of the names of the families present? As well as when they arrived?"

Information instead of introductions—a clear sign of displeasure, and the villagers' blanched faces indicated they understood it.

Kyros inhaled sharply and responded, in an admirably steady voice, "My Lord Lucian, Ideal of Freedom, those present are Khudurile of the families Geriene, Galiene, Enchiette, Asfaliette, Diliette, and Sigiene. They knocked on your door not twenty minutes before your own return." Beneath his even tone, though, ran an undercurrent of anguish and desperation.

Lucian heard it as clearly as I did, for the noble planes of his face hardened. Returning his steel-sharp gaze to the villagers, he said, "Khudurile, have you come to seek an early audience with his Honor? Or with me?"

He did not need to continue. Within moments of his mention of audiences, the villagers stampeded out the door, only pausing long enough to bow and nearly forgetting their shoes.

As the last footsteps faded, the room remained silent as Lucian closed his eyes and visibly composed himself.

Then he said, pained, "Kyros, I ask for your forgiveness. Malika and I traveled farther than three miles in our pursuit of prey."

Kyros shook his head. "I should have called you earlier," he whispered, "and I will be all right." But, from the way his shoulders hunched, curling in on themselves, he was trying to persuade himself more than telling us.

My heart wrenching, I gently tugged him into my embrace. Over the last three months, Lucian's hugs had comforted me on innumerable occasions, so I hoped the gesture would prove somewhat effective for him.

He sighed and melted into my arms, mumbling my name. He seemed reluctant to move.

I tried not to fidget. *Is it supposed to last this long?* I asked Lucian in our private link, as I did whenever I was confused by some form of interaction or alarmed by someone's touch.

It can, Lucian said. His eyes had entirely thawed and now sparkled, affectionate and amused.

Well, when does it stop? I asked.

Let him determine that, Sister, Lucian said, his lips pressed together in an obvious attempt to suppress his characteristic kind laughter, *since you intend to give him comfort.*

Very well, I said, grunting as Kyros squeezed me. I tightened my own arms, as Arista often did, and stroked his back with stiff, uneven motions. When he drew back, I had to stifle a sigh of relief. But my efforts were well rewarded by the smooth contentment of his features.

"Thank you, Lucian, Malika," he said quietly.

I will always defend you, Lucian promised, speaking in the collective link.

Nowhere near so assured of my own abilities, I only forced a smile.

But Kyros, regardless, was pleased, his gray eyes bright and his lips turned up at the corners.

Lucian returned the smile and ordered, *Arista, Elian, Elacir, enter from the north—there are soldiers in your current path. Once you return with those hares, we will have enough meat, so you will not need to leave for a third trip.*

As you wish, Lucian, Arista said grimly. *Though the pickings are quite slim.*

With the bread baked by Kyros and his aunt, Lucian replied, *we will have to manage.*

Then Elian asked, worried, *How is Kyros?* He, Arista, and Elacir had been even further away than Lucian and me when Kyros had called for our help.

Lucian protected me, Kyros answered simply, a statement Elian understood all too well from his murmurs of gratitude.

Where is Kalyca? Elacir asked.

Suddenly realizing I had not seen her, I repeated the question.

Hiding, came her disgruntled answer. *My brother was bullied downstairs, and all I did was hide in the closet upstairs.*

Kyros blew out an exasperated breath. *Kallie, you know that if they saw you with me, they would remember you and turn their anger toward you.*

My fists clenched at the tone of weary acceptance in his voice. The way these villagers treated him and his sister was utterly unjust, no better than how those Bhalaseh residents had treated Elian. But in this situation we could not simply leave and not return.

Kalyca groaned loudly as she appeared at the top of the staircase. "How I want to be fourteen," she muttered.

Kyros' face fell momentarily, and Lucian rubbed his shoulder.

I drew my brows together, then remembered—that gesture demonstrated sympathy, as he had explained before. Since I shared the sentiment, I copied him.

"Come, Malika," Lucian urged, "let us begin with these small deer and these birds."

I helped him gather the rough cotton sacks we had dropped upon our entrance. Removing our shoes, we carried the carcasses to the kitchen and set about processing and preserving them. Kyros and Kalyca returned to kneading the last of the dough.

A few minutes later, Elian, Arista, and Elacir arrived and joined us with their own share of prey. Once we had all exchanged greetings, the cottage fell silent, save for the small sounds produced by cleaning meat and baking bread. But that silence, unlike so many in the beginning of our journey, was companionable, warm with friendship and the sweetness of family.

Only once the last of the chores were completed and we had sat down to luncheon did conversation resume.

For a while, we chattered, discussing minor details of each other's lives, avoiding mentions of our sorrows.

Then Lucian said, neatly laying his utensils atop his plate, "Before we attend the countess' meeting, there is a topic I wish to discuss." He had barely to begin speaking to hold our attention. But, instead of beginning his chosen topic, Lucian stared at the table and tapped his thumbs against each other.

A few moments passed, and we exchanged uncertain looks.

Finally, I asked, knowing the others depended on me to do so, *What troubles you, Lucian?*

He pursed his lips and increased the pace of his tapping, then exhaled, heavier than I had yet heard him do. "Exactly as my Lady said I would," he muttered. Then, raising his volume, spoke, "The incident this morning reminded me of an aspect of your new positions which I have not yet addressed."

Another moment of confused silence elapsed.

He sighed again. "I am surprised that none of you have asked about our names."

What names? I asked, since he, entirely uncharacteristically, seemed to require prompting.

A rather wan smile appeared on his lips. "Our royal names, Malika. Just as my Lady Aalia of Light gave one to each of the royal families of Icilia, so, too, did we, her Heirs, receive one. Although…" His cheeks silvered. "You do not have to accept it if you do not wish."

I raised an eyebrow. *Why would we not wish to share it?*

"Because accepting it means you forfeit your old surname," Lucian answered, "and any rank you previously had." The silver glow of his skin intensified around his knuckles as his hands flexed into fists.

"But you already explained that," Arista said slowly, as confused as I felt. "You already told us that Malika and I forfeited our royal titles when we pledged."

And you explained why, I added.

Though at the time I cared only to bind himself to him and rid myself of the Blood's taint, I had since more fully contemplated his reasoning: the impropriety and unfairness of a Potentate being in line for a throne—or even sitting atop one. My Lady Queen Aalia the Ideal of Light had been wise to separate the Quests themselves from the seven nations' crowns (even if her own descendants were the only ones Asfiya trusted to rule), for otherwise none would have accepted us as independent arbiters of Icilia's laws. Sacrificing our birthrights was only just.

Despite our answers, Lucian pressed his lips together, his shining face openly unhappy.

I could not bear that expression, so I rushed to say, *Lucian, my royal name was my last connection to my family and nation, but your love is my greatest blessing. I am truly happy to sacrifice it for you. I want to be fully part of your family. I want to know myself with your name.*

"Malika might say such fond things," Arista declared, a smirk spreading across her face, "but, as I said then, good riddance! Also, my parents and sisters would be horrified if they knew I had not wholly bound myself to you."

"You know you have no objections from me," Elian whispered, smiling shyly. "My old name carries more bad memories than good. Your name would be redemption."

Lucian's face glowed silver at these words, but he still seemed tense, his posture even straighter than usual and his shoulders rigid. He was waiting, I realized, for Kyros' reaction, because he had more reason than any of us to keep his name. And from the odd unease in Lucian's eyes, acceptance from all his companions meant more to him than he was saying.

Worried, I prepared an argument to, if needed, try and persuade Kyros.

My brother had his head bent toward Kalyca, who whispered urgently in his ear. He nodded twice and then once more. She grinned and kissed his cheek, and he kissed her forehead.

Then, straightening, he said, wearing an unusually bright smile, "Please do not concern yourself over my opinion, Lucian. As Kalyca told me the moment you mentioned names, I would be foolish if I did not accept yours. My parents would probably cheer from the rooftop at my receipt of such exaltation, and Kalyca thinks taking it will enhance my own virtue. My gratitude to you for accepting me as a servant knows no bounds; your name is a boon I do not deserve."

At that, Lucian finally relaxed, and the resultant smile dazzled us like a shock of sunlight. "My gratitude, my companions, and to you as well, Kalyca," he intoned, "and know my name: alongside my titles, I carry the royal name of aj-She-hathar, the monarch's position in the one royal family not forged of blood. Upon your pledge, Malika, you took the name of the monarch's lieutenant, in other families the consort: naj-Shehathar. Elian, Arista, Kyros, you bear the names of the monarch's deputies, in other families the crown heirs, tej-Shehathar."

All four of us bowed our heads and murmured our gratitude.

He braced both hands on the table, leaned forwards, and stated, steel and ice hardening his violet eyes, "So understand, my companions, that when you stand in front of any gathering, whether of the villagers of Tresilt or any other, you are highest royalty, divine-blessed and divine-favored. Let that confidence straighten your spine, and let not one drop of disdain corrode your virtue and purpose. We are come to save them, and no insult or abuse can change the truth. Wear your office with dignity and pride for the Almighty is who trusts in you. We will free them even if they do not yet understand."

The power and strength of his words were the only reason that, hours later, we could walk into that audience.

CHAPTER 25

CONFRONT THE TIMOROUS

Perspective: Graced Malika the Exemplar of Wisdom
Date: Eyyéthar, the twenty-first day of the twelfth moon,
Alshatte, of the year 499, C.Q.

The first thing spoken upon our entrance into Countess Pistiem's home was, "Ugh. That Nasimih boy again. What will it take to get rid of him?"

All five of us stiffened, but our expressions remained, as Lucian had instructed, cool and calm.

Countess Pistiem shot a quelling look at the woman who had spoken. Then, bringing a smile to her wrinkled lips, she curtsied and said, "The Almighty has blessed us with your presence, my *Rulers*. Welcome to Tresilt."

Though all thirty-one people present bowed and curtsied, a few scoffs were audible over the swishing trousers and skirts.

I can already see the factions forming, Arista said as we inclined our heads the way Lucian had instructed.

The nine on the right, Elian asked, *who are standing at attention, favor us, do they not?*

Yes, Arista answered. *As does that other man standing with Khuduya Dinasietta.*

"The Quest prays in gratitude for your welcome, Countess Pistiem," Lucian responded. "Your reverence pleases us, for Tresilt was the home of his Honor Kyros tej-Shehathar."

The villagers either flinched or snorted at the royal title.

Truly? Kyros asked, his gaze sweeping over their faces. *Some of them have always hated me. Although... those heads do look anxious. As though they are about to be tried, judged, and sentenced.*

As Arista began to recite our names in introduction, I displayed images of another set of twelve faces in the link. *These people oppose us, do they not? That is interesting: a couple of the heads who support us had children who were present this morning at your house, Kyros. Or were themselves present.*

Elian and Kyros twitched, as though about to turn their heads but remembering our instructions at the last moment. *How did you know that, Malika?* Kyros asked, startled.

Nice, Arista said, admiring, as she spoke Kyros' name with particular emphasis aloud as part of the introduction. At Elian's questioning glance, she added, *For all that you say you do not remember your childhood training, you have retained enough to distinguish and categorize faces by family.*

I could not protest the praise, because Lucian and Arista had not yet taught us that. Although she was incorrect to attribute the skill to royal training—remembering faces had been essential to survival in the Blood's prisons.

But I fought back the flashes of memory. I never wanted to remember those years, and especially not now.

What was more impressive was Arista's ability to speak both in the link and aloud at the same time.

Countess Pistiem began to introduce the family heads—accompanied by Kyros' silent commentary.

I suppressed a dark scowl and the desire to berate all of these people: Kyros had resisted telling us for weeks, but, at Kalyca's urging last night, he confessed everything about the abuse the village had heaped upon him since his family's murders.

Assigning faces to those names... if not for Lucian's example of iron discipline, even gentle Elian would scream with the desire to have them understand what they had done.

Echoing my thoughts, Arista snarled, *They do not deserve Lucian's presence!*

They took out their fear on innocent children whose parents were murdered in front of them, Elian said, incensed. *They do not deserve this chance at redemption.*

Kyros' arm, intertwined with mine (as Arista's was with Elian's), turned rigid as pain and sorrow flickered in his eyes.

Aloud, Lucian thanked them all for coming, his lordly smile, as Kyros called it, firmly in place. Nothing in his expression or voice betrayed the fury and dislike emanating from his presence in the link.

I adjusted my hand so I could stroke the back of Kyros', as Lucian sometimes did when we walked together. *Lucian truly is partly divine, as the legend says, to give them this chance.*

As I had realized, secrecy was not the only reason why Lucian had not wanted to meet these villagers; as much as they had hurt Kyros, as long as their abuse remained in the past before his pledge, it could not be counted as disloyalty. But doing so now... those who did not accept us today would be counted among the ranks of traitors, and what portion of Khduren's magic that remained would no longer sustain them. Deserted so, they would lose much of the magic of their kind, which allowed them to cultivate the earth with water even as our world collapsed around us.

A drop of compassion diluted my anger. How fear had destroyed them.

Curtsying again, Countess Pistiem said, "My Rulers, I have looked for many years for your coming. As I would always tell my children, the Quest's coming will mark the beginning of our journey to salvation." The smile that lit her face as she spoke these last words...

She is genuine, I commented, surprised. *Considering how she forced your hand, I thought she might actually not be.*

Her only mistake, Lucian said, *is that she overlooked her own judgment in her enthusiasm.*

I nearly turned away from the villagers at the sorrow in his voice.

The mayor continued, "My Lord, if it would be in accordance with your wishes, I ask that you would accept our pledge and set us a task with which we may prepare for your reconquest."

The words resounded in the silence like the first raindrops of a storm on stone.

Then the woman who had uttered that first insult, Cella Dilielta, said, "You presume too much in saying '*our* pledge,' Mayor. My family doesn't want anything to do with that Blood-magnet, much less *pledge* to him." She spat out the word.

'*Blood-magnet*'? Elian repeated, horrified.

"Cella, really," Countess Pistiem chastised, "would you really allow an old grudge to impede you from accepting the Quest Leader's saving hand?"

"Except he is not going to actually save us, is he?" Avel Asfaliett sneered.

"Of course he is!" the mayor exclaimed.

Avel laughed darkly. "If that is so, where is your army, Lord? Where are your soldiers and your earth-shaking magic?" He did not wait for a response. "You cannot produce them because you do not *have* any."

Lucian raised an eyebrow, no longer smiling, yet cool despite the insult. *Do not try to answer, Arista*, he warned. *Do not let him bait you.*

As you wish, she seethed.

Avel continued, "Do you really think us so cursed *foolish*? That we would let you take our children on such a doomed endeavor? Take that Dinasiett boy—we do not want his Nasimih taint here anyway—and stay away from ours!"

Countess Pistiem, eyes blazing, snapped, "You *are* a fool, Avel, for speaking like that to the supreme ruler! And you know our history as well as I do—he does not *need* an army for his success. And that success is guaranteed—he is the divine-favored Quest Leader!"

"You put a lot of emphasis in faith and not enough in reality," Avel said derisively.

One of the women from the mayor's faction, Isella Galiem, stepped forward. Fists clenched, the elderly matriarch responded, "You are the one who ignores reality! We have only survived these last twelve years *because* of the Almighty! Look no further than our farms: we can only still grow enough for our survival because of our kind magic—and that is a gift of the Quest, the Almighty's Chosen!"

Priscella Nostiena, a young widow, added, "Without our faith, we would have collapsed beneath our grief. There is only wisdom in accepting the manifestation of our faith."

She pointed at Lucian. "If we do not pledge to him, there is no end in sight!"

The mayor continued, "And if he asks us for our children's service—which let me remind you, he actually has not asked anything of us; I am the one volunteering—then that is only right! We are his subjects whether we pledge or not; all of our lives are in his hands. We would be the fools to not take the chance to earn his favor at the very start of his Quest!"

Dealla Asfalielta, another widow and in the opposing faction, laughed, the sound bitter and black. "You can say that so easily because you will not be risking your sons in this foolhardy endeavor."

Every single household froze, no matter the faction, and Kyros gasped (though so quietly that only we could hear it).

Why are they so shocked? I asked, wondering if I had missed some social cue.

Because... Kyros blew out a breath. *Countess Pistiem is a widow and was bequeathed the noble title on her husband's death ten years ago. Her son and her daughter became her world... So, last year, when the soldiers began to drag her daughter away, she almost perished right there. She could not argue for Enthella the way she had for all the other taken children. And no one else dared to react.*

The fine wrinkles that lined Countess Pistiem's face deepened, and her blue eyes began to glow with a dark rage. "How dare you," she whispered.

Kyros continued, *In that moment, Ensel, her son, stepped forward and disparaged his sister in such a way that the soldiers' attention turned from her. He drove her to tears, rendering her face splotchy and, so, ugly to the soldiers. At the same time, he casually wiped his face of soot and dirt—and thus captured their attention. We do not know even where he was taken. The last we saw of him was his triumphant smirk as he was stolen. Because Ensel was the future count, very popular in the village...* he swallowed, *the only person who was even mildly friendly to me... he was deeply missed and mourned.*

So Dealla Asfalielta's words trample the line of decency, I surmised, horrified.

"How dare you," the mayor repeated.

And show how against us the opposing faction is, Arista said grimly. *They are willing to ruin even their longstanding relationships in their opposition to us.*

Elian swallowed, that reaction impressed in the link. *What can we do, Lucian?*

Lucian glanced at the mayor and then sent us the impression of a wry smile. *She does not need my defense and would not appreciate it regardless.*

As he predicted, Countess Pistiem roared like a lion. "How dare you! How dare you bring up my *son*—any of our lost ones—as ammunition in your attempt to go unblamed for your cowardice!"

On the heels of her words, Hevel Sigiemt leveled a terrible glare at the other faction. "Most of us have lost a child or a sibling. Are you so ready to accuse us of hypocrisy?" he growled. "If we have no sons to send, it is because we have already lost them!"

Some of the opposing faction winced, for his words particularly stung: the man had lost his only son, the last reminder of his late wife, to the soldiers the year before, and he had switched sides since the morning.

But Dealla, uncowed, responded, "*You* are the hypocrites! Having lost your children, can you blame us for guarding ours so fiercely?" She pointed at the window of the countess' common room. "We have no idea what will happen if they leave here! We have no idea what ills will come if we try to act for the Lord's sake. I, for one, am not willing to risk the two sons who are all I have left in the world!"

In another age, Arista observed, *that would be utterly persuasive.*

But not this one, I agreed.

Apparently sharing that view, Isella Galiem responded, scoffing, "They are at risk within the walls of your home. They are at risk when they walk the streets of our village. They are at risk when they work in the fields. They are at risk even when coated in soot and filth. They are *always* at risk. None of us are safe. Because what happened to the Dinasiette family can happen to any of us at any time. Without reason. Without cause. On a whim."

Both factions froze, stunned.

Kyros blinked. *That is the first time someone other than my aunt and the mayor have ever acknowledged my family was randomly targeted.*

They have never been ignorant of the truth, Lucian said quietly. *But they could not bear the horror of what had happened. They knew the cruelty had been randomly dispensed, so they understood that they could also be so targeted. Unable to withstand the fear and the uncertainty, they seek relief by attributing a cause, by blaming you. Through abusing you, they feel returned to positions of power, as though they regain control of their own lives. And already unhappy with the presence of Nasimih in their Ezulal village, they use the difference in kind to further rationalize what their consciences know to be wrong.* With a sweep of thought, he drew our attention to the villagers' faces, many of which convulsed with remembered terror. *Observe the ruinous consequences of fear unalleviated by hope.*

Cael Gerien spoke, in a quiet yet thundering voice, "You cannot escape the truth: the monster's cruelty has only grown. More and more supplies and shares of the ever-shrinking harvest are demanded every year, and the soldiers, for all that they are lazy, are harassing us more and more. With no provocation they turn to violence. We are not safe. And moreover, our children grow up without much laughter, kindness, or hope. We cannot live any longer in this state. If service to my Lord helps quicken his return and conquest, then so be it."

The countess' faction crossed their arms, their argument complete.

Doubt showed on the opposing faction's faces.

Utter silence.

Lucian said, musical voice calm and even, "The Quest did not come to Tresilt with the intention of publicly receiving pledges. However, since we have granted Countess Pistiem's request for an audience, we will accept pledges as well, if there are any who are prepared to follow us."

Countess Pistiem sighed, relaxing a little, and grinned faintly. "My family and I will pledge to the Quest of Freedom." She knelt in front of him, before the entire gathering.

The ten family heads of her faction knelt behind her and raised their hands as she did.

Lucian smiled, pleased, the silver sheen of his peach-white skin intensifying and dazzling them. *Arista, the pledge.*

Arista dipped her head and recited the pledge that Lucian had said families should use (unlike with the companions' pledges, there were only two portions: the vassal's offering and the liege's receiving). She repeated it three times.

Countess Pistiem and the ten heads proclaimed, "By the Light seen in the Shining Guide, on behalf of my family and my own behalf, I pledge our love and allegiance to you, my Lord Lucian the Ideal of Freedom. We will praise your name in both our homes and among our neighbors. We will live in accordance with the laws of Icilia and with your own commands. In all things we will proffer our best service to you. May the Almighty bless us with success in your Quest."

They barely finished the words before Avel Asfaliett started laughing, loud, contemptuous, and scornful.

CHAPTER 26

WITHSTAND
THE EMBITTERED

Perspective: Graced Malika the Exemplar of Wisdom
Date: Eyyéthar, the twenty-first day of the twelfth moon,
Alshatte, of the year 499, C.Q.

Lucian ordered, *Do* not *draw your swords, Malika, Elian, Arista, Kyros.*

I stilled my hand but did not release my white-knuckled grip on the hilt.

Guffawing, Avel exclaimed, "Really, you pledge to him?"

The mayor and all ten heads shot him dark looks, openly threatening.

He sniggered. "Do you not claim, Lord Supreme Ruler, to walk in the footsteps of the Quest of Light?"

Lucian did not respond, still calm.

Avel needed no reaction. "Then, tell us: why does any besides your Second recite your names and deliver the words of your pledges? Our history is clear: the Second is who speaks for you. Yet you speak for yourself? So, what does that mean?" He directed a mocking look at me. "It means she does not speak. And what does that say about our so-called savior? So few join their names to his cause that he chooses a Second who cannot speak! Whose face so clearly displays her inability to use her kind magic to find water! Why would *anyone* follow such a witless leader?"

I could barely keep my lips from trembling or my eyes from shedding tears, so much did those words hurt.

So much did they remind me of the Blood's favorite taunt, hissing into my ears, "You are a terrible Heir... little Malice... did *I* destroy your nation? Or was it really *you*? Such a worthless Heir, poison to what she loved most..."

Lucian's attempts at interruption and answer of "You know nothing of whom you speak" barely reached my ears. Even the fear radiating from him in place of his usual peace barely made an impression on my mind.

Arista shouted, but her words were entirely inaudible to me.

Ignoring him, Avel continued, gleeful, "And not only the Second is defective! Do none of you see the Sholanar companion's bound wings? What sort of Sholanar cannot *fly*?"

Elian's scales dimmed to a near black, and, unable to control so much of his expression, he looked stricken.

"Do not presume to know why the Almighty chose my companions," Lucian responded, the gold flecks of his violet eyes burning. He drew his sword now. As did Arista.

The clear anger in their words and posture and the fear of Lucian's presence did not reach Cella Dilielta, who added, snickering, "And what of the Areteen? So short, so *puny*, so surely a poor warrior?"

Bronze face hard with rage, Arista only raised an eyebrow. "Really? A kindist slur?" she muttered, unimpressed. The words were clearly audible, despite her low volume.

Even to Cella, who faltered for a moment. Failure in goading her target had more of an impact than the Quest Leader's own words, so far had she fallen.

But, ignoring Lucian's and Arista's interruptions, she regained her momentum and sneered, "And, finally, there is, of course, little Kyros, the Nasimih Blood-magnet. How could such a clueless leader ever be successful when he is accompanied by the Blood-magnet? Kyros will bring the Blood's wrath down on them before the week is out! What a ridiculous idea, to pledge to someone as ludicrous as this so-called Lord!"

Kyros' face coarsened, and he shuddered, his arm convulsing against mine, barely able to remain on his feet.

She laughed again before turning on her heel. "You may be willing to risk your families! But I certainly will not!"

"Never will my children serve the likes of *him*!" Avel proclaimed and walked toward the exit, Cella at his side.

Though unease filled their eyes, the rest of their faction followed.

The final man, Etzel Enchielt, paused on the threshold. "I do not agree with what they said, my Lord," he mumbled, barely able to look at Lucian, "but I will not risk my daughters. They mean too much to me. You ask too much."

The door slammed shut behind him.

All who remained were the mayor and the ten heads mid-pledge, Khudua Dinasietta standing to their right, and four other men and women standing near the back.

One of those men, I noticed dazedly, was unfamiliar, though his youthful face much resembled Kyros' uncle—most likely Kyros' cousin, Solios, for he was glowering at Kyros, his eyes fixed on my brother's anguished face.

Wrath swirled in Lucian's and Arista's eyes, crackling around them like the strike of lightning.

"I do not think I have been so angry in all my life," Arista said, dangerous fury brimming in her even-toned voice as she sheathed her sword. She squeezed Elian's arm and then, leaving aside etiquette, embraced him.

Lucian pressed his lips together, visibly calming himself as the silver of his white skin glimmered like the hard edge of a steel blade.

No one dared to breathe.

Lucian took a deep breath and spooled in the incinerating scorch of his authority, releasing the fear. Then he said, voice icy, "Will you also leave?"

The mayor and her allies shook their heads.

"We are with you always, my Rulers," Isella Galiem vowed, voice trembling yet hazel eyes resolute.

"We proffer our apologies, my Honor Kyros the Exemplar of Strength," Hevel Sigiemt added, openly desperate.

The other heads (including Kyros' aunt) echoed him, heartfelt and fervent.

Though Kyros murmured his acceptance, I doubted he was really listening.

The three remaining family heads hesitated but bowed and left. Only Solios remained in the back—though now he appeared troubled rather than angry.

Lucian sheathed his sword, but his voice was cold as he touched each of the heads' palms and answered, "For freedom by the Almighty, I accept your pledge and promise my support in return. In all things I will be just, and mercy and compassion will always temper my rule. May the Almighty bless us all and be pleased with all that we are. Praised be the Almighty."

Light sparked between his palm and each one he touched, binding the first true group of vassals to the Quest's name.

I was too numb to celebrate.

Once the light faded, Lucian stepped toward Kyros and me and took our hands in his. Without facing the villagers, he spoke, "As you requested, I commit a task to your service: in the months that pass before the Quest's return, train your daughters and your sons for battle so that they may march behind our banner when we reconquer Khuduren." He turned and raised both brows. "Conceal this duty from all but your own families and each other."

The countess winced, openly ashamed.

Lucian nodded to Arista, who stepped forward with the simple silver-and-beryl necklace he had shown us earlier. She presented it to the mayor, who reverently took it and slipped it around her neck.

"The necklace contains a communications spell that consumes much energy but will not leave residue," Lucian said. He stiffened, his eyes narrowing, but continued, "Report to me on the first day of every second month."

Countess Pistiem spoke, presumably assuring him she would. Her words were barely audible through the roaring clouding my mind.

The door flew open.

A young man darted inside and reported, tumbling into a bow, panting almost too hard to speak, "My Lord, I am your vassal, Decel Galien..." The rest of his words were lost amid the screams tearing at my ears.

Then Lucian's sharp words registered clearly: *The soldiers are on their way here, Malika, Elian, Kyros. Listen to me.*

I blinked and focused on his beloved face.

"My Lord," Countess Pistiem said urgently, "my daughter, Enthella, has delivered the three horses under my care to my Honor's house. Please, I beg of you, forgive us and accept this offering."

Lucian gave her a tense smile. "My gratitude, Countess Pistiem. I will not forget your support." He directed a look at his other new vassals. "Act with caution and prudence in the Quest's service. Do not take unnecessary risks. May the Almighty bless you and soon reunite you in our presence."

The new vassals exclaimed tearful farewells.

Solios took a step forward.

"Come," Lucian ordered. Tugging on my and Kyros' hands, he led us out the door and through the shadows of the buildings to Kyros' house.

There, by the gravestones of his family, Kalyca and Elacir waited.

We knelt and offered our respects to his family one last time.

"We have but five minutes," Lucian warned as we rose to our feet, "while Countess Pistiem delays the soldiers."

Kalyca gave him a quick nod and jumped into Kyros' arms. Cuddling into her brother's chest, she asked worriedly, "What happened?"

"Avel Asfaliett and Cella Dilielta," Arista answered, the terse answer still ablaze with rage.

Kalyca inhaled sharply, her gray eyes huge. Then, seeming to steady herself, she kissed Kyros' cheek and whispered, "I love you, Kyie. I will wait for you."

Kyros managed a wan smile. "I love you as well, Kallie darling. I will pray every day for our reunion."

She gave him another squeeze, then leapt from his arms into Elian's and exchanged words of love. Then turned to Arista and did the same. Then me.

My smile was no more than a grimace, my affection so revoltingly voiceless, but the kiss I placed on her forehead seemed to delight her. "I know you love me, Malika, Big Sister, as I love you," she said.

Pressing a kiss to my cheek, she went to Lucian, who knelt and spoke quietly with her while holding her in his embrace.

Arista and Elacir, exchanging worried looks, urged Elian onto a shaggy gray horse. They arranged his wings and bound them while he shuddered and whimpered at every touch. A desolate hatred corroded the beauty of his golden scales and chocolate features.

Once Elian was seated, they settled me at the back of an extended saddle on another gray horse. Clutching the pommel, Arista leapt high enough to mount without aid in front of me.

"I love you, Kalyca darling," Lucian said, words audible now, kissing her forehead. "Remember my counsel."

"I will," Kalyca replied, seeming worried yet determined, as she kissed his cheek. "And I love you, too, Lucian."

Lucian beamed, his cheeks silvering, and cupped a hand to his chest. Then he rose to his feet and approached the third horse, which possessed a white coat. He lifted his palm to its muzzle, and it dipped forward to kiss his fingers, before bowing its head. Lucian nodded, seeming pleased, and mounted, seating himself at the front of his own extended saddle.

Kalyca embraced Kyros one last time. "I will pray every day to the Almighty for you, Kyie, and I know the Almighty will listen to me. The Almighty loves you, you know."

Despite the sweet words, Kyros' smile faltered. "I am sorry for leaving again, Kallie, with even less notice than the first time."

She chuckled quietly and kissed his nose. "Big Brother, you are not the only one with foresight. I love you always." Then she stepped back.

Tears rolling down his coarse cheeks, Kyros only managed to take his seat behind Lucian with Elacir's support.

Elacir spread his wings.

A sad smile now on his lips, Lucian nodded to Kalyca. "Little Sister, retreat inside your aunt's house immediately. She is waiting for you, and I will be watching. We will speak soon."

"I know you will care for my brother, my Lord," she said, bowing formally. The mature smile of a woman far older than her nine years curved her mouth. "May the Almighty forever bless you."

"May the Almighty protect you, Kalyca," all of us responded, no matter how destroyed.

Then Lucian tapped the side of his horse (which was connected by a rope to Elian's), Arista followed his lead, and all three horses stepped into a gallop, racing forwards into the night, Elacir flying over our heads.

Tresilt faded behind us.

But those words… they permeated every bone, every vein, every nerve, crushing what health I had regained.

I was a worthless Heir. And I am a worthless Second.

Because what could a Second who had neither voice nor magic be other than a hardship?

As my birth ruined my nation, my life will ruin Lucian's Quest.

CHAPTER 27

CHERISH THE FAVORED

Perspective: Lord Lucian the Ideal of Freedom
Date: Eyyésal, the first day of the first moon, Lushatte, of the
year 500, C.Q.

The black sky, the smog, and the darkness, congealed
in an alloy of bleak hopelessness, reflected something
of the dimness of my mood. As sunny as my temperament
usually was, bright smiles had become a rarity over the
last nine days.

All the progress I had achieved was unraveling, and all
my efforts to counter that destruction had been fruitless. I
knew I had made the holy choice in not wielding my sword
in vengeful anger or in allowing hatred to taint my soul, yet
I mourned the damage that had been wrought. If only my
companions had listened to me... Even now my voice, for all
its power, did not reach their ears.

"Oh Almighty!" I whispered, desperate, "Sanctuary of the
desperate, Conqueror of the virtuous, Liege of my soul—I beg
the bestowal of Your succor. For the praise of Your name, I

chose whom You chose and nurtured them with all the love You instilled in my soul. My cherishment did not fade, yet I failed to protect them. With tears and repentance, I beg of You the beneficence of Your remedy on behalf of my companions. Give us Your healing Light as you have before!"

Barely had I finished the prayer before a single ray of gray light burst through the smog on the eastern horizon. The solitary beam reached toward me, sheathing me in a shaft of warmth.

Contentment kindled in my heart, and an idea sparked in my mind.

The gray color changed to a muted rose, sober yet sweet.

The light then shifted over my head and stroked the sleeping faces of my family before fading.

"Praised be the Almighty," I whispered with my first full smile since we had parted from Kalyca.

Rising, I prepared for the day.

When sunrise burnished the underside of the smog a dull gold, I roused my family with eager and affectionate words.

Amazed by my enthusiasm, they followed me to the small hillock I had chosen. Then realization, and excitement, lit their eyes, and they quickly seated themselves in a half-circle behind me. They looked east, toward the rising sun, as I did.

The emerging sunlight penetrated the smog as I savored the incense of their presence.

I spoke the ceremonial words, "The Almighty has blessed the people of Icilia with the coming of the Shining Guide and thereafter with the Quest of Light. May the Day of Light, the sacred day on which the Quest of Light ascended and began their task of bringing civilization to our land, mark the Almighty's blessing unto us."

"So may the Almighty bless us," Elian, Arista, Kyros, and Elacir whispered. Malika repeated the same in the link that connected all of us.

I began to sing, my musical voice quiet yet as clear as a bell, the paean written by my Lady Queen Aalia the Ideal of Light.

The simple, harmonious melody filled the air, emitting from my lips but caressing our ears of its own accord. The lyrics, composed in the sacred tongue of Alimàzahre, were beautiful and sweet, with the pure intensity of sunlight. The very sound was reminiscent of reaching one's hand for the stars, the yearning to perceive that which was so much greater than oneself, the wonder of the divine... The song reminded us of holy truth and invoked love for the Almighty in our hearts, rippling out from me to my companions and reverberating from them throughout the whole of Icilia.

I sang the hymn once alone in praise of the Almighty and the Shining Guide.

When I began the second iteration, Elian, Arista, and Kyros joined me with the Siléalaah translation of the hymn. Malika repeated the words she could catch of their singing in the link.

On the third, Elacir joined us, his singing far less perfect than that of the Quest but beautiful to my ears.

I held the final note and let it fade away, then closed my eyes again and enjoyed the sunlight.

I am your Heir, my Lady Queen, I whispered, praying that the Almighty would favor me by allowing my words to reach her. *I will revive your legacy and ensure that your mark does not fade from this land. May the Almighty brighten your gaze, my Mother, with my success.*

As that plea rose from my soul, I said, without turning, "Blessings for the Day of Light, my companions. Blessings for the Day of Light, my vassal."

My family shyly returned the greeting with my reverential address.

I smiled softly.

Then Elian exclaimed, amazed, "I never thought I would celebrate the Day of Light with the Quest Leader himself!"

Arista echoed him with the same amazement, "I never thought I would celebrate the Day of Light as a Potentate of the Quest!"

Celebrating this day with you, my Lord, Malika whispered in wonder, *is a blessing and an honor beyond comprehension.*

"It always meant so much," Kyros said, awed, "but it means even more with you, my Lord. You are their Heir, and we are with you."

Their first words in nine days weighed with neither anger nor anguish.

As usual, the ceremony performs wonders. As all of Icilia is a wonder, I thought, pleased. Then aloud I responded, "We are their Heirs. We are the Quest of Freedom, and we are the Heirs of the Quest of Light."

Malika, Elian, Arista, and Kyros were star-struck.

Elacir merely smiled, affection and gratitude sparkling in his hazel eyes.

"Remember this day," I said, gazing out at the snow-covered plains twinkling under the morning sun, "for it symbolizes our purpose just as our own ascensions do—we are meant to restore the gifts granted on this day: the gift of the faith of the Almighty, the bestowal of which began when the Shining Guide first came to Icilia, on this day five centuries prior according to our legend. And the gift of civilization, the bestowal of which began when the Quest of Light ascended on this day and received their mission to spread the teachings of the Shining Guide to all of Icilia. With our revival of Icilia's faith and civilization, we will bestow true freedom unto her people. For such is the mission with which the Almighty has favored us."

I momentarily glanced over my shoulder at the intently listening faces of my companions. "And remember alongside your purpose that the Almighty gives the favored the tools they need for success in their appointed task. All answers come from the Almighty, as we are the Almighty's answer to the plight of Icilia."

In the wake of my words there was silence.

The sun fully rose above the horizon.

I intoned, "Praised be the Almighty."

My companions and my vassal repeated me.

I rose to my feet, descended the hillock, and walked in a gentle curve, such that my person was angled toward the sun for as much of the turn as possible. My family copied me.

Then, instead of returning to our campsite, I took a seat at the base of the small slope.

Bemused, my family did the same.

A pang of pain pricked my heart as Elacir scrambled to sit behind Kyros, away from the angle of Elian's gaze. Though Elian had never cast him a single covetous glance, Elacir had seemed convinced of Elian's jealousy after Arista told him of what happened in Tresilt. Despite my reassurances, he pushed himself to complete every chore our camps required, as though only such proof of his value stood between him and abandonment.

He had not yet understood that I valued him for his wisdom, greater than his years would indicate, and the magnificence of his soul, so beautifully capable of true freedom. I had needed no other reason to save him and then accept Elian's choice of him as brother.

He will know one day.

Refocusing upon my companions, I brought a smile to my lips.

All four are listening—excellent. For a few moments, the crushing anxiety had disappeared from Arista's eyes, the agonized yearning from Kyros', and the outright torment from Malika's and Elian's.

"On this blessed day, this five hundredth anniversary," I proclaimed, "I gift you the second and third symbols of your office." With easy elegance, I retrieved two athar cloth pouches from the inner pockets of my coat. Opening one, I motioned for them to extend their hands and placed the rings of the first Quest in their palms. Then I dropped the glamor wreathing my right hand and showed them my own.

Each ring had the same base design: a silver band of medium size, featuring delicate golden scrolls carved in relief curving around the outside of the band and the words "The Almighty's Chosen" in sacred Alimàzahre on the inside. Centered amid the scrolls was a small crimson ruby, the size of a teardrop, carved with the Quests' insignia, an elegantly ornate flower-like crown replete with mysterious symbolism.

Lips parted, my companions stared at the rings, which thrummed with power against their skin. Their eyes darted between theirs and mine—in contrast to Elian's, Arista's, and Kyros' rings, the delicate lines of the carving on Malika's were filled with subtle brushes of silver instead of white. Gold accented the insignia on mine.

"Lucian," Arista whispered, numb with shock, "what- what in Icilia did you give us? They cannot be... are they?"

"They are," I answered. "These rings were created by the smith Barracer e'Auros of Etheqa for the Quest of Light in the fourth decade of their journey. The lore states that my

Lady Aalia of Light, pleased by the gift, insisted on requesting two more." I nodded at Elian's. "Malika and I hold our two Queens' rings. Elian has our King's, according the bit of rank existing among you."

Elian squeaked and nearly dropped it.

"Careful!" Arista hissed, steadying his hand.

I chuckled. "Yes, indeed, do be careful. We will wear them until our deaths, but they are only temporarily ours. We must bequeath them to the third Quest, in as pristine condition as possible."

My companions stared at the rings in awe. Only after a prodding look from me did they wear them.

"Now, what is ours," I continued, "are these." I opened the other pouch and placed a necklace in each of their hands. I drew out my own from beneath the collar of my robes.

My companions stared again at the gifts, which my guardians had made to resemble the athar pendants of the first Quest. On each gold chain hung a deep green emerald half the size of my thumb, encircled by a gold setting and carved with the Quests' insignia. Malika's and my own were distinguished from the others' in the same manner as the rings.

"The emeralds," I explained, "contain a number of bases for spells of athar magic, mindlinking, wizardry, and sorcery. These pendants are the central hubs for the communication web I intend to eventually form with gifts of necklaces such as the one I gave Countess Pistiem. The spells, of mindlinking, are my guardians' own unique design and so will be quite invulnerable to interference."

"That is a powerful spell," Arista whispered, awed.

"It let Kalyca contact us yesterday across nearly five hundred miles," Kyros agreed. Then he paused, drawing his eyebrows together. "I do not mean to sound ungrateful, but... why does hers have athar beads and ours do not?"

The rest fixed their gazes upon me as well.

I answered, "My guardians had not completed the requisite research for the pendants prior to Asfiya's capture, and much of the pure athar we carried to our refuge was needed for the basic designs of our various symbols of office. They did not have reserves for beads, much to their chagrin. I intend to remedy that lack upon our future reconquest of Asfiya. As for Kalyca's necklace..." My cheeks cooled so much the silver glow tinted my vision. "That was the token my grandfather commissioned for my fifth birthday."

My companions stared, wide-eyed and open-mouthed. Elacir left aside peering over Kyros' shoulder to stare at me as well.

I shifted uneasily at the regard. "It was but a temporary possession," I muttered. "This pendant is what I am meant to wear."

Kyros wetted his lips and parted them to speak. No words came, and he opened and closed his mouth several times. Finally, he said, his voice quiet yet ardent, "Thank you, Lucian."

I nodded in acknowledgment, relieved both that their scrutiny was fading and that they did not notice what I had omitted: the purpose of the ring. Explaining that purpose would require instruction in the magic of the Quest. I as yet still used too much to wish to reveal the magnitude of my current sacrifices.

Their amazement at a small gift had bordered on horror. Would they not be appalled by the offering of my life?

Glancing at the sky, I noted that the sun was well and truly risen. All the time I was willing to risk lingering in one place had elapsed.

"Come," I urged and rushed us through breakfast and morning ablutions.

Soon enough, we mounted the horses, which I had saddled before dawn. Tapping Rikeb's sides, I spurred the stallion onwards, with Asmarrie, Elian's newly renamed mare, following obediently behind, while Arista directed her and Malika's stallion, Farib, to ride alongside us. Elacir flew over Elian's head.

A grim satisfaction curled my lips. My companions were finally smiling again, and Elacir was less troubled as well. I had much left to do for them, but the ceremony had reversed the tide.

Yet, now that one concern eased, another surged to take its place: someone had betrayed us to the soldiers in Tresilt. And, with Kyros losing progress in his catalysis and my own person unable to sustain the requisite expenditure of life, I could not be certain we were not pursued.

The faster we reached Nademan, the better. Though, in reality, we fled one danger for another, far greater one.

CHAPTER 28

PROTECT
THE TREASURED

Perspective: Lord Lucian the Ideal of Freedom
Date: Eyyésal, the first day of the first moon, Lushatte, of the
year 500, C.Q.

The skin of my back exploded in pain as a sizzling blade pierced my flesh. A scream tore from my lips, and I slumped forwards, my vision a field of lifeless white. Then the white resolved into the sight of a sword plunging into a form clad in midnight blue, dying a red-gold braid with blood.

My vision slowly cleared—and an unwelcome gaze replaced the blade, scalding the tender skin like hot water.

A premonition, I realized. *And an inimical use of farsight.*

My family's panicked voices filtered through the haze, and I noticed the firm arm clutching my waist, the only reason I had not toppled from the saddle.

Shoving aside the pain, I ordered, *Kyros, catalyze for your farsight. Now.*

Instinctually obeying, Kyros invoked his farsight in a tingle of whispery magic.

Sweep the south, I commanded. *Malika, arm the crossbows. Elian, those attack spells Arista taught you. Elacir, fly low to catch our wake.* I spurred my horse, and by extension Elian's, into a gallop.

Arista snapped her reins, urging her stallion to match our speed. *Lucian, what did you see?* she demanded.

Lucian, there are Sholanar troops approaching! Kyros cried.

How many? How far? I asked crisply. Then to Arista in private, *I need you to protect Malika.*

I will, she promised, as firm and focused as I was.

How grateful I was to her parents and her sisters for sacrificing everything so that she could prepare. And to her for her own assuredness.

Kyros answered frantically, *Eighteen miles southwest. Four squads. Forty soldiers, plus the captain.*

Twenty minutes, Arista noted, *at this pace. We have time to set an ambush.*

We also have the advantage of a farseer's spying... I pressed my lips together. *Kyros, I must borrow your farsight.*

He had barely agreed before I invoked a link that allowed me to control the images supplied by his magical vision. Murmuring an apology, I directed it further and faster than he could bear, quickly gathered as much information as I could, and deactivated the link so it would not cause him any more pain. Then I expanded my sense and absorbed every bit of stimuli within my range. Finally, I overlaid the images atop my memorized map of this corner of northern Bhalasa.

Analyzing all I knew, I outlined a plan.

Then I directed us north across the flat plain.

Ten minutes later, I catalyzed several drops of my life and commanded our auric signatures, the pulses of magical energy which demarcated every person, to disappear.

The air grew muffled around us, and the sunlight illuminated my friends' faces as though the rays filtered through a haze. And the sting of hateful eyes vanished, the farsight used by our enemies no longer able to track us.

I changed our course, angling northeast.

We sped across the flat plains, rapidly approaching my goal, a dense cluster of trees that, like their relations less than two hundred miles north, towered over two hundred feet above the snow.

Behind us, the soldiers scrambled to regain our trail, too reliant on magic to be skilled with reading the earth.

The moment we reached the grove, Malika and Arista climbed into the first tree and threw down dry branches. Kyros, Elacir, and I set to sharpening them into crude javelins, while Elian hid his and Arista's horses. Then Elacir carried him and half the javelins into the tree.

Kyros and I rode to the top of a hillock nearly half a mile away.

Hardening our robes, we each wedged five javelins between our legs and the stallion's flanks. Kyros held another two in his hands, while I balanced a pair of throwing daggers between the fingers of my right hand and a javelin in my left.

I reached out with a tendril of mindlinking and touched Rikeb's uneasy mind. Calming at the touch, he swung his head and lipped the toe of my boot, while I assured him that I would protect him.

The soldiers entered the range of my awareness.

Carrying unsheathed swords and glinting spears, they wore gray helmets and black leather armor stamped with the Blood's carmine skull atop the Clawed's maroon daggers.

The Clawed's troops, hmmm? I thought. *Tresilt is under the Slicer's control, which means...* A bitter taste filled my mouth. *The troops in Khuduren actually communicated with those of Bhalasa—something I have not heard of happening in ten years. An ominous sign, and the change occurring in the shadows that has disturbed me these past several months. Which furthermore indicates that our visit to Tresilt was far riskier than previously calculated. These choices were necessary, but they are not ones that I, or my guardians, will repeat.*

Before it could consume my attention, I placed aside that consideration and said in the collective link, *The thin sheets of stretched leather covering their wings are armor, so you will not be able to attack them directly. But, because wing armor always destabilizes flight, a hard blow will disrupt their balance and leave them vulnerable to subsequent attacks. Judging the quality of their armor... your swords will pierce them with sufficient force. As should my daggers.*

How many ranks? Arista asked.

Eight, of five each, I answered. *The captain—marked by a vermillion skull rather than scarlet—is in the second-to-last rank.* My brow furrowed. *An odd position.*

The enemy was almost within view.

I intoned a prayer.

Then the enemy was upon us.

I lifted my hand and threw the daggers at the first rank, the aim and force of the blows driving the blades into two of their throats. Before the corpses plummeted, I tossed the javelin.

The soldier I had targeted tumbled head over heels in the air, his wing pierced through by the javelin. A ball of fire—Arista's—dispatched him.

The enemy dove toward us.

I swiftly pulled more javelins and daggers and threw them, one after another. Supported by Arista's sorcery, one miss, five hits. Behind me, Kyros tossed his own. Two hits, dispatched by fire, three misses. The whole first rank and most of the second.

I wheeled my horse around and tapped him into a gallop. Slipping another dagger from my case, I called out, *Hold!*

Their wings flared tightly against their persons, the troops gained on Kyros and me, their dive sharp, if a bit sloppy.

Just a little further... I whispered.

The trees were but a hundred feet away.

Fifty feet...

Half of the soldiers were flying just above the ground... one soldier of the original third rank almost close enough to touch Rikeb's tail...

Now! Within the shade of the trees, I whirled and flung my dagger into the soldier's chest. Propelled by my strength and momentum, the blade pierced his armor, and blood sprayed Kyros' back.

Crossbow bolts erupted in the chests of two soldiers immediately behind us. Javelins impacted two others with such force that they crashed into the ground. A pair of balls of fire dispatched them.

The third rank plummeted and rolled on the ground by Rikeb's hooves.

As the stallion turned, Kyros and I drew our swords and fell upon the fourth rank as they landed. Their feet sank into the bloody slush, which was melting under the influence of Arista's magic.

But the remaining soldiers, who had not even approached the ground, already flew toward the treetop. The reason why the snow on the ground had melted but not refrozen.

Two soldiers fell, pierced by bolts, but the next two javelins missed.

My family was trapped.

Kyros, help the others. I slashed diagonally with one hand so that the blade bit into the neck of an attacker and threw a dagger with the other. It missed.

Kyros sheathed his sword and, vaulting off the saddle, ran to the base of the trunk. Movements a blur, he climbed it with the precision and speed only one of the Nasimih could have.

I slit the throat of another attacker. Then twisted and stabbed the soldier who had raised his sword to my horse's flank. Squealing, he collapsed backwards.

Increasing the weight of my sword, I turned and cleaved the head of a fourth with a brutal strike. I spun on the fifth just as she pressed a dagger to Rikeb's throat. My blade pierced her armor, killing her instantly.

Twenty-one dead. I threw myself off from the horse. Sheathing my sword and yanking my last four daggers from their case, I raced to the tree and scaled it as quickly as I could.

High in the air and slipping on icy tree branches, my family clashed in a pitched battle with nearly half the enemy force.

Malika and Arista fought back to back, but Elian, Kyros, and Elacir were cornered, alone, without each other's support. Soldiers swooped around them, lobbing taunts with both blades and words.

Reaching the branch Elian had chosen, I threw a dagger into one soldier's back. As he plummeted, I raced forward and stabbed the second. Then, whirling, the third. They fell just as Elian's balance failed, tipping them over the side into the empty air.

I caught the front of Elian's robes and hauled him back onto the branch.

As soon as he was steady on his feet, I leapt for the branch above. Wrapping an arm around it, I cut at the ankles of one of Kyros' attackers. He toppled over the side and, unable to open his wings in time, bruised by branches, died at the impact with which he hit the ground.

Kyros dispatched one soldier. Then froze and stared at the blood on his blade—his first kill.

Seizing the moment of vulnerability, one attacked him, while another struck at my arm.

My blade toppled Kyros' foe, killing her on impact with the ground.

While the sharp edge of my own assailant pierced my flesh, the athar softening only some of the impact.

Clenching my teeth, I swung at her ankles.

She leapt up, wings open, avoiding my blow.

My sword was too far extended to launch another attack.

I braced myself to dodge.

Elian cried out, "Kyros!"

Snapping from his haze, Kyros fell upon the soldier, whirling her around and stabbing her. Her torso slid off his blade with a squelch, the corpse falling to the ground, spraying blood over Kyros' face.

Gray eyes dark with horror, Kyros sank to his knees.

I shifted my grip on my sword and hooked that arm over the branch. Pulling myself up, I ran past Kyros for the tip of the bough, where Elacir lashed out at his attackers.

He was panicking, his blade missing again and again, his fright further fueled by the soldiers' taunts. Blood streaked his plum wings, tattered under the strokes of cruel blades.

Thirty-one—Malika and Arista made two more kills. I threw my final two daggers at two of the three attackers.

One landed in a soldier's shoulder, and he shrieked, dropping his sword, and clutched his wound. The other missed.

Attention drawn, all three soldiers, even the injured one, looked at me—and froze at the sight of my face, lit by the clear sunlight. Before I could attack, they propelled themselves from the branch and tore away from the battlefield.

One was the captain.

Elacir was in no condition to pursue.

And as was true with every one of my misses, with every blow that did not result in death, those opponents were meant to live, for the Almighty had ordained that their lives should not yet end at my hand. Those reasons had not yet been revealed to me, but, as always, I trusted them.

I climbed one more branch to the last fight.

Her crossbow jammed into her belt-quiver, Arista had drawn her sword and was dueling her remaining two attackers, a corpse by her feet. As I approached, she disarmed one, stabbed another, and whirled on her final enemy.

Beyond her, Malika dueled the final two. But with her back pressed against the trunk and her balance shaky, her moves were constrained and uncertain. Numerous cuts bled on her limbs.

The branch quivered beneath my feet as I ran toward Malika.

Her lips moving without sound, she parried another blow.

Both attackers taunted her, their voices shrill with cackling laughter. One raised her blade with both hands for a powerful cleave.

Malika's blue eyes sparked, and, arms a blur, she stabbed the enemy's exposed chest.

The twist left her guard open.

The other attacker raised her sword and swung.

Before I could defend her, that blade pierced Malika's back.

CHAPTER 29

BEHOLD
THE WONDROUS

Perspective: Lord Lucian the Ideal of Freedom
Date: Eyyésal, the first day of the first moon, Lushatte, of the
year 500, C.Q.

Malika screamed.

A dagger flew past me and impaled the last soldier's helm. It sparked with green fire, killing him in a flare of burning flesh.

The soldier collapsed, falling onto Malika and wrenching the blade against her skin. Forcing the edge deeper into her back.

Dangerously unbalanced, she wobbled, her feet skidding and slipping on the blood-drenched wood. Her sword tumbled from her fingers.

Tossing aside my own sword, I pried the enemy's hilt from his dying hand and pushed his corpse away. Hopping on one leg, I raised the other to prevent Malika's fall.

She caught her breath, her screams fading.

As the attacker's body fell with a distant thump, I carefully nudged Malika with both arms and my leg back onto the thickest part of the branch. Then extended my legs and pushed her into a kneeling position. I braced her between my knees.

"This will hurt," I warned.

She nodded and clutched my calf.

I pulled the sword out.

Malika shrieked again, her arms clamping painfully around the limb.

Catalyzing my life, I placed both hands on the gash and began to cast a first spell of disinfection.

Arista and Kyros, who had both reached us, stared at Malika in horror, swords hanging loosely at their sides.

"Arista," I said crisply, and she snapped to attention, her posture stiffening. "Well done in saving Malika. Use the healing salve from my saddle-bag on your injuries and on those of the others. Begin burial and recovery of our weapons. You should find seven of my daggers in the soldiers' corpses. Malika's and my sword have landed on lower branches. Command Kyros; Elian and Elacir may be unable to help."

Arista raised a salute and maneuvered past Malika and me to the trunk. Climbing trees was a difficult task for one of the Areteen in any circumstance, much more this, but she moved smoothly enough for me to relax about her wellbeing.

Kyros quailed under my gentle gaze and followed Arista.

The disinfection spell complete, I drew on yet more life for the healing.

My arm throbbed, the pain blinding, but I distanced myself from it. The bleeding would eventually threaten my life, but Malika's wound was almost mortal. Just a fraction of an inch more, and the blade would have pierced her spinal column. Only the athar of her robes had prevented the injury from becoming so serious. As it was, the gash was deep and wept profuse amounts of her blood.

My robes were soaked with it. Stones weighing my limbs, stark scent overpowering every perfume of the earth.

If I had not been grasping my battle-focus with both hands, I would have melted into an inconsolable mess of tears. Each of my family's hurts and struggles hurt far more than the deep injury that lacerated my arm, but Malika's brush with death was enough to stop my heart. My vision had occurred in truth.

"Lucian," Elacir whispered, and I glanced up to see him collapsing besides me. He inhaled sharply and began to cry. "I failed you!" he sobbed. His wings were stretched behind him and riddled with cuts, more direly injured than on the night we had met.

I smiled as reassuringly as I could with both hands covered in Malika's blood. "No, Little Brother, you did not." I let a sterner tone seep into my voice. "Now go to Arista for treatment."

He took a shaky breath and nodded.

Before he rose, Elian inched around the side of the trunk and paused, pressed against it. He surveyed the scene, and his expression crumpled.

He holds his left arm oddly, I thought. The bond blazed with pain, the pain of something not whole...

I caught my breath, recalling the ways in which the soldiers had taunted him, tortured him... *They deliberately broke his arm...* Rage simmered in my stomach, but it was not useful now, my family already safe from further harm.

Composing myself, I said gently, drawing his gaze, "Elian, my brother, would you go with Elacir to Arista? Malika and

I will be down shortly." He would need support to descend so far, particularly because I was in no position to provide him with a temporary splint. Elacir himself was grievously injured, but I needed for them to help each other.

Elian began to nod. Then his breath hitched, and his eyes widened.

I followed his gaze to my arm and winced. "Yes, it is unpleasant, is it not?"

"Unpleasant!" Elian shrieked. "I can see the bone!" He dropped to his knees beside us.

At his words and pitch, Malika and Elacir turned to see what had evoked such a reaction from Elian's usually soft-spoken tongue. Though the laceration rending her back was still fresh and painful and pulled at the movement, Malika screamed again at the sight of my torn flesh. Elacir looked like he would vomit.

"Please!" Elian begged. "Heal yourself first!"

You need salve! Malika cried. *Or an athar tear!*

"Lucian!" Elacir sobbed.

I smiled, though uneasily. Malika's wound was far more dangerous... and I had not wanted them to know about my injury. I could only estimate what new seeds of trauma it would sow, particularly for Kyros.

Before I could ask them to not worry, Elian's crown-patterned scales flared a bright gold against his chocolate skin and umber hair under the dust and blood that coated his form. His eyes glazed as though in a trance, he reached forward with his unbroken arm and lightly touched the cut.

White healing light emanated from his fingertips...

I gasped, my spine arching, as his magic inundated my body, comforting like the first sweet-scented warm breeze of spring...

The magic brushed every part of my flesh, soothing with a restorative touch, before concentrating on the greatest of my hurts. The nerves and veins of my arm reconnected, the blood flow abruptly ceasing, the muscles knitting together. Skin then spread atop the muscle and joined together, sealed without a scar.

Utter bliss and delight spread a bright, unthinking grin on my lips.

His healing penetrated to almost the deepest part of who I was... and accelerated the regeneration of my depleted life.

Then the flow of it spilled down my fingers and began to mix with my own commanding magic in a warm burst of pale green light. As his healing and mine joined into one, the distinctions between Elian's identity and my own blurred... his green eyes riveted to mine and my violet ones to his, our heartbeats pulsing as one. The combined healing magic, potent unlike anything of which I had ever learned, poured through my fingers into Malika's wound.

The flesh regrew so quickly that within seconds my finger-tips rested on new, unblemished skin, as though the injury had never occurred. Even the blood in her veins was replenished, all infection evaporated.

The drain of my life into her trickled to a stop.

Malika sighed in pleasure and contentment.

Before I could lift my fingers or Elian could move his, a tremor racked her frame, terrifying her.

A crack thundered through our bond.

And, for the first time, I perceived a hint of the sharp edge of her magic, the deadly cool of a blade. The sensation faded as quickly as it had come, but there was no doubt in my mind about what I had sensed.

Though my fingers immediately began to stroke Malika's hair, my wide-eyed gaze remained on Elian.

The magnitude of what happened...

Elian shuddered, ending the connection between us, and fell backward onto his bottom. Awestruck, he shakily examined his still-glowing fingers, then, leaning over Malika and me, reached for Elacir's plum wings. He touched first one and then the other.

Light spread through Elacir as it had through Malika and me, and he sighed, his hazel eyes glazed with the pleasure that came with relief from pain. Within moments, his wings were healed, as though no harm had ever befallen them.

Elian sat back and stared at his hand as its glow faded, along with the shine of his scales.

Malika and I stared at him.

How did you do *that?* she whispered. *Lucian, how did he* do *that?*

I shook my head slowly, as awed as she was. "I am not sure myself... but..." I smiled contentedly. "I think that was a proof of Elian's love for us."

"It cannot be," Elian whispered, flexing his hand open and closed. "I could not heal you, Elacir, when you had that fever. And I tried."

"Perhaps because you did not know how to catalyze then as you do now," I replied. "But, whatever the reason for this blessing, I am grateful." I nodded to Malika's back. "That had the potential to be a mortal wound. Elacir's wings, unlike after his rescue, might never have recovered from the injuries inflicted upon them."

"Your own wound, also, could have been mortal," Elacir said, frowning slightly.

Malika and Elian both gave me sharp looks.

I chuckled, appreciating that they cared so much for me. But, behind my smile and my excitement over what Elian's healing had done, I was starting to dread the repercussions of this battle upon my family. Elian, Kyros, and Elacir had spilled blood for the first time, and many things had happened that would heighten their fears...

Alongside those concerns was another, more immediate, peril: three of the enemy had escaped, having clearly seen my face—the face designed to portray my identity with inescapable clarity—and just as I concluded that the troops of Khuduren and of Bhalasa were communicating. After we had been betrayed.

One of those soldiers was a captain. If he reported to his own commander and was believed (a distinct likelihood), we would be in even greater danger than before. And if they deduced my full identity, though I had not evoked the holy power within my blood, the conquest of Nademan could be compromised.

We had still four weeks to travel before we would reach relative safety at my brother's fortress in central Nademan.

I had much for which I need to pray.

As those pleas for guidance began to form in my heart, I renewed my smile. "Elian, how is your arm?"

Elian's lips formed a mocking grin. "Since I did not heal myself, it hurts as much as it did before."

I nodded and, pulling my legs beneath me, rose to my feet. "To be expected." I offered my hand to Malika. "What you did was miraculous—it would be miraculous even for one who is fully trained. Your healing will come in time, Elian."

He pursed his lips and nodded slowly. "Perhaps, Lucian."

Though his doubt in himself hurt, I did not argue with him. Instead, I directed my efforts at ensuring our safe arrival on the ground and then the cleaning and treatment of all our injuries. Reliable as always, Arista gathered and cleaned our weapons, then buried all of the soldiers' bodies. Under our joint direction, Malika, Elian, Kyros, and Elacir remained focused, despite the sour taste of horror settling into the bonds.

Once we had bathed at a nearby river and my healing had repaired Elian's arm, I had us remount and travel another twenty miles.

Determining we still had time, I then set about repairing our clothes—with athar magic for my companions' and my robes and with thread and needle for the linen-backed leather tunic and trousers Kyros had found for Elacir in Tresilt.

The sun began to set, lighting the smog with dusky rose and gold.

I found another hillock and faced the setting sun, my family gathering behind me.

We sang the hymn of gratitude that my Lady Aalia of Light, my Grace Manara of Light, and my Honor Naret of Light had written in gratitude for their Quest. Three times together we sang it.

I prayed then, "May the Almighty bless you with peace in the hereafter, our Rulers the Quest of Light, Mothers and Father of Icilia. May the civilization you spread in service to the Shining Guide flourish for as long as the Almighty deems Icilia worthy of such blessing. May the day of your ascension be a reminder unto your children of the grandeur of their heritage." I paused and then added my own prayer in a quieter voice, "We are your Heirs and your children, the Quest of Freedom. May we please the Almighty and achieve our victory in the Almighty's name as you did. May we serve the Almighty well."

My companions and my vassal had startled when I began the second prayer. Now, at its conclusion, they murmured with evident passion, "So may the Almighty bless us," using the forms of voice available to them. They spoke in mere whispers, yet that passion was undeniably present.

A wistful smile curved my lips, my eyes on the fading sunlight. "Praised be the Almighty."

Malika, Elian, Arista, Kyros, and Elacir repeated the prayer.

Then, as earlier, I murmured, "Blessings for the Day of Light, my companions. Blessings for the Day of Light, my vassal."

They returned the greeting.

And the sun set on the horizon, leaving the land dark under the night sky and the thin crescent of the moon.

I exhaled deeply and rose. Gathering the ingredients obtained in Tresilt, I prepared the sweet of which was customary to partake on this day: apples drizzled with honey.

With a small smile, I chewed a slice and offered the bowl to my family.

Though they accepted their shares, tormented shame brewed in their eyes.

If I do not want the gains of this morning to be wholly lost, I mused to myself, *I should discuss what troubles them before we sleep. Even Arista is upset.*

Once we had supped, I took my chance: "Sisters, Brothers, what dampens your happiness?"

My family avoided my gaze for several long minutes.

Then the five of them rushed to hug me, sobbing that they had ruined the holy day—the five hundredth anniversary of the Day of Light, no less—for me. I had borne most of the burden of the battle, they said, and I had received injury due to their cowardice.

Gently assuring them, I returned their embraces and said, "Your presence made the holy day perfect. As for the battle itself... Our land is trapped in a struggle for her very soul. Fighting today is fitting. So instead consider that, today, we fought for freedom, for the preservation of Icilia's love for the Light."

Only those words contented them enough that they slept that night. Yet, still, they rested uneasily, tossing with the specters of nightmares, as they had not since they each first began to travel with me. Even my presence was not enough comfort.

Of all things, that is perhaps the most troubling, I thought, my gaze upon the few stars twinkling through the smog. *How I pray that they will become able to withstand the trials that are sure to come. For Malika absolutely must commence training in her magic and rapidly progress...*

I blew out a breath.

What twists the day had taken between the first ceremony and the last!

And the most startling of them was Elian's healing. I had known he was powerful, and the magic of the Quest had only increased the magnitude of his abilities. In our bonding, experiencing the depth of his magic had given me such a profound sense of wellbeing that even I had never known its like.

But what he had done today, out of mere instinct, was... amazing. Unbelievably amazing.

He had regenerated some of my life.

And, when his magic mixed with mine, he had cracked the curse suppressing Malika's magic.

Which hinted that his healing was more potent than a sacred athar tear. Even without amplification.

Despite the pain in my heart and the troubles on my mind, I smiled in wonder.

How beautifully had the Almighty bestowed upon us healing Light.

Only empowered by the magnificence of that blessing would Malika quickly learn to surpass me in battle.

PART 3
DEVOTED

From the writings of Lady Queen Aalia the Ideal of Light addressed to the second Quest Leader:

"Understand, my Heir, that you will face trials beyond your imagining as you endeavor to fulfill your responsibility. You will be tested until exhaustion and then yet further. Do not mistake your trials as a sign of disfavor, for trials come to those who have worth to prove. In every way, strive to inculcate this wisdom in your companions and in the people of Icilia. Gratitude is your greatest quality and your greatest responsibility. In all that you do, in all that you say, in all that you think, do not waver in your gratitude to the Almighty. Only with gratitude shall you demonstrate your worthiness of the Almighty's gifts and ascertain your success."

READ BY LORD LUCIAN AJ-SHEHATHAR

AT THE AGE OF NINETEEN

CHAPTER 30

INSPIRE THE HAUNTED

Perspective: Graced Malika the Exemplar of Wisdom
Date: Eyyédal, the sixteenth day of the first moon, Lushatte,
of the year 500, C.Q.

In spite of all my efforts, not a single word came from my lips. My throat rasped, the vocal cords rubbing against each other, but not a sound came that was more than a wordless utterance—the Blood had not wanted to deprive himself of my screams.

"It does not help you to try, Malika," Elian whispered, green eyes dark with concern.

I dropped my eyes, unable to hold his gaze, as I extended my arms and twisted to the side, stretching the taut muscles.

He was correct, but I could not seem to break the bad habit as both the Blood's jeers and Avel Asfaliett's taunts haunted my ears. Nothing I did could compensate for how I could not perform the first of my duties, speaking in Lucian's name.

Arista really ought to have been the Second. Born royal, well trained, and magically mature, she was the better choice.

But instead I chose to burden Lucian with my unworthy self, seizing what should have never been mine. Just as I stole the crown from my younger brother, depriving Koroma of an Heir capable of protecting her...

I rotated my torso in the other direction and winced at how the scratchy sensation of my scars from the Blood's prisons brushing against my clothes had faded. As much as I appreciated Lucian's and Elian's healing, I deserved every one of those scars for my failure...

"Malika!" Lucian called.

Rising to my feet, I could not meet his eyes. *Yes?* I asked.

Even with such avoidance, happiness welled in my heart, for the shine of his smile today was so bright that the top edge of my vision glowed a sunny gold. As tormented as I was, his joy was mine.

So I could not refuse him when he asked for a duel.

Though I obeyed his every instruction, desperately trying to quicken the pace of my progress as he had begun to demand after the Day of Light, I was nowhere near as ready for our first duel as he thought I was. I could not hope to face him as Arista could—I would fail miserably. But, if the exercise would please him, I would endure the embarrassment of failure.

Drawing his sword, Lucian held it loosely at his side and said in encouragement, according to his custom, "Show me, Malika."

The rest of our family backed away toward the edge of the clearing Arista had thawed for this morning's practice.

Bouncing lightly on my feet, I held my sword with both hands and crouched in a ready stance.

Beams of sunlight, the color of Lucian's hair and beard, streaming through the canopy of the Dasenákder, warmed my neck, and the wind playfully rustled my hair on its winding journey through the tree branches, smelling of rich soil, living wood, and crushed pine. The nearby presence of rivers and streams, chortling merrily as they nourished trees towering nearly three hundred feet above the ground, tingled my senses. The entire forest, though bearing its own ravages from the Blood's cruel fist, emitted palpable delight at Lucian's presence.

Soaking in the stately beauty of Nademan's forest, I managed to achieve a sufficient degree of battle-focus.

Without warning, I sprang forwards and struck at his sword-arm.

Lucian stepped aside, letting me pass him. He swung his sword, still one-handed, toward my back.

I ducked close to the ground, invoked the spell controlling the sword's weight, and sliced toward his ankles. As I did so, I spun my body outward, arching it away from his blade.

His swing missed its target, leaving him unbalanced, but he smoothly jumped over the curve of my sword.

He landed back on his feet and spun toward me in a crouch just as I caught myself with a hand, removing it from my hilt, and vaulted to a standing position.

Before I could take a breath, Lucian struck, lifting his sword with both hands and driving it toward my head in a powerful blow.

I only just managed to lighten my sword and raise it up in a block.

His sword hit mine with resounding force, jarring my arms.

Just as the metal collided, he kicked my ankle, ruining my balance. Between that kick and his powerful blow, I fell backwards.

He swung toward me, but I quickly rolled out of the way, as he had taught me.

His sword came to rest a hair above where my head would have been if I had not moved.

As he turned, swinging his blade up, I used the momentum of my roll to surge to my feet.

"Malika, you can do better," Lucian said calmly as he walked, almost strolled, toward me. Despite the casualness of his appearance, that walk was more of a prowl, like that of the lion we had seen from afar in northern Zahacim.

I controlled my breathing and focused.

Then attacked again, slicing toward his left side.

He moved to block the strike, which was really a distraction for my kick to his right shin—a move I had once seen Arista use.

The kick landed, and he grunted, stumbling forward.

But, before I could press the advantage, he removed one hand from his sword and punched my shoulder. At the same moment, he shoved my sword back with his own and sliced toward my side.

Only my stumble backward at his punch gave me the momentum to dodge his cut.

I quickly disengaged and brought my sword up in a guarding position.

So did he.

"Malika, you can do better," he repeated.

I pressed my lips together.

I did not think I could do better. I truly did not. He surely had his reasons to push me as he did, but I could not fulfill his wishes. As incapable and unworthy as ever.

But Lucian has spoken. And he is always right.

And... had I not begun to win half my matches with Arista?

Perhaps he is right.

He was right.

I could do better.

I could do better.

I could do better.

I can win.

That thought was a spark.

My awareness condensed to the blade in my hand, the strength in my body, and the person of my opponent. My muscles thrummed with energy, and my vision sharpened. I could see, no, *sense*, every shift in Lucian's stance, every dip and rise in the angle of his sword.

I thought of a tactic.

Then moved—and my limbs were but streaks of blue as I twisted my torso away and back, the heavy sword raised with both hands for a powerful blow on his side.

Lucian met the attack with a fierce smile and his raised sword.

Where our swords met, sparks flew from the grating of the metal. My arms did not shake.

"Excellent," he praised through clenched teeth.

I disengaged and then swung again, smoothly ordering the sword's weight to change and feinting toward his shoulder. He moved to block it, and I cut toward his leg.

Lucian blocked my sword again, then kicked toward my left knee.

Somehow, I was fast enough to jump backward and dodge the blow.

He beamed and slashed up toward my left shoulder.

I dodged, curving below his blade and swinging mine toward his left leg. I freed a hand and punched toward his stomach.

Somehow, both blows landed, and he gasped.

Then I did as his sword curved back and hit my left shoulder. The blade did not cut or even bruise, of course, since I was his companion and that was his Quest Leader's sword, but it did momentarily sting.

I tumbled to the ground, then rolled to my feet as he bounced back.

"Well done, Sister!" he called. "Now, can you continue?"

I had not lost my focus.

I streaked toward him again, tucking my arms into my stomach in preparation for a thrust.

This time, he ran to meet my charge, his stride as smooth as the steel of his blade. He raised his sword for a cut toward my left side.

As we met, I angled myself slightly outward and kicked at his right ankle. As his foot went back, putting him off balance, I thrust toward his chest. But just as the tip of my sword hovered above his heart, he twisted his left foot around my right ankle and toppled me.

Before I could blink, I was on the ground, and the tip of his sword pointed at my throat.

The intensity of my focus faded as I stared up at him, and he down at me.

Then his own focus melted into a dazzling smile. He sheathed his sword and scooped me up into his embrace. "You won, Malika!" he cheered.

My eyes widened, and my sword fell from numb fingers.

I won? I asked. *But I ended up on the ground with your sword pointed at me, did I not?*

"Yes, yes, it was a narrow victory," Lucian said, laughing, "but had we been in battle, your final blow would have defeated your enemy before he could topple you." He laughed again and spun me around, then cradled me to his chest, arms tightening in a gentle squeeze.

His enthusiasm was infectious, and, despite all of my doubt, he *was* right. As always. And his laughter silenced the taunts.

Dropping any thought of protest, I grinned shyly and relaxed against him. *You are the best teacher, Lucian. This is only possible because of you.*

He squeezed me again in answer, then drew back and kissed my forehead. "Malika, you are the worthiest Second for whom I could have ever asked." His violet eyes pierced mine.

My face heated. But, for once, I could not help but think he was right.

He *had* been right about my ability to do better. What if he was right about me as a whole?

What if... what if his belief in me was justified? His conviction that I could excel as quickly as he desired well-founded?

It was an overwhelming thought, a diametric contrast to how I had felt mere minutes ago, and too much to comprehend.

So I pushed it aside as our family rushed to us and began to congratulate me.

"You actually beat the Quest Leader in a spar, Malika!" Elian said reverently. "And you've only been training for four months!"

"How did you *do* that?" Arista exclaimed. "Even *I* have not done that!" There was only wholehearted enthusiasm in her voice, not a single trace of jealousy marring her clear eyes.

"Malika! That was awesome!" Elacir bounced up and down, cocoa face shining with childish delight.

Kyros chuckled as he retrieved my sword, wiped it, and somehow maneuvered it into the sheath attached to my belt. Then he hugged both Lucian and me.

Arista grinned and tossed her arms around our waists. Not willing to be left out, Elian did the same, carefully avoiding touching me. After a word of encouragement from Arista, even Elacir joined, snuggling against Elian and Kyros.

Lucian's chest expanded in a deep sigh. He kissed my forehead and then rested his head against mine. Peace radiated from him like warm light from the sun.

Amid such contentment, I could forget the torment. At least for a while.

All too soon, Lucian directed us to prepare for the day's travel. We broke our fasts, packed our belongings, and wiped the traces of our presence. Elian and Arista even spread snow over the clearing. Once the ground appeared as though we had never passed, we mounted our horses and entered the thick pillars of the tree trunks, which gleamed the same gentle brown as Kyros' cheeks.

The odd bare shrub or bush peeked through the snow, itself mostly untouched save for the odd spare twig and the meandering prints of small animals. Even my ears, though nowhere near as sharp as Kyros' in the forest (enhanced by kind-magic rather than farsight) and as Lucian's everywhere, registered the faint strains of birdsong and whispering branches.

But it was no idyllic setting: despite all the water and snow, drought cracked tree bark into masses of wood which often shed splinters at the touch of a breeze. Very few animals stirred, even for the winter, and what few did were nearly skeletal. The rivers flowed at lesser capacity than their banks indicated they otherwise would. And every so often blood marked the trees—the last evidence of untold tragedies.

The scent of smoke assaulting my nose seemed almost appropriate.

CHAPTER 31

SUCCOR
THE TORMENTED

Perspective: Graced Malika the Exemplar of Wisdom
Date: Eyyédal, the sixteenth day of the first moon, Lushatte,
of the year 500, C.Q.

I blinked and sniffed the air. No, I was not mistaken—that actually was the scent of smoke. Leaning around Arista, I opened my mouth to call Lucian's attention. Then flinched at the reminder of my limitations.

Before I could switch to the link, Kyros tilted his head back and asked frantically, *Lucian, is that what I think it is?*

Lucian nodded. *Yes. Follow it with your farsight.*

Kyros grimaced as he closed his eyes. And inhaled sharply. *About seven miles to the northwest, there is a village burning. I think it is why we did not see any soldiers on the border... They are leaving, traveling north...* He whimpered. *They tortured them, Lucian!*

Lucian gave the rest of us a glance, but he did not need to ask, for we returned his resolve.

With unspoken agreement, Lucian and Arista immediately spurred our horses into a canter, the highest speed the horses could achieve amid the trees.

We will not reach them in time to stop the soldiers, Kyros warned as he bounced in the saddle behind Lucian. *They will be gone by then. It is... it is much like Temerilt, and we will arrive at the end of it. Some people still live, but we may only be able to save a few.*

That itself is enough reason to go, Lucian said, his voice tight and pained.

The minutes dragged, hours seeming to pass before we came upon a group of trees, three hundred feet tall and clustered tightly together, separated by a wide swathe of cultivated field from the main forest: a tree-town, composed of covered platforms built high in the treetops and connected by walkways, the bases of the trunks surrounded by gardens and poultry pens. Hedges, reminiscent of those guarding Nademan's border, encircled the cluster.

It was all aflame.

Bodies lay strewn everywhere. Bits of sinew and bone streaked the huts, blood flooded the herbs and vegetables once grown with such devotion... Limbs clung to the sides of the hedges, still hooked around the leafless branches, their lives stolen amid final desperate attempts to escape. The air was filled with the groans of the dying and the tormented. Many of the enormous trees, so precious to the Nasimih, had been brutally uprooted and themselves now crushed the people who had once treasured them.

The image of fire and death wavered, blurring into another city ablaze, the quaint patchwork of humble houses and tall towers crumbling under the blows of brutal fists, smoke and conjury tainting the sky charcoal... screams quaking the earth, shattering the very mountains... sobs shrieking from my brother's mouth, echoing out of sight in the corridors... ruby blood painting the marble floor like a grotesque mockery of a child's painting, seeping from my parents' writhing bodies... Black fingers crushed my wrist and—

"Malika!"

I jerked, the memory of Samaha losing clarity...

Cool fingers touched my cheeks.

My vision cleared.

And I looked up into Lucian's anguished face.

"Malika, I am with you," he murmured and hugged me. "But I need you to stand at my side. I know what you remember, but I must ask for your support."

I shuddered, the memory still lingering in the corners of my mind, but forcibly composed myself. *What do you wish?* I asked.

Lucian helped me off my stallion's saddle onto the ground. Then he took his athar cloth handkerchief from a pocket and tied it over my mouth and nose (though his own face was uncovered). *Wear it until Arista has quenched the fire. Elian and I will heal whomever we can, and Kyros will use the salve. But I must ask you and Elacir to begin the burial immediately. I do not want those bodies to burn if we can save them the dishonor.*

I bowed my head. *As you wish.*

With a nod, Lucian strode into the middle of the massacre. He walked directly to the crashed ruins of a house and threw aside a broken wall. Beneath it lay a woman, moaning in pain, her clothes torn to shreds. Removing his coat, Lucian knelt by her side and covered her exposed body before he touched her forehead and began to chant a spell.

Masking is in place, he said.

A few paces away from Lucian, Elian found another woman, only just clinging to life, and placed a hand on her head. The scales visible above the handkerchief shielding his mouth and nose began to glow—not as potently as on the Day of Light, but enough to show his use of the few spells he had since managed to learn.

Kyros approached a young man and, kneeling, caked Lucian's enchanted salve into a laceration spanning the length of his torso.

Standing in the middle of the flames, Arista raised both hands, palms up and glowing green veined with a fiery cherry.

Elacir and I tied the horses to still-standing trees and strode for the nearest corpse, a man stabbed in the stomach such that his organs spilled onto the snow. Our hands dripped warm blood as we carried him to the spot I had chosen, a bare, unravaged patch at the base of a fallen tree at the edge of the town.

Turning, we retrieved another corpse, brutally murdered after suffering violence.

Then another. And another. And another. Barely pausing to cough out the smoke trickling under the handkerchiefs into our mouths. Not noticing the heat of the flames, blistering despite the winter day.

Arista's spell began to take effect: the fires died, the flames losing strength until only embers smoldered. Then even those were extinguished, and only steam and acrid smoke remained. Then even that, too, was gone, the particles condensing and falling to the earth in controlled showers of soot, melting and mixing with the bloody snow.

I wiped the ash from my face with the clean part of the handkerchief, tucked the cloth in a pocket, and continued.

Lucian, Elian, and Kyros gathered a group of women and men, all of them young, near the horses. None had woken, unconscious from horror and agony, but many seemed to rest easier.

Once Elacir and I had assembled all the corpses accessible from the ground, I located a shovel in a nearby garden. While Elacir retrieved the corpses in the trees, I slammed the metal blade in the mud and began to dig.

Seventy-eight corpses. Men. Women. Children.

Nineteen people, survivors in the loosest sense, all grievously burnt and abused. All but three were women. No children.

Kyros' farsight confirmed what we suspected: no one had managed to escape to the woods. Not a single soldier had fallen.

They had been defenseless.

Tears streaked the grime on my face.

How senseless this cruelty is! Such loss of life—and for what? The Gouge's pleasure?

In the beginning, the Blood and his governors had claimed they would give all who chose them true freedom— freedom from all manner of laws and rules, the freedom to live exactly how one pleased. Unadulterated, unrestricted freedom, they claimed and so persuaded many.

But all their so-spoken freedom had brought was such pain, such destruction.

For when everyone was told to pursue their pleasure without restraint, when there was no law to instill a fear of punishment, the restraints of morality were abandoned. Pleasure was sought at the expense of others. And necessarily those most able to seek their pleasure, the strongest few, seized more of their delights than anyone else.

Who was most able in the Blood's land but the Blood and his governors?

They seized and seized and seized. And no law existed to stop them. No moral code raised doubt in their hearts. So they wreaked untold destruction, all for their insatiable appetites for pleasure. And what was more savagely pleasurable than violence and murder?

They did not have freedom. A land in which everyone was enslaved to vicious appetites, even the tyrants, had no freedom.

No, freedom was held by my Leader, who tirelessly spent his own energy to heal person after person. His face was drawn in focus, his eyes dull and pained, his lips tight, his body stiff and slumping with exhaustion, but still he worked.

He was our freedom. His virtue, his wisdom, his compassion, courage, and strength in saving Icilia, were what gave freedom. His laws, the laws of the Almighty that nurtured such holiness, were what gave freedom.

Indeed, the Blood was mistaken and Icilia a fool to believe any but the Quests. For freedom did not lie in the absence of law and virtue but in its presence.

The Blood's regime needed to be destroyed. And his influence eradicated.

With this conviction crystallizing in clear strands of thought, I understood that I could not flinch from my duty as the Quest Second. No matter the doubt that crippled me, choked my confidence, strangled all thoughts of learning the sword as he wished—no matter what, I had to do better. The freedom of Icilia was at stake. And Lucian had no time for me to wallow in doubting his choice.

Such words were easily spoken. Doubt did not shrivel under the burn of emotion, only under the pressure of sustained conviction. Yet if I truly loved him as I claimed, I could not falter any further than I already had.

The shovel beat the rhythm of battle as it struck the earth.

I memorized that pattern, the memory of my resolve to attain the discipline needed for unyielding faith.

Completing a fifth of the massive grave required, I called out for Elacir in the link.

A moment later, he appeared overhead, informing me that he had gathered every corpse, and began to lower the first of the bodies down to me.

I tucked my unraveling braid beneath the collar of my coat and gently took the man's remains. I pressed him into the earth and took another. Then another. And another.

Once half of the twelve feet of vertical space was filled, Elacir helped me up, found another shovel, and began digging the next hole. I connected it to the first.

Arista joined us once she was sure the fire was entirely quenched. Her magic, used with Lucian's permission, rapidly increased the pace of our work.

Halfway through the burial, a woman shrieked.

The three of us scrambled out of the hole and scanned our surroundings for the threat.

A woman, one of the townsfolk, was scrambling away from Kyros' large form. She appeared to have just woken and seemed wild with terror, thrashing frantically even as her body convulsed with pain. Her words slurred together too much to comprehend.

Lucian ordered, *Malika, Arista, switch with Kyros.*

Wiping our bloody hands on our robes, we cautiously approached the group of women.

As more opened their eyes, they cried and recoiled from Elian as well as Kyros.

Our friends were disheartened, heartbroken, as they retreated. Only Lucian stayed, healing another unconscious woman's arm.

Arista and I halted ten feet from them. Lowered ourselves to our knees. Then began to slowly crawl toward them.

Some calmed slightly at the sight of us, but others still seemed terrified.

I gritted my teeth. *Some of their abusers were female soldiers.*

What? Elian whispered, horrified, his scales almost black.

It happens every way, Elian, Kyros said, watching the cringing women with sorrow.

The women who choose cruelty and malice, Arista said, *like the men, have no inhibitions. Yes, there are fewer women who do this, but only slightly so. They are just as brutal.* Her eyes flashed with the bleak glow of nightmarish memories.

I fought the suffocation of my own.

Concentrate, Malika, I told myself. *This is no time for a second incident.*

But, if I could barely ward off my own terrors, how could I help these people?

Their screams broke my heart as they panicked at the sight of us…

…all of us except Lucian.

None of the women reacted so fearfully to him. Indeed, many seemed to be unconsciously edging in his direction.

Lucian, I murmured, his name a plea on my lips.

He glanced up from where he healed a wound that had riven a woman's torso.

Even in this circumstance, I jerked at the illness apparent on his face. His violet eyes were duller than I had yet seen them, the color closer to black than purple. Bags lined his eyes, and his sunlight hair and beard did not shine. The silver of his beautiful face was the pallid gray of sickness, the same as the tinge still tainting my own.

He is not well! I shouted, though in my own thoughts. *He does too much! But… how could I ask him to stop? He sees this as his duty, and I have no place to question him, even as his Second… Wait.*

From their sharp inhales of breath, the rest of us had seen what I had.

Quickly assembling words, I entreated, *Lucian, if it would conform to your wishes, would you comfort them? I think that, perhaps, they now need that healing most…*

An eyebrow slanted up—a sign that he knew my double intentions—but he nodded.

At the edge of my periphery, the three men woke and shivered as they curled into balls.

Lucian started to rise onto his knees just as the woman whom he had been healing stirred. She instinctually reached for his hand and clutched it, then stared up at him in confusion. She was in pain and frightened yet not terrified to the point of irrationality.

Even amid her agony, she felt the peace and warmth of Lucian's presence.

A grim satisfaction emitted from him in the link. *You discern correctly, Malika.*

I dipped my head to him.

Lucian spoke aloud, "Blessings, my sisters and my brothers." His voice was quiet yet resonant around us, the rich, musical tones vibrating the earth and soothing my very bones.

The women quietened, screams fading. Both the women and the men turned or raised their heads enough to behold him.

Lucian smiled, the expression as gentle as the one he had worn when he had lifted me from the filth. "My sisters and my brothers, I am Lord Lucian the Ideal of Freedom, Heir to the Quest of Light and the supreme ruler of Icilia." He gestured at us. "These women and men are my companions and my little brother."

The dirty faces of the townsfolk contorted in disbelief.

"I assure you that you are safe under our care," Lucian continued. "We learned of your plight several hours ago..." He described when and how we had learned of their village's peril and what we had done since our arrival, and, with each word he spoke, the townsfolk's tense bodies relaxed just a little more.

I dearly prayed that they would not blame him for not arriving in time to save them outright. Just as I dearly prayed that Lucian would not blame himself.

When Lucian had completed saying what he wished, there was utter silence. Even the wind was still.

Then one of the women whispered hoarsely, "Have you really come, my Lord? Is it truly you?" Her expression was difficult to discern beneath the blood, grime, and burns, but her voice sounded desperate.

"I have," Lucian answered. "I ascended in the moon of Marberre in the previous year and have since traveled Icilia in search of my companions, as is my first duty. Now we, the Quest united, have come to Nademan to begin our reconquest. This is the foreordained time."

The woman nodded slowly. Then she lurched forward, dropped her head onto Lucian's folded knees, and began to cry. Heaving sobs racked her frame as she moaned, "You must save us, my Lord! We cannot bear anymore!"

Lucian lightly stroked her hair. "I know. Your pain is my own," he said quietly. From the torment and tears in his own eyes, his sincerity was all too evident.

The other women began to sob as well. Some pressed their faces into my knees, and others placed my hands on their foreheads, and a few touched Arista's hands and knees in the same way. The men cried at Elian's and Kyros' feet. Their wailing, though not loud, shook the very soil of the forest.

The enchantment of Nademan rippled with distress... and contentment. Drinking in the solace of Lucian's presence just as her people were.

CHAPTER 32

SOOTHE THE BEREAVED

Perspective: Graced Malika the Exemplar of Wisdom
Date: Eyyédal, the sixteenth day of the first moon, Lushatte,
of the year 500, C.Q.

As the moments wore on, though, I became increasingly more uncomfortable. I stroked the heads of some as Lucian had and hugged others, but my touch was awkward and uneasy. I had not chosen to touch anyone beside my new family in sixteen years, and I had no voice with which to reassure them.

To my chagrin, Elian was as distressed as I was. Though he had a voice to speak reassurances, he seemed pained by their touch in a way even I was not.

Arista and Kyros were better suited, almost as much as Lucian, to this duty.

Still, incomprehensibly, the women who had come to me clung to my side.

Many minutes passed amid the quiet keening and the soft whispers of my family.

Until Lucian called out, "My sisters and my brothers, please give us time. The sun is close to setting, and I wish to have the grave prepared and a shelter readied by dark."

The townsfolk reluctantly peeled themselves away.

The woman who had spoken before muttered, ashamed, "We should be the ones to bury our family."

Others nodded in agreement.

Lucian soothed them with a smile. "We do this in your place. Honor us so. In the meanwhile, let us share our provisions so that you possess the strength to pray when the grave is readied."

They reluctantly agreed.

Turning his attention to us, Lucian ordered, *You know what to do for the burial. Elian, build a shelter. Large enough for twenty-five people and three horses—there may be snow tonight, if the gray clouds on the horizon are any indication. Kyros, Elacir, follow his instruction. I will distribute food and hunt more if necessary.*

Obeying, we split for our tasks.

Though minutes flew away like the clods of soil flowing through the streams of hot air Arista had cast, within two hours the grave was ready.

Climbing out, I paused to survey the darkening clearing: Lucian cleaned and roasted fresh meat, while Elian, Kyros, and Elacir built a shelter from the town's stockpile of firewood (as Kyros had said in the link), as well as salvageable wood from the ruins. The shelter, stretching over the heads of the townsfolk, covered much of the swathe of open land between the town's trees and the main forest. It would be spacious enough for all of us.

Arista and I approached Lucian.

"It is as you wished, my Lord," Arista reported.

Lucian nodded. "How long until the snow arrives, your Honor Kyros of Light?"

Jamming a sharpened log into the ground, Kyros tilted his head. "The storm is maybe a half an hour away, my Lord."

"We will be ready in time, my Lord," Elian added, carefully sharpening another log. "But we must beg your leave to not attend the funeral."

Lucian gave them a smile. "Excellent. Do as you deem prudent, your Honors." He rose to his feet and paused, a flash of unease crossing his face so quickly that I doubted any but his family had caught it.

What troubles you, Lucian? I asked.

We need warming spells at the beginning of the night, he replied, *because this shelter will not magnify our warmth as quickly as the one in Bhalasa. Only a few minutes are necessary. But...* wryness tinged his voice, *I cannot mask any of your spells, Arista. Would you still be willing?*

Arista radiated alarm in the link. *Lucian, please do not overextend yourself! We can take this risk, but we cannot chance your health.*

Lucian impressed a sigh into the link. *My gratitude.* Then aloud he said, "If you would follow me, my sisters and my brothers, let us honor your families." He offered his hand to one of the women, as did I.

Only with our support did the townsfolk reach the grave.

Most of them collapsed in tears as soon as they were close enough to look inside. The few remaining knelt slowly, their lips moving in silent prayer.

Lucian and I stepped back to afford them privacy in their grief.

We waited—until Lucian cast an uneasy glance at the approaching storm and gently urged the townsfolk to quiet. "Who would pour the first handful of soil?" he asked.

The townsfolk looked at each other and then at him. "You should, my Lord," one of the men whispered.

Lucian dipped his head and poured the first handful from the earth I had displaced for the grave. He nodded to me, and I poured the next.

Then each of the townsfolk scooped up as much as they could and poured their handfuls. They cried as they did so, each sprinkle of earth bringing forth their tears... and contenting them, I thought.

The contentment was clear on their faces, yes, but I also knew that, if I had been given the chance, burying my own family would have eased much of the lingering torment in my heart. But I doubted anyone had ever gone to bury them.

Once each of the townsfolk had taken their turn, I grasped my shovel and filled the rest of the grave. Lucian retrieved a flask to empty into the earth.

When the soil was dark with moisture, he knelt and lamented as he had in Temerilt, chanting first the ritual prayer and the funeral dirge of the Mutharrim.

Clustered behind him, the townsfolk murmured Nademan's versions and their own pleas beneath the soaring tones of his voice.

I grimaced painfully, wistfully, as I accompanied Lucian in the link. These townsfolk, like those of Temerilt, received a blessing amid their horrors in Lucian's performance of these rites. How I wished someone had mourned over the bones of Samaha, my birthplace, with even a fraction of his compassion and eloquence.

As the last note of the dirge faded, Lucian gave his own blessing, assuring the dead of the care he would give to the lives of the few family members who survived them.

Transfixed by the prayer of the Quest Leader himself, the townsfolk were silent for a moment.

One of the women wailed. Followed by another. Then they all began to cry, pressing their hands to the grave's earth and sobbing prayers. Lucian whispered several more of his own, and I gave mine in the link.

As those laments reached their conclusion, cold drops touched my forehead.

Lucian commanded, "Come. The storm is about to break." His words were easily heard over the harshening wind.

The townsfolk hurriedly rose to their feet.

Lucian drew a dagger and turned to the wood Arista had enchanted to serve as a grave marker. *Lead them, Malika.*

Swallowing back a wave of fear, I remembered my conviction and gestured for the townsfolk to follow me.

Though I had no voice, they obeyed and hobbled inside the shelter just as the wind began to howl.

It will be quite a storm, I said, observing the first spatters of snow as I waited for Lucian.

I think it is only the second since the start of winter, Elian commented. *Much of this snow is old and congealed—like what we saw in Bhalasa's foothills and on the plains.*

Arista impressed a scowl. *Neither the lack of storms nor the presence is good. How wonderful.*

Even Lucian and Kyros chuckled.

Turning, I noted that this shelter had enough room for even Elian and Kyros, the tallest of all of us, to easily stand. Each of the walls and the roof seemed sturdy enough, despite their hasty construction out of wood and rope, to bear the wind and snow. In the center of the shelter, the townsfolk huddled, wrapped in our blankets and Lucian's, Elian's, and Arista's coats. Elian and Arista tiptoed among them and distributed shares of meat cooling on thin sticks. Beyond them, the horses lay, dining upon the grain in their nosebags.

Most importantly, heated by Arista's spells, the little hut was warm. Warm like Kyros' cottage, one of the only houses I could remember.

My gratitude for waiting, Malika, Lucian said. The illness on his shining face, I gladly saw, had receded somewhat.

I stepped aside for him as he entered and immediately knelt to carve the last of the roasted meat.

Behind him, Kyros and Elacir inserted the last branches, sealing off the shelter from the chill of the snow-laden winds, and joined Elian and Arista.

Shedding my coat, I retrieved the water flasks from the horses' saddlebags and dampened the sleeves. Then, crouching, I silently encouraged the townsfolk to wash their faces and arms of blood and grime, as well as drink a few mouthfuls of water.

Though urging them to accept my help took several minutes, once they did, they seemed to finally calm.

As always, I thought, *few things match a wash's ability to restore the first drop of one's dignity. How well I remember the first shock of water after my escape. As I will never forget Lucian's offer of protection.*

Across the shelter, Kyros removed his own coat and copied me.

Once the townsfolk had supped and seemed as comfortable as any could be on bare earth, my family and I gathered on the far side of the shelter with our own supper and the last full flask.

Though my family used the last damp patch on Kyros' coat to wash their faces and hands, they did not open the flask.

It is for you, Elian whispered, offering it to me in cupped hands, with the others' agreement.

Thanking them, I smiled wearily and relaxed against the wall. Uncapping the flask, I took a sip—and sighed as the thirst throttling my throat was quenched.

Lucian intoned a prayer for our meal, and too soon we found that we had devoured all of the remaining meat.

Arista sighed and leaned against the wall beside me. *With twenty-five mouths, we will need to hunt again tomorrow. There are only a few pieces of travel bread left.*

We will need to hunt the day after as well, Kyros said, sitting on my other side. *Although how we will track prey in this blizzard I do not know.*

Tilting my head, I realized he was right: while we had been preoccupied in caring for the townsfolk, the wind had quietened outside in the eerie mark of a blizzard (according to Elian and Kyros).

Leaning back on his hands, Elian commented, *Though it does not bode well for Icilia as a whole, I do think we are blessed to encounter only the one blizzard so far.*

Definitely better here than in Bhalasa, Elacir grumbled—his first words since our arrival at Filisso's ruins. While we comforted the townsfolk, he had simply watched, his only reaction the new determination that fueled his efforts.

His dedication brought a fond grin to my lips. *Your expertise would have certainly been useful there.*

Brightening, he grinned at me. *Thank you, Big Sister!*

All of us laughed, welcoming the moment of respite after such a terrible day.

Except—I suddenly realized—Lucian.

Who sat, tensed, head lowered, forearms resting on his thighs.

Drawing my brows together, I straightened and hesitantly touched a finger. *Lucian?* I asked, beginning to panic—what if *he* was experiencing some torturous memory? He had so many from his dreams!

Exhaling heavily, Lucian looked up and smiled at our worried faces. But that smile did not dazzle as the ones he gave us usually did. Instead, pain formed creases in the smooth skin of his face, and tears sparkled in his dulled violet eyes. Then he said, *This day marks the anniversary of my birth.*

We stared at him for a moment of utter horror.

Then scrambled to hug him, Arista, Kyros, and me from the front and Elian and Elacir from behind.

Blessings for your birthday! we cried.

Lucian sighed, more contented than a moment before, and hugged Arista and me. *My gratitude.*

Why did you not tell us earlier? Elacir exclaimed.

We should have celebrated! Elian said mournfully. *I could have made a special meal, somehow. It is the Quest Leader's birthday, and we did nothing to mark it!*

Celebration, Arista lamented, *would at least have given you a different memory for the day than this afternoon and evening.*

I am sorry that all of this happened on your birthday, I whispered. *It is your twenty-third, the first after your ascension. It was meant to be honored.*

Why did you not tell us last night? Kyros asked, echoing Elacir. *We would have found a way to prepare gifts.* He sniffled and tightened his embrace around all of us.

Lucian chuckled, the sound not entirely mirthful. *All I wanted was your congratulations,* he said quietly. *Your presence and your caring about my happiness are enough. And I received the greatest gift I could receive in Malika's victory today and your devotion thereafter.*

My face heated even as my lips parted in wonder. How worthy accepting his challenge had then truly been, regardless of how unprepared I felt to fulfill these new demands of his training.

As beautiful as Malika's victory is, you deserve more, Arista said firmly. *You are the Quest Leader and our dearest brother and savior. You deserve more.*

I added my own unspoken impression of agreement.

Lucian again laughed that not quite joyful laugh. *Perhaps. But this is what I want. Your love is all I need.*

In response, we hugged him more tightly and whispered, *Blessings for your twenty-third birthday, Lucian.*

He radiated contentment.

Then Elacir drew back, stood, and jumped into a low flight above the townsfolk's heads, his wings brushing against the walls. He landed by the horses, removed something from a saddlebag, flew back, and dropped to his knees beside us.

We gave him curious looks.

One of his hands clenched in a fist, Elacir grinned shyly. *We have some honey left from the Day of Light.*

In response, Lucian's face brightened with a dazzling smile, one of utter contentment and joy, one I had not thought I would be blessed to see again this day. *I do love honey.*

We basked in the glow of that smile, warmed as though by the sun, as Elacir uncorked the tiny jar, filled the bowl of an equally tiny spoon, and proffered the utensil.

My gratitude, Elacir, Lucian said as he accepted the handle. Raising the spoon to his lips, he swallowed the few drops it contained.

Blessings for your birthday, my Lord, Elacir whispered.

Lucian smiled softly and closed his eyes. At peace. Despite the troubles that had marred his birthday and the absences of his father and his brother.

Savoring the sight, I vowed to excel in battle as he wished. Regardless of the Blood's taunts. Even if I never understood why he was asking more of me now than he had but a month before.

For his peace was mine.

SEGMENT 1

PROVING COMPETENCE

Perspective: Prince Darian sej-Shehasfiyi, brother of the Quest Leader and auxiliary heir to the throne of Asfiya
Date: Eyyésal, the twenty-second day of the first moon, Lushatte, of the year 500, C.Q.

The sword clunked as it landed on the ground.

"You have not improved, your Highness."

Despite all the confidence I so dearly wanted to portray, my shoulders hunched at those words, fisting my trembling hands, newly bruised from the spar.

"How do you expect to serve our Lord if you cannot equal your mother's skill?" Low, quiet, even, disappointed words.

I did not drop her gaze only because I had been taught that a prince never should.

"When he returns, your Highness," Taza said, "do not be surprised to find yourself without a place at his side." That brutal warning delivered, she walked away, leaving me alone, coated in mud, on the sparring field.

Suppressing my emotions, I waited until the base commander's ring told me she had left the inner circle of the fortress' trees. Then, swiping my sword, I ran for the tallest, the only one with branches sturdy enough to sit upon at its crown that were not visible from the ground.

It had been one of Lucian's and my favorite spots whenever we had visited this base.

And it was the place I now went to remind myself of him.

He never let Taza, or any of his other guardians, treat me so poorly. But, in his absence, there was no one to remember me. No one to see my value. No one to care for me.

I could not remember anything different. From my earliest memories, Lucian had been the center of my family's world. Parents, grandfather, aunts, uncles, cousins, courtiers—those trusted enough to know of him lived and breathed for his sake, devoting every possible moment to his education, training, and comfort. Though he was the youngest of our family, he was our ruler, our hero, our salvation, Asfiya's hope and Icilia's soul. And, in his shadow, amid such enamor for his light, I was forgotten.

Save by him.

Though Lucian was the future supreme ruler of Icilia from the day he was born and I a lackluster spare prince, he had cared for me. He had always included me, always wanted my presence, always comforted me amid my fears and doubts. Even as he prepared for his destiny, he had never treated me with even an iota less than the respect an elder brother should have.

Even after his maturity, when he was endlessly plagued by nightmares so terrible that he roused himself with his own screams, he soothed away my terrors and ensured I received the training I desired.

Even after his ascension, when he became the Quest Leader entire, he remembered to speak to me and fondly bid me farewell.

He had adored me far more than I merited.

Small wonder then that I had never been jealous, in even the slightest degree, of the younger brother who was in every way more than I could ever dream of becoming. Indeed I wholly embraced the role for which I had been raised, his aide, shield, and the herald of his court.

Thus, for Taza, the woman who had come closest to becoming a second mother, to say I had no place at his side... was there nothing I could do that would ever be enough? Even the most rancorous of the guardians, the elderly scholar Ezam Talaméze, called me Icilia's next master of magical scholarship, of such magnitude was my skill in designing and deciphering the inner workings of spells, second only to Lucian's own. Even Taza herself acknowledged my prowess in military planning and strategic command of Lucian's fortresses. Yes, to my frustration as well as theirs, I could not seem to achieve true proficiency in battle—as though there was some unknown *thing* I awaited—but surely what I did excel in was enough? Surely *I* was enough?

The tears welling in my eyes spilled onto my cheeks.

As desperately as I wished to be reunited with Lucian, I feared that, when the moment came, I would find that I truly was *not* enough. For how could an incompetent spare prince retain any worth before the Potentates of the Quest? How could a sibling bond forged by blood compare with those sprung from divine blessing?

I was as Ezam once raged—a burden, valueless save for my blood, and my life would have better served Lucian if I had given it in Asfiya's capture as the other heirs did. Not even my own father saw me as anything more than an unnecessary responsibility.

"Lucian…" I breathed. "Lucian…"

Only his name ignited enough strength in my heart to begin the preparations I had so long delayed: composing the lessons his companions would need.

My lips curved down in a bitter scowl. I did not lust after the Potentates' offices—I would never so disrespect the divine blessing bestowed upon them—but I wanted as little to do with them as possible. Yet, before his departure, Lucian asked his family to help him provide education and training to his companions. And, probably knowing my distaste for the task, the guardians decided to leave the burden of preparation and most of the teaching on my shoulders.

I would fulfill the duty regardless—it was what an aide did. As long as my brother had use for me, I would serve him.

Closing my eyes, I finished a mental list of the materials and topics requisite for history, entrusted the notes to the perfection of my memory, and then turned to literature and the sciences. I would need to confer with Lucian about the topics on which he had already lectured…

As I switched to the subject of magic, the base commander's ring, which linked me with every inch of athar-infused tree and soil that comprised the fortress, heated on my hand.

Ilqan must have returned from his patrol.

Twisting my long slim fingers, I tapped the top of the emerald adorning the simple silver band.

The living base responded, eagerly warming to my attention like the beloved pony of my childhood, recognizing my royal blood, powerful athar magic, and sincere interest in her welfare.

Unable to help a slight smile, I asked for the veins of wood, water, and athar to relay the sounds of Ilqan's conversation with Taza.

Such intrusion, particularly upon spouses, was certainly not a holy act on my part. But they refused every question I asked about the status of the guardians' task, spreading rumors and clandestine aid to Nademan's towns on Lucian's behalf since his ascension. Far beyond simply not involving me, though rumors and aid did not require a level of weapons skill beyond my reach, they seemed determined to keep me ignorant.

The trees shook in disapproval but obeyed, knowing my reasons with the form of sentience they possessed, and brought to me the guardians' voices:

"... yet more evidence," Ilqan was saying, "of the troops' withdrawal to the garrisons at Pethama and the Zaiqani market. The forest is nearly empty of soldiers."

"You also stated the forest is no less safer," Taza said, voice firm and impassive as it was when she spoke in her capacity as general rather than wife or doting guardian.

"It is not," Ilqan said, sighing. "The new commander of the forces west of Ehaya has given direct orders for troops to harass and torment as many townsfolk as possible. Some of the soldiers I attacked were carrying these letters."

A shuffle of paper.

"Is he countermanding direct orders from the Gouge's strategist?" Taza asked, incredulity breaking through her stern focus.

"Quietly, yes, and complicating any sort of aid we might give," Ilqan said. Then he sighed again. "This development atop signs of the soldiers communicating across borders and our attempts to discover more about their plans failing... What are we going to do, Taza? How will Lucian pass safely through these lands?" It was a testament to his fear and concern that he spoke Lucian's name instead of his reverential address.

Though I disliked Ilqan (as much as anyone could detest the man who had held one's hand on countless trips to the outhouse), my heart softened, for I shared the same worry.

"That is something, Ilqan," Taza gently replied, "in which we must trust the Almighty to ensure the safety of the Almighty's own chosen."

"That is true," I whispered, leaning my head against the trunk.

Sensing the intensity of my emotions, the tree swayed gently, trying to soothe me with the rocking motion of a mother's arms.

I could not help a chuckle. "It is not the sort of worry to be rocked away, Arkaiso."

Wind whistled through the trees, blowing my beard and the stray locks of hair leaking from my cap in more attempts at comfort.

My smile widened. Amid all my doubt and anguish, how blessed I was to receive this profound response. Such depth of connection, as Lucian explained, was uniquely mine, unrivaled even among other heirs.

"I know, Taza," Ilqan said, "but it is not easy—"

I noted the shift in his tone, anxious to affectionate, and ended the relay.

Moments later, the emerald pendant pressing over my heart vibrated.

My breath caught. *That is Lucian's pattern! All my gratitude, oh Almighty!*

Fumbling with the silver chain and its amethyst and athar beads, I grasped ahold of the emerald and tapped it.

"Blessings, Brother."

The rich harmony of that voice relaxed all the tension riddling my body, bestowing a peace I had not felt since the moon of Thekharre, when he had informed us of the Quest's union.

"Blessings, Brother," I whispered into the jewel, "and especially so for your birthday." Unable to suppress the words, I then exclaimed, "I thought you would have arrived by then!" I had never been apart from him before on that sacred day, and the guardians and I, unwilling to risk his safety by initiating contact, had had a miserable celebration.

Lucian exhaled a laugh, the most beautiful sound. "My apologies, Brother. I will arrive in time for yours."

Contented, I beamed as I had not in months, despite the spell's drain on my energy. "So I will see you soon?"

"Yes, Brother," he answered. "I estimate two weeks until our arrival."

I nodded. "What do you wish?"

A smile sweetened his beloved voice. "Prepare the rooms alongside your own in the commander's quarters for six. Elacir—the boy of the Sholanar I mentioned in my communication to Father in the moon of Mirkharre—will share a room with Elian. Also prepare the study with all necessary books and the chamber adjacent with the larger maps. As for the kitchens... Darian, I also ask that you welcome my guests."

"How many?" I asked, a bit crestfallen at the thought of more demands on his attention.

"Thirteen," he answered. "Eleven women and two men, whom the Quest saved from the ruins of an Adebani town, Filisso. You might recall the skirmish we fought near her boundary in your eighteenth year."

I gasped. "Filisso is destroyed?" The news was not uncommon, but... though six years had passed, I remembered the town so clearly—I had never forgotten the face of the woman

I had helped save, and it was one of the only twelve missions on which I had been allowed to come.

"Yes," he said, voice grim, "and we could save only a few."

Calculations whirred in my mind, and bile crept up my throat. "Was that day... was it perhaps *after* your birthday?"

Lucian sighed. "We arrived in Filisso on the sixteenth of the moon of Lushatte."

My pulse roared in my ears. "Lucian! Your birthday is meant to be celebrated! The day salvation came! Not lamented upon! Did at least your companions congratulate you?"

"They did," he replied, a smile evident once more in his words. "I am blessed, Darian."

My worry for his sake immediately turned to fear for my own, and I hated myself for it.

"Darian—" Lucian began. Paused. A moment passed. Then he said, sounding distracted, "Brother, I must ask for your pardon. Kyros' farsight is about to fail, and the rebounding magic will have the force to crush bone. I must address this."

"As you wish, Lucian," I forced through numb lips. "Arkaiso will be readied in accordance with your wishes, both for your stay and for war."

"My gratitude, Darian," he said, still preoccupied. "May the Almighty be pleased with you, Brother."

Barely had I returned the greeting before he ended the contact.

I thumped my head back against the trunk, even the trees' soothing whispers bringing no smiles.

I will watch him forget me. And indeed what love would he deign to keep aside for me now that he has his beloved Malika, Elian, Arista, and Kyros? The siblings for whom he spent three years in prayer? I am but a placeholder.

And yet I would obey even when he no longer cared for me.

Lucian was Icilia's savior, but he was my savior first.

CHAPTER 33

THWART THE HUNTING

Perspective: Honored Kyros the Exemplar of Strength
Date: Eyyédal, the seventh day of the second moon, Etshatte,
of the year 500, C.Q.

The catalysis slipped from my grasp just as I saw the soldiers.

I stifled a scream. *Not again!*

A hand touched my elbow. *What happened?* Arista asked.

Though she spoke with only concern, I could not lift my gaze from the leaf litter—but nor could I entirely avoid the question. So I answered, *There are soldiers. About thirteen miles away.*

Your suspicion was correct, Lucian, Arista said, the concern immediately switched for sharp intensity.

We must presume so, Lucian answered, already battle-focused. *We have managed to avoid every patrol since Filisso, and we have adequately concealed our presence throughout this journey, save at Tresilt.*

I flinched.

Arista, noticing the movement, patted my arm. *It is not your fault.*

How I wished I could believe that.

She patted my arm again but turned back toward Lucian, who had called the attention of the townsfolk.

Shoving back my troublesome emotions, I did the same.

"Nademile," Lucian was saying, "as we have discussed, her Honor Arista of Light and I will arm each of you with a dagger. Remember her Honor's lessons on its use, and do not abstain from wielding it if you must. All of these soldiers act of their own will."

The thirteen townsfolk, eleven women and two men, bowed and curtsied with various expressions of resignation and misery.

But then, they were perpetually miserable—as I well remembered, the destruction of one's family was not a pain that shed its poignancy with time. Only Lucian's and Arista's willingness to comfort them at any time of the day or the night had strengthened them enough to come so far. Otherwise, they, too, would have perished, despite his and Elian's healing, like their six more grievously wounded branch-mates.

A shudder rippled up my spine. The memory of that morning, the day after Lucian's so poorly celebrated birthday, was still all too fresh: I would not ever forget the horror of waking to find six of our charges dead. Or the stark grief on Lucian's shining face...

Shaking myself, I steeled myself to try again. Lucian needed more information than merely a sighting. No matter the consequences of rebound, I could not risk harming him again through my negligence as I already had...

The catalysis flickered, veering alarmingly close to outright failing, but then took hold. The overlay of my magical vision fell into place, and I immediately pushed it north.

One mile... Two... I counted. *Three... Four...*

The distance flashed, faster than even the swiftest Nasimih feet could move, until I halted the sweep of magic, reaching the soldiers' position.

The captain, designated by his vermillion skull, was announcing, "— his Depravedness' orders to track large movements after observation. The new standard plan is to attack in shifts: treetops and then the two—"

The catalysis slipped again.

A whimper escaped my lips, the bit of scream I could not repress.

As preoccupied as my family was with arming our guests, all of them gave me looks of sympathy and concern.

My cheeks coarsened, the skin cracking, as shame curdled my melancholy. As always, a burden to those around me.

Lucian frowned and passed a pair of his daggers to Elian. Then he walked toward me and gripped my shoulders. *Kyros, your warning will save our lives. Your value in our family cannot be understated.*

How I wished I could accept his warm assurance. Did my very presence not imperil his safety as the villagers said I had always endangered Kalyca's?

Pain momentarily glittered in his eyes before he nodded, again battle-focused. *What did you see the second time?*

I kicked away my emotions and repeated what I had heard.

Lucian raised an eyebrow. "Shifts, hmm?"

I wrung my hands. "I am sorry I did not hear anymore—" My squeaking stopped abruptly at the grim smile curving his lips.

"Their strategies are deteriorating," he commented, chuckling without mirth. Then, pivoting on his heel, he called, "My family, Nademile, I ask for your attention."

We obeyed.

He spoke, "We have still much of a day's travel from Arkaiso, while the soldiers will be upon us by noon. I estimate that they will attack first from the trees, followed by a delay, then a second attack on a flank, a second delay, and finally a third attack on another flank. With such a three-prong strategy, I estimate a force of at least three squads.

"We will respond in this manner: Elacir, you and I will counter the soldiers in the rooftops. Your focus is to defend against their descent. Arista, counter the first of the two ground attacks. Malika, Elian, counter the second." He paused, glanced at the dim morning light which streamed through the smog above the forest canopy, and motioned for us to resume walking. Then he said, with a gentle smile, "Kyros, Nademile, as soon as the third prong attacks and we begin our parry, I ask that you sprint toward Arkaiso with the horses."

I stumbled and would have fallen but for Malika's and Arista's supporting hands on my elbows.

The boldest of the townsfolk, Halona Tikariat, exclaimed, "My Lord, do you mean we should abandon—" Halting herself, she dropped her gaze, cheeks glossed.

But Lucian seemed to nevertheless understand her heart, as well as mine. "My request is not in the slightest a judgment upon your value in my eyes. I ask this not because I doubt your determination but because I worry for your safety. Your injuries have not fully healed, and I do not wish to risk your lives unnecessarily. And," he turned to me, "your Honor Kyros of Light, I need you to be with them because they cannot pass over the borders of Arkaiso without one of us. Among the Quest, your speed is fastest here."

I bowed my head—he had explained several weeks prior about the poisonous trees and swarms of insects around his fortress that acted as inconspicuous deterrents to townsfolk and soldiers alike. Yet I could not silence the nagging thought that he simply did not believe I would be of use. For he did ask Elian to stay, and I performed better in our training than he.

The unkind thought yielded yet more shame. Elian fought so poorly because his cursed wings ruined his balance, while I actually lacked skill.

The townsfolk seemed contented, however, bowing or swishing the skirts of the clothes they had salvaged in curtsies. The guests assigned to riding the horses this morning bent from their saddles.

So, quashing the errant desire to attempt my own appeal, I murmured only obedience.

Hours passed as the few beams of sunshine strengthened in intensity. The few animals, both predator and prey, which moved about amid the chill rustled leaves and branches. A few deer curiously peeked around shrubs at us—and bowed their heads when they saw Lucian.

Despite the grim air hanging around our company, even the townsfolk chuckled at the sight.

Then Lucian raised a hand. "Ten minutes." Exchanging a nod with Elacir, he reached for the nearest trunk and ascended the tree with greater dexterity than any Nasimih.

I tilted my head back and watched him disappear in the bare branches. If not for the tug of my heart in his direction, I would have thought he had entirely vanished.

Hold your weapons point-down at your sides, Arista instructed in the link connecting the townsfolk with my family.

We obeyed, the faint ring of metal on metal accompanying swords and daggers alike.

Elacir spread his wings and jumped, flapping hard to push himself into the canopy. The towering trees were far enough apart that he could fly almost to the uppermost layers of branches.

Minutes crawled by, too slow yet too fast.

The creak of a crossbow's release began the battle.

Screeches and squeals rappelled down from above as metal rang on metal and bolt after bolt swished from their bows.

How are they? Elian asked, voice desperate despite the firm grip on his sword.

The panic in his eyes and Malika's as they tried to peer through the shadowy branches overhead was enough to try catalysis again. Clinging to the mental exercises Lucian had taught me, I managed to invoke the magic and toss the focus of my vision upward.

I exhaled, relieved. *The soldiers are too disoriented to counter Lucian's attack. The few who try to descend are caught by Elacir.*

Gratitude to the Almighty, Malika prayed. *Please, oh Almighty, I beg of You to continue to protect their lives.*

As Elian and I repeated the prayer, Arista suddenly dashed to the right, and more clashes of metal joined the cacophony.

I flinched yet again and directed my farsight in a scan of the forest. A group of soldiers tried to duel Arista, but several had already fallen to her blade.

A second group approached from the west.

I whispered a warning.

Malika and Elian spun to counter the attack.

I waited until my farsight confirmed that all the soldiers were occupied. Then I said to the townsfolk, *Come.*

The guests on horseback snapped their reins. The rest of us crouched, hands braced on the forest floor, and leapt forwards.

Immediately our kind magic burst forward like the first winds of a storm. Skin glossing, we ran as the wind, dodging trees and leaping over branches with greater ease than any deer or wolf. A freedom inferior only to that of Lucian's presence.

Yet behind us came the telltale whispers of footsteps. My farsight found a pair of pursuing soldiers, as fast on their feet as we were.

I skidded to a stop. *I will rejoin you*, I assured the protesting townsfolk.

The soldiers were upon me in moments.

Spitting vile words, they both stabbed toward my chest.

For the first time, Lucian's and Arista's training meant something to my body.

I ducked, thrust my sword upward, decreasing the weight, and slipped it beneath the first soldier's guard. The flat hit his armored chin with a hard thwack. He stumbled backward, and I swung the blade back down, increasing the weight, in time to counter the other's blow. The soldier's arms shook, and he froze, too shocked to react.

Disengaging, I quickly swept the sword upward and pierced the thin strip between his armor and helm over his throat. Blood spurted over the steel and my gloved hands.

The man fell just as his partner sprang forward, sword raised.

I blocked the attack and kicked at his ankle, one of Arista's favorite moves.

He screamed another vile word as he dodged the blow.

Twisting to the side, I sliced up and then swept the sword down with all possible weight. The force of the strike cleaved his helm.

The soldier crumpled to the ground.

For a moment, the world blurred dangerously around me, the only steady spots the gruesome pools of blood...

Kyros! Lucian called.

As on the Day of Light, the thought of his need was enough to dissipate the horror.

I shook my head, turned, and sprinted after the townsfolk. But my farsight remained behind with my family.

As soon as we had left, Malika, Elian, and Arista had retreated until they stood with their backs to each other. The three of them rotated as they fought so Arista faced the hardest opponents and Elian the easiest. Corpses lay piled at their feet, yet half the two squads remained.

In the treetops, Lucian leapt from branch to branch in veritable circles around the enemy, leaving them disoriented and vulnerable to his harsh blows. Elacir cut down any who snuck away.

Wounds marked some of my family's limbs, yet they steadily proceeded toward victory.

Adhering to Lucian's command (though I longed to return and try to help), the townsfolk and I continued our headlong flight for as long as we could. Without Lucian's protection, even the majestic trees of the Dasenákder were unwelcoming and intimidating, much more anyone beneath its canopy whom we might encounter. The townsfolk were eager to reach Arkaiso, and, though I wished to return to my family's side, I did not blame them.

But they could not sustain such a pace, equal to the horses' canters, for long. So, an hour after our separation, we slowed to a walk while I strained my magic to catch a glimpse of my family.

They were cleaning their swords and preparing for burial. Elian lowered the two soldiers I had slain onto the pile of corpses and offered a flask of water to Malika.

Lucian glanced up and smiled at the focal point of my magic—looking directly into my eyes as though I stood with him.

The smile was enough reassurance to not turn back, though I ached to hear his voice. But, as Lucian had explained soon after I had met him, his links, for all his considerable power, had a range of only ten miles. Which was considered impressive for mindlinking, if not at all for farsight. And, though my magic certainly could relay his words, at least for a time, it was already failing.

I would be bereft of his voice for hours.

Pulling my coat tighter around me, I led the towns-folk onward.

Hours passed in silence, save for some timid questions at luncheon and my equally quiet replies. Without the links, we avoided speech.

The change in our surroundings occurred subtly: we seemed to walk amid the three-hundred-foot-tall trees one moment, and, in the next, the trees soared so much higher that the thick leafless canopy was a blur of sable shadows overhead. So little light lit the forest floor that I relied mostly on my pendant's illumination spells and the sporadic glimpses given by my farsight, which had matured enough to no longer require illumination, to lead the way.

I twisted to check whether we had passed the poison trees.

The moss on that tree certainly is a disturbing shade of green... I mused. *Lucian said the enchantments were keyed to him, and thus also to his companions, and they do seem to be recognizing me... I did not really believe they would, so little do I deserve this connection.*

"My Honor," whispered the youngest of the townsfolk, sixteen-year-old Syona Glikaria. "How much further?"

The fright in her voice pierced my heart. "Not much, Nad-eya," I answered, voice gentle. "My Lord promised the base is only three miles beyond the perimeter."

Her lips trembled, but she seemed contented by Lucian's name. The others remained silent.

As promised, before another hour passed, beams of light pierced the gloomy shadows.

Then the trees disappeared.

And before us, beyond a curving stretch of cleared earth, rose the forest base of Arkaiso.

Trees two hundred feet tall formed a circular cluster that extended as far as my eyes could perceive. Platforms and walkways twined through the highest branches and wrapped around the trunks—which, though shorter than their surrounding neighbors, were as thick as the far mightier giant trees of Lucian's childhood stories at approximately ninety feet in diameter at the base and nearly thirty feet at just below the canopy. Large enough for whole rooms to be carved within yet not impair the trees' natural processes. Even bare and laden with snow, the fortress was magnificent.

Eager for a closer look, I sent my farsight toward the colossal trees. For a moment, something seemed to resist the motion of my magic. Then, abruptly, the resistance broke, and my farsight flew forward.

Though gnarled with age and long abandoned, the trees were vibrant with life. Squirrels chittered and scurried along branches, birds chirped and swooped from their nests, and even the occasional deer wandered amid the trunks.

"How big is it, my Honor?" Syona breathed.

"About two miles in diameter," I answered, distant in my wonder. "There are no doors, though. I wonder—" I paused, breaking my own sentence.

"What is it, my Honor?" Ronna Pastarias asked, anxious.

A nervous smile curved my lips, and I bowed my head just as a woman and a man appeared in front of us.

CHAPTER 34

HAIL THE COLOSSAL

Perspective: Honored Kyros the Exemplar of Strength
Date: Eyyédal, the seventh day of the second moon, Etshatte,
of the year 500, C.Q.

Before I could speak, the couple dipped quick bows and then wrapped me in a tight embrace, their touch enough reminiscent of Lucian's that I did not resist the show of affection.

I could not help but wonder if they were anything like Aunt Cyanna.

Finally, some minutes later, the woman and the man drew back and bowed again. "Blessings, my Honor!" they exclaimed.

My smile was probably too shy as I answered, "Blessings, Safira Taza Palanéze, Safiri Ilqan Palaneze." Their faces were quite distinct from Lucian's: although their skin was cream and their green eyes jewel-bright, their faces had a subtle metallic green sheen. White and gray liberally streaked their sandy-brown hair, and faint wrinkles touched the corners of their eyes and framed their lips. Both had the similarity of feature that often emerged from years of shared life rather than blood. For, as Lucian had said, they were wife and husband.

"I see our Lord is as thorough as always," Safira Taza said, laughing. "But, please, address us as he does: Taza and Ilqan. We have long since left our old positions of high general and chief scholar of arms magic; we are solely his guardians now." Her expression, like Ilqan's, had that odd, contented, selfless tinge of true parents.

Many times had I seen it in my own reflection...

Swallowing my ever-present longing, I asked, "Should we wait for my Lord here?"

Ilqan grinned. "If we left you waiting on the edge, he would give us that awful, disappointed look that brings us to repent of killing hornets."

I exhaled a chuckle, knowing which look he meant. Thankfully, I had received it only once so far—when, in a fit of melancholy, I had told him he should break his bond with me because of the harm I had caused him.

"If it would please you, please follow us, my Honor," Taza said. "And blessings and welcome to you, esteemed guests of the Quest."

The townsfolk seemed too shy to do more than bow and curtsy.

Chattering in loud, excited tones, the two guardians urged us across the cleared arc and into the colossal trees. Though each tree looked the same, they directed the townsfolk to a specific one about half a mile into the cluster. In a whirlwind of activity, they settled all thirteen guests across three floors of quarters, with a promise of supper once Lucian arrived, and then worked to stable the horses into the hollowed space beneath another tree.

Craning my neck, I wondered how that tree could possibly remain upright when its base was mostly missing.

Once the horses were fed, Taza and Ilqan scooped up our saddlebags and turned to me. For the first time, a hint of displeasure crossed their faces, but so quickly that I almost did not believe I had seen it.

Lighthearted chatter obscured all sign of discontent as the couple opened a door recessed into the wood of a third tree and beckoned for me to remove my boots and enter.

Unlike the other trees, the staircase was inside, hidden within a narrow wooden shaft at the center of the hollowed trunk.

Rapidly we climbed upward, passing five stories of mysterious rooms, until the top floor. There, the guardians ushered me to one of the four doors, which was marked with my name and title in an elegant script. The only door bearing a single name.

Holding back the unnecessary nerves, I stepped inside.

My mouth dropped open.

As large as my parents' bedroom, the chambers boasted a pair of the softest beds I had ever felt, a bathing room with actual pumped water, a large closet filled with sets of spare clothes (*three* were robes of athar cloth) alongside a veritable armory of weapons, and a balcony overlooking the forest canopy. The views offered by that balcony meant that this tree was among the tallest...

Commander's quarters, I thought, dazed, as I washed and changed. But, as luxurious as it was for a mere orphaned peasant, it was nothing I could enjoy without my family. How I wished Kalyca would appear in a blaze of turquoise and bounce on the second bed...

Holding back tears, I tapped my pendant, into which Lucian had pressed the connection for Kalyca's communications spell.

Vibrations leaked from the emerald until a sweet voice answered, "Kyie! Blessings! How are you?"

Smiling shakily, I relaxed at the beloved sound. "Blessings, Kallie. The Almighty blesses me daily. Particularly so today with our arrival at Lucian's base. How are you, my darling?"

"Oh! Kyie, what does it look like?" she demanded.

Closing my eyes, I described everything I saw with both visions. Then, at her harrying insistence, told her something of my troubles.

Though I treasured every word of her rather pointed encouragement, the wounds on my heart refused to heal. But, with the sound of her voice in my ears, I managed to wait until, finally, I spotted our family's entrance into the base. Which was accompanied by the cool restoration of Lucian's links.

Assuring Kalyca I would contact her later, I rushed down the stairs.

Only to almost collide with a slender form waiting on the final step.

I gasped an apology. Then choked as the man turned.

He was Lucian's mirror image. And yet not.

Demure white-blond hair and beard instead of radiant sunlight, lavender eyes instead of violet, cream skin shining with chips of white instead of silver, handsome instead of divine-favored beautiful... he resembled Lucian as a child's drawing could be called similar to a master's landscape. But, just as a child's drawing was treasured by those who loved her, so also could I see why Lucian adored him—for piety and wisdom shone in Prince Darian sej-Shehasfiyi's eyes despite his young age. As did the fire of utter devotion.

But not for me, I realized as those eyes cooled.

For, though the prince revealed no other sign of his dislike, it was all too apparent. Unlike Taza and Ilqan, his love for Lucian did not by default extend to me, Lucian's companion.

The stiff formality of Prince Darian's bow as he moved aside for me throbbed like a wasp's venomous sting.

All the more so because he was right to despise me—my actions had *hurt* Lucian.

Though repressing tears, I gave him a warm smile as I walked to the door.

Then everything else fell away as Lucian, Malika, Elian, Arista, and Elacir entered—weary, filthy, but triumphant.

Kyros! Malika cried as she tossed aside her boots and threw her arms around my waist just as I bent in a reverence. *I was so worried!*

Quickly straightening, I pressed her to my chest and kissed the side of her head. *I was more worried for you, my Sister.* Brown flashed in the corner of my vision, and I twisted slightly so I could examine the dark stains on her arm. *Were you... were you badly injured?*

No, only minor cuts and bruises, Arista said dismissively as she joined the hug. *Elian managed to heal some, and salve took care of the rest.*

Malika pulled me toward her and tucked her head beneath my beard. The soft cloth of her cap and the still-coarse strands of her red-gold hair tickled my chin.

Elian's scales flared gold against his dark skin as he rested his arms over my upper back (the only hug he could give while avoiding brushing against Malika). *I only did a little,* he muttered.

He understates, Elacir grumbled, awkwardly patting my elbow—until Arista wrapped an arm around his waist and yanked him against us.

What you did was valuable, Elian, Lucian said as he hugged all of us. *Kyros, my gratitude for bringing our guests to safety.* He gestured with a wave of thought to the tree's door, where the townsfolk had gathered. *I am glad to see them well. And even more so, I am glad to see you.*

My face moistened in a gloss at the undeserved affection.

Lucian beamed and stepped back. He turned and greeted Taza and Ilqan with hugs and affectionate words (he did not wait for them to bow first), his cheeks faintly silvering under their delight. Then he strode across the room.

The five of us disentangled ourselves.

Whatever cool dislike they had held before, the prince's eyes now burned with an almost desperate fear. As though whatever happened next was sure to shatter his heart, and he was helpless to stop it. And yet could not look away.

He stared as Lucian halted a pace away. Lips trembling, the prince tilted forward in a bow.

"Blessings, Brother," Lucian greeted, chuckling. "Since when have I asked my elder brother to bow to me?" With a gentle tug, he tipped the prince into his loving embrace.

The utter relief on Prince Darian's face was heartbreaking. Closing his eyes, he melted into his brother's arms, hands unsteady and shoulders sagging. "Blessings, Lucian," he murmured, his voice a light baritone that sounded shrill in comparison to Lucian's rich voice. But still musical.

I wonder, Arista said, a bite of anger in her tone, *how many times he has been compared to his incomparable brother and found lacking?*

Following her gaze, I noted Taza's and Ilqan's faces, which, while adoring toward Lucian and affectionate to the rest of us, bore a steely disapproval as they watched the prince stutter shy words of welcome.

Too many times to count, Lucian answered, weary and sorrowful though his face showed only joy.

No wonder he did not seem to like us, I muttered, suddenly understanding something of the prince's mind.

He did not seem to like you? Lucian asked sharply.

I panicked—I had not meant to say that in the link! *I beg you to not scold him*, I pleaded.

Though his expression did not change, Lucian impressed a sigh into the link and then an amused smile. *He is more blessed than he realizes to already have your loyalty.* Before I could process those words, he said aloud, "Come. There is a matter I wish to immediately discuss. Our guests, if you would proceed upstairs, you will find the dining room, with an adjoining kitchen, on the second floor. You may begin supper without us."

Spinning on his heel, he directed his family up to the third floor and into a semicircular room half the size of the trunk. A long oval table, ornately carved oak, was positioned in the center and surrounded by ten chairs. A large map of Icilia lay on its surface.

Lucian waited until all nine of us were seated (even Elacir, dismissing his anxious protests) and until a link was established among all of us. Then he stated, voice icy yet tightly controlled, "We have a failure of intelligence."

The guardians shrank in their seats, their faces silvering in the same manner as Lucian's despite the difference in sheen. Still, Taza's voice remained admirably steady as she reported, "As you commanded in your contact following the Day of Light, my Lord, we suspended all rumor missions. Your father, Hasima, Da'ana, and Eloman remain active in their missions of aid in western and eastern Nademan, as do Ilqan and I here. Ezam and Almana pursue the threads of research you ordered. However, the rest of us await your next command." An odd emotion shaded the last sentence.

A wry smile quirked Lucian's lips. "Your attempts at gathering better intelligence failed." He spoke the words as a statement, not a question.

Taza's answering smile was just as wry. "Farsight and shadows are not enough to infiltrate the enemy bases which would have the information you desire, my Lord." She spread her hands. "In this area, our kind fails you. We cannot pass for the other kinds; the few illusion spells perfected before the Blood's subjugation do not adhere to our skin. In Khuduren, Mutal attempts a new form, but he does not expect success in these conditions. You need better spies, my Lord."

Leaning back in her chair, Arista tapped her plates and muttered, "Which means we must recruit and train spies in each nation."

How I wished I had the courage to speak as she could.

"Exactly so, my Honor," Ilqan replied, lowering his green gaze. "Gathering an army is already a task of great magnitude; we had hoped we would be able to spare you this trouble."

The dissatisfaction on Lucian's face faded to gentle reassurance. "I do not blame the guardians, Taza, Ilqan. We presumed that we would be able to act in each nation independently because of the enemy's longstanding habits and reputation, as well as the history of our ancestors with regards to the first conjurors and to the age before the Quest of Light. Only civilization binds a people well enough for harmonious life. And, indeed, this belief is correct: for many years we have resisted the enemy, and they have been blind to our pattern. Our decision to spread rumors in Asfiya while I traveled and in Bhalasa and Khuduren after the Quest left those territories was sensible and should have posed no substantial risk to our safety. But…" He sighed and pressed his lips together.

You think the soldiers' communication is not a good sign, Malika completed his sentence, speaking in the newly formed collective link including the prince and the guardians.

Lucian gave her a brief, rare grin. "How well you know my thoughts, Malika."

The terrible grayness of her cheeks eased as she blushed, beaming with delight.

The rest of us smiled as well—except Prince Darian.

I blinked, trying to clear my vision. Apparently I needed to rest my eyes, for they told me something that could not be true. There simply could not be *jealousy* in Prince Darian's eyes. His character was surely too pure for such sin. And, regardless, what reason could he have? He was the Quest Leader's own brother and adored by him as well; his place at Lucian's side was guaranteed.

Lucian caught my gaze and raised an eyebrow.

I impressed a shake of my head into our private link. *I do not want to say.*

Lucian responded with the sense of a nod. Then he said, his smile fading, "Malika is correct." A strong, elegant hand rubbed his forehead. "There is some deeper plot at work which we have not yet perceived. A goal powerful enough to motivate those who hate each other to cooperate. For sharing news of us cannot be the full extent of their communication; it is merely a secondary ramification. Yet, even if this conclusion is false, we must consider that news of our presence may have already reached the governors' ears. If not the Blood's own."

Even the guardians looked frightened at the thought.

"What adjustments could we make for your safety, Lucian?" Prince Darian asked, the desperation on his features far exceeding what had burned in his eyes at Lucian's arrival.

Another wry smile crossed Lucian's face. "None."

Prince Darian sputtered an objection. And he was not the only one—the rest of us, even the guardians and Elacir—entreated him to reconsider. Only Arista did not speak.

Raising a hand to quiet us, Lucian stated, "I designed our plans from my ascension until this point with our safety as a primary consideration because our travels precluded the refuge of a fortress. Now that we have arrived at Arkaiso, we have such a refuge." His violet eyes flashed, yet his baritone voice remained even. "We are at war. War, my family, is unsafe. But without war, we cannot free Icilia."

None of us could speak against those words.

"Then, Lucian," Arista said, her voice calm, "if it would accord with your wishes, I ask to hear your next plans in detail. How do you intend to balance our training with a campaign?"

Lucian nodded, pleased, and exchanged a cryptic glance with her. Then he rose slightly out of his chair and drew a circle around south-central Nademan on the map. "While the guardians present in Nademan, Asfiya, Bhalasa, and Khuduren begin again to spread rumors, we begin our reconquest in this part of the province of Zaiqan, in the forest surrounding Arkaiso."

CHAPTER 35

WITNESS THE DESOLATE

Perspective: Honored Kyros the Exemplar of Strength
Date: Eyyéqan, the twelfth day of the second moon, Etshatte,
of the year 500, C.Q.

Despite Arista's warning, the girl yelped as Lucian swept her off the mare. She clutched at his collar and then seemed to relax, recognizing his blessed touch.

Though shafts of sunlight warmed the branches of the tree-town ahead, tension and a coiled rage burdened the air.

Shouting drifted to our ears on the breeze.

"Papa," the girl whispered, milky hazel eyes filling with tears.

Casting my farsight in that direction, I smiled reassuringly, though she could not see it. "He is attempting to rally your neighbors into rescuing you, Nadeya Basarias."

Breana smiled but her voice was laden with sorrow as she replied, "He would try, but no one would dare to risk the wrath of the soldiers for anyone, much less a blind girl

of fifteen years. Well, no one but you, Lucian, Arista, Kyros."
Awe filled those last words.

"To do so is our pleasure," Lucian said, chuckling. He
pressed a brotherly kiss to her head and strode into the clearing.
My voice, Arista. Unload the stolen supplies, and ready the horses.

Obeying, we removed the sacks of dried meat and vegetables from the saddlebags and carried them to a spot just
within the shadows of the main forest. Simultaneously, Arista
cast a spell that, according to what she had described earlier,
would vibrate the particles of the air in accordance with the
cadence of his voice—thereby amplifying his words.

A moment later, Lucian called out, "Ruyisso of Zaiqan!
Your daughter, Breana Basarias, has returned!"

Silence.

Dozens of fingers and shoes scraped over tree bark as
a group of men and women rushed down the trunks. They
gazed wildly around the clearing until their eyes met Lucian's
shining form.

A couple detached from the group and ran toward him,
unheeding of their neighbors' shouted orders. They flung themselves at Lucian, who held steady as they pulled her from his arms.

"Mama! Papa!" Breana cried as her mother cradled
her. Her father embraced them both and squeezed them to
his chest.

We grinned.

We must tell Malika, Elian, and Elacir all about this!
Arista declared as she and I remounted our horses. Her face
was almost as bright as Lucian's with bliss at the sight of our
people's happiness.

Yes, I agreed, alit with the same glow despite my own pain.
*Seeking out a squad of soldiers was certainly not as terrible
as Elian and I were expecting.* Except for how many times

my farsight had failed as I searched for the ones we wanted to confront. Lucian offered to ask Taza, a farseer herself, for help via communication spell, but I persevered. Burdened as I was by my substandard weapons skills and my hesitance in battle, my magic was the only way I could serve him.

Though I doubted even such service could remedy the lack caused by my fear of spilling blood—a fear so great, so in excess, that innocence and true esteem for life could not justify it. For when I indulged it, I stood aside while my family and my people faced danger—as I had on the Day of Light.

Despite the weeks that had passed, Lucian's blood glinted shining crimson on the backs of my eyelids... *I* had wasted that sacred blood which concealed divine Light...

The townsfolk drew near the reunited family. One of the women hissed something, and the man whom Breana had called Papa raised his head and looked at Lucian, who stood so close to him. He caught his breath.

The rest of the villagers, reaching them, did the same.

Breana's mother glanced up and visibly swallowed.

Lucian smiled in his lordly way and calmly stated, "Blessings. My siblings and I return your daughter and six sacks of stolen supplies to you in the name of the second Quest Leader, Lord Lucian the Ideal of Freedom, Heir to the Quest of Light and supreme ruler of Icilia. May the Almighty shelter you." Before anyone could react, he spun on his heel and strode toward the glade's edge.

As he passed into the shadows of the forest, Breana twisted in her mother's arms and exclaimed, "Lucian!"

Lucian's only answer was a light peal of laughter as he mounted Rikeb's back and flicked the reins. Arista and I nudged our own horses, and we disappeared southwest into the snow-covered trees.

Once we were far enough, Arista threw back her head and laughed. "That was amazing! The look on her face! When she realized that the Quest Leader himself had held her like his sister!"

Lucian laughed also. "It was indeed satisfying."

My lips spread in a grin. Their happiness was the honey atop the pastry. As much as I found reward in caring for our people, the greatest fulfillment was in their smiles.

Waggling an eyebrow, Arista teased, "So, Kyros, do you dread your next turn so much now?"

I shook my head. "Not as long as you are with me."

Dropping the playfulness, she promised, "Always, Kyros. Always."

Contentment soothed some of the turmoil in my heart. As much as I missed Kalyca, as much as I doubted myself, I had to remember that I was not alone. I had Lucian, Malika, Elian, Arista, Elacir, and even the guardians now. The long years of enduring abuse without any hope of defense were over. My shortcomings would not repulse them. Amid my torment, they were my strength.

Beaming as though he could hear my thoughts (I was not sure that he could not), Lucian nudged his white stallion closer to mine and momentarily clasped my shoulder. Then he asked seriously, *What is your evaluation thus far of my plan?*

Arista scratched her plates. *Hmmm. I must admit that I was slightly skeptical. Attempting to patrol even fifty miles of territory around Arkaiso is ambitious, much less the hundred miles' radius with which we are starting. But, considering the two days Kyros needed to even find any targets and how spread out the tree-towns are… if we tried for a more manageable distance, we would take months to generate an impact. What worries me, though, is the strain these constant rotations will* place on us. *Managing exactly where each of us are in our studies will prove a challenge, yes, but far more worrisome are the physical and emotional burdens.*

I added, though with more hesitation, *Elian is terrified he will not have any chance to see you. And as much as the Filisso townsfolk trust us, they need your presence more.*

Lucian pressed his lips together. *Your arguments have merit. But there is little more we can do other than including a week at Arkaiso between each series of rotations. We must not delay.*

Arista nodded. *That would be sufficient. And if Taza and Ilqan would be willing to go in our stead, your plans would not suffer any delays as well.*

Lucian tilted his head and then nodded. *I will order these changes.*

Arista and I exchanged looks of delight—the Quest Leader's value for our opinions never ceased to be a wonder.

Lucian chuckled. *Now, come. I do not want to miss Darian's birthday celebration.*

We spurred our horses in response.

The miles flew away as we raced the darkening of the smog, reaching Arkaiso but two hours before sunset.

We paused only to stable our horses and for Arista to quietly assure Ekhittie, the newly renamed mare she had taken from the soldiers, of the improvement in her circumstances. Then we sprinted to our chambers for a change of clothes before descending the stairs to the dining room, where the others had gathered.

As festooned as the room was with tendrils of ivy, holly, and pinecones, the smiles on the Filisso townsfolk's faces were the greatest decoration of all. They had cried when Elacir had accidentally mentioned Lucian's birthday, so today was the first celebration they would have since they had lost everything. I was glad their grief did not so consume them that they forgot how to express joy.

And from the soft expression on his face as he entered the room, Prince Darian agreed. Though he quickly focused all his attention on Lucian, who hugged him with a murmured, "Blessings for your twenty-fourth birthday, Brother."

The words seemed to mean the world to the prince. Though he thanked the rest of us for our wishes, they were mere side notes to the tome that were Lucian's. Indeed, throughout the feast that followed, his focus remained solely on his brother—ignoring both the guardians' ever-present dissatisfaction and Lucian's companions' attempts to engage him in conversation.

It is, I thought, *understandable: Lucian seems to be the only one who does not neglect him. But as much as I understand it, I wish he would accept us. Malika and Elian say he is calm and attentive as he tutors them and Elacir, never cross or disrespectful, yet cold. As though he cannot help but wish us gone, yet only does not act on it to avoid causing Lucian pain. He accepts Elacir better than he does us. And, despite my friends' hopes, our organization of this celebration has not in the slightest changed his regard.*

Only with my usual tranquil façade donned could I manage the walk to the spacious training arena that lay at the center of Arkaiso. Not until I sat on the benches Elian and Elacir had arranged here last night did I remember why I was present.

I scooted to the edge of my seat and ignored the discomfort apparent in Prince Darian's posture beside me.

It is about to begin, Arista breathed, wiggling in her seat on my other side.

Here they come! Elian cheered.

Lucian and Malika strode, steps attuned, into the arena. The sun and the sky together. Gold athar cloth rimmed his midnight blue collar and cap just as silver lined hers.

Prince Darian frowned. "What is happening, Brother?"

Lucian smiled, shining even more than usual in his excitement. "My companions and I present a tradition of Asfiya in honor of your birthday." Then, drawing his sword in a smooth whoosh of metal on metal, he turned to Malika.

Unsheathing her own sword, she bowed to him, and he inclined his head. She straightened and stepped back so that she stood six feet sway.

Both Lucian's and Malika's features set into expressions of immense concentration.

And what followed was... more breathtaking than anything I had ever seen before.

For ten minutes, longer than any previous match, their swords crossed in pattern after pattern. When Malika threw a punch or a kick, Lucian dodged sharply to avoid the blow. When Lucian sliced or thrust at her, Malika parried to deflect his attack. Together, they ranged across the field in a blur of motion that only resolved into clear strikes and counters at the culmination of each move. A harmony of graceful yet deadly motion.

Sparks flew and the field rang.

Undoubtedly Lucian was more skilled, for he launched more successful attacks against Malika than she did against him, and he countered more of her attacks than she did of his. But what was equally apparent was that, in the scant weeks since her first narrow victory on Lucian's birthday, she had rapidly grown more powerful, rising to the new pressures of his training like a bird adapting to the necessities of flight.

Indeed, she was giving Lucian almost as much trouble to defeat as Taza, his teacher.

None were able to look away from the show of martial prowess.

Malika threw herself to the ground to dodge an attack and simultaneously hooked one leg around Lucian's ankle. His knees nearly buckled, and he stepped back with the other foot to steady himself. Malika used the moment to launch a thrust upward toward his stomach.

With a powerful kick, Lucian swept back the foot tangled in her hook, thereby pulling her toward him. He blocked her blade and immediately thrust in the direction of her throat.

Untangling her legs, Malika rolled to dodge and then rose into a crouch.

They faced each other.

Malika charged forward with her sword lowered to her right and arching upward.

Lucian leapt back to dodge and then swung upward himself.

Malika leaned to the side, causing his swing to miss wildly, and brought her sword down from the pinnacle of its previous swing.

Lucian twisted around her to dodge and lifted one hand from his hilt to solidly punch her back as he fell to the ground on his side. Malika stumbled forward, and Lucian used a combination of punches to the back of her thigh and a sweep with his leg across her ankles to bring her to her knees.

Recovering faster than I could blink, Malika twisted and brought her sword to his heart. Before he could raise his to the back of her neck.

A clear victory.

Yield? she asked, panting wildly.

"Yielded," he agreed calmly, only slightly out of breath. A dazzling smile curled his lips. "The Almighty has blessed us with your fifth victory."

Malika stared at him in wonder. *I won? Truly won? Outright won?*

Lucian laughed and rose. Sheathing his sword, he offered his hand, and she accepted it, blue eyes still wide with disbelief, drawing on his support as he lifted her to her feet.

"You have fulfilled the mandate of my training," he said, his rich voice quiet yet resonant, "in but six weeks' time, though you did not understand why. I am pleased, Malika, my Second."

A blush colored her face crimson, and she laughed sweetly as she lovingly sheathed her sword and embraced him. Then, a smile as dazzling as his on her lips, she began to walk toward Elian, Arista, and me.

In that moment, as everyone leapt to their feet and began to cheer, I believed what had before been too great for my broken mind to fully comprehend: I believed in the future, in the power of choice, in hope and wonder, in the Almighty's favor.

For I had just beheld Malika, who had cowered, alone and beaten, not five months ago, defeat in battle the Quest Leader, he who was both supremely well trained and blessed with immeasurable skill.

She had won. For the fifth time.

That was not supposed to be possible.

But I had seen it.

The Almighty had brought this to fruition.

So what else could be possible?

Could my becoming worthy be possible?

Could peace and freedom be possible?

If the Almighty could, through Lucian's hands, raise Malika from the desolation to which she had been consigned, then what could not happen?

I believed in possibilities and the power of my choice to accept Lucian's hand.

I saw the potential within my own future.

And my foresight sparked, my focus riveted to Lucian and Malika.

So I saw what happened next seconds before it did.

CHAPTER 36

SAVE THE CURSED

Perspective: Honored Elian the Exemplar of Esteem
Date: Eyyéqan, the twelfth day of the second moon, Etshatte,
of the year 500, C.Q.

One moment, the air was bright with laughter and celebration.

In the next, Lucian and Kyros screamed.

And in the third, Malika wailed, her voice high and keening. Her eyes rolled upward, leaving only white in her eye sockets. Her knees buckled as she began to collapse.

Lucian and Kyros streaked toward her from opposite directions.

Kyros blurred, tapping his kind magic, and managed to catch her just before her torso slammed the ground. Inserting his legs beneath her, he bore the full brunt of her weight. His skin was both coarse and glossy.

Lucian skidded to a stop beside him and fell to his knees. The silver of his face had become gray.

Her eyes open and white, Malika lay still and crumpled in Kyros' arms.

Then her limbs began to twitch. And convulse.

Her mouth opened wide in a shriek, an endless, ear-bursting shriek, as though she had fallen beneath the torturer's blade...

The sound ripped away my own breath, agony freezing my limbs, my scales black and cold.

Kyros could not hold her as she writhed.

Lucian snatched her from his arms and pressed her to his chest.

Her convulsions did not end. She did not regain consciousness.

Eyes overflowing with tears, Lucian desperately clutched her to him, her shakes vibrating his person as well. His voice escalated from quiet prayer to screams that matched hers in volume and pitch and agony—

Pain tore through my heart, burning the shock from my limbs.

Arista and I shot from the log to where Lucian and Kyros knelt in the dirt. We fell to our knees as well but hesitated, uncertain how to help.

Kyros, his gray eyes glowing oddly, stared at Lucian and Malika. Then he ordered, "Hug them."

Without a moment's hesitation Arista threw her arms around them. The convulsions spread to her, and her screams joined theirs.

I wrapped my arms around Lucian's waist, careful out of ingrained habit to not touch Malika.

Kyros hugged all of us from around Arista's back, his long arms reaching my shoulders. His voice, too, rose in a scream, our friends' torment becoming his own.

But I did not share in that torment. Not beyond the agony of seeing those whom I loved most in unbearable pain. Their screams echoed those of my parents as the Blood cursed me and of mine as he tore out their beating hearts... Desperation consumed my mind as I feared a second loss of all I had.

Oh Almighty, I beg You!

Warmth ignited in my heart, spreading through the vessels of my blood, bringing pleasure and relief in its wake, reaching my fingertips... my healing, which had awakened to this degree only on the Day of Light. It had the strength to save them.

My scales glowed gold, and white light gathered in my palms.

I willed it toward my friends. *Anything to help you.*

The light began to soak into Lucian's back.

Lucian and Kyros suddenly cried out, the wordless screams condensing into gritted words, "No, Elian, no!" With a harsh push, Kyros shoved my shoulders away, and Lucian twisted an arm around to wrench my right one from his waist.

The shock of their attack was enough to break my hold on the healing light.

"What?" I whispered, my eyes suddenly, shamefully, welling with tears while my friends were falling to pieces.

Kyros managed to bring the scream under control enough to say through gritted teeth, "If you heal, you will worsen it. Only touch us!" His voice rose back into a shriek on the last word.

The explanation did not ease the hurt, but I retained enough sense to obey. I slipped my arms around both Lucian's and Kyros' shoulders. I did not want to be anywhere else while they were in pain.

Hold onto them!

Still they screamed.

Still Malika convulsed.

I could not share their pain.

Hold onto them!

Tears spilled from my eyes as I sobbed. I did not know what was happening, but I wanted it to cease. Their pain was shredding my heart. I would rather it shred my heart than afflict them even a moment longer.

Hold onto them!

I would never leave them...

Hold onto them!

Even though Malika's shakes had spread to my wings, and each vibration was a hot dagger digging into the tender flesh, beyond the threshold of what I could bear—

Hold!

But that was nothing compared to their pain.

Hold!

The moment was endless.

Hold!

Then the feathers shaking on my wings began to settle. The shakes receded, and the screams lowered in pitch, until my friends were still and quiet.

Holding my breath, I peeked over Lucian's shoulder at Malika's almost translucent face. Her skin had lost so much color that the pulsing of her veins was visible beneath it. The balls of her eyes were rolling back into place, her irises visible once again, blue amid blood-streaked white...

The fear and pain contorting her expression devastated me.

Lucian stroked her back. "My sister, my heart, I am with you," he whispered, his voice so hoarse that it had nearly lost its richness and melody.

She shivered, her eyes glazing. Then they cleared. She blinked and looked around her. Her lips parted, and she tried to speak. Then she remembered the links. *L-Lucian?* she ventured.

My heart, I am with you, he repeated and pressed her face into his neck. *I have been with you for every moment. I have not left.* The music of his voice would have been wholly comforting... if not for the stark anguish and agony within it.

But Malika still seemed to calm. *Lucian,* she murmured contentedly. Then she asked, *E-E-li-li-an? A-Ar-is-ista? K-Ky-Ky-ro-ros?*

We are with you also, Arista replied, defeated. *Sister, our Grace, we are here.*

Our Grace, Malika darling, we are here, Kyros whispered, heartbroken.

I wanted to stroke her head but refrained. *Malika, our Grace, my friend, I have not left you either.* My voice, even in the links, wavered unsteadily.

If anything had happened to her... I treasured her so much, so much more than my own life. I had not known her for six months, but she meant Icilia to me. As Lucian did.

I had withstood my parents' murder and thirteen years alone, cursed, helpless, tormented. But I would not be able to withstand her loss. Any of my family's, yes, but particularly hers.

She sighed contentedly, the sound rough against her throat, and relaxed in their arms. *I dreamt of the fall of Koroma...* she murmured, more coherent. *But I woke up with you and not with him.*

We stiffened at the words.

My breath hitched in another sob. *She thought she was waking in the Blood's prisons... after watching her family's and home's destruction all over again...* I could not withstand the horror of such thoughts.

Arista whimpered, and Kyros muffled a cry.

Lucian, however, asked urgently, *Was it vivid, my heart?*

Seeming confused, she answered, *As though it had just happened. As though I had just lived it.*

Lucian inhaled sharply. Then he spoke, his voice booming and powerful, the roar of a wrathful lion despite the audible scratch of his throat, "*I will enact justice for this.*"

It was the first time he had raised his voice in all of these months, and it frightened me to my bones, even though I knew instinctively that it was not directed at me.

Arista and Kyros squeaked in fright.

From the shocked and petrified faces of Prince Darian, Taza, and Ilqan, he had never displayed such anger before.

Malika quailed but only pressed further against him.

No one dared to ask him about whom he would punish. We knew the name too well.

I ventured a peek at his face and then almost wished I had not.

Haloed by dim yet piercing sunlight, his beloved, radiant face was a fear-provoking mixture of the deadly silver of a blade and the gray of illness. His dazzling violet eyes were hard and colder than ice yet drowned with sorrow. And his blessed mouth was both spread in a grimace of pain and a snarl of anger. His was the face I revered, that I knew better than my own, but I could not understand what I read upon it.

Lucian seethed for a moment. Then he kissed Malika's forehead, exhaled a sigh, and said, "My heart, my Second, that attack was caused by your curse. The curse that cages your magic."

What? she whispered, drawing back so that she could tilt her head and meet his gaze. *It has never attacked me before!*

Arista, Kyros, and I choked, unable to breathe at the horror of his words.

Lucian smiled without humor. "No. This attack is a new torment. And…" he sighed, "it happened because a drop of your magic has been freed."

What! she exclaimed. *How?*

"Elian cracked your curse," he answered grimly, "when his magic mixed with mine on the Day of Light."

I reeled back, head spinning, and fell on my bottom. "This is my fault?" I gasped.

I had done this to her? My treasured friend, my dearest partner?

Lucian turned away from Malika long enough to smile at me, the expression grim yet brimming with reassurance. "No, Elian. The blame for this attack is the Blood's alone. In his contempt for the laws and gifts of the Almighty, he suppressed her magic, blaspheming in his intention to cripple her. And, Malika," he returned his attention to her, "in more ways than merely by the cage itself.

"When such blocked magic flows free, it scalds the veins in which it flows, for neither the mind nor the body are accustomed to its presence. What this means, as my guardians Ezam and Amalna have conferred with me, is that spell rebound is catastrophic—and almost guaranteed. Even when the magic released is but a few drops.

"But the Blood devised a still deeper assault: he congealed your curse by placing a contingency, an illness that would fester with every drop of magic freed—an illness born of a spell designed to invoke your worst memories. It would destroy every part of your identity by tormenting you with the loss of your family and home if you ever escaped and discovered a way to free yourself. It would taint the joy that you found in the freedom of your magic. And it would retaliate if even a drop was released. This attack was inevitable."

"*Inevitable!*" all four of us exclaimed, and Arista added, "Why did you not tell us? Or at least tell Malika?"

"Because, Malika, you needed to focus upon your training," Lucian answered, his tone calm though he remained visibly incensed. "Living as we do in an age of war, I calculated that the possibility of an uncontrolled use of your magic, and subsequent rebound, was high. However, the chance of rebound was something we could mitigate with proper training. Thus, I have placed every emphasis upon it so that you would learn to control your magic and thereby protect yourself from this consequence.

"In addition... I seized the opportunity to train you while you have access to only some of your magic rather than all of it. On the day we break your curse, the control you have learned in these past weeks will serve you well and safeguard your life. In a similar manner, suffering the curse's retaliation today will, if the Almighty blesses us so, enable us to better address the aftermath of the curse's full severance.

"Finally... Malika, my Second, this is how you have learned to believe in your own strength."

Malika's lips parted, wonder and gratitude glimmering in her eyes as she gazed up at him. *That is why you commanded me to learn to defeat you.*

The fury on his shining face brightened to such a look of affection and love that it lit up the dark world beneath the smog like the sun had come to walk amongst us. And, though his violet eyes were affixed to her blue ones, that adoration was radiant for Arista, Kyros, and me as well, embracing us as though our souls were one with both his and hers. His empowerment of her lifted us alongside her.

Though tendrils of suffering still permeated my being, I was contented. So, though I noted what Lucian did not explain and what Malika did not ask, I raised no question. I trusted that whatever secrets Lucian kept was to our benefit, as his silence about my parentage was to mine. If he did not reveal the type of Malika's magic, then it was not yet time for us to know.

That same peace and unwavering belief shone on Arista's and Kyros' tear-streaked faces.

Lucian bent his head to kiss Malika's forehead, the white-gold of his beard mixing with the red-gold of her hair. Then, shifting his arms so that he could carry her, he said, "Malika must rest, as must we all, despite the early hour. Let us retire together. Elian, Arista, if it would please you, assemble blankets. And Kyros—" a smile curled his lips— "I praise you for your stable use of foresight at the perfect moment."

Laughing amid the horror, we repeated that praise until his cheeks switched from coarseness all the way to gloss. Bowing his head, he cupped a palm over his heart, gray eyes glowing—though with a different light than what I now realized to be the sign of his magic.

Lucian indicated then that he wished to stand, so we scrambled to our feet.

One arm beneath Malika's knees and the other around her upper back, Lucian rose onto his knees. Then he winced and abruptly sank back onto the ground.

We rushed to help.

Letting us bear his weight, he staggered as he raised himself enough that he could place one foot upright on the ground.

Malika's feet scraped harshly against the earth, but she did not complain, instead clutching the front of his robes with both hands, shaking knuckles white with the force of her grip.

He managed to attain his feet, then staggered again as Malika's limp weight in his arms upset his balance. But he did not drop her.

We steadied him, Kyros' and my arms around his back and Arista's on Malika's waist and his side. My wings shifted, but I shoved away that pain.

Only when we were all standing, clinging to each together, did we turn.

Only then did I realize that Prince Darian, Taza, Ilqan, Elacir, and the townsfolk were still present, gathered around us, watching, standing frozen with horror and anguished pain.

Discomfort thrummed through the Quest's personal link.

The townsfolk abruptly dipped reverences and ran for our tree.

Grimaces twisting their lips, Taza, Ilqan, and Elacir wrapped their arms around us, solidifying our balance.

Prince Darian, however, did not move. Fever glittered in his lavender eyes, and the white chips on his skin were nowhere to be seen. "Lucian…" he whispered.

Forgive me, Prince Darian, Malika said quietly, *for tainting your happiness.* She attempted to turn and meet his gaze but instead just slumped into Lucian's chest.

The prince frantically shook his head. "No, no, please do not apologize! It is only…" His lips trembled. "I would rather have perished than see you, any of you, in such pain."

I repressed my disbelief from emerging in my expression. Was he not the same man who had watched us with cool dislike and contained jealousy since we had arrived?

Lucian tried to smile, mouth twitching, but could not bring his usual gentle curve to his lips.

Prince Darian flinched and then drew in a deep breath. "My Grace, I will labor day and night until your curse is broken," he vowed, the words filled with the solemnity of pledges. "May the Almighty transform my oath into truth."

Gratitude brimmed in Lucian's eyes, and Malika said, overwhelmed, *May the Almighty bless you, Prince Darian.*

The prince dipped his head and joined the others of our family in supporting us.

With their help, we limped back to our tree amid the waning sunlight, dimmed though hours still remained before sunset.

At the tree's base, Elacir insisted on flying all five of us, in turns, to Malika's and Arista's bedchamber, while the others sprinted up the stairs.

Once there, Lucian gently laid Malika's form in bed and tucked her beneath her blankets. Then he collapsed beside her atop them. Prince Darian collected additional quilts from the townsfolk, who peeked in through the door, and spread them over his brother.

Before her eyes closed, Malika asked Kyros to sleep on her other side. As soon as the words left her lips, Taza and Ilqan layered enough sheets on the floor to serve him as a bed. Murmuring his thanks, Kyros intertwined his fingers with hers.

In the same moments, Arista reclined on her own bed and, at my desperate plea, allowed me to sleep beside her, angling my body around the curve of hers over the coverlet. Elacir untied my wings so they would not come beneath me and cocooned me in still more blankets.

My eyes closed on the terrified expressions of my family, who watched us as though fearing that, once we slept, we would not wake.

CHAPTER 37

IMPEL THE DAUNTED

Perspective: Honored Elian the Exemplar of Esteem
Date: Eyyésal, the thirteenth day of the second moon, Etshatte,
of the year 500, C.Q.

L oathing for myself roaring in my mind, I clutched Arista's hand as though the grip would prevent me from
being blown away—

"Elian," Arista soothed, folding her muscular arms around
my waist, "I am with you. The Almighty has dispelled those
thirteen years like dust on a breeze."

Choking, I fell to my knees and buried my head in
her shoulder.

"Elian," she sighed. "What prompted this?"

At the gentle but direct question, I poured out, "I am to
blame, Sister. If not for me, if I had but reined in my magic,
Malika would not have suffered, not have dreamed the terrible
nightmares she had last night, and Lucian would not appear
as though his heart was broken, and—"

"Elian," she repeated, tipping up my chin so that I did not escape her gaze. "Your actions provided Malika an advantage: if you had not cracked her curse, she might have been saved yesterday's pain, but she would have no defense when her curse would be broken. You will have protected her on that day."

"But Lucian did not let me heal yesterday!" I protested, unable to believe her. "And I was useless in his endeavor to save her!"

"Well," a slight smirk drew up her mouth, "he could not let you accidentally crack her curse *again*, could he? Balance, Elian. And as for your aid yesterday... I would advise you to not presume." Disquiet flashed on her face, passing too quickly to understand.

Exhaling, I looked up at her, drawing strength from her beloved amber eyes, so quick to seethe like molten gold at the merest hint of injustice.

"Brother, Hally," Arista said, grinning as she used the Zahacit endearment, "you do understand what support you gave Malika, do you not? With but a drop of magic, she defeated the Quest Leader himself! Five times!"

I could not resist a smile. "She is certainly amazing."

"Divine-blessed so!" Arista exclaimed, laughing. Then she dragged me to my feet and pulled me after her. "Lucian said to *reach* the training arena! Not to delay in front of the stables!"

The sound of her mirth buoyed me like the breezes that had lifted the wings of my childhood.

Reaching the arena, Arista whirled me around, wrestled my limbs into a kneeling position, locked an arm around my neck, threw off my cap, and rubbed my head with a fist. All despite my much greater height and weight.

"Arista!" I gasped, laughing, even as my wings overflowed with agony. "That was my last clean cap!"

She moved her fingers to my collarbone and tickled the soft scales there.

"Arista!" I exclaimed again amid uncontrollable giggles.

"Haaaallyyyy!" she sang several times before finally releasing me, letting me fall into the dust.

Despite the pain, I could not contain my grin, scales shining gold, as I lifted myself onto my knees. "Is that what playing is like, Hanny?"

"That is certainly how Areta and I played, whenever we had the opportunity," Arista answered as she flopped down beside me and offered a plain cotton handkerchief.

"Areta is the name of your twin," I remembered as I accepted the cloth and wiped my face and my cap.

A sad smile curved her lips. "My best friend before the Quest."

I opened my mouth to attempt words of comfort.

A voice cried, "Elllllll-i-annn! What have you done to your wings?" On the heels of those words Elacir dropped to the ground and stood, struggling to maintain a scowl.

Merely the mention of the cursed flesh seemed to heighten the throbbing. Still, I forced a smile as I replaced my cap. "To what do you refer?"

Though his scowl was turning into a grin, Elacir managed a stern tone as he scolded, "Your wings must be cleaned! It has been two weeks since Lucian last washed them. And, since the Almighty has blessed you so much, I have decided to offer my help!" He brandished a pair of flasks and a sheet.

I did not want him to clean my wings. Not merely because of the pain but because, once he experienced how helpless I truly was, he would certainly lose whatever esteem he still possessed for me. He had hardly met my gaze since leaving Tresilt; even now that we shared a bedchamber, he rarely spoke to me. This conversation was one of the longest we had had in weeks.

Yet how could I refuse? How could I beg Lucian to care for this humiliating need when Malika required his presence so? Particularly when I had not told him, or anyone, about the true reason I could not clean myself as even children could?

Clenching my hands into fists, I braced myself and said, "If it would please you, Elacir."

"It certainly would!" he proclaimed as he spread the sheet behind me. Without a moment's warning, he carefully opened the ties, letting my wings fall loose onto the cloth, and tipped water onto the first feather.

Tapping my cheek, Arista joined him and began on the other wing.

Though my siblings were gentle, dipping each discolored quill into a cupped palmful of water before lightly massaging filth from the delicate scales and the brittle shaft, it was agony. Sharp knives scraped at and stabbed my skin, as though they were digging each feather into my flesh before yanking it out entirely.

So much pain...

Nearly fourteen years to adjust, I thought bitterly, *yet I still cry like a temperamental child.*

Sweat dripped down my forehead, my teeth clenched so tightly that they seemed on the verge of cracking.

So much pain...

Then a hand, soothing with divine-gifted light, touched the tops of my wings.

I gasped, spine arching, as the pain vanished. And, opening my eyes, beheld Lucian.

He was stroking my feathers.

I froze. *By the love of Icilia! He knows!*

Lucian smiled gently and straightened my cap before turning and beckoning the rest of our family closer. Yet the relief of his touch remained, numbing the hurt from Arista's and Elacir's.

Blowing out a breath, I did not know what to do. I should not have been surprised, for he knew everything, and indeed I should have realized he knew from his solicitude, but... the shame of my weakness suffocated me.

"Hally, Elacir and I have finished," Arista said, breaking the pall of torment, as my wings were tied in place, just enough sensation remaining that I could distantly feel what happened to them.

It is the perfect state to cut them off... the unbidden thought brought yet more shame, for such desires would anger Lucian...

A pair of hands appeared in my vision, Arista's small but powerful bronze and Elacir's cocoa (which was starting to exceed my own massive ones in size).

Though those same hands had inflicted pain, I accepted them gladly, curving my lips in an attempt to allay the worry in their expressions.

Lucian glanced back at us, a silent order for us to join Malika, Kyros, Prince Darian, and the guardians.

As I obeyed, I directed a look at Malika, examining her gray face as she lay cradled in Kyros' arms, her limbs too weak to support her.

Though the illness and shadow of horror on her features hurt, I only thought, as I always did, *She is beautiful.* Like Lucian himself, the new day's sunlight caressed her hair, the red shining under the light like rubies set in gold the color of purest honey, itself a symbol of her virtue. Her radiance lit my world, warming my scales to a pale gold even amid the whirl of loathing in my mind. I still did not dare to reveal my secrets to her, but she was my dearest friend for as long as that friendship lasted.

Perhaps noticing my gaze, she turned her head slightly and beamed at me, bleary blue eyes warming.

How I prayed I would never lose that friendship…

"My family," Lucian spoke.

Something in those quiet words snapped our attention to him.

A gray tinge like Malika's marked his usually silver cheeks, and dark circles like fresh bruises lined his eyes, but his expression was stern, radiating power and authority.

He spoke, "We have suffered much in these last weeks. Wounds and curses drown us in torment and threaten to break our spirit. There is much cause amongst us for doubt and loathing—enough cause for us to slip from our path, to cower in fear rather than rise in hope." He gestured around us at the arena. "There is much reason for each of us to never wish to return here."

My breath caught for he seemed to directly address my torment.

"But, my family," he said, "we must not slip. Much depends on our success, much beyond what you know, much even beyond what has so far been revealed to me. We must fulfill the trust placed in us by the Almighty just as we trust the Almighty to bless us with the heart to continue." An eyebrow slanted up. "Do you trust in the Almighty, my family? Do you keep your faith in me?"

"Yes, my Lord!" all of us cried as we scrambled to bow in acknowledgment. Kyros steadied Malika on her feet long enough for her to proffer a reverence before sweeping her back up into his embrace.

Lucian nodded, pressing his lips into a thin line. "Then listen to my command: your Grace, I forbid you to wield, hold, or touch a weapon of any kind for as long as I wish. Obedience, your Grace, in this matter is loyalty to me."

Mouths dropping open, we stared at him—even as Malika pushed aside Kyros' arms, tumbling out of his grip and landing with a jarring thud on her knees. Despite the pain twisting her lips, she bent her head and intoned, *As you wish, my Lord.*

"My Lord?" I whispered, not understanding as easily. He had not merely given an order—he had bound his command to her allegiance!

"My Lord, Malika's new skill is a major strategic asset!" Arista exclaimed, bewildered. "Why did you order her to excel as you did if you do not intend to use that skill in our battles? Why—"

Kyros jabbed her side with an elbow as he helped Malika stand. Arista's eyes widened, and, silencing her protest, she immediately said, "As you wish," and I echoed her.

Though his eyes had flashed with pain at Malika's fall, Lucian's expression remained stern. "I asked Malika to train not for Nademan's conquest but for control of her magic. A second retaliation is not inevitable, and this is the necessary step." The words rang with displeasure.

I grasped Arista's hand, and she clung to my fingers in return as we bowed, then knelt and murmured together, "My Lord, we beg your forgiveness in asking." This had not been the correct moment, and our offices required that we perceived that distinction.

Lucian seemed appeased. "Listen to my next command: your Honor Elian of Light, your Honor Kyros of Light, Prince Darian-asfiyi, and Inase Elacir bi-Dekecer, you must achieve mastery in the sword and the bow and in the use of your magic for battle. Additionally, your Honor Kyros of Light, you must excel such that you attain magical maturity, for her Grace and his Honor cannot. Though I desired to allow you the time you needed to flourish in your studies, our need of strategic preparation is a higher priority. My guardians, Safirele Palanézes, you will aid them in obeying my command."

His requirement terrified me, and the acknowledgment of what I lacked hurt, but I did not hesitate. The sacred response, "As you wish, my Lord," spilled from my lips as quickly as it came from the others'.

Lucian inclined his head and then focused his piercing gaze on his brother.

The prince froze, a deer blinded by intense light.

"Prince Darian-asfiyi," Lucian said, "I give you a third command: teach my Second everything you have learned and understood about military strategy and the Quest's fortresses. Make her my equal in these matters. And, your Grace, surpass me as you have in battle."

Though anguish creased his features, Prince Darian bowed and murmured his obedience as promptly as Malika herself did.

Satisfaction lit Lucian's face, followed by a dazzling smile.

And I could finally breathe. I loved his majesty with all the fervency of devotion, but I had erred. His delight was true redemption.

My family relaxed as well.

A footstep sounded behind us.

Arista and I leapt to our feet.

"Blessings, Nademile," Lucian greeted, inclining his head with his usual kindness. "What brings you to us so early in the morning?"

Faces glossing, Halona Tikariat and the townsfolk of Filisso dipped reverences. They seemed too frightened to speak.

"There is no cause for hesitation," Lucian said, chuckling. "Speak. Ask of us what you desire."

Halona took a deep breath, calming her usually steel-wrought nerves, and responded, "My Lord, my Grace, my Honors, Inase bi-Dekecer, you are the reason that we still live, that our families rest in peace, that we have hope for the future. Thus... after much conversation and deliberation, while we treasure the name of our town, we have decided to leave it aside in favor of the name of Arkaiso. For as long as your war lasts, we will be behind you. Every army, even yours, requires support. We will be your staff, and, though we are not nearly so skillful in your martial training, we will fight for you as well."

In unison, they bowed and curtsied again.

Even Lucian appeared shocked by the pronouncement. His scales an iridescent plum, Elacir affixed his gaze to his boots.

"We are grateful for your words of support," Lucian said, "but what prompts such a vow?"

"Leaving aside Filisso's name is no small matter," Arista added. "Do you not intend to return after Nademan is reconquered?"

The townsfolk vehemently shook their heads, and Halona answered, pale brown eyes flashing with both determination and sorrow, "My Rulers, we understood on that very day that we owe you everything. Our undying loyalty. But yesterday..." Many of them shivered, pained, and she continued, "Your agony made our own love for you inescapably clear. We will not leave you even after you reconquer Nademan. You gave us back our lives. My sisters, my brothers, and I want to tie ours to yours, as we should already have done."

"You even wiped our tears amid our grief," Deanna said. "The least we can do is help you do that for others."

"Our families would be proud of us for doing this," Memona declared.

That started a clamor from all of them, even quiet Syona, of what we had done for them and how determined they were to see our war through with us.

We will show them all they need, Ilqan said with clear approval.

When each had spoken, Lucian beamed affectionately. "We accept your promises, and we will welcome your pledge, with favor, when I am well enough to receive it. My guardians will help you prepare for your duties."

The townsfolk—no, *staff* members—returned the beam and hurriedly bowed and curtsied again. They begged leave and, as soon as Lucian gave it, left for the commander's tree, all the while assuring us that they would immediately take charge of our kitchen, laundry, farmyard, and stables.

In the sudden silence, Kyros commented, "I am glad they are finding purpose again."

"They are very sweet to offer this," I concurred.

Our family murmured their agreement.

Then Prince Darian said, a glimmer of excitement cracking the impassivity of his expression, "So now you have a proper staff and the beginnings of soldiers, Brother. Any thoughts on an army?"

Lucian smiled in response. "May the Almighty show us the moment to gather one soon."

CHAPTER 38

UPLIFT THE TAINTED

Perspective: Honored Elian the Exemplar of Esteem
Date: Eyyélab, the ninth day of the third moon, Zalberre, of
the year 500, C.Q.

The hymn, 'In seeking the Almighty's wishes, there is fulfillment,' reverberated in my mind. As it swelled into true conviction, I catalyzed physical energy in a rush of warm wind, streamed the power through the emeralds of my pendant and my sword, and spoke in the sacred tongue Alimàzahre, "Simit pe saneru u'wurqet ai teku u'nabtet, taz simirim zidilëm, kaferim ó saneh Dalaanem-ik." Then, holding onto to those words, I reached for the breeze.

Though faint, merely brushing against the tall pillars of the forest, the streams of air responded to me like my horse, Asmarrie, reacted to a rub of her muzzle. Eager, ready to listen, affectionate, yet easily distracted, combing through my hair, beard, and feathers.

I pressed my spell into the white-hot power and the willful wind, more smoothly accomplishing imbuement than I ever had before.

The air crackled with power, my command swirling on the flows and eddies.

Then a force of air burst out toward the soldiers.

I opened my eyes as the gale ripped through the cordon, tossing some out toward the forest and others into the town's massive trees. The soldiers, no longer sneering, could not stand steady, their kind magic ineffectual in front of my cyclone.

"Excellent work," Lucian murmured.

Arista flashed me a proud grin. "That was your best spell yet, Elian! Even better than the one you used to deflect the arrows directed at Nadeya Penna Zitariat," she said, referring to the woman we had saved three days prior.

My scales flared as I streamed more power into my spell, directing it with additional commands to spin around the townsfolk and pry the soldiers off the women they had captured.

"Continuous imbuement," Darian commented. "Impressive."

Finally earning that elusive praise brought such a glow to my scales that the gold edged my vision.

"My gratitude, Elian," Lucian stated, clapping my shoulder. "Arista, Darian, come." Spurring his horse, he rode into the clearing, our siblings mere paces behind on their own horses.

I maneuvered the wind around them, keeping even the smallest eddy from mussing Darian's blond hair or the white mane of Rikeb, Lucian's stallion. Not a single current hurled the last slush of winter; not one breeze disturbed the first shoots of the town's crops and the first buds of spring adorning the trees.

Leaning in the saddle, my family swung their swords down on the soldiers, killing them with far more mercy than they would have shown the townsfolk. Matching her mistress' battle-rage, Ekhittie lashed out with her hooves at any whom Arista's blade missed.

A woman's screech drew my attention. Swinging her arms wildly, she attempted to throw off the much larger soldier crouching over her.

With the flick of a gust, I tossed him directly into the path of Darian's blade. Then, turning, flung another man into Lucian's blood-dyed sword.

Several soldiers, spitting out their own spells, pushed back the force of my magic and ran toward the edge of the forest.

Remembering what Lucian had said about no one here bearing the taint of manipulation spells, I tapped my horse's sides, nudging her into a canter. Then, trusting my seat to her, I unsheathed my sword and sliced the throats of two of the soldiers and pulled the air from the lungs of the third, killing her instantly.

Blood splattered my feathers, the sticky liquid dripping down to the skin, each drop a knife to the cursed flesh. A shudder of both pain and revulsion rippled through me. But my focus on the spell did not waver.

Spinning my mare around, I noticed that my family had caught most of the soldiers and dueled the last few. Another was attempting to escape, but with Arista and Ekhittie on his heels, he would not reach my blade.

The skirmish ended with Lucian delivering the last blow.

The townsfolk, windblown and rumpled but uninjured save for a few bruises, stared at us.

Considering we saved them, I observed, neatly pinching off the flow of power for my spell, *from a massacre like the one at Filisso, they seem quite upset.*

Irritated, really, Darian agreed.

Though he had surely heard our observations, all Lucian said was, *Come, let us bury the enemy.* Dismounting, he hefted the bulk of a particularly large man into his arms.

That monster does not deserve the Quest Leader's cradling arms, Arista grumbled as she selected a shaded spot just beyond the town's boundary.

Darian copied our brother in lifting a scrawnier soldier.

Sharing their opinions, I cast another spell and carried a group of the corpses in the arms of the wind. I piled them by Arista's fire-forged shovels and then paused. *May I continue casting my spell?* I asked.

On our way back toward Arkaiso, we were now within the boundary of the territory we had set out to control, in which Lucian had mentioned not masking, and so attracting more soldiers, was now to our advantage. But this skirmish was unlike the others we had recently fought, near a town instead of the open forest.

Delivering a soldier to Arista's pile, Lucian replied, lips pressed together, *I have cast masking. Please continue, Elian.*

I nodded and moved more corpses.

Between my wizardry and Arista's sorcery, within half an hour we had the grave dug, filled, and sealed.

Lucian knelt to pray while Darian climbed into his saddle. Cleaning our swords, he murmured thanks to the few townsfolk who had helped us. Arista and I remained mounted, guarding both brothers.

A woman of somewhat advanced years asked, drawing our attention, "Who are you?" Dressed in leathers a touch more refined than her branch-mates, she stood at their head.

Arista responded, suave yet polished, "Blessings, Countess Strofaria of Prochisso."

The woman, despite her crossed arms and lifted chin, flinched, as did the townsfolk around her.

I smiled, proud of how Arista had so quickly mastered this fraction of the magic of the Quest. Lucian had instructed her only yesterday in the way to learn the name of anyone she met, and already she progressed to discovering the names of neighborhoods. My own disqualification for magical maturity because of my curse, and thus for wielding the magic of the Quest, did nothing to tarnish my joy.

The countess managed to summon another question: "How do you know our names?" Slightly more wondering than suspicious this time.

Arista waited until Lucian had finished his prayer and remounted his horse. Then she proclaimed, "We are servants of the second Quest Leader, Lord Lucian the Ideal of Freedom, Heir to the Quest of Light and supreme ruler of Icilia. We act in his name, seeking the glory of the Almighty."

The townsfolk's mouths dropped open.

Lucian nodded in his lordly way. "May the Almighty safeguard you." Wheeling Rikeb about, he rode into the forest.

Arista, Darian, and I silently spurred our horses into following.

Only when we were over a mile away did I dare to ask, *Lucian, why did you not ask for their pledges?*

They would not have given their allegiance had I asked, Lucian answered, more weary than the silver of his shining face suggested. *As terrified as they were of the soldiers, they thought our actions would bring more on their heads. Between fear and suspicion, little gratitude remained.*

Then they do not deserve to pledge to you, Darian muttered.

Just as fiercely protective, Arista proclaimed, *We need to look for the perfect town to join your army. Only the purest deserve your presence.*

We might protect everyone, I concurred, *but only because of your divine mercy.*

Lucian did not answer, though his lips quirked into an amused smile. Instead he asked, *Elian, would you rather press for Arkaiso or clean your wings immediately?*

I glanced at the blood staining my discolored feathers and tried not to recoil. After two weeks of Ilqan's gentle prods, I had finally begun to rebuild the shambles of my value for myself, clearing away the ruins of my hatred, but I still abhorred any mention of my wings. They represented, as my magic and kind did, the taint of the Blood's relation and my parents' murder.

As Ilqan had urged me to realize, I loathed my magic. Magic was, actually, the way in which the Blood had found my family: my father had cast a single spell of sorcery outside my mother's shelter of athar-based protection to save me from a mountain lion. Ever on our heels, the Blood used the speck of residue to locate us and revealed all too clearly the source of our doom amid his tortures.

So, alone and afraid for years on end, I had rejected my magic, healing and wizardry alike. As I had rejected my wings. Both were cursed by the Blood, though not in the same way, and I had been able to use neither, not even for my family's needs, much less my own. I could not break the mental association I had given them with the Blood, no matter how much my family needed me.

Such depth to my torment was not surprising.

Did I not hate myself for my shared ancestry with him?

Had I not longed to commit violence against my own life?

In sowing such acrimony, the Blood had cursed me almost as effectively and completely as Malika.

The only part of myself for which I cared was the rope that bound me to Lucian. And it was that rope which had been my lifeline to freedom—and to competence.

Once Ilqan had coaxed out these excruciating realizations, and I had confided them to Lucian, I made rapid progress. An arsenal of wizardry spells and a compendium of healing now lay at my fingertips, and my feet retained balance despite the drag of my wings, allowing me to manage the currents of battle. I still had not mastered using jewels for amplification, but I moved with more grace than ever.

All because of Lucian's and Ilqan's patience.

My torment was by no means eradicated or even greatly lessened. But cutting open the festering wounds had finally given me a chance to heal, to truly begin to recover for the first time in thirteen years. The Almighty had blessed me indeed with such an opportunity. And perhaps someday I would be healed in full. Cleansed of the taint of hatred spawned by my torment.

I could finally taste the hope of Lucian's presence. For if he could heal the four of us, what truly could he not do…

Elian, Lucian called, jolting me out of my thoughts.

I ducked my head, my scales hot. *Sorry for not answering.*

Did your contemplation yield anything of value? he asked, amused.

Daring to peek up, I gave a tiny nod. Every reminder of my gratitude for his love was valuable, a weapon to beat back the melancholy.

Then do not apologize, he said. *Tell me instead of your conclusions, if that pleases you.*

Only that I love you even more than I did four weeks ago, I muttered, aware that we spoke still in the collective link.

The affectionate smile curving his lips, lit by the silver glow of his cheeks, was the reward I wanted, the sight for which I had not bowed to my embarrassment.

I love you, too! Arista declared. *And if I did not fear alarming you, I would jump horses to prove it! As Areta once did!*

Darian and I twisted in our saddles to stare at her, while Lucian gave her a look of reproach.

Your sisters cannot have taught you that, I said, disbelieving.

No, she replied with a wink, *my mother did!*

Lucian tilted his head back and sighed. *Mother Serama, of all the things to encourage the twins to do...*

Darian glared at her. *Do* not *do that!*

Why, Prince Darian, Arista teased, *with such words one might think you were concerned for me.*

Grumbling, the prince averted his gaze, unable to hide the slow spread of silver across his face and neck. Still, his eyes contained less dislike than in weeks past.

Exultant though I was at that victory, I turned to Arista and pled, *Please do not take such risks, Hanny.*

Only if you promise me a duel, Hally! Arista sang out and began to snicker.

Glad to finally be something of a challenge, I acceded and then could not help but join in her laughter.

And finally I believed that it was within my place to do so as a worthwhile Potentate of the Quest.

SEGMENT 2

PROVING WORTH

Perspective: Prince Darian sej-Shehasfiyi, brother of the Quest Leader and auxiliary heir to the throne of Asfiya
Date: Eyyélab, the ninth day of the third moon, Zalberre, of the year 500, C.Q.

"My Lord," Taza said as soon as Lucian turned away from greeting his companions, "I beg your pardon. The guardians outside Nademan beseech you to grant them an audience—Amalna and Fozala have news of a rebellion fomenting in Khuduren and only an hour in which to present it. They fear that any longer will expose them to the enemy's patrols sweeping their surrounds."

Lucian pressed his lips together, an odd light shining on his beloved face, which still retained a shadow of gray. "Such news certainly requires immediate discussion." He started to swing his heavy saddlebags onto his shoulder.

It was an opportunity. So, before anyone else could offer, I blurted, "I can carry your packs to your quarters!" We actually shared a chamber, as I had arranged and Lucian had allowed, but I was careful to avoid any such mention—after learning of Lucian's imminent arrival, Taza and Ilqan instructed me to give up my room in the commander's quarters entirely.

They had not even asked where I had slept in the month since.

Pushing aside that hurt, I let my eyes drink in the sight of his smile as he allowed me to take his bags.

For one moment, the world held only us, brothers forever.

Then Lucian gave me a single nod and, beckoning Arista and his guardians, walked briskly in the direction of the training arena. "Khuduren is not the only nation with a possible opposition. Etheqa, too, seems…"

I was left staring after him.

Why did you not ask me to come with you?

"Prince Darian," Kyros said, using the little formality a Potentate was required to use for an auxiliary heir, "would it please you to join Malika, Elian, Elacir, and me for supper?"

'No, it certainly would not!' was what I desired to say every time one of them asked. But that was disrespectful, and Lucian would hear of it. So, instead I dipped a reverence, murmured a polite refusal, fisted a hand in Farib's reins, and strode as fast as I could toward the stables.

The horse dragged me to a halt and, flicking his tail in my face, trotted back to whicker at Malika, his mistress, leaving me scrambling to remove my saddlebags.

Neither the Potentates nor Elacir nor the staff said anything, but, from their sympathetic glances, they clearly noticed my humiliation.

Such an embarrassed chill spread over my face and neck that it almost burned my skin.

Once I managed to retrieve my possessions, I clutched all four bags and, leaving aside the horse, trudged toward the commander's tree.

How pathetic you are, Darian. A caricature of Lucian's virtue and dignity like your appearance suggests.

Hunching my shoulders, I stared at the ground, the sight of Lucian walking away flashing repeatedly before my eyes.

It was just as Taza had predicted: I was losing my place at his side. Oh yes, he had thought to include me when he issued his commands for excellence, and he did ask about how his companions' lessons progressed—but those were the demands of office. He had only a few minutes for me otherwise. Nothing like the long hours we had once spent together on this very base, laughing as we studied, practiced, and prepared...

Even to the fulfillment of my role he gave little relevance: as the herald of his court, *I* should have presented the townsfolk's proffering of service. But I had not had the chance to even open my mouth before he spoke. As his aide, I should have been in attendance at every meeting. But he had not called me even once.

He was losing interest in me.

Small wonder then that I could hardly bear the sight of the Potentates. Outside of lessons and training, I wanted as little to do with them as possible. I avoided even Elacir for his presence usually meant Elian or Kyros were but a step behind.

Amid such aversion, the last two weeks—spent watching Lucian lavish all his time on Elian while being expected to somehow survive as Arista eked more skill out of me— stretched my nerves almost beyond what I could withstand. And, now that I had returned, I would be required to continue Malika's lessons in strategy and fortress command.

Yet another sign of how Lucian was replacing me.

As she excelled in the few areas which I had mastered, he would have less and less need of me. Soon enough, with the rapid pace of her learning, Lucian would order me to surrender the commander's rings and keys in my custody, leaving me almost entirely without use.

I had only one way left to prove my worth—the fulfillment of the vow I had made regarding Malika's curse.

Though in truth my motivations were many: my own place, certainly, and the admiration for the Potentates that had rendered their suffering, particularly Malika's, heartbreaking to witness. But most of all was my fear for Lucian's health.

The plan we had begun nearly a decade ago for Nademan's reconquest was no small endeavor, requiring massive effort from both he himself and all of his vassals in every area from military action to magical preparation—but what Lucian was doing now was several steps beyond. The demands he heaped upon himself, as he had done since the retaliation from Malika's curse, were so great as to be unhealthful. That was apparent even without giving credence to my suspicion that he was concealing something from none less than the Potentates themselves.

My place at his side was too uncertain, however, for an objection. The best I could do was relieve a fraction of his burden, and the most effective manner in which to do so was the application of all my skill in magical scholarship to the breaking of Malika's curses.

Connected deeply enough to my will to sense the sway of my thoughts, the trees of Arkaiso whispered in appreciation of my intentions.

My embarrassment fading, I could not help a soft smile. From the way they had overwhelmed me upon my return with even the smallest sensations, the movements of butterflies and bees, the trees of Arkaiso had truly missed me. They were becoming as attached to me as the histories said they had been to their first commander, the legendary Prince of Virtue, the Asfiyan king who was Lucian's and my ancestor.

Reaching the commander's tree, I climbed the stairs, two at a time despite the heavy packs, to my shared bedchamber. Once there, I quickly refreshed myself and arranged Lucian's possessions, separating out the weapons and clothes that needed cleaning. Gathering the bundle in my arms, I left to bring them straight to the laundry and the armory. Though Halona Tikariat, the woman whom I had appointed as chief of Arkaiso's staff, would collect such loads tonight, Lucian's belongings had first priority.

Caring for such minute matters was what an aide did.

Upon my return to the commander's tree, as I crossed the common area among the suites, footsteps on the stairs caught my attention.

The athar in the wood thrummed in delight, shining white in my magical vision.

"Arkaiso, *every* time one of the Potentates walks anywhere?" I asked, quietly chuckling as I retrieved my research journal, my preferred quill, and a half-empty inkwell. "Particularly her?"

The fortress drenched me with a sort of smug satisfaction, before posing a question.

"No, they cannot see your greetings yet, darling," I answered, "but may the Almighty soon bestow those gifts upon them."

The trees creaked a little and then settled, praying in their own way.

Prince Darian, were you speaking to Arkaiso? Malika asked in our private link as she stepped into the common area. Her eyes were bright with curiosity, as eagerly attentive as during any lesson. Gratitude to the Almighty, she did not find my most cherished subjects boring.

"Yes, my Grace." I bowed and then elaborated, unable to resist that enthusiasm for knowledge, "Living fortresses always respond more faithfully to those commanders who treat them as incé."

The tree groaned softly, an agreement.

I impressed a smile into the connection as though it were a mind-link. "The original design of these Nademani clusters was that living trees, able to recognize friend and foe, would serve a chosen commander's will. But, because they are indeed living, the trees soon began to exert their own judgment. Thus, although usually merely possessing the commander's ring allows access to the base's defenses, the trees may choose to entirely revoke such access. Or, conversely, with pleasure and trust they may grant near total impunity. Much as incé themselves do."

And you are one of the commanders obeyed with impunity, she said, gazing at me with a sort of... that could not be admiration, could it?

Cupping a hand over my heart, I bowed slightly and replied, "Yes, my Grace... my Grace, might I implore you for a few minutes of audience?" I could not hide the hint of fluster in my tone.

Malika nodded and led the way to the chairs Kyros had arranged for us by the tall, narrow window that gave a view of Arkaiso almost as spectacular as the one from my most favored tree.

Dipping another bow, I sat across from her, opened my journal on my lap, and began, "My Grace, I beg your indulgence in answering a few sensitive questions."

Please ask, Prince Darian, Malika encouraged, smiling kindly, hands clasped over her lap. Though I only ever spoke with her out of duty, she always radiated such comfort and peace...

I swallowed hard at the similarity to Lucian. "If you would deign to tell me, my Grace, I would like to ask about the curse on your voice."

Malika froze, and that easy smile fell from her lips. Shuddering, she wrapped her arms around herself, then sighed and nodded. *Of course, Prince Darian... I confess that I am not all too sure when he placed it. I only know that, sometime after I found I could not speak, he told me that I would never become a magician. Much... many of the memories are too dark to understand. Without light as well as without... compassion.*

Flipping to a fresh page, I recorded her answer. "That itself is most illuminating, my Grace..." I paused and cracked a wry smile in an attempt to soothe her nerves in return. "That choice of word was not intentional."

She chuckled, her shoulders relaxing, and asked curiously, *Why do you inquire about this curse though? Is not the one on my magic of higher priority?*

"I have decided to try something different, my Grace," I answered. "I theorize that, of the three curses between you and our Honor the Exemplar of Esteem, this one may be the simplest. Diseases that affect the vocal cords do exist, while nothing natural impedes the flight of properly formed wings and the use of one's magic. Thus, I hope to gain a proper taste of his magic from this curse."

Malika nodded. *Hmmm, that is quite reasonable...*

I tried not to silver at the praise like the neglected little boy I was.

Any other questions, Prince Darian? she asked.

"Yes," I said. "If you would indulge me, my Grace, I would like to observe you attempt speaking. By sight as well as by feeling your throat as you attempt the sounds. Please do not think the request to be one made with improper intentions."

She nodded, a bit hesitantly, but with enough decisiveness to convince me of her consent.

I moved my chair a bit closer and placed a cool hand on her throat, slipping my fingers beneath her high collar. "If it is in accordance with your will, would you try to speak the alphabet?"

Malika grunted and then opened her mouth in pronouncing the first rune.

Vibrations met my fingers, rippling through the delicate tissue. *She laughs and screams and sighs, so indeed the cords do work, and well. I have noted in the past that her muteness concerns words. Speech. A reasonable conclusion because the Blood hates language... of course he would attempt to ruin her dignity as an incé by taking away something as fundamental as speech.*

"Please continue," I encouraged, masking my rising ire.

She formed the next runes, and more vibrations met my hand as they should have. Yet...

There is something... odd *about the movements of her mouth. I know what she is saying—I know the history behind every one of these runes—but if I did not, would I be able to tell...*

At that precise moment, Elian, Kyros, and Elacir emerged from their rooms.

"What are you doing, Malika, Prince Darian?" Elian asked.

Only curiosity filled his tone, not the suspicion and anger I expected, but I could not help the defensive response: "I am only attempting to learn more about my Grace's curse."

"Ohhh..." the three brothers breathed and gathered around us, sweet smiles curving their lips.

Even as those smiles warmed my heart, I opened my mouth to shoo them away (though it would be disrespectful). Then paused. *What if I...* "My Honors, Inase, can you guess what our Grace attempts to say?"

They intently examined her face, then shook their heads.

"Sorry, Malika," Elian muttered.

My eyebrows drew together. "Hmmm... my Grace, would you switch to the names of the Quest? But not in order?"

Malika did as I asked.

"I cannot tell," Kyros said, cheeks coarsening.

"Nor can I, your Highness," Elacir said, scales dimming.

"Sorry, Malika," Elian repeated.

No need to apologize... Prince Darian, Malika asked, *what did you conclude?*

Withdrawing my hand, I pursed my lips. "Nothing definite yet... but..." *She can utter the words, but those words do not make sense on her lips... what if...*

My gaze shifted to Elian, and I remembered Lucian's description of the magnitude of his healing. Then scrambled for my quill, ink, and journal. As I scribbled my thoughts with perfected elegance, I wondered, *If what I am starting to hypothesize is correct... could we actually break this curse?*

Nothing would please and aid my savior more. And nothing would do more to secure his regard for me.

CHAPTER 39

AWAIT THE ERRANT

Perspective: Honored Arista the Exemplar of Bravery
Date: Eyyésal, the eleventh day of the third moon, Zalberre,
of the year 500, C.Q.

I jabbed my finger at the map, plates buzzing. "Over the last month, we have appeared in *all* of these towns. Between your patrols and the guardians, that is *all* of the towns within 150 miles of Arkaiso! And yet no one has pledged! Not a single person, much less a town!"

Lucian retained his serene expression, hands clasped atop the table.

Our family was not nearly so tranquil.

Even Elian seethed as much as I did, grumbling, "I am still upset over Prochisso."

Kyros muttered, "How many rescues must we perform before they do more than stare at us?"

The rumors must have spread from town to town already, Malika said, *so they must know by now that we have a pattern. That you are sincere and not buying favor with one specific region.*

"And they all know what the news of your name means!" I exclaimed, plates vibrating. "Even now, their households must treasure the Quest of Light's prophecy. They do so in Zahacim despite their treason; certainly the Nademani do so as well!"

"They do," Darian said. "We have years of intelligence to confirm that impression." He shifted and muttered a word that sounded like 'ingrates' beneath his breath.

"His Highness has a proper point," Ilqan agreed (even amid the heated discussion, my heart twanged at the shock on Darian's face). "All our prior research confirms that the people of Nademan, like those of Khuduren, Bhalasa, and Asfiya, long for your coming. The pledges of a part of Tresilt's families are yet more evidence."

"The people should have rallied behind you already!" Taza declared, slamming her hand on the table.

Her words prompted an outpouring of vehemence from all of us, wildly upset on Lucian's behalf. For he was spending the silver glow of his health in the protection of these neighborhoods...

Lucian raised a hand and asked, entirely calm, "Elacir, Nadeya Tikariat, why do you think we have not received any pledges?"

We twisted to face Elacir, who squirmed in his seat between Elian and me, and Halona, who waited at the door to receive any orders for refreshment. Under the pressure of so many gazes, neither seemed willing to speak for a long moment.

Elacir sighed and met Lucian's eyes. "My Lord, you are gracious beyond imagination to ask. To fulfill your wish... My Lord, I beg you to remember that your people are traitors. Your inner circle, your companions and family, are pure of such fault, but your people are rife with flaws. And..."

Someone has been refining his eloquence, I commented, impressing a snicker into the Quest's private link despite my anger.

Remember that speech at Temerilt? Elian said, relaying both exasperation and amusement. *He naturally speaks like this! And he is not yet seventeen!*

Elacir glanced at Halona, whose face coarsened as she stepped forward. "My Rulers, the people of Nademan refuse you because of both guilt and fear. Guilt because, since that wretched monster's conquest, the towns have actually tried to live with it. They harden their hearts to the suffering of their neighbors, their relations, even their own children, so that they might somehow survive. Though even the quietest submissiveness, the complete willingness to surrender every shred of dignity, will not ward the tyrant away for long. That is," her eyes brimmed with tears, "what happened to Filisso. We did everything they asked, yet they did not spare us."

"And the fear?" Lucian asked gently.

The chief of the staff wiped her tears with a faded cotton handkerchief. "My Rulers," she said, swallowing thickly, "fear because the wretched Gouge has trampled us under his heels. He has so far destroyed us that we are afraid to accept your hand in fear of him. The thought of what his troops might do haunts us. The western commander has stricter policies every year about dissent, and the Gouge's chief strategist is ruthless and cunning in her shrewdness. And we are also afraid because we know we do not deserve you. Even... even I did not want to pledge in fear of what the magic would show you of my heart. I f-feared your re-rejection. It is why, though we received so much aid over the years from you and your guardians, even Filisso ignored the rumors of your coming.

Until you saved us in your bountiful mercy." Seeming overcome, she cast a desperate look at Elacir.

Our little brother concluded, "So they will delay pledging to you as long as they can." He visibly shook and shrank in his seat. "May the answer please you, my Rulers."

As I considered his words, plates calming to a lower hum, a wry smirk twitched my lips. "And already understanding all of this, perceiving more than we can comprehend with your divine-gifted awareness and reason, you are more patient than your vassals, Lucian."

One corner of his lips curved up. "Yes."

Taza snorted and leaned back in her chair. "You always did wear that knowing smile whenever we gave our reports. Ilqan, how did a boy of seventeen know our findings better than we did?"

All of us laughed, and the remainder of the tension drained from the air.

Then Lucian stated, gesturing at the map, "We need to plan a bolder move. Something that assures the people that there is power behind the name of the Quest."

Malika frowned. *Do you mean a sort of public announcement?*

"That would be very dangerous," Darian warned.

"But necessary," I replied. "Perhaps the conclusion the towns are forming is that, beyond a few marginal operations, we do not have the resources for a direct confrontation. And well," I laughed without mirth, "they are not wrong."

"Even at the apex of our abilities," Taza agreed, "your circle does not have the resources alone to reconquer Ehaya. You need a true army for that."

Lucian raised an eyebrow. "In only one version of the plan, Taza. There are other options."

"Riskier options!" I scoffed.

"Gathering an army would be better," Kyros agreed. "Nademan is not worth risking your life in a scheme of infiltration." Though he usually spoke at a volume only a few pitches above a whisper, in that moment the stern set of his brows and the firmness of his rumbling voice attested how much of a father he was.

If I had not already been opposed, I would have certainly dropped the idea.

Though not intimidated as the rest of us were, Lucian gave him a slow nod. "As you say, Kyros. Then we must plan for a major maneuver with the intention of securing more pledges."

Elian bit his lip. "What about attacking one of the province's garrisons?"

Of the three... Malika drew her brows together. *These two, the ones in the north and east, are too isolated. And the one at the city of Pethama is again too risky.*

"What about the province's market?" I asked. "It is nearly five hundred miles north, but it would be ideal, unless... Nadeya Tikariat, does that practice still remain?"

Her cheeks glossed at the weight of our attention. "Umm, yes, my Honor, though most attend now because the soldiers harass anyone who does not attend. They are... well, hunting grounds for the soldiers."

All of us tensed, infuriated.

"Zaiqan's market on the twentieth of the moon of Likberre is our target," Lucian said decisively. "Malika, as your first assignment, I ask that you present the Quest with a plan when we gather after the next rotation. Learn well from my brother so that you may succeed."

Malika startled but then nodded eagerly. *As you wish, Lucian!*

He smiled at her and rose, prompting us to leap to our feet. "Malika, Elian, Arista, Kyros, come. I have a matter I wish to discuss. Brother, Taza, Ilqan, Elacir, Nadeya, you have leave for the rest of the day. We will see you at supper." He strode toward the door that led from the strategy room (as Kyros had named it) to the library.

We scrambled to follow on his heels.

As the door swung shut, I glanced around us and snickered quietly. "This is the first lesson since the moon of Thekharre without Elacir."

Whatever will we learn without Elacir? Malika jested, chuckling softly as she took her seat, a slightly more ornate chair than the others, in front of Lucian's veritable throne and large oak writing table.

"He is the source of your learning, Elian, Kyros," I teased.

Kyros merely smiled, much like my father would at such a comment, as he settled in his chair and bowed his head to Lucian, who wore a patient air as he selected a book from the shelves behind the desk.

Elian shot me a dry look, an unusual expression for my Sholanar brother, and then stepped to Malika's side and offered a flask, his emerald eyes bright.

No, sweet as always, I thought, my smirk warming to an affectionate smile.

Malika beamed, accepting the offering. *My gratitude, Elian.*

Elian examined her face, noting as all of us did that the gray tinge was finally fading, before returning her grin and turning to his seat.

I quickly darted forward and unbound his wings, carefully angling them around the chair so that he could sit properly. Then I sauntered to my own just as Lucian seated himself on his throne.

The four of us gave him attentive looks.

Lucian's gentle smile transformed into a dazzling one. "In honor of Elian's birthday tomorrow, we will today begin our study of the lore of the Quest, from the volumes written by the Quest of Light."

Our attention sharpened.

"Finally," I breathed.

Lucian opened the book he held so very reverently. Anticipation tinting his expression, he spoke, "The first topic I wish to discuss is the requirement placed upon us, for it is essential to understanding our purpose. When you consider this, it will make complete sense. We are the rulers of Icilia—though the same term, 'ruler,' that is used for the seven nations is also used for us, we are different. We are so much more powerful and possess much greater authority. Why are we entrusted with such power? What is the guarantee that, regardless of our initial thoughts, we would not be corrupted by the arrogance of possessing power?"

We blinked, entirely confused.

He chuckled. "My Lady Queen often asks questions and then answers them herself. That, alongside passages of direct address to me, is the style of her work. Bear with me, my companions."

We nodded.

He continued, "The answer is that our power is tied to our character. All of us must have absolutely stellar character—especially me. The slightest wavering is unacceptable; the slightest occurrence of arrogance, greed, jealousy, or impiety is not permitted. To feel such things and to rationalize them with thought, much less to act upon them, would shatter our power and position. Such is the expectation placed upon us. And thus we may be trusted above all others. For the rulers of the seven nations would not lose their power, barring a ruling from us or some form of interference, even should they become corrupted. But we would. We have power because we have characters that are as close to perfect as is possible for incé."

Silence as we processed those words.

"Is this true," I asked slowly, "of *all* of our magic or only our pledges and the magic of the Quest? Is the magic which connects us to the seven nations' enchantments, for example, also tied to our character?"

Lucian grinned. "Excellent question. All of our magic is so bound. We were born for this task, remember, so even our personal magic, like my mindlinking and your sorcery, and our birthright magic, like my athar magic and your characteristic Areteen abilities to sense how stone may best be cut or carved and to find good soil, is tied to the magic of the Quest. This connection for me was present at birth, hence why my guardians devoted most of the lessons in my early years to ethics. Only when my character was fully matured did I begin to receive the Quest Leader's magic. For you, the connection, while inherent at birth, solidified only when you pledged to me and ascended."

"How are we supposed to maintain such perfect character?" Elian asked, worried. "Making mistakes is easy."

"Your anxiety is itself an indication that you will make few errors," he pointed out. "Moreover, understand that the divine favor upon you eases your adherence to this rule—and indeed makes such adherence possible. Your character is inherently pure and has been so from birth."

But what if it has already become corrupted? Malika asked in a subdued voice.

Lucian gave her a smile brimming with compassion. "Understand that your pledge formed the bond between us only because your character has remained uncorrupted."

"But it is impossible to remain entirely free of sin!" Kyros exclaimed. "How can we meet such requirements?"

Lucian's eyes sparkled with kindness. "The requirement is not to remain free of all sin—that is too far beyond the capability of us as incé. Only the Shining Guide was so pure.

"Though the expectation placed upon me is greater than it is for you, even I am not asked to be free of all sin. Rather the requirement is to be free of major sin, such as those that come from impiety, arrogance, greed, and jealousy—the sins that corrupt character. As examples, we must never knowingly shed innocent blood or commit violence against someone, and we must never utter blasphemy." He raised an eyebrow. "Those are things you already would not do."

The four of us considered his words. Then we jumped to ask him more questions.

And all the while, I thought to myself, *If only the people of Nademan knew how stark the contrast is between the tyrant to whom they cling and the Lord who wishes to free them!*

CHAPTER 40

CONNECT THE SEEKING

Perspective: Honored Arista the Exemplar of Bravery
Date: Eyyéqan, the seventeenth day of the third moon, Zalberre,
of the year 500, C.Q.

I heaved my aching body into the saddle. *Yet another day in the saddle*, I thought, sighing. *But at least I convinced Lucian to stay back this rotation. All these sores and long days are worth giving him a chance to rest. He truly has not seemed well these last weeks...* Frowning, I called over my shoulder, "Kyros! Elacir! Is it only my skewed perception, or has Lucian seemed ill recently?"

Kyros wrung his hands, shifting them over Farib's reins. "I have the same perception, Arista, and I am *very* worried about him."

"He has pushed himself since that duel," Elacir observed, scratching the thin reddish-brown patch of adolescent beard covering the sides of his face. "In his plan after that, he dropped the thought of week-long rests between rotations. Even after his previous acknowledgment of your concerns."

Rubbing my plates, I said, "It is as though he is aware of something, something alarming, that he has not told us… Something frightening enough to prompt him to ride for weeks without rest… Even when he is on base, he is constantly teaching or planning or discussing Malika's curse with his guardians—" I startled and twisted in the saddle. "Do you think he knows something about Malika's curse?"

Kyros' lips curved in an uncharacteristically wry smile. "Arista, I think Lucian and Malika have hidden almost everything about what happened that evening. You, Elian, and I experienced only the margins—we did not see what they did."

"What of your foresight?" Elacir asked.

Kyros shook his head. "My foresight glimpsed only what we should and should not have done. Nothing beyond, nothing to explain the gravity of the circumstance."

I exhaled a mirthless chuckle. "So we still do not know what, precisely, Lucian did to save her. We do not know what, precisely, provoked that… the *depth* of his wrath." I shuddered at the memory and at the echoes of the pain that still racked my entire being…

"So, there is much we are missing," Kyros agreed. "Although…" a laugh rumbled in his chest, one far more genuine than mine, "I do not know your opinion, but I am inclined to not ask. The very thought of such a confrontation terrifies me, yes, but I trust him entirely. If he keeps a secret, he does so for our sakes, with our welfare as his foremost concern."

I pursed my lips and, unwilling to quarrel, did not speak my own thoughts: *His secrets protect us, yes, but what protects him? Without knowing the full scope of the situation, how can we protect him?* The more I dwelled on these thoughts, the more anxious I became…

Miles of forest passed, and the three of us marveled at the first sights of spring in the Dasenákder. Spring had always meant tiny splashes of vivid flowers adorning thorny shrubs and gnarled trees to me, meadows of wildflowers to Kyros, and hardy blooms amid squelching mire seen from the sky to Elacir. Yet here the elegant pastel blossoms twined around the massive tree trunks, climbing more than carpeting, releasing a sweet perfume unlike any I had smelled before. Our joy was tainted only by the effects of the Blood's tyranny—and Lucian's absence.

"It truly is beautiful despite the destruction," Kyros breathed, though the faint wobble of his voice betrayed his own longing. "How I wish Elacir and I could share what we see with you."

Giggling, concealing my own concern and yearning, I leaned to the side and swatted his shoulder. "Savor it for me instead, Hally!"

"Do *not* tilt out of your saddle!" he exclaimed. "Elian told me about your suggestion of 'jumping horses'—do not *dare* attempt that, Sister!"

I exploded with laughter, doubling over and clutching my middle. Tears streamed down my face, winding through my plates. Ekhittie pranced beneath me and tossed her head back, neighing in what sounded suspiciously like chuckles. *A distraction for all of us, at least for a while.*

Elacir joined me, muffling his snickers in Asmarrie's gray mane.

"Your safety is no laughing matter," Kyros said, voice stern, though his lips twitched.

"It is not, but- but- that expression!" I gasped. "Kalyca simply must hear of this!" Then straightening, I chirped, "Yes, Big Brother."

Kyros smacked a hand over his mouth, muffling what had to be his own chuckle. Then he froze and dropped his hand as his eyes glowed.

Elacir and I sobered, immediately straightening and grasping our hilts.

Kyros blew out a breath. "Hmmm. There is a group of seven Nasimih men and women traveling in our direction... but none of them wear the uniform of the Blood's soldiers. Or, indeed, have a soldier's bearing. They carry sticks for makeshift weapons, and they seem... frightened... and yet... determined... as though looking for something. At our current pace, we would encounter them at sunset."

I traced the edges of my plates. "What does your foresight show? And, also, my praise for using your sights concurrently."

His cheeks glossed as he replied, "I am focusing my foresight on you, Arista..."

I nodded, perceiving the intense scrutiny of his magic, with the sweet tinge of the gaze of someone I loved, as Lucian had described I would be able to sense as a fully mature Potentate. Though I had achieved magical maturity before my ascension, only now, under Lucian's guidance, was I beginning to access my full Quest-gifted magic.

"And... well, if we meet them..." His glowing eyes widened. "Arista! They might actually pledge!"

"Then we must meet them!" Elacir cried. "Oh please, can we, Arista?"

I grinned. "Yes, indeed. Though I will contact Lucian to ensure I know exactly what I need to do..." Nudging Ekhittie in the direction Kyros indicated, I invoked one of the communication spells my pendant held.

The emerald vibrated, and Lucian spoke with clear concern, "Blessings, Arista! What support do you need?"

"Blessings, Brother!" I laughed as I savored the sound of his voice. "Should I consider it a slight on my competence that your first thought was that I required aid?"

He chuckled, seeming to relax. "Of course not. But what else would I ask first when half of my heart is riding through dangerous territory without me?"

Kyros and I exchanged delighted looks, while Elacir shifted Asmarrie closer to me. "Do I count in that part of your heart?" he called out.

"Yes, Elacir, you do," Lucian said, a smile evident in his voice. "Now, tell me, what do you need?"

"Well…" A grin split my face. "Kyros foresees the possibility of a pledge!"

"Excellent," Lucian stated, pleased. "Would a review of the necessary ceremony be of use to you?"

"Yes," I replied. "I can receive the pledge, can I not?"

"You can," he answered, "though remember that any pledges made to us must be bound with life. That is what allows us to truly assess and observe loyalty. And this is how…"

Between his detailed instructions and my questions, much of the time passed until Kyros asked me to call a halt for the evening. Promising to contact him on the next day, I farewelled Lucian and led my brothers in establishing a defensible camp: makeshift alarms in the trees for any Nasimih movement, carefully trimmed bushes to allow maneuverability, and our blankets themselves at the base of a wide trunk clear of branches until the canopy. Open ground for me, climbing access for Kyros, flight space for Elacir.

Satisfied, I brushed off my hands and accepted supper from Elacir.

Then, chewing on hard bread and dried meat, we waited.

Restless, I prodded Kyros into granting me a duel. He had excelled enough to give me a decent challenge (once he had found his spark, when he beheld Malika's fifth victory, he began to rapidly improve), and the exercise refreshed my cramping limbs and further refined his skill.

I was raising my blade to Kyros' chest when I heard the crunch of fallen twigs.

'They are here,' Kyros mouthed through heavy wheezes.

I nodded and sheathed my sword. Then I reached for the magic of the Quest, holy and warm, reminiscent of the patient compassion of Lucian's violet eyes. As it blazed through my mind, I tapped Nademan's magic, the sighs raised in repentance and the shamed murmurs reminding one's own heart of decency and modesty... Brushing through the rustling magic, like leaves in the wind, I came to the place where I stood and touched the auric signatures of the ones who approached. In the whirl of energy, I found their names.

Opening my eyes, I said, "Blessings, Count Ciro Tolmarie, mayor of Jurisso. And to you as well, Countess Belona Tolmariat. How is Nadeya Penna Zitariat?"

The man and the woman, who had approached us with makeshift spears raised, froze. Their mouths dropped open as they fixated on our faces. Without warning, they rushed forward a few steps—prompting Elacir's hands to tighten on his sword—and flung themselves at Kyros' and my feet.

"You were with him," Count Tolmarie breathed, his voice a pleasant smooth baritone. "Ten days ago, at our town. Please, I beg of you to tell us: was he truly the Lord Quest Leader?"

Sheathing my sword, I dipped my head. "The shining man was the second Quest Leader, yes, and we," gesturing at Kyros and me, "are his companions. I see that his words achieved their objective. Though, why are you so far from home?" We were nearly forty miles south by southwest of Jurisso.

The golden tan of their faces glossed completely. "We were searching for our Lord, my Honor," Ciro muttered.

Already using the reverential addresses, I noted, *and he and his wife seem terribly flustered. Good signs, as Lucian explained. As for their words...* I declared, "My Honor and I are glad then, to have been found by you."

Only days ago we had lamented the lack of adherents to Lucian's cause, and now we met those who had gone looking for us! How the Almighty had blessed us!

They blinked, startled again.

Donning a regal smile, Kyros prompted, "Would you introduce us to your comrades?" As he sheathed his sword, he covertly stroked the surface of his pendant, activating the link Lucian had bound within it for us. *What do you think, Arista?*

Ciro and Belona seemed to shrink in mortification. They glanced at the forest, but they did not need to speak, for the other five women and men were already emerging from between the trunks. Cheeks glossing, they knelt in front of us.

Recognizing one of them without the use of magic, I curled my lips in my own regal smile. "Blessings, Nadeya Zitariat. How are you? How is your recovery?"

Penna seemed too shy to speak, though she had chattered for much of the ride to her town not many days before, in Lucian's own presence.

Greeting the other four by name, I listened to my instincts, as Lucian had taught. From what I read of their auric signatures and the impressions given by Nademan's magic... they were capable of true freedom, of true faith in the Almighty and trust in Lucian. Pleased, I then communicated all of those impressions to Kyros.

Excellent, he said and, following my unspoken cue, introduced the three of us.

Then I asked Penna, the only one I had met previously, for a proper introduction.

Despite my gentle tone, she seemed utterly embarrassed as she rushed to obey, stumbling over even the name of her husband.

All of them seemed awed—though only Kyros and I were present from among the Potentates.

That alone shows that they will be worthy vassals, I asserted.

From the quiet murmurs in the link, my brothers were as satisfied as I was.

The light of the setting sun, I noted, was painting the portions of the western sky visible amid the tall trees a sorrowful crimson and a joyous gold, the colors bright despite the smog, and the shards of eastern sky were already a deep indigo. So I proclaimed, with my brothers' agreement, "Rise, Nademile, and, if it would please you, retrieve your supplies. If you would join our camp tonight, we can speak tomorrow about why you searched for my Lord."

Unusually, none of them rose. Instead, they glanced at each other, apprehension wrinkling their foreheads and coarsening their faces. Ciro opened his mouth to speak but hesitated.

He seems to think you will refuse him, Kyros commented.

"Ask," I said, curious.

Ciro blurted, "We want to pledge!" Then he ducked his head, frustrated at the crudeness of his own words. Belona elbowed him, the gesture so smooth I almost did not notice it.

"Truly?" I questioned, surprised. The political customs of Icilia dictated immediate acceptance, and regardless we truly did need their pledges, but… "You have not yet learned of the Quest's purpose, nor of our choice of methods in achieving it."

They do seem a bit hasty, Elacir agreed. Then he impressed a wrinkled brow. *Wait, what does that make our pledges?*

Love at first sight, I suggested, prompting snickers from all three of us in the link, though we were careful to keep our expressions tranquil.

The townsfolk glanced again at each other. Then Ciro responded, "Forgive me, my Honor, but your purpose is obvious. We ask to follow you in it, with whatever methods you choose." Anxiety and apprehension coated the words, but they were resolute themselves.

I raised both eyebrows. "Are you certain?"

They nodded.

The pledge itself will tell me of the strength of their conviction, I said. *Continue, Kyros, with your part.*

Dipping his head, Kyros inquired in his rumbling bass voice, "Do you pledge individually, Nademile? Or on behalf of your town?"

"On behalf of my town," Ciro replied immediately. The fading gloss of his skin returned.

Kyros nodded and explained the proper words and position.

Once he had explained three times, Ciro and his comrades held their hands up as Ciro recited, "By the Light seen in the Shining Guide, on behalf of the town of Jurisso and my own behalf, I pledge our love and allegiance to you, my Lord Lucian the Ideal of Freedom. We will praise your name in both public speech and private discourse. We will govern ourselves in accordance with your will and uphold your commands and laws. In all things we will proffer our best service to you. May the Almighty bless us with success in your Quest."

Taking a steadying breath, I placed my hand on Ciro's and recited, "For freedom by the Almighty, in the name of my Lord Lucian the Ideal of Freedom and with his favor, I, Honored Arista the Exemplar of Bravery, accept your pledge and promise his support in return. With the testament of love, I say that in all things he is just and that mercy and compassion will always temper his rule. May the Almighty bless us all and be pleased with all that we are. Praised be the Almighty." Simultaneously, as instructed, I accessed the font of my life (reachable without perversion only because of my maturity as a Potentate) and, with the same sensation as pricking my own fingers, catalyzed a portion.

Drops of life, equal in number to the lives of the ninety adults whose hopes were joined to Ciro's, spilled into my palms as the ruby of my Potentate's ring began to glow.

Light flashed around Ciro's and my hands and then around the hands of each of his comrades. Forty miles to the south, the townsfolk of Jurisso froze and startled as light wreathed their hands. In that light, all of them caught a glimpse of Lucian's character and power, as well as my own. Upon their hearts dawned the truth of who we were and whose power spread around them.

As I in turn beheld who they were: their fears, cares, loves… their identities and the quality of their virtue… their convictions. Lucian's return of their daughter had convinced several, and Ciro had persuaded most of the rest to follow us. A few remained uncertain. But, regardless of their prior thoughts, all of them immediately accepted the duties of their pledge. Desperate hope flooded our fledgling bond.

So, knowing what Lucian would say, in turn I accepted all of them. They were capable of being truly free, and tying them to the banner of the Quest, for both our mission and their salvation, was worthy of the sacrifice of my life.

With a silent prayer I sealed the pledge.

And then I watched in wonder as my power infused them with the drops of my life, enhancing their strength and magic, tying them irrevocably to *me*, as well as to Lucian, their obedience to my command as well as his required of their loyalty. The connection coalescing between us would tell me always of how they fared and whether they required aid. For the townsfolk of Jurisso had become my vassals as well as Lucian's.

My first thought was of gratitude, that finally Lucian's army had begun to form.

Ciro and his comrades fell back onto their bottoms and stared star-struck up at me.

The second thought was a slow creeping horror... Binding this one pledge had cost me enough to make me lightheaded and unsteady on my feet. Ninety-one drops of life—and the bond formed was powerful, potent, and yet merely a fraction of the bonds among the Quest.

So, exactly how much had Lucian sacrificed for our bonds?

CHAPTER 41

ACCEPT THE PLEADING

Perspective: Honored Arista the Exemplar of Bravery
Date: Eyyédal, the nineteenth day of the third moon, Zalberre,
of the year 500, C.Q.

Ciro choked and wheezed, gasping great amounts of air as he swayed back and forth. Only the arms of his much calmer wife kept him in Asmarrie's saddle.

"Count Tolmarie, our Lord is not *that* scary," Elacir chirped.

Belona cast him a rueful smile and retorted, "You say that because you have traveled with him for months on end!"

Unable to resist, I teased, "And because he lets you make all the mischief you want, Hally!"

Elacir grinned and flapped a wing an extra time, aiming a gust of wind in my direction.

Not one mahogany curl fell loose from the tight loops of my bun, nor did my cap tilt so much as a single degree.

I smirked at his frustrated groan and then turned back to the countess. "But, truly, Count Tolmarie, Countess

Tolmariat, my Lord will welcome you. Indeed, he knows you already."

At those words, even the countess lost the serene, amused expression she had worn. "How?" she gasped.

Kyros gave Elacir a quelling, if amused, glare as he answered, "In the same way as my Honor did when she sealed your pledge. Just as you glimpsed our Lord's and her character, so did they see yours."

"That does not help me feel better, my Honors!" Ciro wheezed.

I chuckled and gave him a fond smile.

In the two days we had traveled together after the pledge and the others' return to Jurisso, Kyros, Elacir, and I had come to intimately know the noble couple, as they had us, and we had quickly formed a friendship. The countess was very much a kindred spirit to me, as the count was to Kyros. Our time together had confirmed much of what I saw in the fires of the bond, and I was convinced that, as we had prayed, Lucian's first allegiant town was truly worthy of his presence. They deserved the audience Lucian intended to give them.

"Jests aside, though, Count Tolmarie," Elacir said, gliding above the man's head, "our Lord is truly kind. Only his companions and his family actually deserve his compassion, but he still lavishes his care upon all of us."

Ciro exhaled heavily but nodded. "Thank you, Inase bi-Dekecer."

I winked at Kyros and activated Lucian's link. *As always, my gratitude to the Almighty for you, Elacir. And not only for the praise and the soothing words—I know it is not easy to fly amid these trees. Thank you, again, for allowing them to ride Asmarrie.*

Elacir's plum scales flared, the heated color rippling from his face down over his arms and wings even as those same limbs scraped rather painfully against several tightly clustered branches.

What did you want to discuss? Kyros asked, amused and just as appreciative.

Warmth filled my heart at how well he knew me. *Would you deign to look ahead, Kyros? I do not want to bring our new vassals into any danger. Or bring any to Lucian and Elian.*

He indicated a nod, and whispery magic ignited around him.

I raised an eyebrow. *Sensing catalysis. That is new,* I thought. *Yet another ability Lucian said I would develop as a fully matured Potentate... which renders my need to acquire answers about the magic of the Quest all the more important. Because there is something missing about his explanation...*

It was the conclusion I had reached after a day of reflection on my questions about the companions' pledges. Yet, as much as I reflected and considered, I could not fathom how to actually *ask* him anything.

The pace of his campaign would increase now that a town had pledged, and I did not want to add to the burdens on his shoulders. Moreover, his decision to keep certain matters secret was more justified than my desire for answers—as I remembered with Elacir's illness, he placed his family's needs clearly above his own. My questions arose only for the sake of his needs—a reason that, unlike with anyone else, would not find favor with Lucian.

Though immersed in these contemplations, I maintained a steady flow of conversation with the nobles, as my training in diplomacy ordered.

So the hours elapsed until Kyros alerted us that Lucian and Elian approached.

The links snapped back into place with a wave of cool magic.

Blessings, Arista, Kyros, Elacir, Lucian spoke. *How are you, my Sister, my Brothers?*

Blessings! Elian added. *I missed you!*

I tilted my head back as I relished the sincerity in those words. *Blessings, Lucian, Elian! We missed you, too, and we will be well when we see you.*

Lucian laughed, and the musical sound, as pure as the ring of a great bell, drove away the vestiges of the pain I had suppressed in our days apart.

With their progress toward us and ours toward them, the miles thankfully passed quickly amid our questions about Malika's, Darian's, the guardians', and the staff's wellbeing. Soon enough we rode into the same clearing.

Dismounting, I ran to Lucian, and, with not a thought for decorum, he swung me into his arms, spinning me in a circle and kissing my forehead.

I beamed, enjoying the sense of comfort and peace that radiated from him. How had I ever lived without him?

You know that I share that sentiment, Lucian murmured, briefly resting his forehead against mine.

That is honestly too much to believe, I admitted as I drew back and flung my arms around Elian's waist.

Lucian impressed a smile. *You will know your value in my eyes someday.*

Confidence in your love would be a blessed relief, Kyros said, accepting an embrace and then stepping aside for Elacir.

I know you laugh at my audacity, our little brother whispered, snuggling into Lucian's arms, *but I sometimes wonder when you will realize that I do not belong with you. I am not a Potentate to deserve your love.*

As if we deserve your love ourselves, Elian muttered with a flash of melancholy.

You will believe me soon enough, Lucian said as Elacir moved back.

Perhaps, Brother, I replied.

Assured as always, Lucian took a step toward the nobles. Then suddenly froze. Anguish tore through his presence in the links.

Lucian! Elian, Kyros, Elacir, and I exclaimed, ears ringing as pain blasted through our hearts.

Lucian shook his head, as though to clear his thoughts. *My apologies—an old memory consumed my attention for a moment. I will tell the story to you on another occasion.*

At the tacit undertone of dismissal in his voice, the four of us reluctantly put aside our questions. Though my alarm lingered, I focused on him as he began to speak.

Hands folded over his waist, he was saying, "May the Almighty bless you, Countess Belona Tolmariat, Count Ciro Tolmarie. My boundless gratitude for the sparks of loyalty that led you to seek me."

The charmed smiles Ciro and Belona had worn amid our personal moment, which had faltered slightly in Lucian's momentary pause before addressing them, transformed into pure, star-stricken awe. They were too dazed to even bow.

Lucian chuckled softly and gestured for us to seat ourselves on the grass-covered ground. We obeyed, forming a circle in front of him, but, before he himself could bend, I cast a spell I had designed several months prior.

A chair, formed of tiny links of fire, bloomed in a rush of warmth by Lucian's side.

"For the love of Icilia," Elian whispered, his fascination bringing a new buzz to my plates.

Quirking an eyebrow, Lucian accepted the seat, smoothing the fall of his robes over his knees. *My gratitude. Though it was unnecessary.*

I impressed a smirk, noting that he seemed entirely at his ease once more. *Not for your dignity perhaps, but certainly so for ours!*

Laughter sparkled in his eyes, dispelling the last of my anxiety. *The spell is well done, Sister.* Then said more seriously, *Kyros, Elacir, observe the forest. Much of this territory is clear, but we have our vassals' safety as well as our own to consider.*

The two farseers indicated obedience.

Arista, the introduction, Lucian ordered.

Recalling the ceremonial words, I presented the nobles to Lucian and Elian.

Satisfied, Lucian then said, "Count Tolmarie, Countess Tolmariat, I would listen to your requests first."

The couple exchanged glances. Ciro motioned subtly to Lucian, and Belona gave him a pointed look. He nudged her side, and she rolled her eyes but nodded and pursed her lips, seeming to gather her words. Then, bowing her head, she spoke, "My husband proposes that the townsfolk of Jurisso become soldiers in your service, my Rulers. Alongside that plea, we have several favors we desire to ask, though we know our place at your feet is new."

Lucian nodded. "Ask."

"We seek the shelter of your base," she said, her husky contralto voice steady despite the fluster of her glossed cheeks, "wherever it may be. Exposed as our town is to the soldiers in our own trees, your service would place our families at greater risk than they already are. In the hope of your acceptance, our families are already prepared to move.

"Our second plea is that, if you allow us to come to your base, you also bestow upon us land to farm and raise our chickens. We will provide for our own meals through hunting and gathering, but such continuance of agriculture is necessary to refine those skills in our youth.

"And in a similar thread is our third plea: the exemption of our matrons and elders from your army so that they may teach our children. In the last seven years, with the wretched Gouge's demands ever increasing, our children have lost much of their chance to learn. We would hope that, in the safety of your base, they would regain the opportunity.

"We leave the acceptance of our pleas at your feet, my Lord, my Honors."

Her entreaty, Kyros remarked, *exactly match what Malika and Darian are preparing.*

It is what I would insist, I agreed. *Also, Belona speaks very well—as well as you, Elacir! Do not impress that playful scoff in the link—you know she included all the right appeals.*

Lucian's lordly smile widened a little. "The Quest grants all of your appeals, Count, Countess."

The couple sighed, relieved.

"Though, with one condition."

They stiffened.

"We ask," he said, "that our own scholars, my brother and fortress commander Prince Darian sej-Shehasfiyi and my guardians Safirile Taza and Ilqan Palanézes, be welcomed in your lessons. One of the intentions of our reconquest is to restore the Quest of Light's standard of education; speaking to your children and youth would fulfill the beginnings of our plan."

Ciro and Belona nodded, stunned.

I affirm your judgment, Arista, Elian said, delighted. *They truly do seem to be worthy first vassals.*

Then he asked, his tone grave, "What is your opinion of how far the Quest's name has spread?"

Elian, Kyros, Elacir, and I leaned forward.

The couple's expressions darkened. "My Rulers," Belona answered, "as much as we wish otherwise, we are the only town within our acquaintance who has been ready to pledge. The rest are..." She paused and seemed to struggle to find the proper words, scratching the thick, ropy scar that crossed from the corner of her right eyebrow to the side of her chin.

"We are planning," I said, "to reveal ourselves more publicly at Zaiqan's annual market. Would that generate a difference?"

She spread her hands. "Perhaps? We, your new vassals, would certainly be honored to support you in such an appearance... but I fear that the difference among the towns is one of leadership. Everyone suffers, and everyone fears the wretched Gouge and his strategist, but the mayors and their families, both noble and no longer, have mostly managed to ward away tragedy by offering up their own people to the soldiers."

My family and I said nothing, but our fury was palpable.

Belona winced, even as the same anger lit her sky-blue eyes. "Saving women like Penna certainly gives the townsfolk themselves hope, but without their leaders... Ciro and I led our tree-town to pledge allegiance only because of personal experience." Her shoulders slumped as she uttered that last sentence, and Ciro rubbed her back.

Sorrow bled into the wrath on Lucian's silvery beige face. "Witnessing the state to which the people of Icilia have been reduced grieves my heart." His violet eyes took on a distant quality, as though they gazed into the past, beholding something none of us could. "The Quest of Light wished for Nademan to be a nation of art and commerce, of elegance and novelty, in its whimsy a bastion of the decency and shame of civilization." Those purple jewels snapped to our faces, breath-taking in their intensity. "This is what I intend to restore."

Ciro and Belona seemed enamored, expressions bright with the same wonder as Lucian's own family.

"Only our Lord could dream of such things," I said, a sad smile curving my lips. "We are too crushed to even imagine the assuredness of true security."

The others breathed echoes of the same sentiment.

"It is my place to wish for more for my people," Lucian stated, the steady assurance we sought in his gaze.

That wonder and enthrallment intensified.

Amid that amazement, a thought coalesced in my mind, and, frowning, I asked, "What could possibly motivate the Nademani to fight then amid such circumstance? The Nasimih are not inclined to war; would a display of the Quest's power truly be sufficient motivation?"

Ciro and Belona exchanged uncertain glances.

"Would power not counter the fear and guilt Nadeya Tikariat described?" Elacir asked hesitantly.

Elian tapped a crown-patterned cluster of scales on his cheek. "Should it not be a display of strength instead? So that they see the refuge your strength will provide?"

"That seems more reasonable," Ciro offered.

"Perhaps," Kyros said, twisting his fingers, his eyebrows drawn together, "but it still does not seem… right. And there cannot be any error in this presentation." He pursed his lips. "The question we should ask is this: what does strength mean to the Nademani?"

"And moreover," I said, turning to Lucian, "how do you wish, my Lord, to demonstrate it?"

Lucian gave us an approving smile. "Nademan's redemption, as the Quest of Light foresaw, is ever in shame, the whispers of conscience that prompt decent thought, belief, and action. Shame is what permeates the soil and flowers in the trees. Thus, the people of Nademan must be given a reminder of their errors through the display of our power. And then, when shame is ignited in their hearts, they must bear witness to our forgiveness. With such awakening of their conscience, they will return to the Almighty and become ours once more."

CHAPTER 42

REVEAL THE SHINING

Perspective: Lord Lucian the Ideal of Freedom
Date: Eyyéthar, the twentieth day of the fourth moon, Likberre,
of the year 500, C.Q.

Closing my eyes, I examined all of the stimuli offered by my sense. The twenty-nine trees of the market, each towering six hundred feet above the ground, all together forming a perfect circle... the townsfolk preparing wares on the lower branches and at the base of twenty-two of those trees... the six empty trees... the last tree, the watch-tree, thicker than the others, holding six squads of enemy soldiers...

Oh Almighty, Liege of my soul, I prayed in my own thoughts, *I beg of You a victory.* Then I reported in the collective link, *Your Grace, your calculations are correct. Sixty soldiers are stationed within the trunk of the watch-tree, fifteen move into position on the towns' various trees, and ten more roam the central sward. Only two are of the manipulated, standing on the highest level of the watch-tree.* I impressed images of both.

Aglow with excitement, Malika spoke with the assured tones of a commander, *Then, my Honors, Prince Darian, Inase bi-Dekecer, Guardians, Jurisso, let us proceed.*

Indicating their obedience, our forces split: Elacir flew Kyros to the very highest branches of the watch-tree, directly above where the great bell hung among the leaves. Arista and Taza led the force of thirty townsfolk from Jurisso, former soldiers and determined farmhands alike, to the tree's base. On Jurisso's tree, Elian and Ilqan settled among the large rolls of cloth arranged by ten loyal cloth-weavers to conceal them from view. Darian and Ciro positioned themselves around Malika and me.

My Lord? Malika asked, twining her arm through mine.

I intoned another prayer, this time in the collective link, and proclaimed, *With my favor.*

Movement flashed in my awareness as the attack began.

And Malika and I stepped onto the sward.

Dark hoods draped our faces, hiding our conspicuous Muthaarim and Ezulal features, so we attracted no more opposition than a few hastily averted glances. Until a soldier stepped in our path.

Before he could utter a challenge, Darian thrust a blade through his heart. A wind from Elian whisked the corpse past the edge of the market's glade, thereby concealing our attack from the patrols inspecting the towns' wares.

A second soldier appeared on the heels of the first, and Ciro dispatched him just as quickly.

Thus we progressed.

Around us, Elian and Ilqan siphoned air from the soldiers on the trees, while the others felled soldier after enemy soldier within the watch-tree, all under Malika's orders via the link. The battle was almost entirely silent, beyond the townsfolk's skittish notice.

This is the first battle in nine years that I have not led, I thought, amused. *Indeed, I do not even have the role of wielding my blade. And rightly so—between Malika's coordination and the skill of my family and soldiers, I am not needed...* How I enjoyed this proof of their excellence.

If not the reason why such competence had needed to form.

In the months of my travels before reaching Arkaiso, I had prepared a detailed plan that would allow my companions the opportunity to develop their skills and flourish in a timely yet unforced manner. Until the crack in Malika's curse, of such benefit in the years to come yet painful in its inevitable consequence, changed my every calculation.

After the Day of Light, I had ordered Malika to learn to duel and defeat me—with this mandate changing her training with the sword from martial prowess to careful direction in the use and control of her magic. Though I gave no explanation, her trust in me was such that she strove to excel in response to my increasing requirements and quickly succeeded for the first time on my birthday. Thereafter her triumphs grew more frequent and more impressive, reviving her confidence in ways unmatched by what I had done before. She blossomed, the excellence in training translating to her studies of rulership and the disciplines of civilization, well on her way to surmounting my standard (though not magical maturity itself because of the impediments of the curse).

Then the curse had struck. With repercussions for which even I could not fully prepare.

On the day of that duel... the activated curse had torn her apart, burning every organ, muscle, vein, and nerve with greater lethality than any flame, all while tormenting her with visions of the fall of Koroma as understood through a mature mind... She relived every act of violence, every drop of spilled blood, every violation of sacred intimacy, every desecration of family, home, and nation... It would have broken her sanity.

But I halted it. With nearly everything the wellspring of my life had to offer.

I had exchanged her illness for my own.

Yes, I was in no danger of losing my mind, much less the exalted holiness of my soul. My gratitude and trust in the Almighty did not waver, far more unshakeable than the foundations of Icilia.

Yet I felt strained for the first time in my life. For, though my Lady Aalia of Light had warned me, I had used too much of my life. I ignored the whispers of overextension, pushing myself against the limit to protect my family after the Day of Light and even harder to save the townsfolk of Filisso. I catalyzed for healing, training, masking, and spells of concealment, forcing myself beyond what I could easily regenerate. And then I had shattered the limit for Malika.

Oh, in appearance, yes, I had recovered enough to depart on rotations and instruct my family and vassals. But my movements slowed, my limbs weakening, and neither rest nor nourishment nor the consumption of athar tears sustained me, only slowing my decline and not reversing it. Fever smoldered in my head, and wheezes cramped my lungs.

And yet duty drove me forward. I had no time to care for my own health, for the people of Icilia needed the Quest Leader, and Malika herself needed my achievement of Nademan's reconquest in order to fulfill her destiny.

Thus driven, I pushed my brothers, Elian, Kyros, Darian, and Elacir, to train and advance, refining their skills at a much faster pace than what would allow for progress without strain. Simultaneously I urged Malika to advance in her studies of military operations, both fortress management and combat strategy—areas that were meant to be my responsibility and not hers. All of these changes had been necessary yet remarkably disregardful of their needs. But still my family admirably rose to the occasion prompted by my command.

The command haunted by premonition and spurred by dread...

My Lord, Malika said, drawing me from my thoughts, *we are almost ready.*

I nodded, appreciating the reminder though my sense had kept me well informed of our progress. Taza and two of the Quest's soldiers pursued the last of the enemy within the watch-tree, while Elacir, Ilqan, and the rest began to clandestinely remove and bury the soldiers' corpses, walking carefully around the market's boundary line. My companions waited in the shadows of Jurisso's tree.

Displaying his marvelous new skill, Darian whirled and tossed an unerring dagger at the final soldier. *Ready, my Lord, my Grace*, he said, as Ilqan blew the corpse directly to the burial site he had chosen some three hundred feet away from the market's circle of trees.

In position, my Rulers, Ciro said, slipping into the stirring gathering, who were turning toward us.

Together, my Second and I stepped onto the circle burned in the sward that marked the central locus.

Speaking with the voice of my soul, I called out to Nademan, invoking far more than magic.

She immediately clutched my feet like a child desperate to atone for her sins, her grass green form visible to my eyes alone.

Mother, I spoke, amused, *I do not forget who nurtured me. Only if it would please you do I ask for my wish to be brought to fruition.*

Answering in the rustles of leaves and creaks of branches, she inquired about what would please me.

I responded, and she agreed.

A groan sounded from deep within the earth.

Then the place where we stood shot into the air.

When the dust cleared, a solid column elevated us fifty feet above the forest floor, with space enough atop for all five Potentates of my Quest.

Praised be the Almighty, Malika breathed.

Indeed, praised be the Almighty, I stated in our private link, *and my gratitude, Malika. Despite all that you suffer, you have done better than I could, one more effort toward fulfilling my deepest wish—for you to be better than me, in battle, strategy, and every aspect of rulership.*

Her cheeks flushed, the peach and pink finally unmarred by gray.

Blessings for your twenty-third birthday, Malika, I added. *May what is cemented on this day benefit you for decades to come.*

She beamed, bowing her head and tightening the arm twined with mine. *At your side, Lucian, forever and always.*

Wearing a smile slightly softer than my lordly one (as my family had named it), I turned my attention to the gathering.

Grouped around the column, the townsfolk clasped their hands over their hearts and gripped their hair, setting their hats and bonnets askew.

Rising on a gust of wind, Elian landed by my side. Arista flew to us atop a cloud of heated air. Kyros appeared in a flash of green besides Malika.

Silence, for the townsfolk were too frightened to even whisper. The only motion was one at the edge of my periphery, an elderly man racing toward the watch-tree.

Is he not the Keeper of the Market? Arista asked, tracking the same man.

Yes, I replied. *Watch for us, Kyros.*

He murmured his obedience.

Then, at my signal in our link, the five of us tossed back our hoods and our cloaks, revealing the last symbols of our office.

Arrayed in supple athar cloth robes of glittering green, rippling from the color of the richest emeralds to the pale pastel green of the magic of the Quest, we shone as the pillars of the life of Icilia, the essence of the land given incé form. And upon our heads gleamed the crowns of the Quests, forged by the order of the first Quest and far grander than any worn by the rulers of the seven nations.

A ridge of graceful scrolls, white athar inlaid with clear diamonds, leaped and soared from each circlet. At the center, over our foreheads, those scrolls peaked to form a delicate circle that held the insignia of the Quests, the mysterious elegantly ornate flower-like crown, formed of yet more white athar and clear diamonds. Durable translucent white athar helms connected the peaks of the scrolls, forming the tops of the crowns, and against their curves rested the circles of the insignia. Though each circlet was forged of athar and embedded with vibrant rubies and emeralds, Elian's, Arista's, and Kyros' circlets were white, as was the athar of their crowns' insignias, while silver athar distinguished Malika as the Second and gold athar marked me as the Quest Leader.

On that gold shine focused the townsfolk's eyes.

And then I spoke:

"Praised be the Almighty! Know, people of Nademani Zaiqan, that we are the Quest of Freedom, Heirs of the

Quest of Light and the highest rulers of Icilia. In obedience to the command of the Almighty and bearing divine favor, we have arisen to bestow true freedom unto the people of Icilia. We come to cleanse the taint that mars the hearts of our people and to break the chains of the tyranny brought upon our land by the Blood-soaked Sorcerer. We come with the promise of wise laws, esteem for each of your souls, bravery for your defense, and strength to succor you amid your sufferings. So do we pledge without question for your allegiance, our souls committed in entirety to the cause of your freedom. May the Almighty shower blessing upon all of you."

I let my voice echo into silence.

No one moved.

No one spoke.

No one blinked.

Until Ciro called out, "My Rulers! My Lord the Ideal of Freedom, *I* am loyal to you! On behalf of Jurisso, I, Count Ciro Tolmarie, pledged to you when few else did, and I will uphold that allegiance on every day of my life, for however many days the Almighty grants me. I am your loyal vassal, always and forever. True shame dictates that I declare so publicly, not conceal my fervor behind dithering hands."

That is not what you prepared to say, Malika remarked.

I asked to speak, he stated grimly, *mustering my courage despite Belona's absence, and now I ask to say more. Anything to prod these cowards into acting.*

My gratitude, Ciro, I said, my voice as calm as my heart, *though that is rather harsh.*

But true, Kyros muttered. *I am almost ashamed of my own kind in this moment.*

Indeed, Ciro grumbled. *As I am of my own nation.*

The market grounds remained silent a long moment more.

An elderly woman cried out, "My Rulers! I beg of you: why have you come? We have failed you! As much as we hide our shame in our hearts, we know this to be true—we welcomed your enemy, defying your laws and discarding your name. Why have you come, my Rulers? Why would you promise to save us?"

In answer, I sang a verse from the translation of my Grace Manara of Light's paean:

> *Guidance You bestow upon the unworthy and the ingrate*
> *The insolent and the impatient, the blasphemous and*
> *   the insouciant.*
> *Knowing their defiance, why do You not leave them to*
> *   their fate?*
> *Why do You seek to enlighten those who forfeit*
> *   their sight?*

Then I asked, "Nadeya Mikaria, what was the next verse?"

The elder lowered her head. "I do not dare to sing it."

"Does anyone dare?" I asked.

Silence.

"My Lord," a young girl beseeched in a loud but trembling voice, "I would like to answer... but I do not know all the words."

None seemed willing to support her.

Then Kyros declared, gaining her name from Arista, "Sing with me, Nadeya Pantarias." He shifted a few steps and knelt, facing Malika and me. "My Rulers, I ask that you count my answer as hers."

Sobbing, Adanna Pantarias bowed and knelt. And, with Kyros' support, sang:

Guidance, oh Almighty, You give in purest unsought love
Sweeten justice with compassion, brighten judgment
  with patience
Rewarding compliance with ordeals witnessed from above
In the crucible You refine within our souls the poten-
  tial to be whole.

As the words rang in the glade, a beam of sunlight pierced the smog overhead and touched my crown, refracting through the rubies and emeralds into a dazzle of color caressing the silver-gilded creamy brown of my face.

Lucian, Elian asked in the Quest's private link, *why... why is your skin... Is it a different color?*

Malika and Arista startled, and Kyros tilted back his head to examine my features.

Yes, Arista breathed, *a different color. It is almost like...*

Like Kyros' color, Malika whispered. *Your color matches his.*

How can this be? Kyros gasped.

An exhale of a chuckle left my lips. *I wondered when you would notice. Remember, I am the Quest Leader for all of the five kinds, all of Icilia, though I am of the Muthaarim by birth.*

My companions stared at me as the townsfolk did.

Many began to kneel.

Until another person asked, "My Rulers, as honored as we are to be the first to witness your coming, can you truly protect us?"

Before we could answer, Ciro pivoted and shouted, "Countess Strofaria, do not dare attempt to trap *our Rulers* as you do everyone else! You know as well as I that this is the age of war! We will *not* all live to see the age of peace the Quest Leader will bring! We will die in battle, both in our own nation and in others, and our bodies will have little more mark than a stone atop a mound of earth. We will *not* all live!

"But of what value are our lives if we do not act in this moment? What sort of a life is cowering in our homes waiting for the monster to drag us out? What value is life without virtue and purpose? What value is life without the Quest Leader's guidance? So do not ask for his protection. Ask for his favor!"

Spinning back to face us, he dropped to his knees and held out his hands.

The countess would be proud, Arista remarked.

Around him, all the townsfolk swayed and fell to their knees and raised their hands, not even the most cynical remaining behind.

She would be, Ciro agreed. *But are you?*

It was the miracle of the Almighty, the first of the wonders I longed to see, the faces of Nademan's children glossed with hope. Wind, one not borne of magic, whirled around the clearing, brushing the Quest's robes and stroking the people's hair. Droplets of rain, not borne of storms or smog, sprinkled the tops of our heads, wetting our crowns and dampening their caps.

A true dazzling smile blazed on my lips. "Behold the Almighty's favor." And to Ciro, I answered, *Yes*.

Light, wondering laughter swirled through the gathering.

The clock set within the watch-tree chimed. Twelve high-pitched rings of minor bells. Noon.

On the edge of the market, the rest of my family and vassals appeared and knelt. Tears glimmered in Darian's, Taza's, and Ilqan's eyes.

Malika whispered, *May the Almighty bless you with many more days such as this one.* She, along with Elian and Arista, knelt to me and touched my feet. Kyros rested his hand on my booted toes.

Nademan sighed her joy.

Then the bell tolled.

The deep, rich sounds vibrated through the trees, the earth, the very people, reaching my feet.

Twenty-one tolls of the great bell.

Seven each for the Potentates of the Quest of Light and for the three ranks of the Quests. Seven each for the Quest, the rulers of the nations, and the people. Three each for the seven nations. In annunciation of my Quest's reign and recognition of my Quest's presence, as the bell had been rung for each visit of the Quest of Light.

On each toll I chanted a prayer: "May the Almighty bless the people of Icilia."

Hayàsimimas hayye ó rohilele, e'Kairie, ru a'hayàsimeh en zatelem.

PART 4

RUNG

From the writings of Lady Queen Aalia the Ideal of Light addressed to the second Quest Leader:

"Know, my Heir, that you yourself are ultimately responsible for your name. You must yourself give it worth, spread it, and maintain its majesty. Accept aid from your companions and your allies, but understand that you alone bear the responsibility of achieving victory in your mission. Your name, my Heir, is intended to be the beacon of light in dark places, hope and peace to the despairing, and the bell of freedom to the destroyed. Ensure that your name is indeed perceived this way, and correct the reasons that it would be otherwise. And, above all, trust in your own promise. The Almighty entrusted you with an enormous task; the Almighty will not abandon you in its prosecution."

READ BY LUCIAN AJ-SHEHATHAR AT

THE AGE OF SEVENTEEN

SEGMENT 3

CONTRIVING STRATEGY

Perspective: Nadeya Tahira Enarias, citizen of Nademan
Date: Eyyéfaz, the tenth day of the fifth moon, Marberre, of
the year 500, C.Q.

Though my heart burned at the act, my face was blank as I curtsied to the Gouge. "Your Depravedness," I said, my voice perfectly emotionless, "I have prepared a suggestion for the next set of orders."

His head leaning on one fist, he waved at me and yawned. "Hurry *up*, Enarias," he drawled.

I knelt before his throne and offered up the stack of documents.

He seized them, scowled at me, and flipped through the pages. "Withdrawing to the provincial fortresses?" he muttered and cast me a sharp glance. "Why?"

I held steady—such was his usual manner. He hated reading, so he only skimmed my proposal, picked out a few key words, and then demanded an explanation. Since he never actually read the documents, there was much I could slip past him.

"Several of the lieutenants' reports show that the rebels are attacking our supplies." This was true. "By gathering together, the squads will pose a more tempting target and so will be better able to lay ambushes." Such attacks would have been effective... but not with the methods I had outlined in the orders.

"Will they get rid of the nuisances faster?" he asked lazily—a ploy for luring his less competent soldiers into self-incrimination.

Well accustomed to his games, I answered, "The rebels will pursue larger caches of supplies, in a continuance of the pattern that they have shown in pursuing the smaller. Your soldiers will draw them in like flies to honey and so conquer them." The fortresses contained far more than supplies, so I had no doubt that the silent heroes would attack, rescuing the captives within while also decimating the Gouge's forces.

The Gouge's soldiers were no match for these heroes: since the first moon, quite a few of the patrols had gone missing across Nademan. Only a few ever escaped, the few whose records were marked in the barracks for special food and drink—the magically manipulated. Their testimony indicated that their attackers rarely numbered more than three. Indicating the heroes were exceptionally powerful warriors.

As should be expected of the Quest Leader and his servants.

But the Gouge and his commanders were too stupid to draw such educated estimations, and I would not help them. If they did not read their own military's reports and analyze the whispers catalogued within, then I would not do it for them.

For indeed, as much as I could, I was sabotaging the Gouge. I had never been loyal to him: I served him only because he held my little brother Kanzeo hostage, threatening to wreak the worst sorts of violence against his life and sanity in order to ensure my obedience. But even in that service, I had always walked a fine line—I constructed his strategies and managed his troops but with only slightly more creativity and efficiency than what he and his colonels could manage. And because they underestimated my brilliance, and that of women in general, they had never guessed that I produced plans beneath my own standard.

Yet now I did more. Halfway through the first moon, I had heard confirmation of the Quest Leader's coming in the form of his name, a name too resonant in holiness to be fabricated. So I had not hesitated.

My Lord Lucian the Ideal of Freedom was the one who possessed my loyalty. Though, should I have the blessing of entering his presence, he would certainly regard me with suspicion and censure.

Indeed, my Lord likely already did—according to what Kanzeo had once heard and told me with a sob during one of the few meetings we were allowed, I was infamous among many of the towns.

But still I did not hesitate.

As long as I continued to leave no evidence and provided partially viable strategies, I could balance long enough on the edge for the Quest Leader's reconquest to reach Ehaya.

It was a risk, but a calculated one—not taking such action would slow down my Lord's reconquest, each passing day another that left my brother and me exposed to the Gouge's whims. Moreover, inactivity would leave us without a defense in my Lord's court. Not to mention how each further month of the Gouge's rule cost the blood of innocents.

I was all too aware of that. Though the military was nominally in my hands and though I controlled their postings, I did not control their movements. I had not been able to stop their pillaging before, and, now that I was shuffling forces to create vulnerability for the Quest Leader, I could not stop the amassed forces from... *enjoying* their pleasures. Like the destruction of the town of Filisso—which I suspected my Lord had seen, from the reports of residue there. Yet another accusation against me, yet more blood unnecessarily spilled.

Bile rose in my throat, but my expression remained even as the Gouge perused the documents again.

"Enarias," he drawled, "what about the border? You want to withdraw forces?" The edge of danger to his tone threatened a display of conjury, the soot-like blemishes on his void-black skin shimmering like mirages of water.

In the corner of the throne room, a man, little more than skin stretched over bones, jumped. He glanced frantically around himself and then scrubbed the floor with renewed fervor.

Crown Prince Eligeo tej-Shehennadem—the son of the man responsible for our troubles, abused and tortured and *hated* so much that it was impossible to believe that he had once been called the hope of Nademan.

The man from whose situation I would do anything to protect my own brother. Including both serving the Gouge and walking the line of betrayal to him in order to usher in the rule of the Quest Leader.

If my life was forfeit, so be it.

With that strength starching my spine, I responded, "Your Depravedness, the forces were withdrawn because your spies in Bhalasa assure you that your inferior rival the Clawed is feuding with your inferior rival the Slicer over failed intelligence. Your inferior rival the Clawed has transferred his own forces from his border with you to his border with your inferior rival the Slicer. Thus, it is proffered to focus on the threat of these rebels, to crush them and show what they blindly ignore, your awesome might."

The anger cooled on the Gouge's face. "Hmmm. Fine, Enarias." He tossed the papers at me and leaned forward as I caught them, the cracked edges of his lipless mouth spread in a leer. Then he said something that scalded my ears, despite the five years I had spent in such close quarters to his court.

I did not flinch, unlike the broken figure of the crown prince. "Your Depravedness," I calmly replied, though what I wanted to do was scream that I would *never* willingly accept such a lecherous invitation, "I must beg your forgiveness. There is much still to do to bring about this strategy such that it does credit to your glory, and a single moment of distraction might threaten all of your stunning achievements. And I would certainly be... *distracted*."

The flattery worked as it always did, and he leaned back, appeased. "Off with your boring self then, Enarias," he snickered. "Make my glory obvious in front of my rivals. And give your brother my greetings." He repeated his usual threat, though it was becoming more absent-minded as the years of my seemingly flawless service passed.

I curtsied from my kneeling position, picked up the papers, and stood. I backed away from him, never turning away and never straightening as I moved toward the double doors of the throne room.

The Gouge smirked after me, then cast the broken crown prince an amused look. He rose from the throne and kicked the poor man in the ribs, drawing a shriek. Laughing, he leaned down, hooked his fingers into the piteous prince's collar, and dragged him along the floor toward the small room behind the throne's dais. The door clicked shut on both the governor's massive figure and his pathetic captive.

I suppressed a wince. For all that Crown Prince Eligeo tej-Shehennadem was hated, for all *I* hated him, I pitied him also. I was under no illusions about what the Gouge did to him. The crown prince was the living remnant of the civilization that the Blood and his governors so despised—the Gouge took out all his hatred on him. And that hatred, that utter disdain and contempt, was like the unfathomable pools of molten rock beyond Icilia's borders: unextinguishable and unbearable.

The prince deserved pity. All his siblings, but him especially.

Perhaps my Lord would deign to free him as well.

Because, I thought dryly as I finally left the throne room, ignored the guards' sneers, and walked to the commanders' war chamber, *no one else will lift a hand to protect him. Not his siblings, not his former staff, not I.* It was despicable, but in the Gouge's court the freedom that nurtured love and compassion did not exist.

The only person I cared to save was Kanzeo, and that motivation still smoldered because the Gouge had not yet beaten it out of me.

I sighed and checked my papers one last time outside the chamber, ignoring more sneers from both these guards and passing soldiers. Frustrated at my lack of a reaction, several of them tried to tug loose the tight blonde braids of my bun, unprotected by cap, bonnet, or handkerchief as my hair was. I ignored them as well.

My Lord's location, I had deduced, was in southern Zai-qan, and he was amid a transition in operations from clearing a swathe of area around his base to reconquering provinces. He possessed the beginnings of a military force, but it seemed reliant upon his and his servants' skill. He certainly did have a secure fortress.

If the Almighty blessed us so, his progress would soon accelerate with my planned vulnerabilities. Surely the townsfolk of the various provinces would not be so foolish as to avoid pledging much longer.

And soon, if the Almighty blessed us, my Lord would be on the way to Ehaya.

Then freedom would be within my grasp.

Neatening the stack of papers, I entered the round chamber. The men inside grudgingly quit their crass exchanges and turned to me with snorts, sneers, or leers. Not one of them rose from their seats around the rectangular table. Indeed, per his habit, one of them kicked my assigned chair as I moved to sit on the right-hand side of the head.

My expression did not change as I smoothly steadied the seat and handed the papers to the top general, who took them with a roll of his eyes.

"His Depravedness approves?" he grumbled.

I dipped my head. "Yes, Sir General."

He grunted and began to distribute orders according to my proposal, with many a sideways baleful look directed at me.

Indeed, I thought with an inward grim smile, *though the townsfolk hate me for this, like they do the crown prince, my place is timely for the Quest Leader's service.* I laughed within the privacy of my thoughts. *How ironic. The commanders hate me for my position, and the townsfolk do the same, but I am the one with the power to remove obstacles from my Lord's path. Such power that I may do so with near impunity.*

The commanders grumbled and growled but could not find fault with the orders. But many still cast me lascivious glances or glares of murderous wrath.

I suppressed a sigh. For all of my bluster, how I hated my place. Other than those brief moments with Kanzeo, years had passed since anyone had treated me with kindness and respect. Well, also since I had deserved such treatment.

But still how I longed for esteem.

As I always did when such yearning came upon me, I subtly moved my hand to the stomach of my simple gray gown, where a tiny emerald hung from a long cord looped around my neck. Trembling slightly, my fingers stroked that emerald, caressing the perfect half-sphere.

The round shape reminded me of laughing violet eyes lit with brotherly affection and set in a shining silver-cream face adorned by sunlight hair and the thin wisps of an adolescent beard. Instant comfort from the memory of the only person whose kindness remained untainted in my mind.

Warmed by solace, I dreamed of the coming of the Quest Leader.

CHAPTER 43

SECURE THE NEGLECTED

Perspective: Honored Arista the Exemplar of Bravery
Date: Eyyéqan, the twenty-seventh day of the fifth moon, Mar-
berre, of the year 500, C.Q.

The nausea roiling my stomach threatened my iron grip on the spell. As if to compensate, my limbs tightened around Duena's torso.

"Are you all right, my Honor?" the soldier asked.

I grumbled wordlessly, then muttered in her ear, "I think there is a gap in my training, Nadeya Narichias: I should have asked Inase bi-Dekecer to carry me while he performed his aerial exercises. It is disappointing that I can withstand windstorms but not these heights."

Duena reached for another handhold on the trunk as the winds howled past us again, only just deflected by my shields. "My Honor, you would be an inspiration in whatever you chose to do." Quiet words, earnest and without flattery. Genuine admiration—startling from the taciturn woman.

I shifted my head on her shoulder so my vibrating plates would not disturb her helm. Then, biting back a swell of panic, I tilted my head to see how far we had left to climb.

While I had been clenching my eyes shut, my squad of fifteen soldiers had neared the top of our target, an unoccupied tree tower somewhere between too decrepit for use (or withstanding the wind) and sturdy if worn. It was both the most accessible tower to my troops from the castle-tree's wall and the closest to the commander's offices according to my scout. The eight other towers that grew vertically from the tree's massive trunk, which formed the main section of the castle, were in poorer condition. Like the city of Tadama, a quarter of a mile to the southeast, whose four-hundred-foot-tall trees had sprouted very few leaves this spring. The four watch-trees that guarded the city's boundary stank of unnatural rot.

The gale swept over us again, battering my shields and bringing the peculiarly icy scent of Mutharrim magic to my nose.

"Come, Ilqan, not when we are so close," I muttered. But, considering none of the enemy had noticed us clambering up the side of the castle in the middle of the day, his distraction was proving effective.

As almost everything in our operation had been so far, beginning that blessed day of Malika's birthday when an entire province had pledged to Lucian.

Once the ceremony of allegiance was performed, Lucian declared the market open, presiding over the trades and reminding anyone who asked about the traditional laws and customs regarding economy—the purpose behind the timing of his revelation. Then, after our family had privately celebrated Malika's birthday, he announced our plans for multiple operations: recruiting soldiers from the towns, he sent each of the Potentates to different parts of Nademan—Elian to western Adeban, Kyros to central Gairan, and me to eastern Makiran and Buzuran, while he and Malika remained in Zaiqan.

Gathering thirty soldiers from the townsfolk attending the market, as well as the squads we had brought from Jurisso, Ilqan and I had left immediately for our first destination, the western city of Tadama, which was controlled by the largest garrison other than at the capital. Over a thousand miles and a month's journey away.

Those miles were oddly empty of most patrolling squads, but still enough soldiers roamed the forest to prove a challenge to my new troops, mostly former farmhands rather than members of the old military in hiding.

The scale of those skirmishes had been barely blips of action, but that month reinforced for me the common perception of the Nasimih: with a few exceptions (mostly the enemy's servants), they truly were the least warlike of all the kinds, as my ancestors had complained. However, like Kyros, the Arkaiso staff, and the Jurisso soldiers, their devotion and determination to be of service to the Quest and their nation was enough for excellence.

Duena jumped over the railing of the open window at the top of the tower and, without pausing for a moment's rest, scurried inside, into the stairwell, and shut the door on her comrades. Then, away from the wind, she helped me release my cramped limbs, carefully steadying me with respectful hands. Only once I was standing on my own strength, my shielding spell properly concluded, did she open the door for her peers—who had waited patiently.

Touched, I gave them a smile before splitting them into two squadrons. One would attack any enemy soldiers near the designated entry points for our troops, while the other would come with me to find the commander.

As soon as my soldiers indicated they were prepared, we sped down the stairwell into the main section of the castle. There we separated, and my squadron immediately came upon a group of enemy soldiers.

Before I could raise my sword, my soldiers dispatched all of them. Cleanly, efficiently, avoiding blood splatter—though not without the shudders that had characterized each attack since we had left the market. A mark of restraint.

It is sweet, I thought as we darted forward. *And these are words from the daughter of a particularly bloodthirsty clan of Areteen who enjoyed provoking fights with their neighbors at every level, even before the Blood's rise. Which honestly shapes a greater appreciation. For, of course, my blood-dripping ancestors could not understand the value of variety in their pursuit of warrior excellence.* I flicked a dagger at a lone soldier charging at Duena, killing him on impact. *Useful today, yes, but not all important.* I retrieved the weapon and wiped it on his trousers before continuing onward.

Hallway after hallway we passed, confronting our enemies where we had the numbers to match theirs and slipping away where we did not. Nothing impeded our progress as we marched toward the commander's quarters in the precise center of the castle, above the grand atrium and stairwell that formed its official entrance.

Three hallways from our destination, Ilqan spoke into the link Lucian had bound for my detachment, *My Honor, a contingent exits the castle and is charging toward where my squads await your command. Your permission to engage?*

Granted, I answered, peering around a corner and beckoning my soldiers forward. *But quickly, Safiri, and not with the whole force.*

As you command, my Honor, he said and withdrew.

While my squadron sprang upon a group of enemy soldiers, I took a moment to contact the watch-tree captains. All four responded that their positions, which we had taken with a combination of frontal assault and subterfuge, remained secure. Only a handful of soldiers held each, but they seemed to trust my wards and shields enough that not the slightest waver in their resolve was perceivable even within the intimacy of the link.

Satisfied, I opened my eyes in time to slay an enemy soldier about to stab one of mine from behind.

The woman crumpled, and I cleaned my blade before leading us into the final hallway.

There waited four enemy squads, crouched in front of the commander's doorway.

"My Honor?" Duena whispered, unconsciously gripping my hand. Her face glossed then beneath the shadow of her helm, and she let go.

I squeezed her shoulder as I assessed the scene. *Of course not a direct attack,* I muttered to myself, *and they would not fall for magical residue as a distraction a second time... there are shields—not especially strong ones but cracking them would alert the casting sorcerer... the position is too defensible to attack from behind... they know to watch from above... or do they? Hmmm...*

The enemy soldiers looked to their left and their right but never checked the tightly woven branches of the ceiling.

Adherence spells easily clung to wood. Particularly the living wood of a tree. And my comrades were of the Nasimih, known for their natural capabilities in climbing.

With a brush of thought, reciting the hymn ordained for my magic, I catalyzed physical energy, amplified the power with my emeralds, and imbued the words, "Sholit ai sholeh, ashoneret é enerel, nazneremas sasholeh ó sasholeh, i'silih wes abile ai nazhanlile."

The traces of temperamental heat in the world around me received my command, a distinct deference accompanying the affectionate acceptance. Drawing upon the powers of my office, I then invoked my soldiers' kind magic and connection to the magic of Nademan and amplified both.

Once the elements of the spell were in place, I guided Duena's hands to the wall. A faint gasp left her lips as her gloved hands warmed and molded to the wood.

I moved a hand and nodded at how the fingers slid over the bark, not fused yet not easily detached.

Despite their alarm, my seven soldiers understood. Pressing their hands and legs against the wall, they began to crawl... upward. Then upside down on the ceiling. Defying the attractive pull of the earth.

That is actually disturbing, I thought, carefully balancing the flow of power to their limbs and the branches, the particles heating and cooling under the influence of my magic.

Moving cautiously, my soldiers crept around the corner and over the enemy.

Now, I ordered.

They dropped atop the squads, blades plummeting and killing many of the enemy before they could react.

Then the rest recovered and, screaming, attacked my soldiers.

Ending the spell, I gripped my sword in both hands and twisted them in opposite directions. At the pressure, the sword divided smoothly into two, one blade in each fist. I raised both into an attacking position, then sprinted around the corner and channeled my momentum into a leap.

At the pinnacle, I arced both blades outward, cleaving the heads of two soldiers from their necks, and ejected two balls of fire from my palms, tossing them like daggers at two more opponents.

Blood sprayed the hardened athar of my cap and robes, and the odor of charred flesh singed my nose.

I kicked off the falling bodies into another leap and slew yet more in the same manner. Then, switching tactics, I weaved through the greedy hands and thirsty blades of my enemies, using my lesser height to its advantage as I pierced their chests with steel and flame.

A trail of corpses lay in my wake by the time I reached my beleaguered squadron. I pushed through their protective circle and attacked the soldiers on the other side.

When only blood, smoke, and death remained, I turned and surveyed my soldiers. Three had fallen to their knees, deep lacerations glistening red, while the remaining four looked stricken at the carnage surrounding them.

I offered them a grim smile. "I know," I said quietly, feeling the same horror on their faces in my bones, "I know. They are our wayward siblings, children of Icilia, incé whose lives have meaning. But do not forget what I told you before this mission: all of my analysis of Nademan's magic show that they chose the Gouge's service of their own will, none bearing the taint of magical manipulation. They betrayed Nademan and Icilia, and so my Lord and ultimately the Almighty and the Shining Guide. We mourn them, and we will respect their bodies, but their blood is not spilled without cause."

My soldiers nodded, appeased though still sickened. As they should have been.

Avoiding the mess of limbs, I strode back to them and ordered the squadron leader, the one soldier present who knew a bit of medicine, to tend the injured.

With the remaining three at my back, I dismantled the shields, melted the lock on the doors, and threw them open.

Beyond the threshold, the commander scrambled to stand from where he crouched over a woman behind a monstrous desk. Eyes hard, he spat words of abuse as he catalyzed for a spell. A dangerous one that would leech all moisture from our flesh.

As I streaked across the room, I heated the wood beneath him, breaking his concentration.

His spell rebounded, crunching bone and bruising, causing such pain that the man cried out and crumpled to his knees.

Letting the enchanted edge of one sword slice through his personal wards, with the other I cut his throat.

The head toppled from his body.

I immediately strode around the desk.

The woman clutched her torn dress but seemed too frightened to whimper.

Softening my robe-coat, I knelt in front of her and said, voice calm enough to hide my fury, "Nadeya Sianna Sezarias, I am a Potentate of the Quest of Freedom. You have nothing to fear."

She sobbed once before scrambling to her knees and falling at mine.

"My Honor, if it would please you?" Duena whispered, holding out the coat she had assembled from rabbit skins on our journey east.

I accepted it with a tight smile and draped the material over Sianna's shoulders as I asked in the link, *Do you see the commander's ring?*

Yes, one of my soldiers responded. A pair of leather boots clicked against the floor, and she appeared before me, kneeling and offering up the silver emerald ring in cupped palms. *I washed it,* she added.

My gratitude, I said with a fuller smile and slid it onto my fourth finger, by my Potentate's ring. Remembering Darian's instructions, I catalyzed, activated the emerald with a drop of power, and imbued my will into the heat of the living castle-tree as I would for a spell.

The entire castle vibrated, shaking around us.

The immense tree seemed to actually whimper.

Sensation slammed into me, the movements of water coaxed through trunk and limb, the sway of thousands of branches, the swish of countless leaves, enjoying yet dreading the push and pull of Ilqan's gale. Then came voiceless cries, complaints of inadequate care of towers and trunk, of evils witnessed, of gore staining proud wood, of a perversion of purpose. Living but powerless to protect itself from harm, its only possible choice a refusal to allow the enemy use of its defenses.

For long minutes, I murmured soothing words, as Darian had advised, assuring the castle of my office and my intention. I poured a portion of my reserves into steadying the six-hundred-foot-tall tree's wavering foundations. Then, my voice as gentle as the hand that stroked Sianna's dirt-smeared hair, I asked the sentient castle to help me.

The tree immediately opened the side stairways for my squads outside. Then it began to slam doors and draw out air, herding the enemy toward where my soldiers would confront them in the atrium. Stairs under enemy boots grew slippery, and a poison spread through the air, wafted directly toward their faces.

Done, I breathed to Ilqan and my forces.

The whistling winds rocking the castle faded bit by bit into stillness.

Then Ilqan led his charge, the contingent that had challenged him outside the castle lying dead behind him.

I exhaled and leaned against the wood beneath the study's window, still holding Sianna.

Not long now, I thought, finally feeling my exhaustion. *Next to secure Tadama's people, and then east to Buzuran.*

As my muscles uncoiled, my mind turned to my two families, one whom I had not seen for a year now and the other embroiled in battle after battle. Elian, Kyros, Elacir, and Taza, securing the west and the center, Malika and Darian, managing new vassals, troops, and supplies...

And Lucian. For whom I worried without end. Whose secrets were starting to scare me.

When I had last seen him, he had ordered me to accept the pledges of Zaiqan in his stead.

In the weeks since, I had pieced together his unspoken plan. For, though he had not said it, his actions were clear: he was training all of us, from Malika to me, to act without him.

I refused to believe he would leave us so soon.

CHAPTER 44

MEND THE SHATTERED

Perspective: Honored Elian the Exemplar of Esteem
Date: Eyyéala, the seventh day of the sixth moon, Kadsaffe,
of the year 500, C.Q.

A heavy blow slammed into the athar cloak covering my back. I lurched forward, then spun and stabbed my attacker, sword clutched in one hand. Twisting and curling the fingers of the other, manipulating the contours of my wind spell, I swept another soldier off his feet, straight onto the waiting blade of Lucian's father.

Quick and efficient, Prince Beres dispatched the man. Then his lavender eyes widened—one of the few flickers of emotion I had seen from him since he had met me on Adeban's border. As uncannily similar as his appearance was to his sons', the prince was usually entirely impassive.

I need your help to pull the spear out, I said, abashed, in the prince's link. There was enough of a lull around us to tend to my need as my soldiers pushed back against the swarming enemy.

Prince Beres dipped his head and grasped the weapon's handle. I braced myself, and he tugged it from the hardened silver athar, spun it around, and flung it with deadly accuracy at another soldier.

My scales flared as I gave him a shy smile. *Thank you again, Prince Beres-asfiyi, for the cloak. My wings might have been shredded*—not just inflamed by the jostling—*if not for your gift. With every battle, I am all the more grateful that you gave me your own royal armor.* An action that I thought spoke of deeper similarity than appearance between father and son, for Lucian had given his royal token to Kalyca in the same manner.

A spark of warmth lit the prince's eyes for a brief moment before he returned to the attack.

If Lucian had not warned us, Elacir grumbled in the link Lucian had bound for the two of us, *I would think he did not care at all about you. He is even colder than Prince Darian.*

Not colder, Little Brother, I said, plunging back into the battle, *but consumed by grief. And you understand that as well as I.*

Elacir was quiet for a moment as we cut and thrust in tandem. Then muttered, *Yes, I know it well.*

Focused though I was on simultaneously wielding my sword and my magic, I still impressed my sympathy into the link.

In the six weeks since we parted from our family in Zaiqan's market, Elacir and I had gone through much together. We had traveled across hundreds of miles, rallied soldiers from Lucian's pledged villages, designed training for them, and attacked both garrisons and patrols, confronting the western regional commander on several occasions.

Together, sweeping west and north, we cemented the decade of protection Lucian had given this province into commitment and allegiance. Prince Beres, who had spread Lucian's name in this province since Lucian's ascension, guided and supported us, but the work was in my name and in Elacir's.

The winds influenced by my ongoing battle-spell pushed away the three enemy soldiers attempting to strangle my subordinates.

The breadth of our newfound experience of reconquest strengthened Elacir's and my relationship beyond the loose brotherhood it had been before. Though we avoided any mention of my wings, save when he insisted on cleaning them, I had come to believe that I had his unwavering support. As he understood he had mine.

I stabbed a soldier, my blade at the precise angle necessary to pierce through his armor (which Arista had taught me) and tossed aside another.

With that trust, on the night of his birthday in the middle of the moon of Marberre, Elacir had finally told me his history: the story of his parents' deaths and the ways in which his own family had subsequently exploited his grief, stealing his reputation, his home, the romantic attentions of the future countess of his aerie, and ultimately his liberty—they had committed their own relation to the soldiers' torture and abuse. Unable to see a means of escape, he thought himself lost until he glimpsed my face amid the rain and sleet. And now he served the Quest because we were all he had, his second family.

Elacir would be my kindred spirit if only I could muster the courage to tell him of my own history.

I slew a soldier who was stalking my brother's movements and then stepped back and assessed the battle. My three-and-a-half companies were steadily pressing the remaining four of the enemy against the doors of their shacks and the bases of the enormous trees. However, though our victory seemed likely, my soldiers, on the third skirmish of the week, were exhausted, suffering more and more injuries and moving with less finesse and skill than before. In contrast, the enemy was fresher and fought manically, seeming to have abandoned any expectation of reinforcement—the squads lying in wait outside the fort's fences were the first we had attacked.

My soldiers could not continue for much longer. They would not be able to cope if the enemy retreated onto their platforms (dozens dotted the trunks' eight hundred feet) and harassed us at their leisure… and neither would I—despite all my stamina, I had only enough energy remaining for one or two more spells. Since there would be much to do even after the battle ended, I needed to conserve my strength. Which meant choosing something simple but effective…

Prince Beres-asfiyi, I asked, *are the conditions suitable for a modified sandstorm?* Lucian had mentioned that his father could wield some wizardry of the soil alongside his powerful athar magic and middling mindlinking. It had once made him an effective orchardist in the athar orchards.

In response, the prince retreated from the battleline and crouched beside me. Burrowing his fingers into the soil, he chanted, "Hayàretet ai saretet, ramireh é silérohile, chilerim an lanerelum." Silver light trickled from his fingers and spread out over the yard enclosed by the walls.

Though still pouring power into my battle-spell (augmented by the jewels I finally knew how to use), I recited the hymn of my magic again, catalyzed, amplified, and whispered, "Simit pe saneru u'wurqet ai teku u'nabtet, sasiren-errim a'hayàretet, sanerrim a'saretet, zulàsimirim a'simih sir zidilëm."

While the battle-spell's winds sought to topple as many of the enemy as possible, new winds arose. Whirling and twirling, they stripped soil and dust from the surface of the yard. Small twisters of an ominous beige color, like the tornadoes Kyros had once described, coiled and rotated around me.

Shield your eyes, I ordered in the link the prince had made for my troops. Then I lifted the twisters up over their heads and dropped them amidst the enemy.

Growls and screams erupted from their ranks as they tried to shield their eyes.

Brace yourselves, I ordered. *Five seconds.*

My soldiers brought their swords up to attacking positions.

I quenched the twisters.

They attacked, falling upon their dazed opponents.

Within minutes, the battlefield was clear.

I exhaled and prayed, *May the Almighty return me soon to Lucian and Malika. May this victory be another step on my journey back to her side...*

While those thoughts lingered in my mind, I ordered my soldiers to search the buildings and begin burial. Cleaning and sheathing my own sword and ending my spells, I went myself to lift the bodies of the thirty-seven soldiers of the Quest who had perished in the battle.

How I abhor their deaths, I thought, wiping tears from my dimmed scales. *They paid for this victory, important though it is, in blood... I must check my records for their towns and write letters of condolence. And speak to their relations and friends among my company—*

"Elian! Watch out!" a voice called. Elacir.

I turned.

An arrow passed a hair's breadth from my ear.

Tracing its arc, I looked up.

Two squads of enemy soldiers stood on the second lowest of the platforms, high enough to have escaped my twisters. Bows drawn and arrows nocked, they aimed for my people.

One woman fell, an arrow piercing her throat.

Opening my mouth, I blew out a breath and intensified it with catalyzed power into a wind rushing toward the enemy.

Elacir flared open his wings and jumped into the wind. Riding it upward and dodging arrows, he swept under the platform.

Prince Beres and three squads of my soldiers sprinted up two stories of ladders.

My gusts spun into a cyclone, catching the enemy's arrows mid-flight, before they could reach my troops.

Elacir emerged behind the platform and descended on the soldiers.

The prince and the troops reached his side.

Within a few flashes of steel, the attack was over.

A young woman being escorted out of the shacks heaved a loud gasping sob. Pulling her arm away, she ran to the body of the woman who had just fallen.

Though numb with shock, I dropped my spell and moved to comfort her. Then the other captives my troops had found. Then the relations and friends of my companies' dead. All thirty-eight of them.

Tears soaked my shoulders and knees, yet I continued, offering what solace I could. While ignoring the storm brewing in my mind.

Summoning my healing, I knelt by the injured and poured power into mending potentially fatal wounds. Then cleansing and soothing the smaller. Dozens of cuts, pierces, and massive bruises were brought to me as I was our only healer.

You will *accomplish your duties*, I said to myself. *Lucian trusted you with this!*

When the burials were complete, I knelt and led my companies in prayer for our fallen with the funeral dirge Lucian had taught me. Then I alone prayed for the enemy.

Rising, I examined the documents my captains were collecting from the fort. Distributed the weapons found in the armory among my soldiers, replacing broken swords, dulled daggers, and spent arrows. Allocated portions of the recovered supplies for each town within a week's travel.

Not yet, Elian, I entreated. *You do not have time to fall apart!*

Gathering my soldiers and our guests, I led them back to our campsite and instructed them to clean their armaments and prepare a moonlit feast. For both the funeral and the victory.

Only once my soldiers had relaxed enough to chatter over their meal did I retreat. Tightly gripping myself together, I lit my pendant and walked back to the conquered fort under the darkening sky. I found the ladder and climbed, beyond the platform used in the attack, to one high enough to see over the border.

Sitting hunched at the edge, I beheld, under the dimmed light of the moon, my first glimpse of Asfiya: verdant forests that decreased in height until they met the base of the first white mountain.

The first of the hallowed mountains, formed of white stone covered with sparse woods of silvery trees and crowned by sparkles—the easternmost athar trees.

Though smog covered the skies of Asfiya as it did those of Nademan, moonlight glistened on that distant peak. Reminiscent of the glory of Lucian, and of Malika.

Entranced, I noticed the tears only when they cooled my scales.

I swallowed, my focus broken.

Then burst into sobs.

Only you, Elian! I screamed. *Only you could be so blind as to forget to check whether the soldiers had climbed the ladder! You worried about it, and you did not check! At the cost of Geanna's life!*

I pressed my face into my hands. My scales were shocks of chill amid burning skin on my palms.

It is all your fault, Elian. All of it. You claim to have adjusted to your useless wings, but you forget the lessons of your kind. Useless, worthless—what is the point of one of the Sholanar being part of the Quest if he cannot even remember to look up? *Stupid Blood-spawn!*

A roaring echoed in my ears.

Then those dread voices, whose poison I thought I had escaped, taunted, "*You are nothing, Blood-spawn! Nothing. You deserve nothing. Even the Almighty does not want you!*"

Over and over the words repeated.

Clamping my hands to those abused ears, I screamed. Twisting, writhing, trying to shake them away, while the curse incinerated my wings.

Wetness welled from the places where my fingernails dug into my scalp.

My shaking body slipped off the platform.

Only for a strong hand to haul me back.

That same hand dragged me across the platform until I lay against the side of the tree.

"Elian!" a voice exclaimed as hands pried my own from my head. "Elian! What were you thinking? Even with your magic, these platforms are so high that you might have broken all of your limbs before you caught yourself! Brother! Look at me!" Two fingers tapped my eyelids.

Reluctantly I opened them.

Plum scales dull, Elacir sighed and shifted from his crouch over my person to my side. "The troops have not yet noticed your absence, but his Highness and I did," he said, explaining his presence. Then he scowled. "Elian, you have not cleaned your robes? What about your sword? And your wings are a mess, even with the cloak!"

A sob ripped from my throat at the reminder, and I curled into myself, hiding my face so I could avoid his gaze.

As much as I loved him and valued his contributions to the Quest, I could not stand the sight of his wings. Not then, not amid my torment.

"Elian!" he exclaimed. A hand removed my cap and combed through my hair. "Oh, Elian…"

I shifted away from him.

"Brother?" he asked, voice breaking. "Please do not reject me, too. I know losing any of your soldiers always hurts—"

Jolting upright, I spun around and yelled, "Your wings work! You saved them instead of putting them at risk! What do you know of hurts?"

Elacir winced, recoiling.

I realized what had spewed from my mouth and crumpled. "Sorry, Little Brother," I whispered, ashamed. My scales cooled to black, too unworthy of any warmth.

He sighed and shuffled closer. "I suppose, finally, it is time." Hooking a finger beneath my beard and chin, he tilted my head upward.

I averted my gaze.

"No, Big Brother, look at me," Elacir said, hazel eyes brimming with compassion. "There, that is better. Now. I have dreamed of saying this since Arista told me of what happened at Tresilt, but I did not want to accidentally add fuel to your torment. There simply has not been the right moment. But I think this is it." A soft smile shone on his lips as he reached beneath my cloak for my wings.

Shuddering, I nearly recoiled. But then I remembered how I had hurt him. So I sat still as he touched a dull golden feather. Unknowingly igniting a ripple of pain.

Elacir's smile brightened. "No matter what you do, I can never be upset with the man who saved me and gave me both purpose and a new family. In your service, Elian, I have found all the healing for which I could have prayed, if I had known how to ask. All the pain of my history has faded in your company."

He chuckled. "Elian, Brother, you are truly my world now." A stroke across a discolored quill. "That is why I want to tell you this: Elian, my wings are yours." Another stroke. "Whatever service I render to Lucian with them is done in your name." Another stroke. "I think the Almighty saw your suffering and decided to give you another pair of wings, and I was chosen for the honor. Just as Lucian gave Malika back her voice." He brushed dirt away from another quill. "I pray that someday soon the Almighty will ensure that your curse is broken. But until then, and even after, my wings are yours."

Pulling back his hand, he grasped my wrist and guided it so that my limp fingers brushed the glowing plum scales of his wings.

Fresh tears spilled down my cheeks.

"Touch," he urged.

I hesitated but then stroked one of those soft scales. So unlike my quills and yet so similar... the slender muscles rippled under my fingertips, a strength I had never known. Yet he offered it to me... To me of all people.

Silencing the shrieking taunts in my mind.

Smiling shyly, I whispered, "My gratitude, Little Brother."

His scales shone at the endearment, and he pulled me into a hug. "You do not need to yearn for something that is already yours," he whispered in my ears—such a diametric contrast from what those ears had just suffered.

I melted into his embrace. "I was never jealous," I admitted, "because I desired from the very hour we met for you to serve Lucian with your wings. But I have often wondered whether you despised me for my weakness." Despite my blossoming contentment, the end of the sentence squeaked like a question.

"Never," he swore. "Never."

And, believing him, relishing that confidence, even with the lamentation in my heart, I was beaming as we returned to camp and prepared to report to Lucian via communication spell.

Only for that smile to shatter as I heard the pang of exhaustion in his voice.

CHAPTER 45

REFRESH THE DRAINED

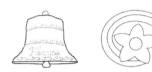

Perspective: Honored Kyros the Exemplar of Strength
Date: Eyyéqan, the eighteenth day of the sixth moon, Kadsaffe,
of the year 500, C.Q.

The men roared like bears and hefted their heavy swords over their heads.

One magical overlay of my vision blurred their movements forward, simulating the exact angle of their strikes. The other overlay showed Taza moving away from my back as she cornered her opponents against the far wall. The rest of the area around us was clear, my soldiers focused on scouring the rest of the tower.

Catalyzing and amplifying, I chose a spot behind my enemies and added the requisite belief in the Almighty's miracles to the ones on free choice and purpose. Then I stood in place as my four opponents swung their swords down in brutal cleaves. Just before the blades touched my cap, I teleported in a flash of green light.

They stumbled, the missed blows shaking their balance.

Raising my own sword, I struck a precise hit on the back of one man's neck. He collapsed, and his comrades lumbered around, growling like wolves.

Checking both sights, I teleported again, appearing behind another man, and cut his throat beneath his helmet. Then did the same to the third.

Only enough for one more transfer, I thought, blinking back a wave of exhaustion.

The final soldier snarled and swung his sword, aiming for my chest. I dodged to the side, slipped beneath his guard, and sliced his neck. Still snarling, the man teetered and began to collapse over me. The wicked edge of his sword fell toward my back.

I teleported one more time and reappeared by Taza just as she slew the last of her opponents. Turning, she caught me as I stumbled and patted my shoulder.

"Well done, my Honor!" she praised. "That was your best attempt yet at simultaneously balancing all three types of magic and contemplating all three necessary beliefs. You must mention it in your next report to our Lord! He would be glad to hear of your prowess. Particularly against the plains outpost's four most infamous soldiers."

My cheeks moistened in a gloss. "My gratitude, Taza. Though what about magical maturity?"

Taza tilted her head to the side and examined my face. "Hmmm. Soon I would say. Since the standard you must meet would be only a few degrees below our Lord's... and our Honor Arista the Exemplar of Bravery did confirm that her own standard was far higher than her sisters'... I would think you still require a month or two more of training. You have not quite reached the level in which you contemplate the beliefs without conscious effort. Also, though you have mastered the use of jewels for amplifying your teleportation—and, remember, the nearly five miles you manage is one of the greatest ranges of which I have ever heard—you have not quite done so for your sights."

I pressed my lips together but nodded and gave her a wan smile. "If you would deign to train me still further, Taza, may the Almighty grant my swift success." Without meeting that standard, I could neither fully serve Lucian nor truly claim to have upheld his command.

Similar to how potential heirs were required to attain magical maturity in order to receive their ranks and royal abilities, the Potentates needed to achieve that standard for access to the magic of the Quest. Among Lucian's companions, however, only Arista so far had that status. Since Malika and Elian were disqualified due to their various curses, the pressure was on my head to excel as fast as I could.

Without that sacred magic, the only pledges I, or Elian, could receive were ones sealed by our birth-magic. While such pledges did forge a bond between allegiant and liege, they did not provide any endowment of strength or assessment of loyalty. So, though Lucian was confident in his ability to later change what Elian and I received into the correct form, I needed to attain maturity to fulfill my office—and my pledge to Lucian.

Taza squeezed my shoulder, sympathy bright in her eyes. Then she asked, voice crisp, "What are your next orders, my Honor?"

Rotating my head on my neck, I closed my eyes and scanned each room of the tower. The battle was over with our duels won, and all eight companies had immediately turned to their usual tasks: freeing captives, gathering documents, finding the armory, burying the enemy's dead, guarding the fort, caring for our injured—thankfully, between our unexpected attack and our superior tactics, we had not suffered any losses.

As necessary as I knew each part of this conquest was, I could not sleep after attending my own soldiers' funerals. I had finally managed to adjust to the cost of shedding blood, through sheer breadth of experience, but I could not, would not, become accustomed to the deaths of those who died while fulfilling my orders.

The burden was a massive one to withstand, but it was my place to bear it.

Satisfied with my assessment of the outpost itself, I turned my attention to the surrounding plains.

After parting from our family at the market, once we gathered a sufficient number of troops from the pledged towns in northeastern Zaiqan, Taza and I had begun a vast and comprehensive sweep of the province of Gairan. Skirting Ehaya, we had traveled east and south, conquering every outpost, defeating every patrol, and returning both captives and supplies.

Through an appearance at Gairan's annual market in the middle of the fifth moon, we gained additional pledges and soldiers, enough to defeat the major garrison nearby. Since then, we had angled south, a strategy that culminated with this battle and accompanying reclamation of the plains that formed Nademan's southern border—a deeply consequential move, as the Nasimih of these plains cultivated the second-largest strip of Nademan's fertile land and would, without the soldiers' arbitrary seizures, trade enough grain to feed the nation once winter came.

"This second look confirms," I said, "that these plains are slightly healthier than Khuduren's."

Taza nodded. "I concur. What is your opinion of the central farming town, Somisso?"

Directing my farsight east over the flat terrain surrounding the fort, I examined the cluster of multistory houses, each built in the image of large trees and surrounded by a thorny hedge, which much resembled the thick barrier grown by the Quest of Light along the southern edge of the Dasenákder. Despite their varied circumstance, the Nasimih congregating on the central sward of their town dressed and acted much like their siblings of the forest. Except…

"They look more unhappy," I observed, "than anyone else I have seen in Nademan." A frown tightened my lips.

"Indeed," Taza said, her eyes on my face (her range did not extend so far). "But what is your opinion of their willingness to pledge?"

"Hmmm… they seem rather weary. Drained." I blew out a breath. "Considering how Elian and Arista confirmed last week that it is even more difficult now to secure pledges than it was three months ago, despite the benefits we have given in returning captives and supplies… and the resistance we faced two hundred miles north… as well as even Lucian's experience with their unwillingness… I do not think it likely. Indeed, for all the ways in which you have helped them and we now support them, they seem increasingly unwilling to give anything at all. Zaiqan was truly exceptional."

"Indeed…" Taza sighed. "But I advise you to at least try, my Honor. Perhaps we may have success this time."

I doubted we would but dipped my head, for her counsel often proved invaluable. "I will order messengers to be sent to Somisso, along with a share of the supplies recovered here and any of our new guests who would like to return." A messenger instead of traveling myself, for, after Elian's last report, I did not want to give anyone the chance to smear the Quest's dignity.

Smiling gently, Taza patted my shoulder. "No, let me, my Honor. You could use a moment of rest."

As much as I wished otherwise, she was right. So, acquiescing, I dipped my head again and watched her descend the stairs and gather a company of my troops.

As she began to speak, I turned my attention to the windows. Panes of glasses fitted each of the room's walls, allowing a wonderful view of both the vast forest to the north and the expansive plains to the south.

As beautiful as those forests were, even faded under the dominion of tainted rain and the enemy's careless logging, the plains called my heart. For, despite their yellowed grasses, they reminded me of Kalyca.

Too many days have passed since I last had the time to contact her. I hope she does not think I have forgotten... but, with all the tasks we have to do to secure this fort, I am not sure whether I will have more than a minute or two to myself. But I certainly should on Eyyéthar... the second year of two that I have not spent my birthday with her... How lovely it would be to see Lucian, Malika, Elian, Arista, Elacir, and Darian on that day...

Though, yes, these struggles in gaining allegiance complicated an already difficult campaign, the worst part was the distance from my family. I heard their voices regularly in our weekly reports, but it was not enough.

How I missed them.

Tipping my head back, I closed my eyes and exhaled. *Not too much longer, Kyie... Once this southward sweep is complete, Lucian might send me to reinforce Arista... Even seeing one of their faces would content me. How I wish we were ready to retake Ehaya...*

Footsteps pattered in the stairwell.

Reluctantly, I blinked open my eyes and turned.

One of my eight captains burst into the room and immediately fell into a bow. "My Honor," he managed to say clearly amid his pants, "I beg your forgiveness for the interruption. May I have your leave to speak?"

"You may," I said, "and please, Captain Nesaries, rise and breathe first."

He inhaled deeply, filling his lungs, and straightened. "My Honor, General Palanéze requests your presence at the tower's entrance."

"Did she provide a reason?" I asked, curious. *If there was an emergency, she would have activated Lucian's bound link, even though its energy is nearly depleted. But this still sounds urgent...*

He hesitated, biting his lower lip. "Ummm, she mentioned, my Honor, that your magic would give a better answer than she could."

"Very typical of her," I replied, offering a comforting smile. "Thank you, Captain." I wiped my sword on the trousers of one of my dispatched opponents and sheathed it. I moved toward the stairwell, then paused and added, "Captain, if you would, I would appreciate a notice from you to the squads on burial duty for the corpses here. Depending on what the general requests, I may not have time to return."

He snapped a salute. "As you command, my Honor!"

I inclined my head and descended the staircase. With every level I passed, my soldiers paused their tasks and bowed to me, most wearing enthusiastic, deeply adoring smiles.

At least our soldiers are loyal. How the Almighty has blessed us with their willingness to follow us, leaving behind their towns... regardless of their pledges, such loyalty is a blessing.

Recalling my farsight, I sent my magical vision to the tower's entrance. Frowned and examined the scene with my foresight. Then ran down the remainder of the stairs and into the large hall of the fort's entrance.

There, squirming as he stood beside Taza, waited a boy. A boy whose face was covered in purple-green bruises. Dressed in perhaps the most tattered rags I had ever seen, his trousers barely covering his shins and his ripped tunic flashing large amounts of inflamed skin. So malnourished that his ribs were visible, his gangly limbs little more than twigs. His tan cheeks as coarse as drought-stricken earth, a sign of desperately poor health among the Nasimih. With the faint blond stubble on his upper lip and his height of five-feet-two, he was on the cusp of adolescence yet had the shape of a child.

But as I approached, his bloodshot ice blue eyes brightened. "My Honor," he breathed and tossed himself at my feet.

I glanced at Taza and raised an eyebrow.

She shook her head.

"My Honor," the boy whispered again and promptly began to cry.

Suppressing a wince (all children's tears reminded me of Kalyca's), I knelt in front of him and gently drew him into my arms.

He cried harder and clutched my waist.

"My little brother," I soothed, stroking his back, "darling boy, may the Almighty forever protect you. My brother..." I repeated the endearments, over and over, until he calmed, sniffling with the odd hiccup.

Taza approached with a handkerchief (athar but plain unlike Lucian's) and dropped her gaze meaningfully to the boy's clothes.

'Salve, too,' I mouthed as I handed the handkerchief to the boy.

She nodded and left the tower for our campsite.

The boy blew his nose and wiped his cheeks.

Pasting a smile on my face, concealing my anger over his condition, I asked, "Nadeyi, would you give me the pleasure of knowing your name? I gather you know who I am?" *If only I could discover names like Arista...*

Fidgeting with his hands, the boy inhaled, as though seeking courage. Then he whispered, barely able to meet my compassionate eyes, "My Honor, my n-name is Kanzeo Enaries. And, if you would let me, I have some in-intelligence for you ab-about the wretched G-Gouge's court. A-and, also, a p-plea."

Just how would he know about the enemy's court? I wondered, horrified. *Just what am I about to hear?*

Yet all I said was, "I am pleased to speak with you, Nadeyi Enaries. My soldiers have cleared a few of the second floor's offices; let us retreat to one, if it would please you."

Kanzeo's head wobbled in something of a nod.

So, hoping he would not mind the blood on my robes too much, I lifted him in my arms.

He squeaked but clung more tightly and melted into my hold.

Settling his weight, I carried him to an office and placed him in one of the only two chairs there. The soldier rummaging through the desk left at our entrance, pausing only to grin in quick (but anguished) welcome at the boy, like the others we had passed.

I took the other chair and clasped Kanzeo's hand between both of my own. Refreshing my gentle smile, I encouraged, "Speak to me, my little brother."

Kanzeo clenched his other hand into a fist. Then, with another deep breath, met my eyes and said, "My Honor, my sister, Tahira Enarias, is the Gouge's chief strategist in appearance, but truly the Quest's devoted servant. I beg you to free her."

CHAPTER 46

PERSUADE
THE RELUCTANT

Perspective: Graced Malika the Exemplar of Wisdom
Date: Eyyésal, the twenty-sixth day of the sixth moon, Kadsaffe,
of the year 500, C.Q.

The creaks of the tree's branches and the shift in the walls' luminescence sent me squeaking beneath my blankets. My heart thumped rapidly as I desperately tried to calm myself. For the third time that night.

Come, Malika, I groaned to myself, *what sort of adult woman is afraid of the dark? Far, far less what Potentate?* But after the last two months of again sleeping without one of my friends nearby, I could not deny that I had become so.

It was the least destructive change brought about by the curse.

Since that disastrous day and the horror of what I had seen... I had become, for all of my cultivated physical strength, fragile. Every minor illness traversing the staff or the soldiers afflicted me, leaving me abed and too sick to move. Each monthly cycle brought more pain and blood. My concentration broke often in lessons, requiring copious notes on the scarce supply of paper to maintain. My emotions were raw, often driving me to tears at the slightest upset. And, in every shadow, I saw flashes of the fall of Koroma.

Hence my fear of the dark. A fear I had not had to this degree even after escaping the near-perpetual darkness of the Blood's prisons.

And hence I did not dare to think of defying Lucian's command, however much I longed for the sword locked in his wardrobe.

Truly, Lucian had favored me with a miracle beyond what I deserved in saving me that day.

Yet, though I knew the consequences were far less than they could have been, I was ashamed. So, despite lingering guilt, I had begged Lucian to conceal my fragility from our family and staff. Only out of necessity had I told Halona, and Darian after the market.

I sighed and gave the door a wistful look. *If only the prince would call himself my brother as Lucian and Kyros do...*Though Darian and I spent all of our time together, from lessons to training to developing strategies for our family, he still maintained a cool distance, always using my reverential address and never my name. Whatever affection he held for me was no more than a rare flicker in his eyes.

I could not be less than patient with him though, for I well understood how abuse warped one's mind. Neglect had often equal power.

Blowing out a sigh, I calmed enough to remove the blanket from over my head. Staring at the faint glow of the ceiling, I counted each ring of the trunk.

Just as my eyes began to close, a series of sharp raps roused me and brought me running to the door. Pulling it open revealed Darian.

Face grim, he stated, "My Grace, Arkaiso is under attack."

What! Where do they attempt entry? I grabbed the cap that matched the robes I wore for sleep and exited my room.

"The eastern quadrant," he reported, rushing downstairs, "near where Tapisso is housed." Tapisso was one of the five towns who had petitioned me through Ciro for living quarters like Jurisso's at Arkaiso.

Have the townsfolk been alerted? I asked. *Do you know who is attacking?*

Yes to the first, Darian replied, switching to the link Lucian had refreshed for me on his last visit. *I ordered them via the fortress' internal communications to leave for the central arena. The three companies present also gather there.*

I offered him a smile. *Well done, Prince Darian.*

His cheeks silvered. *As for the identity of the attackers… the trees send me impressions of axes and torches.*

The two enemies of any trees, likely wielded by our enemy, I mused as we started to walk toward the central arena. How glad I was of his company, for very little light pierced the smog. The trees lit our path with luminescent twigs, but it was not enough to banish the shadows. *Do the defenses hold?*

They do, for now, he said. *The outermost trees of the ring began shedding poison, in the form of pollen, as soon as they appeared. The magic woke me not moments after, and I came immediately to you. The insects are now stirring.*

So not much time has passed, I noted. *What do you suggest for a counter?*

He gave me a rare smirk. *Should I not ask you that, my Grace? Are you not the supreme commander?*

I chuckled at his use of Lucian's new endearment. *It does seem the ideal opportunity to test what I have learned all these months at your side, Commander.*

And, to my wonder, his lavender eyes shone for a brief moment with brotherly love.

My own sisterly adoration welled in my heart.

I snapped my attention back to our discussion. *Prince Darian*, I said crisply, *I do not want to rely on the fortress defenses to ensure that none of the enemy survives to spread our location. Thus, I suggest a physical attack as well as a magical one: let us station the soldiers in the border trees and have them pick off the attackers. With an extension of the proper access, they would remain unaffected by the poison and insects, as well as the gloom of the boundary ring. The assault would also allow them the chance to practice their archery on the battle-field. Does that plan please you?*

The remnants of his smirk shifted to a wry smile. "You sound exactly like Lucian does in a battle. Tone, diction, expression—a perfect mimicry."

This time I was the one who blushed.

Darian actually grinned, flashing his white teeth, before resuming his usual impassive regal composure as we arrived at the arena.

The Tapisso townsfolk bowed and curtsied as soon as they saw us, while the soldiers (all trainees from Zaiqan) hurriedly formed ranks before dipping their own reverences.

The prince and I exchanged glances, and I nodded. Then he commanded, voice quiet yet clear, "Arkaiso is under attack. We will supplement the fortress' response with an attack from the trees. Captains, have your troops retrieve their bows and quivers and meet my Grace and me at the eastern boundary. We leave a choice of post in the trees to your discretion; you may fire at will as soon as you reach your desired location. If your targets are marked by magical manipulation, I will warn you. Each squad sergeant must approach me for access before their subordinates climb. Nademile, prepare meals and medicines as you were taught. So wills my Grace."

Curtsies, bows, and salutes indicated their obedience.

Inclining our heads in acknowledgment, we resumed our walk to the boundary, carefully circumventing patches of the towns' crops.

Prince Darian, I said once we had passed the arena, *this attack only strengthens Kyros' and my argument. We cannot delay an attack on Ehaya.*

He raised an eyebrow. *How do you conclude so?*

Arkaiso is well masked and has been undetected for almost a decade, I opened my argument, while praying silently in gratitude for my unusually clear mind. *The Nademani towns-folk know better than to approach such poisonous trees. Thus, it was found likely because of some careless or traitorous whisper. Such whispers, from our family's reports, abound still because the Quest has not commanded widespread loyalty and allegiance. Do you not agree?*

Indeed, I do, he said.

We will not be able to gain such adherence, I continued, encouraged by his reply, *without the show of our prowess reconquering Ehaya would necessitate. For as long as Ehaya remains under enemy rule, the towns will easily be able to point to the capital and say that we lack strength. A third of the towns and half the cities' boroughs have not pledged, and only about half of those who have are truly loyal. And even that number may be suspect because Elian's and Kyros' pledge-bonds do not allow for such analysis. Without Ehaya, the situation will not improve.*

But would it improve even then? he countered. *The issue seems to be one in the hearts of the people, unalleviated by the benefits they have all received from the Quest's nearly solid control over four of the five provinces. If we wait another three months as originally planned, we would have more trained forces drawn from your existing vassals for the attack. With our Honor the Exemplar of Bravery's retake of easternmost Buzuran, the Quest would have the control to corner the enemy in Ehaya without an avenue of escape.*

Where *will we find these additional soldiers?* I asked pointedly. *The fifty-two towns under Lucian's rule have at most sixty men and women each to spare, some far less, and we have already summoned all of them. And you have heard Arista's reports on Buzuran's stubborn unwillingness as well as I. Even with two more months, she may still not hold sufficient confidence in their readiness to remain loyal so that she might return.* A difficult implication to digest, for I missed her.

He stationed himself at the base of the first tree of the boundary ring, while I started to climb it. At my touch, the tree ceased secreting the black particles that clouded the air and produced the spine-chilling gloom within the ring. Though this specific pollen was not toxic, unlike the types discharged by the outermost trees, it would still complicate our defensive operations.

As the murkiness receded, I relaxed a little, despite the faint cries drifting from the boundary proper. Yet the glow of my pendant did not banish the darkness well enough to soothe my raw nerves. Every single shadow contained flashes of blood and bits of brain and bone...

Malika, Darian said, and I startled. He impressed a reassuring smile. *Lucian would be proud of you.*

I sighed. *My gratitude. Please, if you would, continue your response.*

Darian extended his sleeved forearm as the first of the sergeants arrived. The woman brushed the underside of his with her own armored bracer. A glowing spark transferred through the touch, and the sergeant stepped back, saluted, and proceeded into the trees, her nine squad members following. The next sergeant approached, bowed, and held out her arm.

Two of thirty-two, Darian muttered. *They seem to remember the procedure well.*

Captain Zitarie has truly excelled in his position as trainer, I commented as, with a few nudges, I began to coordinate the insects' counter with the trees' bursts of poison. After as many drills as Darian had had me perform, the orders required little thought to give. Provided my concentration remained so clear. *Now, your answer.*

Well, Darian considered, *I would have argued that another three months would allow our soldiers to further improve. But the facility with which they have already begun to pick off enemy targets tonight indicates that they may not require so much time. None of our Honors have spoken of incompetence amid their ranks. And two more months has even less of a chance to solidify the people's loyalty than the retake of Ehaya. But, truly, my Grace, do you believe the reconquest would change this? The Quest cannot proceed to other nations if Nademan refuses to be loyal.*

I stroked a knot in the bark as I directed the insects to avoid several flung torches and then smothered the flames with a spray of the trees' specially nonflammable sap. The Mutharrim who had built this fortress two hundred years ago for Nademan's queen had been exceedingly thorough in their design.

Once the threat of fire was eliminated, I answered, *As you often say, Prince Darian, the question is one of history: the people of Nademan remember all too well the horror of their last ruler's weakness. As our vassals confirm, they fear such frailty even with us; they are terrified that we do not have the power to fulfill our promises. We need to disprove such allegations. Only then can we gain true loyalty—beyond the truly exceptional people of Zaiqan.*

Darian impressed an agreeing chuckle as he climbed his own tree (a curious move, for he, as the fortress commander, did not require touch to communicate with Arkaiso as I did). *How should I feel about you using my own words to prevail against me?*

That you taught me well? I suggested, gritting my teeth as the trees rippled in alarm at the bite of an axe.

Darian coolly dumped a shower of poisonous leaves on the axe-wielder, which caused death with but a few brushes against exposed skin. Then he muttered, *I am beginning to see what Lucian means.*

What? I asked.

Ah, not so relevant at the moment, he said. *Do you still maintain that Nadeyi Enaries conveys the truth of the matter?*

I nodded. *Yes. His supposition that his sister is sabotaging the Gouge accords well with our analysis of glaring vulnerabilities among the enemy's movements. The lack of significant patrol activity, the faltering efficiency of their tactics, the massive presence at garrisons… all of it marks a departure from years of strategy. We had begun to suspect that the strategist's reputation did not match the reality, and Nadeyi Enaries' message confirmed it.*

Certainly it is the western regional commander, Darian agreed, *not the central command, who has been the guardians', and now Lucian's, primary opposition.*

Until Lucian slew him four days ago in the siege of Pethama. I grinned, remembering the relief of that news.

Gratitude to the Almighty for that, as he was singularly cruel, Darian said fervently before impressing a sigh. *I must confess that even before we began this topic, my mind was changing. If Nadeyi Enaries' intelligence is correct, we owe the facility of the reconquest to this woman. Moreover... my Honor the Exemplar of Strength's description of the Enarios' health and situation touches even my heart.*

And if the Gouge realizes what she has been doing, I observed quietly, *both her life and the life of the crown prince would likely be lost.*

Indeed, Darian whispered, as solemn as I was.

We both well understood the desperate straits to which that crown prince and his siblings must have fallen. He and I had argued since the middle of the third moon for Crown Prince Eligeo tej-Shehennadem's eventual restoration, provided that he did pledge and that Lucian did not detect any taint in the man's heart, in spite of the distaste on the staff's and the mayors' faces.

Silence spread between us as we directed a few last bursts of poison and insect venom at the attackers. Then Darian relayed the stimuli provided by the base of the last few invasive auric signatures fading under attack from arrows.

That could have been far worse than it was, I remarked, exhaling as my muscles loosened.

Undoubtedly, my Grace, Darian concurred, an unspoken simmering tension disappearing from his presence. *Though I do not know if I can return to bed tonight.*

I could not sleep at all, I muttered, mocking myself as I struggled to repress an episode of unprompted tears. *After the burial, I intend to begin drafting my proposal for the reconquest.*

If the Almighty blesses us, Lucian will deign to hold a conference in two days, and I would like to have an idea prepared for it. I did not really expect a reply.

But, though his gaze remained on the pair of soldiers awaiting our descent, Darian spoke, *I will join you. You have my support, my Grace.*

Those words meant the world to me amid my torment.

CHAPTER 47

COMMAND THE RESOLUTE

Perspective: Lord Lucian the Ideal of Freedom
Date: Eyyéfaz, the twenty-seventh day of the seventh moon,
Narsaffe, of the year 500, C.Q.

A warm smile on my lips, I acknowledged each bow and curtsy with a tilt of my head, savoring the hope brightening the awed faces of my vassals. Though we were but an hour away from battle, they looked at me as though the glimpse was enough to fulfill all of their longings for freedom.

Praised be the Almighty, I thought, contented amid my lingering fever, as I gave their readiness and equipment a final inspection. *And gratitude to the Almighty for how well my companions have prepared them.*

Indeed, there is no difference between my troops and theirs. I reveled in the sight of three of my companions, who walked in a single rank behind me. *How far in this year the Almighty has brought Malika, Elian, and Kyros, transforming them from desperate youths to commanders capable of ruling provinces in their own right. How great is my homage for Kyros' achievement of magical maturity! How admirably they have excelled in upholding my command.*

Sensing my gaze, my companions lifted their heads from their ongoing discussion with Father, Darian, Taza, Hasima, and Elacir, who walked behind them. They flashed me adoring smiles—a sight relished by their watching soldiers—and returned to the debate in my father's link.

Though I listened to their arguments, the majority of my attention remained on my soldiers. Throughout the camp, on every platform around every tree, they scrambled about, donning armor and checking weapons, bidding their families farewell and storing provisions in their belts. The few magicians among them, many of whom my family and I had trained, practiced the incantations they would use. Many repeated the prayers I had given this morning, for the day was a holy one, the anniversary of my Lady Queen Aalia the Ideal of Light's birth, and so chosen for this attack. But, regardless of preoccupation, all bowed and curtsied as we passed, even my own troops amazed at the sight of me.

We have come so far, I said to myself, *even with all our struggles of gaining loyalty. May the Almighty reward their devotion.* More prayers coalesced in my thoughts, alight as I was with happiness. Indeed, no matter what came of the attack, the day was perfect—save for Arista's absence.

Though Malika, my brother, and I had reunited at Arkaiso before beginning the journey to Ehaya, and Elian and Kyros had joined us on that path, along with my father and two of my guardians, Arista had remained in the east, another two of my guardians with her. The campaign she now waged in Buzuran was essential to Nademan's future stability, but I wished she was at my side on this day.

How I missed her.

So many months had passed since the Quest stood together in Zaiqan's market. Weeks upon weeks of campaign, conquest, and mission, asking for allegiance and overthrowing the enemy's hold. Freeing Nademan with every square mile and every heart touched.

While my companions had traveled east and west or returned to Arkaiso after the market, I remained in northern Zaiqan. With Ciro at my side, I gathered and trained a new division of younger troops, four companies of men and women who had only just reached adulthood. When they proved themselves to my satisfaction in tournaments, I led them southward, defeating garrisons and patrols alike, until we reached the southwestern city of Pethama, Nademan's second-largest. Once Hasima, my father's cousin and the guardian assigned with him to Adeban, had joined me, we laid siege to the city—a long, grueling, costly operation that was all too necessary for the city housed almost a full enemy legion and the only blacksmiths in northern Icilia.

We had triumphed, ending the threat posed by the western regional commander, only to almost immediately march northeast: my companions and Darian had presented a most persuasive argument regarding the benefits of attacking Ehaya now rather than in the autumn. Having already considered the value of such a plan, I agreed—and then watched, full of pride, as my sisters and my brothers prepared the entire operation under Malika's leadership.

I had needed the chance to rest. For though I was delaying the ratification of Elian's and Kyros' received pledges,

I had still taken many myself while traversing hundreds of miles of territory and leading in dozens of battles. With such strain, I was not recovered from dispelling the consequences of Malika's curse and my previous overreach. I conserved as much energy as I could, even ceasing the flow consumed by my sense and my dreams and limiting the use of my mindlinking, but the font of my life and my physical strength remained depleted.

And still the greatest expenditure was yet to come: while my companions and my soldiers would retake the royal castle and scour the city, my task was to slay the Gouge. Every plan for his defeat required much from me.

I would offer whatever sacrifice was necessary.

My family turned to another topic, the precise timing for addressing the city after the battle. Kyros insisted a delay would serve our purpose better, but Elian and Darian thought the opposite.

Pleased and amused, I listened, speaking only when a decision was required or my opinion asked. My father was similarly quiet (though less from pride and more from temperament), but Taza and Hasima participated with as much fervor as Malika and Darian, whose proposal formed the foundation of our strategy. Every so often, Elacir muttered aloud that he should be anywhere but walking in a line with princes, as though he were their equal.

We completed a full appraisal, climbing temporary stairs built around each tree chosen for the camp's platforms, and were halfway through the return walk when a soldier approached Elian. Bowing, she mumbled something, her cheeks glossed and expression full of shame.

Elian smiled, offering comfort, and answered, "You were right to bring this issue to us, Sergeant Frorarias. My Lord, if it would be in accordance with your wishes, would you deign to answer a plea?"

The woman's cheeks coarsened with apparent fright.

"Of course, your Honor," I replied. "What troubles you, Sergeant Frorarias?"

She squeaked and gave Elian a desperate look, stepping slightly behind him.

Though his forest-green eyes filled with anger, Elian chuckled quietly—much as I had often soothed his distress—and said, "My Lord, my Grace, my Honor, a man has appeared at the camp's gates and demands an audience. The soldiers initially denied him entry, considering how little time remains, but he continues to heckle them."

I nodded, pressing my lips together, and asked, *Kyros, if I may borrow your farsight?*

Kyros drew his eyebrows together but nodded without apprehension for the connection itself—both he and Elacir had gained enough stamina in the use of their sights that such sharing no longer brought any difficulty upon them.

Activating the necessary link, I sent his magical vision toward the edge of the camp. Beyond the gates stood an angry man, dressed in clothes of finer linen than the Nademani usually wore. His bearing, the thin circlet upon his brow, and his auric signature, though not his choice to spew insults, spoke of his position in the old nobility. An old servant of Nademan, though no longer.

He is someone to meet... I spoke, "The man is the old duke of Ehaya, the city's governor. I will grant his request and meet with him at the pavilion, though I am displeased. Sergeant Frorarias, if he says anything more to you and your squad, tell him that I will remember his words."

A glad relief brightened her face, as she saluted, to both Elian and me, before returning to the gates.

Turning fully, I requested, "Your Grace, if it would please you, attend me. Your Honors, Father, Brother, Guardians, Inase, if you would be willing, please complete the remaining preparations. I will rejoin you in the first rank." In the link, I added, *The fourth, seventh, eighth, ninth, eleventh, and fifteenth companies require additional weapons; the eleventh and fourteenth require more armor, as well as assistance in wearing it as instructed; and the third requires a healer for minor ailments. See to that, please.*

Bowing, my family murmured their obedience, and Malika and I resumed our walk.

Below the tree reserved for my family and the captains, the soldiers had assembled a large tent comprised of fine, heavy material, woven by the townsfolk living at Arkaiso. Shading five specially carved thrones, it was intended for speeches and audiences, a reminder of the Quest's grandeur even amid these circumstances to our people and a sign of our vassals' love to me.

Taking our seats, Malika and I did not wait long before Sergeant Frorarias returned with the governor. The man still griped, but with more unease than vitriol.

Tapping just enough magic to discover his name, I said, "Blessings, Duke Foltariet."

He startled and examined my face a second time. Then he swallowed and bowed. "May the Almighty bless you, my Lord the Quest Leader, my Grace the Quest Second."

I raised an eyebrow at the reverences. "Rise, Duke. For what reason do you request an audience?" I allowed a hint of chill into my voice and forewent a formal introduction.

The nobleman quailed slightly before he rallied and answered, "My Rulers, I learned of your presence and the possibility of your attack through some of my city's farmhands. I beg leave to offer a few thoughts."

Is he actually saying he wants to give you advice? Malika asked, incredulous.

Impressing a nod, I answered, "Speak."

Drawing himself up, the duke declared, "My Rulers, in the formulation of your battle strategy, I beg you to show that you possess the will to do what is necessary. Without such demonstration, the people of Nademan will never fully respect you."

"What would such a showing require?" I asked.

"It may displease you to hear it," he stated, "but ruthlessness is what is required. The monster won this land because of his savagery, while the good people of Icilia crumpled before his power. Our own king did not have the will to truly act, and all the whispers indicate that you do not either."

Malika's hands clenched into fists over her armrests, and Ciro, who had approached during the noble's response, seemed ready to draw his sword.

Still calm, I inquired, "From what whispers do you draw such a conclusion?" Though the appointed time for the attack drew near, this was a blessed opportunity to disseminate my response to the concerns of many.

"The folk of my city tell me that you bury the soldiers," he responded, "and you do not kill the tainted, instead letting them go so they can carry tales of you to the enemy. My Lord, such actions will never inspire confidence in the hearts of the people, for nothing less than brutality can effectively counter this monster. Only with a brutality matching his own could anyone hope to decisively win against him, without wasting lives and resources." He raised both eyebrows. "My Lord, the only way to kill the Gouge is to destroy Ehaya's castle."

Malika, Ciro, and the sergeant choked, horrified.

I clasped both hands together over my lap. "Would you like to hear my response?"

The governor hesitated but nodded.

I spoke, "The extension of burial to all enemy soldiers, children of Icilia and our siblings save for their choice of allegiance, is one of the rituals given by the Quest of Light. It is no sentimental act, Duke Foltariet. Each death, no matter the reason behind it, places a burden of justice upon the killer. The more just the reason, the less the weight of that burden—but it must be fulfilled regardless.

"The burial of our enemies, accompanied by prayer, fulfills this burden in one stroke and thereby lessens the trauma that comes with the shedding of blood. Refusing this ritual spreads a taint in the soul, a curse of blood that brings upon one suffering in this life and a loss of the Almighty's blessing in the hereafter. Do not mistake me: the corpse of those who wield conjury must necessarily be handled differently—they must be burned, so that the residue of their magic does not pollute the earth. But, otherwise, though adherent to evil, the enemy must be given a mass grave, as we would to our own soldiers.

"For the same reason, we do not kill the magically manipulated. These women and men do not act of their own will, so to kill them would bring upon us the taint of murder of the innocent. Yes, because we do not have the means to imprison them, we let them go, using at most a spell or a hard blow to disorient them. But rather we engage in this seeming imprudence than bring the accusation of unjust death upon our heads.

"Finally, again within this understanding of justice, I answer that ruthlessness may seem expedient. The Blood and his deputies conquered and now tyrannize Icilia with atrocity upon atrocity. But do not mistake their victory to be anything other than hollow and ephemeral. Cruelty brings with it a corruption of the soul, born of violations of the Almighty's laws, and such a burden of justice as to stifle any possibility of a contented life, as well as salvation in the hereafter. I will not lead my people down such a path, Duke Foltariet. Death is preferable to such damnation."

My vassals grinned, vindicated and proud.

Cheeks coarse, the tinge of arrogance in his bearing vanished, the governor fell to his knees and bowed his head. "I beg your forgiveness for my disrespect and impertinence, my Lord, toward you and your soldiers... but, still, please, will you not destroy the castle? My city-folk will leave with one order, and the soldiers' remains can be interred afterwards. Will you not guarantee the wretched one's destruction?"

In the link Kyros said briefly, *Lucian, we await you.*

Acknowledging him, I smiled at the nobleman. "I absolve you of your disrespect, Duke, though my soldiers' willingness to do so is their own choice. As for your plea... this I cannot fulfill, and not only because of the castle's own sentience. That castle, Duke," I gestured toward the massive tree with a finger, "is Nademan's heart. It may seem a mere building, simply one of many trees, replaceable, but its loss would destroy the very people I hope to save. As for the Gouge... my plans for his destruction will not fail."

Duke Foltariet swallowed as he bobbed his head in a nod. "May the Almighty bless you, my Lord."

"May the Almighty bless you as well," I said and rose. "Now, Duke, I offer you two choices: either to stay here under watch or to be escorted out the gates. Many matters demand my attention."

Scrambling to his feet, the governor bowed again. "I would ask leave to return home, as well as the opportunity to apologize to your soldiers."

I nodded. "Sergeant Frorarias?"

The soldier saluted and escorted the noble back to the gates.

With a smile to Malika and Ciro, I quickly climbed the stairs to the Quest's platform. There, once I consumed an athar tear, I drew out the sack containing my own version of the leather armor I had commissioned at the market for each of my soldiers.

Lucian, Malika whispered, arriving behind me, *let me help you.*

I hardened my robes and held my arms out for her.

With a kiss to my cheek, Malika draped the athar-soaked chainmail over my head. The steel-backed athar vambraces were buckled to my arms and the similarly made greaves and cuisses to my legs. A gorget was fastened over my neck, and gloves were slipped over my hands. Then, finally, she placed my crown upon my lowered head.

Stepping back, she bowed. *I beg the Almighty to protect you.*

"All will be as the Almighty wishes," I murmured, caressing her beloved face. "Do not allow your faith to waver, my darling Sister."

Never, she vowed.

Together, we descended to the base of the tree.

Upon our arrival, Ciro kissed Belona's cheek and his infant daughter's forehead, then ruffled Kanzeo's hair. Malika clasped Belona's arm, and the two women and the children watched as Ciro and I walked toward our assigned posts.

Someday, I promised, glancing over my shoulder, *someday, you will walk again with me, my Supreme Commander.*

And until then, I will watch over you, my Supreme Ruler, she pledged in return.

Those words gave new vigor to my spirit, such was their power.

As we reached the last ranks, the soldiers bowed, murmured their prayers for my triumph, and stepped aside, following with bright eyes our path to the first rank.

Upon my arrival at the front, Elian and Kyros bowed and briefly embraced me, both wearing their crowns as I was. At my nod, they walked to the heads of their contingents, while Father, Darian, and Hasima formed a row behind me. Catalysis sparked around each of them.

For a brief moment, I activated my sense. And, with it, I gazed upon Nademan's jewel and my beloved vassals.

Beyond the edge of the forest, amid a great greensward nearly two miles in diameter and encircled by a thick hedge almost fifty feet tall, stood the city and castle-tree of Ehaya. The city's trees, towering over their surrounds at a height of seven hundred feet, clustered in a mass of vibrant green and rich brown the shape of a gibbous moon. In the northwest of that formation, the tree-line curved inwards to cup the massive castle-tree, half again as tall as her neighbors. Like her peers in Tadama and Pethama, Ehaya's castle-tree was composed of a hollow trunk and a set of nine towers, each half of the full tree's height. All of Ehaya retained a lushness the yellowing forest had long since lost because of the magic with which the capital had been planted.

A mile west by northwest of the castle-tree was the Quest's campsite. There, in a large glade just within the shelter of the woods, flew upon a great staff the flag of my Quest, the mysterious flower-crown on a field of rich green trimmed in gold. Directly behind that blessed banner was the platform on which Malika stood to command our forces, and beneath it were assembled her soldiers, one-and-a-half thousand in number, their resolute faces and polished weaponry shining amid the trees under the morning sun. Five companies formed ranks behind Elian, nine behind Kyros, and the last behind Ciro, while Taza, Kanzeo, and the women with small and nursing children flanked Malika. Each determined to uphold their orders in accordance with my wishes. Each prepared to sacrifice their blood in my name, for our cause.

Honored, I bowed my head as a smile of pure wonder curved my lips.

Then I proclaimed, letting my voice ring like a bell over the army: "Oh Almighty, Guarantor of prayers, Vanquisher of the vicious, Liege of our souls—I beg of You a victory as You once gave my Lady Queen Aalia the Ideal of Light. I beg Your succor as You once gave Icilia with the birth of the first Quest Leader. Praised is your name."

The faint sunlight dewing the bottom of the smog brightened, forming true beams, then hardened, blade-sharp.

Turning my attention to the towering expanse of the castle-tree, I spoke, "With my favor."

Fifteen hundred voices bellowed, "For the Lord of Freedom!"

SEGMENT 4

INTENDING SERVICE

Perspective: Crown Prince Eligeo tej-Shehennadem, Heir-apparent to Nademan
Date: Eyyéfaz, the twenty-seventh day of the seventh moon, Narsaffe, of the year 500, C.Q.

For countless minutes I was in too much pain to think. Agony ripped through my limbs and coiled through my torso... at once too much to bear yet all too familiar.

But, though the Gouge's cruelty had not abated one degree, this time was different. For I had something to which I could cling: the Quest Leader's name.

As I returned to a state of coherence, my lips fluttered with that name, like a prayer.

I opened my eyes and cautiously tested each limb, before inhaling deeply.

The expansion of my torso sent pain shooting through my chest.

I winced. Those were definitely broken ribs. The Gouge's kicks had fractured the healing breaks from his last blows,

and my ribs were dreadfully fragile. But, from the dull familiarity of the pain, the injury was not more serious—no bones
piercing my lungs, for one. Whenever that happened, I had
to grovel for healing from the one elderly staff member who
had the magic. She was always disinclined to help me, and
only taking on chores that I could hardly afford to shoulder
ever persuaded her...

I tested more of my body, twitching my hands to pat my
sides and my skull. There were bruises and bumps, but no
cuts or burns. Which meant that he had not gone beyond
conjury and his usual tortures.

Blessed.

I moved to push myself up.

"I do so think your little checks are hilarious," said *that*
voice, menace given the form of sound.

I froze. Whatever calm I had evaporated. *He has not
left yet!*

That voice, so full of desire that it was cold, continued,
lifting into a mocking croon, "Pathetic little prince, poor
baby without protection, heir to nothing."

His taunts turned so crass that I wanted to burn the ears
that had heard such things. Then he stepped forward... and
his boot, the sole lined with metal nails, hovered over my
exposed left hand. Taunting with the cruel prospect of escape.

There was no escape to be had.

His boot stomped down over my bloodstained fingers.

Audible snaps mingled with my scream.

The Gouge laughed and walked away.

My chest heaved as I tried to come to terms with the pain,
but each breath only increased the agony.

Lord Lucian! my mouth uttered in a silent screech. *Oh
Almighty! Please do not abandon me!*

Again and again I repeated the words... until the pain did ease, enough that I could regain control of my breathing.

Whimpering, I cradled the broken hand to my chest.

Then, bracing the one working hand against the hard wood, I pushed myself into a sitting position.

Oh, gratitude to the Almighty, he is gone, I thought, sighing—and winced again, regretting that sigh.

My head swam with pain, but I forced myself to stand. He had not dragged or summoned me to his personal chambers in several weeks, so I needed to take this opportunity. These rooms were the best place to search for information. The Gouge despised written messages, but he did keep them. The most important of those papers were likely to be here—he did not trust his soldiers, he did not use a study, and the rest of the papers were anyway handled by Tahira Enarias.

Tahira Enarias—the Gouge's brilliant chief strategist, who was trapped here just as much as I was.

Though my siblings, the staff, the soldiers, even the Gouge himself, thought she delighted too much in the challenge of her position to care about the implications of her actions, I knew her true motivation: her brother's life and sanity. For I had been present, scrubbing the floor in a corner, on that day five years ago when the Gouge ordered her and her brother to be dragged in front of him. I had seen the expression on her face when she accepted his offer of a position. And I heard enough from the Gouge and the soldiers to know that she still visited her brother, as often as she was allowed.

She was better than I: she was not so ruined by the Gouge's cruelty that she had forgotten her sibling, whereas I... sometimes I had to rack my memory for the names and faces that had once been so precious to me. But moreover, she used her position in the Gouge's court to protect the people of Nademan—my mind was not so far gone as to not realize that the strategies she presented the Gouge were only just more efficient than what he himself knew how to design.

She was only a commoner, her noble title and duty destroyed with her village, while I was the crown prince. Yet she acted for the whole of Nademan while I had done nothing for my people.

If anyone at all in the capitol deserved salvation, Tahira Enarias did—even more so now as she attempted to render the Gouge vulnerable to the Quest Leader's conquest. She was risking both her brother and herself, but that did not cow her into abandoning the Quest Leader's service.

I admired her, though I had never spoken to her—the Gouge scrutinized every person to whom I spoke for any stirring of sympathy toward me. She had too much at stake to risk such examination.

Though, perhaps, if I found any useful information, I would consider hoping that she might take that risk. The Quest Leader's reconquest was of paramount importance.

Clinging to my conviction, despite the pain, I shuffled to the nightstand, the desk, and the dresser. With my one working hand I pulled out each drawer and scanned the jumbled contents.

As I did so, a memory bubbled up in my mind: as a child, long ago, I had poked through these same drawers, in search of clues and trinkets at my father's behest. On one rest day he organized a treasure hunt for the children of the castle, and we giggled as we scampered through the castle. Indeed, the halls rang with joy—my parents, aunts, uncles, staff, and the visiting nobles laughing uproariously at our antics. The day had been so much fun...

Where had that father and king who had cared for his family and his people gone? To where had that man who desired to bring joy to his loved ones disappeared?

He had vanished long before his murder. All his murder had done was end his body; the man himself had already died. His name was unsalvageable—there was no question in anyone's mind that he started us down this path. This was not a story of eventual discovery of his blamelessness: his guilt was clear. Even I, once his most devoted son, hated him for what he had done.

He had stood by and let Nademan be destroyed. He was just as much a traitor as the royal families of Zahacim and Bhalasa. And with his treason came my own damnation. His actions had cursed all of his blood.

No matter what I did, how could I expect the Quest Leader to ever accept me? I did not deserve forgiveness; I was not like the long-lost Heir to Koroma or the massacred heirs of Asfiya—my parentage was not of heroes but of traitors.

I had not even tried to compensate for that. Instead, I had allowed sin to consume me.

I was too unworthy to look upon the shoes of the Quest Leader, much less his face. He was mustering an army, but I had no place in its ranks.

A pain even greater than my broken bones skewered my heart.

Curling my fingers around the knob of the last drawer, I opened it and spied the edge of a stack of paper, just as a few muttered words reached my ears.

I froze. I knew the Gouge's voice better than my own—undoubtedly, he was the one speaking.

I should have scurried away by now! Regardless of what he did to me, he always expected me to be gone within minutes of his departure!

Closing the drawer and lifting my other hand to my mouth, I frantically looked around the room. I needed to hide; I could not even imagine what would happen if he caught me snooping...

There was no space behind the furniture, and he could come and sit on the chairs in the corner—

My eyes lit upon the athar cloth bed-skirt. Moving as fast as I could, I limped over to the bed, lay down on my back, and scooted underneath, letting the drape fall to cover my body.

My heart thundered in my ears as, but moments later, the door slammed open.

Heavy footsteps thumped across the wooden floor and made a shrill screech.

Then a hand, blacker than night, appeared beneath the cloth.

I bit my lower lip, the faint taste of blood filling my mouth.

The hand groped about under the bed and latched onto something near my head and pulled it out. Stones collided against wood.

Remembering my conviction, I raised the drape by a fraction of an inch, just enough that I could peek out from beneath it.

The Gouge was taking a blue stone from a wooden chest—presumably what he had removed from below the bed—and lifting it to an eye. He examined it, then grunted in satisfaction. Replacing the stone, a sapphire, he pocketed the chest. With a growl he spun on his heel and left the room.

Outside the door spoke another voice—certainly the voice of one of his conjurors, though I could not tell which.

The Gouge responded in his bone-crushing timbre, "Of course not; we have her brother. And anyway that—" he used a foul word that demeaned women— "enjoys what she does. She gets pleasure, somehow her—" foul words regarding intimacy and what ought to be private about a woman's body—"so I will let the generals use her plans. But I will not stay for this battle, as much as I want to confront that upstart. His Viciousness requires this to be delivered."

The other voice mumbled a few words.

The Gouge snarled, "I am the master of this territory; I control it, and I will not lose it to some—" again, a foul term, this one demeaning men.

Then several sets of boots thundered away.

Silence.

I dared to shuffle out from beneath the bed.

A bellow pierced the walls of the castle: "For the Lord of Freedom!"

A smile, the first in a decade, spread across my lips. *He is here.*

I scrambled to my feet. Limping over to the dresser, I pulled open the last drawer—in answer to my prayers, it contained sheafs of documents.

They were not important enough for him to take, but perhaps they might still be of benefit?

Making a quick decision, I stuffed the papers down the collar of my tunic and more in the waistband of my trousers. A few remained, so I shoved them into the sleeve of my useless arm, which I pressed against my heaving chest. Glimpsing the knife lying carelessly atop the nightstand, I clutched it in my working hand, though I could not repress a shudder of horror—the blade was stained with my blood.

No! Keep your focus, pathetic little prince, I chanted to myself.

Then I shuffled out the door as the walls began to glow.

I did not know what would become of me by the end of this day, but these papers would reach the Quest Leader's soldiers.

And, if she allowed, I would help Tahira Enarias do the same.

CHAPTER 48

ATTUNE

Perspective: Graced Malika the Exemplar of Wisdom
Date: Eyyéfaz, the twenty-seventh day of the seventh moon,
Narsaffe, of the year 500, C.Q.

"For the Lord of Freedom!"

Laughing in pure delight, I activated Lucian's bound link for sharing magic and nodded to Taza.

Grinning herself, she catalyzed for her farsight and bowed her head as I took control.

Blinking, I wondered for a moment how Kyros managed *two* overlays when I had such difficulty grasping the notion of seeing something with anything other than my eyes, even after so much practice.

Taza squeezed my hand, and I focused.

My Lord, I said in Prince Beres' link, which connected the commanders of each contingent and all the captains. *If it is your wish to proceed.*

In Taza's farsight, I observed Lucian stride into the open, his father, his brother, and his guardian flanking him, passing from the woods amid which our army had assembled into the vast ring of open grass around Ehaya.

Guards stirred at sentry points over the vast expanse of the castle's walls. Nocking arrows, they aimed for the person of the Quest Leader over the barrier of thorny hedge which protected the castle-tree and the city cluster.

I held my breath.

Then Lucian, the princes, and Hasima sprinted toward the massive hedge, long, even strides rapidly crossing the mile between our camp and the capital.

Count Tolmarie, proceed, I ordered.

Ciro dashed out into the open, leading his company toward the city. Leather armor well-oiled, weapons well secured, the only sound was of their footsteps.

The city guards did not see them until the company was nearly upon them. Scrambling for arrows, they did not notice a squad skidding to a stop and arming bows. They fell, skewered against their own defense.

My Lord, Count Tolmarie has nearly reached the hedge, I reported.

Lucian flung himself headlong at the hedge.

A squeak left my lips, though I knew his plan.

The enormous hedge shrank, the entirety of it around the castle and city crumbling to a fraction of its height before a single thorn could touch his skin, removing a barrier our forces would have otherwise crossed with great difficulty.

Lucian sped over the tiny row and continued toward the castle, his visibly alarmed detachment on his heels.

Taza shuddered. "If I had not known all of Nademan's hedges were attuned to the Quest Leader's will..."

Exhaling, I said, *Count Tolmarie, the way is yours.*

Ciro reached the city's trees and climbed, his contingent following.

Lucian was nearly at the castle's base. The guards were still recovering from their shock.

My Honor Kyros, proceed, I said.

Kyros streaked pass the edge of the forest. His contingent followed, tapping their kind magic, formed in three rows.

The castle guards shot a volley.

His eyes glowing, Kyros raised his hand, and, as practiced, the companies halted with enough distance that the arrows landed harmlessly several feet short of their boots.

Kyros led them forward again.

The guards shot a second volley.

Kyros signaled a second halt.

Switching Taza's focus, I observed as Lucian arrived at the castle's base. Prince Beres, Darian, and Hasima placed their hands against the bark. Eyes wide and silver, they channeled their prepared spell of athar magic into the living wood, prompting it to glow.

The tree resisted, pushing back that glow toward them.

Then Lucian spoke, "Treasured castle of Ehaya, gift of my Mother, allow me entry."

The giant castle, a thousand feet tall amid a sea of far shorter peers, a gift of the Quest of Light, shuddered. Then the glow spread rapidly over the trunk, into the branches, the tree shining like a pillar of light, a defiant torch challenging the smog.

A doorway opened before Lucian's team.

Two-thirds of the way across the field, Kyros called encouragement to his troops as they skidded, starting and stopping repeatedly to avoid the arrows.

The way is yours, my Honor Kyros, I said.

Kyros acknowledged the words as the guards focused all their attention upon his detachment.

My Honor Elian, proceed, I said.

Stepping out into the open, Elian blew out a breath and released his spell. A breeze stirred in the forest, an ominous rustle of leaves. Then winds began to gather, shaking even these towering trees, circling over Elian's head. Soon, great bursts of gale winds swirled above him, forming a funnel that rivaled the castle in height. A giant twister, yet one polite enough to only ruffle leaves.

I chuckled, shaking my head. Only Elian would make a considerate tornado.

Winds howling, the twister shifted and began to lean sideways, the motion visible as a shuddering mirage of the air. Its top loomed over the crowns of leaves and branches that capped the castle's nine living towers.

The guards stood frozen in shock.

Kyros and his force arrived at the castle's base. Side doors, comprised of planks of bark, opened at their touch, while three stories of windows, panes of translucent wood, crumbled in the tree's welcome. Half of the nine companies entered from the first story, while the second half scaled the walls and followed Kyros inside through the second and third.

Elian, Elacir, and a half-company stepped into the twister. The circling winds swept them up off their feet, spun them through its massive length, and dropped them atop the central and highest tower, the royal quarters. Balancing carefully, they descended the branches to the first window, which melted at their touch.

Glossed faces bright with awe, the rest of Elian's four companies followed, the twister carrying them to the ring of surrounding towers.

Excellent so far, I said in the link. *All forces have achieved entry. Speak if you require support.*

"My Grace?" Belona whispered, standing beside me as she gently rocked her sleeping daughter.

Remembering my promise, I smiled over my shoulder at the two companies of women and their children. All two hundred and twelve of them had chosen to accompany their spouses for this battle, deciding both that such an endeavor was safe for their families, allowing them to remain reunited, and that they would be the staff of the camp. Lucian had entreated them yesterday to also be my final support should the battle go poorly, for they were as well-trained as their spouses. In agreement, choosing their favored weapons to carry, the women had made only one request: candor regarding the direction of the battle, at least through my expression if nothing else.

I held great respect for them, knowing them to be warriors in their own right. And, like my friends, I enjoyed how their presence turned our camp from a somber place of death into a lively neighborhood lit with the laughter of little children.

Correctly interpreting my smile, the women gasped and cheered.

"Praised be the Almighty," Belona breathed. "How quickly they achieved entry! Within fifteen minutes!"

A bright grin spread Kanzeo's lips as he clung to Belona's side.

I dipped my head and returned my attention.

His hand brushing against the wall, Darian had found a series of empty corridors, and Lucian was allowing him to lead their squadron through the maze of passages.

Though I dearly wished to help them, finding the Gouge was not my duty, nor within my capacity. So, with a prayer for their protection, I turned to observe Kyros' progress. Speaking in his own link, he directed his soldiers through their respective floors, the combination of his sights warning many in advance of the enemy's ambushes.

I directed Taza's farsight up through the walls. The tree resisted such passage for a moment before relenting, only allowing the movement because of the accompanying tinges of Lucian's mindlinking and my auric signature. Much as Arkaiso had checked Kyros' magic when he had first arrived.

Elian's companies crept quietly down through the towers, avoiding the staff's chambers and slaying many enemy soldiers as they hurried to arm themselves in their living quarters. Every so often, Lucian spoke directly into their link, ordering them to spare one of the manipulated. At each such order, the captains wrestled the targeted soldier into a chair and restrained his limbs. With their advantage of surprise, though the enemy outnumbered us with a ratio of two to one, Elian's contingent progressed rapidly downwards, tearing through the thirty floors.

Be wary when you enter the main castle, I warned. *My Honor Kyros is still on the first three floors. You will encounter resistance.* Then, glimpsing enemy movement, added, *My Honor Kyros will be attacked from above in thirteen minutes. Reinforce him.* Switching links, I informed Kyros of the same. Then I turned to find Elian.

Unlike his troops, he, Elacir, and their squads had not yet crossed the topmost ten floors. Standing in a clump, they discussed something in quiet, heated voices.

My Honor Elian, why have you stopped? I asked in the commanders' link.

My Grace, I require support, he said anxiously. *Some sort of magical trap lies ahead, and Elacir and I cannot coordinate with my contingent while we attempt to defuse it.*

Though worried, all I said was, *As you say, my Honor.* Switching again, I told his captains of the change in command. The captains fretted but immediately focused again on their own movements as I guided them through the corridors and stairwells.

The contingent had reached the main castle when Ciro called, audibly distressed, *My Grace, I need support!*

My Honor Elian, can you resume? I asked.

Yes, my Grace, he answered.

Informing the captains of the change, I sent Taza's farsight to the flicker of Ciro's auric signature in the link.

Jars, sticks, and slabs of bark flew through the air, pummeling my soldiers. I staggered, the bruising collisions sharp across my own body as tears amassed in my eyes.

Taza squeezed my hand, and I focused and examined the situation.

The city-folk, the Nademani of Ehaya, threw projectiles from the sides of their platforms at Ciro and his company. The onslaught halted every attempt my soldiers made to proceed across the branches of the city's dense cluster, cornering them in a knot on a confluence of hanging walkways.

While, in response, all my soldiers could do was bat away the objects with their sheathed swords, too honorable to harm their fellow citizens.

Nine hundred feet away, three companies of enemy soldiers swarmed toward my troops.

Frantically flipping through the tactics from my lessons, I activated the bound link for speech with Taza and ordered, *Taza, send someone to contact Sergeant Frorarias. I want the marquis found immediately.* In the commanders' link, I acknowledged Kyros' news, though not without a shudder of fear.

She murmured her obedience and whispered to one of my defenders.

"My Grace, what is happening?" Belona asked, clutching at my arm.

I gave her a frown as I said to her husband, *Count Tolmarie, I have sent someone to find the marquis. Order half your company to form a circle around the rest. Rotate your swords in the joined ovals you were taught as a dueling defense—the involutes you form should deflect more projectiles.*

He relayed my orders. Four squads abruptly pushed themselves to the edge of their huddle and sketched the joined ovals with their swords. Another squad elbowed their peers back and joined the perimeter.

"My Grace," Taza reported in my ear, "Nadeya Thrasaria has returned. Sergeant Frorarias has sent half of the gate guard in the direction the marquis chose."

I hissed a breath and muttered to her in the bound link, *I understand why Lucian wished for him to leave our camp, and it was indeed a wise move, but his departure adds an extra issue.*

"Do not worry, my Grace," Taza assured, voice quiet. "We will find him."

Flashing her a smile, I adjusted the last elements of a plan, even as I took command of Elian's forces, and said in the commanders' link, *Count Tolmarie, I give you the following tactic.*

The mayor listened intently as the city-folk's barrage increased, joined now by crass taunts. Then, aided by his familiarity with Lucian's preferred methods, he began to arrange his company as I ordered.

The outer circle stepped forward, allowing room for two columns of two squads each to assemble. Those columns drew their swords as, upon a shouted command, the circle snapped into two lines, on either side of the first two, and continued to deflect projectiles. Ciro and the last squad formed a final file in the middle of the four columns.

On my mark, the columns charged east over the branches and walkways toward the enemy.

Within arrow's reach, the enemy raised their blades and let loose a massive cry.

My troops responded with Lucian's name.

Lucian briefly assured me that none of those soldiers were manipulated.

Then the enemy was upon them.

The outer columns fell back, still defending from the city-folk's attack. The first soldier of each of the two inner columns engaged the enemy, dueling a single opponent each. Immediately, the second soldier of each column split off to the side and attacked another. Then the third and the fourth, until the entire mass of the enemy queued to fight twenty soldiers, funneled to them by the narrowness of the approach across the branches. Single slashes were enough to topple the enemy, who plummeted to their deaths, impaled at the high speed by lower branches.

Excellent defense, Nademile, I praised—which Ciro repeated aloud, heartening the men and women.

The city-folk, cheeks coarse and eyes wide, drew back, fewer sticks and jars leaving their fingers.

One of my soldiers fell, head cleaved open by a brutal strike. Leaping over her body, another filled the empty place before the enemy could press an advantage.

Save for a few deaths, the Quest's soldiers, better armed, better trained, and wholesomely motivated, fared far better.

I confirmed that Elian and Kyros did not require additional support: although Kyros faced a major battle in the lower levels, his magic gave his troops a distinct advantage. Similarly benefited by Elian's ingenuity, his troops combed the upper levels, preventing any additional reinforcement from reaching Kyros' opponents. Elian himself scoured the royal tower.

Pleased, I turned to Lucian, who fought near the throne room. And stifled a shriek, clutching my pendant.

For Lucian dueled more than a squad of conjurors. The athar of his armor and the light of his person dissipated any of the black smoke cast in his direction. Even as I watched, he slew two and stalked the remaining thirteen. A harrowing sight.

Indeed, from just my distant view, I felt the cold burn of the evil...

"He will be all right," Taza murmured, squeezing my hand, though she sounded as frightened as I. As terrified as the princes and Hasima appeared, pressed against the wall and only able to support Lucian through shields of athar magic.

Yet even amid that terror, I marveled at Lucian's prowess.

He had faced conjury only once before, but he knew precisely how to counter each dark blow, wielding the sunlight of his presence as a weapon. The fear could not touch him. And the conjurors fell at his feet.

Giving a grim smile to my defenders, I shifted Taza's far-sight back to Ciro, assessed the situation, and ordered, *Switch.*

The latter squads of the inner columns surged forward from behind their peers, driving the enemy back several steps and allowing the first nineteen to rest.

The enemy began to edge around the blockade, climbing onto higher branches.

Arrows, I ordered with an image of the maneuver as I answered a question from one of Elian's captains.

The front squads of the deflecting columns sheathed their swords and drew their bows in two smooth moves. Nocking arrows, they snapped their heads up and shot all of the enemy soldiers who had tried dropping down on my troops.

Tilting his head back, eyes glinting beneath the shadow of his helm, Ciro examined the enemy's swarm and ordered, "Volley over our heads!"

The archers shot another set, this time arching above our soldiers into the mass of the enemy.

Shrieks as more fell.

Ciro ordered a second volley.

The city-folk retreated into their huts just as Taza reported, "The marquis has been found and informed, my Grace. He will speak to his people and ensure they do not resume resistance."

I exhaled as my shoulders relaxed. In the bound link I murmured, *Gratitude to the Almighty that Lucian bothered to entertain him. My gratitude to the defenders and the guards.*

Taza bowed her head and conveyed those words to the women, heartening them as they scrutinized each of my expressions.

I informed Ciro of the development and then said, *Only a company remains. Angle your front-facing squads and charge. Tip and arrow.*

At his orders, the two squads dueling the enemy moved forward in step, angling outwards in the form of an arrow-point until a slight gap remained at the tip.

Ciro ran into the gap, sword unsheathed, a squad behind.

The remaining seven squads threaded between their comrades into the mass of the enemy.

Divided by Ciro's charge and overwhelmed by rested swords, the enemy succumbed in bursts of red.

The last enemy soldier collapsed as Marquis Foltariet's voice emitted from the treetops, welcoming the Quest.

The city of Ehaya was won.

Now for the castle.

I pivoted to support Kyros just as conjurors appeared before him.

CHAPTER 49

CONCORD

Perspective: Honored Kyros the Exemplar of Strength
Date: Eyyéfaz, the twenty-seventh day of the seventh moon,
Narsaffe, of the year 500, C.Q.

The gentle pressure of a beloved gaze nudged my back. The sensation brought a momentary smile to my lips, a reminder that Malika watched over me.

The thought occupied but a drop of my concentration as my mind split in a dozen ways: with one thread, of catalysis and the conviction on free choice, I predicted the actions both my opponents and my captains would take. With a second thread, of catalysis and the conviction on purpose, I peered around corners and spotted ambushes and overhead attacks. With a third thread, I maintained a connection with Nademan's magic, which alerted me whenever my forces faced one of the manipulated or found the hiding spots of the staff.

Through the one link Lucian had agreed to actively power, I relayed all of this information to my soldiers, coordinating our progress as we scoured the first three floors.

Like an exhibition duel, my captains and I, accustomed to battling together, moved in synchrony, dispatching enemy after enemy while shielding ourselves from unnecessary risk, suffering few casualties though far outnumbered and constricted by narrow passages.

As I had hoped, the training that had led to my maturity and subsequent receipt of the Quest's gifts in full made such massive harmony possible—with immense concentration, such as what I invoked for battle, and the amplification provided by my jewels, I could direct my farsight in a dozen directions and observe possible futures for a dozen people, simultaneously beholding multiple images alongside my physical vision.

Both hands on my hilt, I slashed at an enemy soldier's chest, piercing his armor. Blood pooled around him, dying the living wood red. A floor below, a spear-wielding squad impaled their opponents, spilling more blood over the luminescent walls. That squad crouched, and their peers released a volley of arrows, piercing throats in sprays of blood.

I winced but did not hesitate, stepping through the pool and informing the two companies on the floor above of an ambush lying around a corner. I ordered the two companies moving through corridors parallel to mine to spin around and look up moments before the enemy swung into view. Blurring my own actions forward, I noted the possibility of an assault from an approaching stairwell. Turning to the squads who accompanied me, I instructed one on how to safely find the mirroring stairs and sent those soldiers to counter the assault from above. Streaking forward, I waited with a squad on either side of the stairs. When the enemy appeared, we attacked from three directions, decimating all but two in minutes. Those last two, of the manipulated, were tied to the stairwell by my soldiers. Then I led the way onward.

My Honor Kyros, Malika said in the commanders' link as I surprised another ambush, *you will be attacked from above in thirteen minutes. I have ordered our Honor Elian's troops to support you, but they will not be able to eliminate the entirety of the reinforcements.*

With your will, my Grace, I said, and she withdrew.

Switching links and searching ahead, I ordered my captains, *My Grace has warned me of reinforcements in thirteen minutes. We will counter in the atrium. Captain Nesaries, that door to your right, the embellished one, will lead you to a balcony overlooking the atrium. Shoot several volleys at the two squads already gathered there. Clear the space.*

And the rest of us, my Honor? Captain Pantaria asked.

With one thread, I inspected each of the balconies for the thirty floors of the main castle and, with the other, predicted the enemy captains' movements. *They will attack from either the balconies or the central grand stairs, depending upon where they find us.*

They have the advantage of high ground... Captain Berdariat mused. *Could we attack from the balconies' shadows?*

That is what I intend, yes, I said, stabbing one enemy soldier and parrying a blow from another. *I can teleport perhaps two squads, but I would rather keep that tactic in reserve. It would drain much of my strength.*

Indeed, yes, my Honor, Captain Pantaria said. *Our move-halt maneuver would be sufficient counter-advantage.*

The other captains indicated their assent.

Then we are agreed, I said. *Captains, direct your soldiers onto the balconies or out the doors as soon as the hallways are clear and Captain Nesaries reports. Conceal yourselves in the balconies' shadows.*

While Captain Nesaries and the seventh company unleashed volley after volley outside, six companies huddled around the doors. The remaining two and my squads dashed through the halls while the enemy's reinforcements drew closer.

Clear, Captain Nesaries reported.

The six companies emerged outside and pressed themselves against the living wall. Nocking arrows, they readied themselves for the onslaught. Moments later, the final two dispatched their opponents in a shower of blood and did the same.

Skidding to a stop in front of a balcony door, I prepared to follow them when the flicker of my own actions changed. If I delayed but a few minutes...

Flexing my fingers over my hilt, I ordered, "Sergeants, proceed without me. I will follow you in seven minutes."

The three sergeants exchanged worried looks but saluted and led their soldiers onto the balcony.

I raised my sword into a guarding position and spun so my back faced the wall beside the door. With one thread of thought, I examined my soldiers' position.

The atrium was a vast space, thirty stories high, formed from the inward curve of the main trunk beneath the nine tree-towers. Its ceiling was the base of three of the towers, one wall the concave façade of the lower castle, and the other open air facing the city.

Five massive balconies extended from each story into the atrium, and ten vertical sections of the wall were composed of nearly transparent slabs of wood. Decorated with trimmings of gold and rich banners of linen, silk, and athar, the atrium represented the ease with which any citizen of Nademan could approach the crown, as well as the crown's own commitment to be candid about its actions.

Or, at least, so its majesty had once been—many of those banners now hung stained and in disarray, the gold accents tarnished, and the translucent wood dirtied by paint, soot, and blood.

Despite our battle-focus, anguish burned on my soldiers' faces, and my own heart wrenched in my chest.

Lucian will heal all of this, I told myself. *Icilia is changing. Hope returns in his wake, and all of us will no longer be alone.*

The portion of farsight scanning my surroundings followed the confident walk of a woman as she strode into my presence.

Bold and assured, butter-blonde hair coiled into a tight knot beneath a rag of a kerchief, the woman wore a tattered brown dress with all the dignity of athar robes. Steel glinted in her icy blue eyes, the mark of a warrior more fearsome than all but Malika and Arista. Though her hands trembled around the strap of a sack and a dull knife, and her bronze cheeks were as coarse as her brother's, she was strength incarnate.

I smiled as I dipped my head and lowered my sword. "Blessings, Nadeya Tahira Enarias."

She startled, eyes wide and lips parted, then smoothed her features into expressionless composure as she offered me a curtsy. "May the Almighty bless you, my Honor."

"I am delighted to meet you, Nadeya Enarias," I said, exhaling a chuckle. *The shared resemblance with her brother is remarkable... and of course she has the knowledge to discern my exact position in the Quest from a glimpse at my crown. Lucian will be glad we found her.*

Her expressionless mask faltered again, a polite disbelief creasing her lips, before returning. "The distinction is mine, my Honor. And, if it would be in accordance with your pleasure, I ask for a moment of your time."

I nodded. "Speak." In my companies' link, I ordered, *Brace yourselves. Two minutes.*

She inhaled deeply. "My Honor... the Gouge's squadron of conjurors plan to approach your position."

My smile slipped as I sent my farsight to comb the lower floors. "There are conjurors by the throne room... but my Lord engages with them." I suppressed a shudder, more terrified by his battle than by confronting them myself. Lucian had taught Elian and me how to face them, as well as trained our troops on what measures to take. But nothing could prepare me for *his* battle with them.

For the briefest moment, Tahira seemed to share my fright. But her voice was steady as she reported, "My Honor, the Gouge has three squads of conjurors under his command. He sent two squads, divided into four squadrons, to find my Rulers, per established plan. The remaining squad, his elite, is... not in the castle."

"Hmmm... If they are not in the castle," I considered, "the best we can do is inform our Lord. As for the ones coming in my direction..." I exhaled. "I can address their attack."

Again, for the briefest moment, the corners of her lips curved up. "As you say, my Honor."

Though aware the enemy was nearly upon my troops, I switched to the commanders' link and reported, *My Lord, my Grace, my Honor, I have received a warning that a squadron of five conjurors approaches my position. An entire third squad, the Gouge's elite, is missing.*

I acknowledge, your Honor, Lucian said tersely. *I will support you as soon as I can.*

As I thanked him, Malika and Elian acknowledged as well, frightened for my sake.

Better me than Elian. Or Malika, I thought. Then spoke aloud, "My gratitude for this warning, Nadeya. It is invaluable." As I had learned during those terror-filled weeks in Bhalasa before Lucian had found me, my sights could not detect conjurors until they actively used their magic, and my access to Nademan's magic could find them only once they were almost upon me.

Lucian had the magical capacity to track conjurors, but it required much skill—more than I could have learned so newly into maturity. Yet we had so many reasons not to delay this battle…

Remembering one such reason, I requested, "Nadeya Enarias, if it would please you, I would ask that you wait here, wherever it is safe." I only waited for her nod before slipping onto the balcony.

In that very moment, the enemy arrived, screaming war cries, upon the higher level.

Focusing on my flicker of foresight, I ordered my soldiers to hold their places while the enemy rained arrows upon us. Then, as they reloaded, I commanded a volley. Several exposed enemy soldiers fell. My soldiers retreated just as the next enemy volley was fired. Then I commanded a second.

Several repetitions followed, until half the enemy force tossed aside their bows and clambered down the sides of the castle to meet us, digging brutal knives and axes into the living wood.

Spears, I ordered.

The spear-wielders dashed into the open, dodging arrows, and flung their weapons, impaling many, before unsheathing their swords.

The enemy drew closer to our levels.

Hold…

The enemy landed on our balconies and on the ground beside us.

Bolts. Then swords. Sides and circle.

My soldiers fired a series of crossbow bolts, dispatching several squads, and then rushed out from the opposite sides of the balconies' shadows, forming two columns that encircled each group of attackers and pressed them inward toward the balcony doors, where yet more of my soldiers waited. The two-pronged move dispatched many before they could return blows.

Prepare for a second wave, I warned.

Unable to clearly see our response, the enemy repeated various versions of the same tactic, again and again, with both the castle wall and internal staircases, as they attempted to surprise us from above… Their numbers felt nearly endless, despite the efforts of Elian's troops. Amid the spinning and the slaughter, the sprays of blood, the constant twists of my sights and the frenetic pace of my orders, I nearly forgot about the conjurors.

Then the magic of Nademan churned around me.

Snapping my head up, I located the conjurors approaching from a door on the opposite side of the atrium. *Inside! Conjurors approach! Climb up to these upper floors and attack from behind.*

My captains ushered their soldiers away. Resistance tinged many of their expressions, but none disobeyed.

Sheathing my sword, I jumped onto one of the castle's walls and climbed down, then ran into the center, all while dodging arrows. Running my hands over my chest and legs, I checked my armor, a match to Lucian's and salvaged from the guardians' belongings—Prince Beres had labored for days to infuse it with athar magic for this battle.

Focus, Kyie, I commanded myself as I drew my sword again. *Conjury is terrifying, yes, but you are not the pitiful boy you were when you first choked on it. The Almighty's blessing and Lucian's favor shine within your soul. Do not let it trigger your memories; do not let it overcome you. You, a Potentate, can withstand. Focus, Kyie!*

The door opened, and four figures in vermilion armor stepped onto the atrium floor.

The enemy soldiers squealed, retreating from the balconies.

The blacker-than-night spots of soot on the conjurors' glossy brown skin shimmered. A cloud of malevolent shadow rose up from their skin and swept toward me.

Please, my Grace, my troops, I beseeched her, my sights showing how the enemy soldiers would fall on my uncoordinated troops.

I will watch over them, Malika assured me. *Fight well, my Honor.*

Strengthened by her words, fixing my faith in the Almighty and in Lucian in my mind, I dove into the cool well of my life and catalyzed a portion with the magic of the Quest that now pulsed through my blood, forming power that crackled like lightning. A numbing haze clouded my thoughts as though blood gushed from a wound. Then the crown on my head and the ring on my finger warmed and restored my strength.

I commanded, "Alaëh alasir ai hasnir, daileh é a'ezahram, pisterim u'onem!"

White light coalesced in a shield just before the black magic engulfed me.

Almighty, Shining Guide... Aalia, Manara, Naret, Lucian, Malika, Elian, Arista...

The dark magic receded, and the conjurors snarled.

I intoned a second command, and the white light spun into a halo around my sword.

The conjurors cast another cloud.

In a flash of green light, I teleported and appeared behind one of them.

Tendrils of smoky cloud, tracking me despite the transfer, snaked around my limbs. The armor flashed, and the icy perfume of athar magic sliced through the odor of charred flesh.

Before the man could turn, I poured more life into the magic and swung, removing his head.

The conjurors spun and cast another cloud.

I teleported to avoid it. Appearing behind them, I beheaded another.

The cloud overtook me, exhausting the magic in my armor, seeping into my lungs as shadowy daggers pierced my heart and my mind. Resistant as my Potentate self was to the spell of fear, the magic sought to overwhelm my organs and shred them to pieces...

Chanting the divine names and the names of the Quests, I switched the light from sword to shield and pushed out the cloud, the pain, straining the air of the smoke so I could breathe. Sweat poured down my face, stinging my eyes and soaking my collar.

I teleported again, appearing behind the third conjuror. Drawing yet more life, I coated my sword with light and swung again.

Missed as he pranced away.

Before I could teleport or even move, the cloud swallowed me. And pain burned me alive.

Collapsing onto my hands and knees, I screamed, *Lucian!*

Kyros! he answered.

And light pierced the cloud, consuming it in a burst of white flame.

Panting, I staggered to my feet and swung my light-infused sword again.

The head of first one, then the other, rolled across the grass, shock their last expressions.

Beloved gazes touched me, Malika and Elian, but not his...

As I incinerated the blood on my sword with the remnants of the light, I searched the atrium for the face I most desired to see.

It was empty. Save for me and piles of corpses.

My farsight found Lucian still dueling seven conjurors, wielding both athar magic and light formed of the magic of the Quest, far more skillfully than I, though it was only his second experience with conjury and his first ever actual battle.

Thank you, I whispered, awed.

Always, Lucian answered. *Burn them.*

Remembering his instructions, I called my soldiers, who immediately ran back onto the balconies. Their expressions of terror faded only when their eyes alit upon my intact person. Despite the aftershocks of pain and my immense exhaustion, I smiled in reassurance. "If you would, please burn their bodies. Gather ours and watch for more reinforcements."

In the link, I soothed my friends' worries over my health as Malika returned command of my troops.

Captain Berdariat saluted and ran for a broken piece of spear. Her soldiers, as well as Captain Nesaries', scrambled for more discarded shards of arrow and bark, enough for four stacks. The rest collected those who had fallen in this skirmish or spread back into the corridors of the castle.

Soon, the conjurors' corpses, along with the pools of blood around them, began to burn, aided by fire spells Lucian had bound for me. Count Kartaries, a sergeant and a minor wizard of the breeze, directed a shaft of air to carry away the smoke, pushing it high into the sky where it would dissipate safely.

Satisfied, I strode toward where a figure in brown waited in the shadow of a balcony.

Upon my approach, Tahira offered me a second curtsy and a wan smile. "Praised be the Almighty," she whispered.

"Indeed, praised be," I replied, bowing my head and smiling. I considered her face and then added, "Nadeya Tahira Enarias, I have met your brother, Nadeyi Kanzeo Enaries."

She choked, composure shattering as both fear and relief contorted her face and fell at my feet.

Laughing softly, I knelt in front of her. "Please, Nadeya, this is not necessary. Nadeyi Enaries explained, and the Quest knows he speaks the truth." My own perception of her heart, a gift of my maturity, confirmed my initial confidence in Kanzeo's words. "For that reason, I offer you my pendant as a sign of safe passage." I slipped it from my neck and clasped it around hers, careful to avoid contact. "Show this to any who stop you and use it to ask for direction to my Grace. She will protect you."

Tears trickling down her coarse cheeks, fingers instinctively curling around the emerald, Tahira stared at me. As though I had given her dignity when she had thought it forever lost. Her lips moved, no sound coming, until the words spilled, "My brother?"

"Safe with my Grace and one of her guards and awaiting you." I beamed at the thought of their reunion.

She swallowed and nodded. Then she tilted her head. "My Honor, those are four pyres. Where is the fifth?"

Leaping to my feet, I spun and counted the pyres. "Seek my Grace, Nadeya." Though I watched her leave with a bit of farsight, I focused my attention on scouring the castle.

A black cloud blew toward Elian.

CHAPTER 50

COHERE

Perspective: Honored Elian the Exemplar of Esteem
Date: Eyyéfaz, the twenty-seventh day of the seventh moon,
Narsaffe, of the year 500, C.Q.

Starting catalysis, I blew out a breath, both for my magic and as a sigh. I abhorred placing an extra burden on Malika's shoulders, but I desperately needed the whole of my concentration and Elacir's help to break this trap.

Though I had learned how to command soldiers and use my magic for their benefit, I was still untested in the discipline of combatting magic with magic: in the few months of lessons I had received, breaking spells of wizardry and sorcery with those same forms of magic was not covered with much depth, both because not many trained magicians had survived the Blood's conquest and because little scholarship existed at all on the subject.

Without Arista's support, my soldiers would have been defenseless against the magic.

"My Honor, we have the water," Elacir reported, holding a large vase as he stopped beside me. Behind him, the rest of my five squads carried dozens of delicate, decorative bowls and jugs.

Massaging my forehead, I nodded to him and spoke into my pendant, "Would you have any other suggestions, my Honor?"

"No, my Honor," Arista answered, clear voice emitting from the emerald. "Cast the spell—I have every confidence in your abilities. That is, of course, why I did not tell you to ask Lucian or the guardians for help."

That blunt reassurance calmed much of my rising anxiety. "Thank you, my Honor."

"For your happiness," she responded. "As a last warning, let me remind you to be wary of the caster. The wizardry of this spell and the lack of gems signify that the trap must have been freshly laid."

"I will, my Honor," I replied, and, at her acknowledgment, closed the connection, which ended a considerable drain on my strength.

Behind me, my soldiers, who had waited patiently, smiled in encouragement. After months of fighting together, they knew me quite well—indeed, I still wondered at how they had not yet lost all respect for me.

Elacir raised both fists in a cheer as he turned and spread his wings. At a nod from me, he began to flap them, sending gusts of air into the tiny mirage that marked my incipient twister.

I catalyzed, streamed the power through my jewels, and chanted, "Hayàsimile é a'hayitos, sasholos ne zazatet, enisimirim ai unisimirim, kasirenerrim zulluh kasholir ai akasholir." I blew, emptying my lungs, as did the soldiers, while Elacir quickened his flaps.

Channeling those breezes, I formed a twister that was large enough to resemble a person.

As soon as the swirling shape steadied, Elacir and the squads flung the contents of their vases, bowls, and jugs at it. Rotating so fast its winds were translucent blurs, the twister sucked up all the water and, at my direction, moved out over the trapped section of corridor, scraping the floor as it passed.

The spell activated and pulled the water, drying the twister until it collapsed. A muddied green mass writhed over the floor and then dissipated. My magical senses, honed somewhat by Ilqan's lessons, indicated the trap was gone.

Signaling my squads, I moved forward cautiously, wary of more traps.

When two floors passed without further incident, I accepted my command back from Malika. My captains informed me that they had reached the main castle, so, with a bound link and Elacir's farsight, I directed them to the reinforcements who were marching toward Kyros' troops. Like Malika and Kyros, I warned them of upcoming obstacles and ambushes even as I crept through the royal tower.

Though I was petrified by the thought of crossing the Gouge's path, I prayed I, rather than Lucian, would do so. The brief flashes of Lucian's fight with the conjurors that Elacir's farsight had given me as I directed my troops around the area chilled my spine, evoking memories that I had long suppressed…

When Kyros spoke of conjurors in the commanders' link, my heart stopped.

How I wished I could support him! How I wished I could do *anything* so he would not have to confront this threat alone. But, without magical maturity, I would be little more than someone else to protect. I had neither access to the magic of the Quest nor his level of resistance to conjury. All

I could do was acknowledge his news, pray, and continue on my own mission.

Slaying the oddly few squads of enemy soldiers we encountered, my half-company and I had nearly reached the lower third of the tower when the hum of arms magic drew my attention.

Invoking the magic in my blood, I let a substantial amount pool beneath the plane of my concentration before I imbued it with my will. The magic spread along my nerves, infusing every sense, so that I could perceive magical residue as though it were a sprinkle of tangible particles in the air.

Another trap spread in front of me—from the inspections made by my probing wisps of wind, it would not be disarmed as easily as the last one. Nothing less than a person's passage would suffice.

I explained this to Elacir and my soldiers, who immediately began to confer in low voices.

The swish of a dress caught my attention.

A woman appeared at the end of the hallway. Her auric signature matched the one mixed into the trap. A wizard of water, and no middling or minor one at that.

Get behind me, I ordered in our bound link. Then, switching to the commanders' link, said, *My Grace, I urgently need your support.*

Malika acknowledged the plea and took my command.

Cackling, the woman lifted her hands and chanted a spell. A murky green miasma formed from moisture drawn from the air and the living wood around her. The color leached away, forming a shimmering vapor tinged with green. Then it spread toward us.

"Poison," I breathed. My breezes were clear that none of us would survive that cloud's touch.

Immediately, I began to spin a shield of wind.

Elacir ran to open a window.

Pulling air, I formed channels which leached bits of poison from the cloud, drew them outside, and dissipated them.

The pungent fumes cleared—only to reveal a streak of greasy green shadow nearly at our feet. A swathe of charred, bleached wood marked the path it had taken across the floor.

A tendril reached for Elacir's ankle.

Terrified, I shrieked—and used that air to form a mist of flexing currents, which slid beneath the burning shadow, scraped it off, and flung it outside.

"You need offense, Brother," Elacir whispered.

Clinging to my focus, I cast a gale.

The first drafts swept inside the window. Eddies tumbled through the castle corridor. Spinning and swirling, the first currents coalesced, thick ropes unseen yet unmistakable in their passage.

More and more wind came.

Soon, massive gusts wreathed my person, howling and screeching, mussing my hair and beard, yet pliable to the slightest drift of my thoughts. Not a single whisper ruffled the feathers beneath my cloak.

I thrust the cyclone at the enemy magician.

The second cloud of poison floating toward us streamed back over her body. Burning the flesh off her bones and clawing at the inside of her lungs.

She screamed as the gleam left her eyes.

Her bleached bones tumbled to the ground, mere seconds after her own magic had touched her.

Horrified, I pushed what remained of the poison outside. Then I fell to my knees and stared, my scales dim and cold. *That was not what I wanted to do... How could I do that!*

"Elian?" Elacir asked, touching my shoulder.

"A moment please," I whispered, numb despite the angry irritation of my jostled wings. "The trap perished with her, so you may continue if you would like."

"Never without you," he stated and crouched beside me.

Boots tapping against the ravaged wood, my soldiers arranged themselves around me, enclosing me amid their ranks.

The beginnings of a smile softened my lips, the horror starting to fade as warmth lit my scales.

Then I froze, scales cold, as the turmoil in the commanders' link pierced through my thoughts... "Kyros," I breathed. "My brother confronts conjurors! His battle began, and I did not even notice!" *What sort of brother am I to not notice...*

Elacir's hand tightened on my shoulder, drawing my attention. Despite the fear in his own eyes, he whispered, "You can continue, Brother."

Heartened by his strength, whispering prayers, I stood. "Let us continue forward. Sergeant Ekesarie, please note the position of this body. Ideally, I should be the one to return, but if I cannot, then, please, one of you should, to fulfill the burden of justice."

The sergeant bowed, and the rest of my soldiers saluted.

I contacted my captains, who had been fearfully demanding answers of Elacir in the bound link even as they followed Malika's orders. Reassuring them, I accepted the return of my command and led the way forward—with one change: as the battle heated below, Elacir's farsight needed to be dedicated to my captains' aid, so my own comrades were left vulnerable to the enemy's approach. Thus, I decided to send a pair of my soldiers with minor farsight as scouts. Returning periodically, they confirmed when the way was clear and warned me when they spied soldiers.

On the last floor, outside a despoiled sitting room, they returned with a young man escorted between them.

"A captive," Nadeyi Poleries murmured as he lightly nudged the man in my direction.

Before I could fully note his face, the man fell at my feet—with a brief yelp of pain, the odd crunch of crinkled paper, and a shudder, as though even the summer heat could not warm his skeletal frame. Though that form held the lines of adulthood, he was short for one of the Nasimih and desperately malnourished, more so than even Kanzeo, from the coarseness of his honey-brown cheeks. His golden-blond hair and beard were so sparse that he appeared half-bald. Brown streaks of drying blood covered more of his body than his rags did.

Sympathy warmed my heart, for I knew misery and desperation well.

So, with a gentle smile on my lips, careful of my wings, I crouched and tipped his head up with one finger beneath his chin. "Blessings, Nadeyi," I welcomed him, even as I alerted my companies of a cunningly arranged ambush on the twentieth floor.

His lips trembled as tears rolled down the bumpy skin of his cheeks. "My-my—" he stuttered, fixated on my crown.

"My Honor," Elacir helpfully supplied, tone compassionate. "You speak to my Honor Elian the Exemplar of Esteem, Potentate of the Quest."

The man shivered, gray-green eyes as frightened as they were relieved and hopeful. But he had at least not recoiled from me.

"What is your name?" I asked. Lucian and Kyros were engaged in dreadful battles, so asking was my only option, however much a disservice that did to the Quest's majesty.

His lips parted, about to answer.

Around us, the soldiers shifted, and several grunts of disapproval reached my ears.

Resignation souring his hope, the man cowered and crossed his arms over his chest, hugging himself and hunching his shoulders over the papers he held.

Alarmed, I looked up at my soldiers. "What disturbs you?"

Every member of my five squads was glaring balefully at the man.

"What is the reason for such a reaction?" I asked.

They exchanged glances. Then Sergeant Dideriat exclaimed, furious, "My Honor, those eyes are a clear sign! This man is the former crown prince, the firstborn son of the shamed king!"

I frowned. "The shamed king... who is... oh."

The man, Crown Prince Eligeo tej-Shehennadem, Heir-apparent to Nademan, flinched as though struck. Though he did not recoil, my finger on his chin not the slightest bit shaken, he seemed to withdraw into himself. Preparing for a beating.

I had done the same countless times. For the same reason—the sins of my relations.

Though I knew the soldiers had reason to feel such rancor, I opened my mouth to defend the broken man.

A scream—Kyros'—echoed in the commanders' link, *Lucian!*

In answer, Lucian shouted, *Kyros!*

Light filled my vision, then faded.

Frantic, I grasped Elacir's farsight and sent it to Kyros.

Who slew the last of four conjurors. Alive, upright, unharmed except for the lingering creases of pain and exhaustion on his features.

I clutched my heart, dizzied by the intensity of my relief. My scales glowed golden, bright enough to light my vision.

In the link Kyros whispered, voice full of awe, *Thank you, Lucian.*

Which meant that, without doubt, Lucian had somehow saved him when he had asked. Yet another indication of how blessed I was to have him as my liege and brother.

Always, Lucian responded, confirming the thought. *Burn them.*

Though reassured, I waited until Kyros himself promised Malika and me of his well-being before returning to coordinating my companies, who were nearly as relieved as I was, as well as my current situation.

"What happened, my Honor?" Elacir and several soldiers cried.

I beamed. "My Honor Kyros of Light defeated the four conjurors who had attacked him."

Elacir and all of my soldiers sighed, shoulders slumping, sharing that relief. Even the crown prince relaxed slightly.

Tilting my head then, I considered the Nademani. *Angering them and ignoring their emotions is a poor return of their loyalty and care,* I thought. *As much as this man's situation draws my sympathy, I do not know him, and I do not have the magic to judge his heart. But, to be compassionate toward all of them...*

Elacir drew my attention with a tap on my shoulder and offered me a trusting smile.

Warmed by his confidence, I declared, "Nademile, let us take Nadeyi Eligeo—" I hastily composed a temporary address— "with us, back to the camp."

The crown prince froze.

"My Honor!" several soldiers protested, and Sergeant Ekesarie added, "He is unworthy of your presence! Much less your care and attention!"

"That is for my Lord to decide," I replied calmly, "not us. And regardless, my Lord would be appalled if we left him in this condition, when he has not raised a weapon or uttered an insult. Until and unless my Lord says otherwise, Nadeyi Eligeo is to be treated as a freed captive, a guest of the Quest's army."

The soldiers bowed, reluctantly but without hesitation.

His eyes welling with more tears, the crown prince looked as though redemption had come. Though I had not been able to give him any guarantee.

Elacir squeezed my shoulder, and the pang of guilt faded. I had done the best I could without the magic to assess his heart.

Smiling again, I moved my hands to touch Prince Eligeo's shoulders.

A whimper escaped his shrunken lips.

That smile disappearing, I examined him... and saw his hand.

The fingers were crumpled, as though crushed beneath something heavy, the joints bent in unnatural directions. Broken. Almost beyond repair.

My lips twisted in a scowl, I concentrated on the conviction that the Almighty held all cures, catalyzed, and amplified, preparing enough power for a massive healing spell. Scales and fingers glowing, I touched Eligeo's forehead and whispered, "Kazaqer lamile ai akakaser hadile, damile unuzuler ai lananareh ider, paresilerim, pariderim, parobanerim, parejiderim, pareneru be ore anemizu kanne."

The green light glistening on my fingers sparked and then permeated him.

Prince Eligeo gasped, back arching, as the light swept through his entire body. Bones snapped into place and rejoined into seamless wholes, flesh knitted together over cleansed wounds, fresh blood trickled from his marrows into his veins, and, most of all, the pain ebbed, fading until it almost vanished. Ribs, fingers, opens cuts, bruises and tears both internal and external... I guided my magic over the worst of it, intent on giving what comfort I could, vowing to see to a full healing as soon as the battle ended.

All the while coordinating with my troops, who had nearly reached Kyros'.

The healing light inspected Prince Eligeo one last time before returning to my fingers and disappearing.

Scales dimming, I exhaled sharply, despite the amplification more exhausted than I had anticipated, though still quite far from reaching the dregs of my strength. But the momentary flash of pure, unburdened joy on Prince Eligeo's face was all the confirmation I needed for my choice.

If Lucian judged this man to be pure, as I suspected he would, the best path toward the restoration of his heart and mind began with healing his body. As I knew all too well.

Breathing deeply, freely for the first time in perhaps years, Prince Eligeo bowed his head and whispered, "Thank you, My Honor." Only four words, half of it my address, yet brimming with loyalty and hope.

Chuckling softly, I helped him to his feet. Then I glanced at Elacir.

My little brother dipped his head and drew the crown prince to his side, with a firm grip on his arm.

I nodded to my soldiers, who wore expressions of both awe and loathing, as they saluted. "Let us continue," I said. "The rest of us are but a floor above my Honor Kyros' troops. The castle is nearly cleared."

The soldiers pivoted on their heels and marched forward.

Though I led them, Elacir fell back behind the last rank with Prince Eligeo.

We had barely crossed the threshold into the main castle when a voice called out, "My Honor, I have to tell you something!" Prince Eligeo's squeaky rasp.

I turned just as a black cloud spread in our direction. *Conjury.*

I blew a breath and, with the last of my strength, flung my brother, my soldiers, and the crown prince toward the far wall.

The cloud consumed me. Slithering into my lungs, into my blood, through my organs.

My heart felt as though it would explode as the beats quickened. Breath, the life of a wind wizard, disappeared from my lungs. Pain, hot as a fever yet cold like the direst chills, spread down my spine and curdled my stomach. Agony, burning me alive and clouding my mind.

Potent fear. Crushing fear. Devouring fear.

And yet my will remained my own, my world still Lucian and Malika, Arista and Kyros.

Lucian, Malika, Arista, Kyros...

Almighty, Shining Guide... Aalia, Manara, Naret... Lucian, Malika, Arista, Kyros...

The names, sacred and most dearly beloved, empowered me. Enough to turn.

Enough to fling a dagger.

Enough to stand upright as the conjuror screamed, clutching the blade in her shoulder.

Footsteps thrummed on the living wood as Lucian burst from a nearby stairwell. Sword dazzlingly bright, he sliced the conjuror's head from her neck. Whirling around, he leaped forward and swung at the six conjurors who had followed. Shields of white light and silver athar magic flashed around him as he deflected spells and attacked, never caught within their clouds.

His features as frigid and hard as ice, the silver of his skin the glint of steel, he was the wrath of the Almighty, terrifying as he shone like sunlight.

Eyes wide, I slowly retreated to where my comrades were starting to sit upright, dazed from the collision with the wall. A soldier began to speak when I pressed a finger over my mouth. Following my gaze, they fell silent and still.

We did not dare to move as Lucian slew conjuror after conjuror.

When all seven lay at his feet and his sword was cleaned, he turned to us. Breathing heavily, he wiped perspiration from his forehead as he commanded, "Burn them. As well as the ones in front of the throne room. Now. The pollution has already reached the castle."

My troops and I scrambled to obey.

Gathering arrows, linens, anything flammable we could find, we built pyres, and I filtered smoke out an open window.

Halfway through the task, a movement attracted my gaze.

Prince Eligeo crawled across the floor to Lucian's feet as he leaned against a wall, eyes closed in evident exhaustion. But at the crown prince's approach, Lucian tilted his head down and smiled warmly.

"May the Almighty bless you, Crown Prince Eligeo tej-Shehennadem," Lucian greeted him, his musical voice brimming with compassion. "I wondered when I would meet you. His Honor has certainly performed a thorough healing."

My scales flared.

Though overwhelmed, the crown prince seemed intent on speaking, opening and closing his mouth.

"Speak," Lucian encouraged, kind as always.

At the encouragement, Eligeo cried, "My Lord, the Gouge is gone!"

CHAPTER 51

BALANCE

Perspective: Honored Arista the Exemplar of Bravery
Date: Eyyélab, the twentieth day of the eighth moon, Belsaffe,
of the year 500, C.Q.

Sword-tip resting between my boots, hilt held by my clasped hands, I faced west, as solid and silent as the stone sentinels of Zahacim but far more vigilant. Several dozen feet behind me, equally watchful and unmoving, were Eloman and Da'ana, Lucian's warrior guardians assigned to the east. Three thousand feet away waited Ilqan and my five companies, shielded by a fortification camouflaged in the trees.

Overhead the smog lightened from abyssal black to the shade of night and then to a charcoal gray.

Still we did not move.

Today would be the culmination of weeks of planning and months of struggle. Today Lucian would defeat the Gouge.

Immediately after what the soldiers called the Battle of Ehaya, Lucian, Elian, and Kyros had departed for the east in pursuit of the Gouge. Hundreds of miles had flown by beneath the hooves of their horses, but they could not catch him, for the monster had nearly half a day's start and far less concern for his horse or the townsfolk he robbed. But, tracking him with the skill only he possessed, Lucian had estimated that the Gouge ran east and south toward Koroma. Between his predictions and the guardians' and my knowledge of the eastern provinces, we had chosen a site in Makiran for an ambush.

Not long now, I thought.

Already Nademan's magic whispered of the approach of chaos. Birds shrieked, deer and wolves alike fled, trees trembled. The very air heated, a scalding temperature rather of agony, fever, and molten rock than anything resembling the warmth of life.

The smog lightened yet further to the color of lead, signaling that the first rays of dawn lit the sky above.

The gaze of someone whom I dearly loved, Kyros' farsight, caressed my face and back.

Perspiration gathered beneath my crown and collar and dewed my arms as the pleasant balm of late summer was consumed by the unnatural heat.

"The plan?" I spoke.

"As you say," Da'ana and Eloman answered, though with great reluctance. Like Taza and Ilqan, they bore the same affection for me as they did for Lucian. But no stringent argument of theirs and Ilqan's had convinced me there was a better way. So they would obey, loyal servants and soldiers at their core.

The magic of Nademan began to writhe, inaudible shrieks shaking the earth.

I tensed, plates stretched tight over my skin, and flipped up my sword. My crown and my ring warmed in anticipation.

Hooves thundered against the ground. Branches cracked and snapped in a rising wind. Approaching closer and closer...

"Brace," I said.

Lucian's long-dormant links with the guardians and me fell into place. And with them came a wave of terror mixed with grim determination. As well as the voice I had most missed.

Hold! Lucian ordered. *Arista! Hold!*

The very world darkened, the smog unalleviated by the rays of dawn.

A swarm of black and red horses burst into view.

"Alarim." At Eloman's command, lucent athar magic shields sparked around the clearing. Sealing me inside with the conjurors.

The horses reared in alarm, neighing loudly at the sudden enclosure.

Two more light-shield spells, fire sorcery and the magic of the Quest, ignited at my command, reinforcing the athar magic.

Three total rings. It would be insufficient unless I succeeded.

The riders yanked their horses under control. Then the foremost tossed back his hood.

Revealing the soot-stained, blacker-than-night face of the Gouge.

Irises the color of the abyss set amid bulbous gray sclera. Nose protruding and pointed like that of a wolf. Lipless gash of a mouth parted to reveal red elongated fangs. Black hair sprouting from skin that should have been coated only with gloss. A beast on two legs who had once been incé and a child of Icilia.

The face of my nightmares, for only the pattern of soot and hair and the absence of plates and scales differentiated him from the Choker and the other tyrants.

We are almost there, Arista! Kyros shouted. *We need only a few minutes of delay!*

Raising the knobby ridge of a brow, the Gouge raked his gaze over my face, my person, and the crown atop my head. Then threw his head back and laughed, loud and scornful. "So this is where you've been, little Arista! Hiding in my territory, playing at rebels—and abandoning your family." He sniggered. "Does your family know what you've done? So appalled they would be to know you've betrayed your masters!"

"You are not my master," I said, clinging to my composure with every drop of discipline I had. Even as I realized he was saying they knew I had escaped... "As you are not the master of this land."

"Such a bold thing to say for such a tiny, pathetic, weak little girl," the Gouge said, sneering. "Do you really think you can challenge me? Your own family, those proud warrior princesses, succumbed to our vice. What, do you think you have more virtue than they did? You are as inferior, as easily crushed beneath my heel, as they are. After all, why else did you escape Choker's court only after seventeen years under him? Remember that I am more powerful than he is—you will not escape me. You are made for rape and abuse. And now you are mine. My slave."

You can hold him, Sister! Elian called. *And you are* more *than capable of protecting yourself!*

Despite my brother's words, I swallowed as thousands of horrifying, bloody memories besieged my mind, a life empty of all but pain and degradation... Everything he said was something I had heard countless times. Every sentence, every word, dug its vicious claws into my deepest fears about myself—that, despite all the pride I had in my reliability, my power and skills, I did not deserve to be free... that I really was unworthy of Lucian's favor...

The thought of his name called forth his face. The memory of his love. His pride. His trust. Four months apart had not changed his regard for me.

Exemplar of Bravery, I said to myself. *Remember what Lucian titled you, what name came for you from the Almighty's blessing.*

Arista, you are Icilia's paragon of courage, Lucian said, as fiery as the summer sun.

The embers of my courage kindled and flared, blazing into a roaring inferno, a conflagration fueled by faith and love. The sun rising within my soul.

Straightening my back, I responded with all the ferocity of a lioness, "I can and I will challenge you, Gouge. You and your cabal do not own me, for I choose to be a servant of the Almighty and a vassal of my Lord Lucian the Ideal of Freedom. And upon his blessed name, you will not escape him!" Then, catalyzing life faster than I had yet done, I flung three bolts of pure light at him and the closest of his thralls.

The two conjurors toppled from their horses, smoking holes bored through their chests. While the Gouge snarled as it crashed into him but remained otherwise unaffected.

"You will pay for that," he seethed. "Your Quest and laws are but worship of weakness. I will show you what real power is." Dismounting, he strode toward me. The massive girth and hulking height of his body seemed to swell in his anger, leeching light and warmth from the world like a void, a black mass of monster intent on shattering my soul with his violence.

I braced myself. "Real power, Gouge, is finding freedom in the Almighty."

What are you doing, Arista? Lucian asked, wary now.

A cruel leer curved the Gouge's maw. "Is that so? Will you believe that still when conjury breaks all your claims of free choice and becomes your only divine?" Black smoke undulated around his hands and snaked through the grass.

"Yes," I said. "For I will withstand anything to protect my Lord and Icilia!"

The Gouge barked a disdainful laugh.

Arista! my brothers screamed.

The smoke swallowed me. Piercing my nose, mouth, eyes, passing through every pore and around every plate of my skin.

Pain.

Endless pain.

Pain gnawing on every organ and bone, sucking my blood. Devouring my entire world, as though doused in molten rock. Seeking subjugation, if not by fear, then by agony...

No. I am dedicated to Lucian's service, and his service has set me free. For his sake, I bear this pain. With every drop of conjury I absorb, I protect him! I lessen the sacrifice he must give!

Better me than him!

I began to laugh.

Hands tight on the hilt of my sword, body stiff as stone, I stood and laughed. Even as the conjury permeated my flesh, attempting to wring out every drop of hope and love.

How could it ever succeed? For my hope and love resided in Lucian!

The Gouge snarled, long and low, absolute malice.

My laughter only grew louder.

"Idiot girl," he spat. More smoke, blacker and more venomous, spewed from his fingers.

I grinned. "Do your worst, pitiful beast."

What are you doing, Arista! Lucian shouted. *This was not our plan!*

The Gouge roared in uncontrolled rage—the paltry squeal of a tantrum compared to my Lord's wrathful words.

"Losing your edge, are you not?" I taunted. "I am not the least bit afraid!"

The squad of terrified conjurors scurried to the far side of the enclosure.

Breathing heavily, the Gouge stalked closer and, looming over me, grasped my chin with searing fingers. "I will teach you your place at my feet if it's the last thing I do!"

Please hold! Elian begged. *Just five minutes!*

I snickered. "So you will *fail* in the last thing you *ever* do, because *my* place is at my Lord's feet! Not yours!"

We are coming, Arista! Lucian screamed.

The Gouge's sharpened nails dug between my plates, drawing blood. The soot-like smears on his face shimmered, ash and scalding smoke made flesh.

And conjury spilled directly into my veins.

CHAPTER 52

HARMONIZE

Perspective: Lord Lucian the Ideal of Freedom
Date: Eyyélab, the twentieth day of the eighth moon, Belsaffe,
of the year 500, C.Q.

We are coming, Arista!
Agony boiled my blood as the darkness of conjury in its most potent form entered Arista's veins. Poison unlike any other—and yet she laughed.

Laughed.

Laughed because she had *intended* this. Intended to goad the Gouge into wasting as much of his magic as possible to lessen the weight of my task.

Arista! Elian and Kyros sobbed.

The thought of her sacrifice, the validation of the glories of her character, held no pleasure for me. I had planned to face the tyrant myself precisely because the cost was mine to bear. My companions were not yet capable of withstanding his magic, and I refused to demand of them what they could truly not give.

Yet Arista had given this sacrifice regardless.

I would not let it destroy her.

I am almost with you, my darling Sister, I whispered.

Then I called out to Kyros, "We have just passed the limit of your range. Teleport us both." It might drain strength that we could not spare, but Arista needed us...

Kyros did not hesitate. Nudging his horse closer to mine, he grasped my extended hand and catalyzed. Within a blaze of green light, he transferred us from our horses' backs to a patch of blackened grass enclosed by three shields.

Paces away from the beast digging his claws into Arista's throat.

Yanking his arm away, I tore the Gouge from her and threw his monstrous form against the side of the shield.

He screeched as the athar, fire, and light scorched his flesh.

I drew my sword as the Gouge struggled to stand. *Kyros, the other eight. Eloman, bring Elian here. Da'ana, Ilqan, shield my companions.* With the awareness provided by my sense, activated again for this battle, I watched them act on my orders.

Gently pushing Kyros' bloody handkerchief away, Arista lifted her sword and moved her feet into an offensive stance. *Lucian, please do not dismiss me.*

I will not interfere with your judgment of your own abilities, I said dryly as I invoked the first of my prepared spells, *and I respect your choice. But please do not shred my heart.* My crown and my ring warmed, ready to relieve the sharp pain from the massive amounts of Quest-gifted magic I would need to use.

I will not! she declared, remarkably cheerful even as black lines spread between her plates.

Despite the crushing anxiety in his expression, Kyros scrambled to stand beside her without protest.

Nearly uprooting a sapling with the pressure of his hand, the Gouge attained his feet. Then, growling, he raised fists shrouded with black smoke and charged toward me.

The smoke, I noted, was perceivably dimmed by the attack Arista had prompted. Though I abhorred the risk she took, her reasoning was sound.

On the far side of the ring, Arista and Kyros, backs together, attacked the conjurors. Outside, Eloman arrived with Elian, who, along with all three guardians present, catalyzed for spells of shield and support. Our horses, cajoled by Elian via my mindlinking, trotted in the direction of the ambush.

The Gouge leapt into the air, reaching for my face.

I jumped back and slashed my light-wreathed blade at his shoulder.

He dodged and unleashed a blast of conjury.

I raised a shield of light, blocking the blow and balancing out a fraction of his magic.

Then I began to sing:

Freedom by the Almighty, light of the shining sun
Blesséd by divine choice, chosen of our own accord
Discord healing by our hands, standing once more as one

The melodious words, my promise to Nademan and to Icilia, given in the common tongue of Siléalaah, soared above the battle, filling the forest, resonating with the land itself. The calming tones countered the conviction behind conjury, the frenzied desire to relish fear and pain, and the thread of Quest-gifted magic in my voice directly negated the chaotic energy.

My companions and my guardians beamed, joyous laughter radiating from their lips. Soothed, assured, heartened, the force of their blows increased, the speed of their movements augmented, the potency of their magic enhanced, for they were in harmony with me and what I represented.

Shock froze the shimmer on the Gouge's face. He ducked to avoid my thrust only at the last moment. Then contempt contorted his features. "You're actually *singing*? What kind of witless battle tactic is that?" Even as the black smoke around his fingers lost some of the depravity of its color.

On the other side, the conjurors looked terrified. All eleven of their horses clustered, eyes rolling widely and flanks heaving, fleeing as far as they could from the fighting.

Lifting a hand from my hilt, I punched the Gouge's stomach, provoking both a wheeze and a shriek. Then leaning back, I kicked a foot into his knee before pushing off, flipping to a handstand, and slamming the other foot into his chin. Every blow burned him, neutralizing some of his magic.

As I flipped back to my feet, the Gouge stumbled. Then screamed and charged again.

I sang the next verse in the sacred tongue Alimàzahre:

Lightning bursting in the sky, sign of soothing drops of rain
Refreshed under the renewal, renewed of broken hope
Rope for the searching hand, standing once more as one

The trees, the animals, the air, Nademan herself exhaled a sigh of contentment, while all the conjury paled.

The Gouge unleashed a storm of punches and kicks. Weaving and dodging, I avoided all but one, an uppercut to my chin.

I winced, but the skin only stung with the beginnings of a bruise. His conjury had no effect. No pain, much less fear.

Disbelief pried open his lipless mouth.

I swung up, and the blade pierced his vambrace and bit into his upper arm. Light gushed down the steel into the wound while I sang the next verse.

He screamed. Shoving the blade away, he lunged for my throat. Rage mixed with disbelief.

I ducked, extended my leg, hooked it around his, and wrenched.

The Gouge toppled to the ground—and kicked my shoulder with a flailing foot, sending me sprawling.

Quickly extricating my limbs, I swept my legs beneath me and leapt to my feet.

Just as he did. Hollow eyes on level with mine, he stared for a moment. "You simply cannot be him."

I continued to sing.

"You are a worm! A worm to be smushed beneath my boot!" Snarling, he swung both fists at my head.

Streaking around him, I struck his back, cutting through the armor to the flesh beneath.

He howled and whirled, aiming a punch at my ribs.

I darted backwards, but the punch landed, fracturing the bones. Pain crossed my features, lancing through my body, though my singing did not end and its effect did not falter.

"*Lucian!*" my companions screamed, though they remained focused on their own battle.

The Gouge grinned. "See, you're not that special."

Then the white-hot bolt of pain rebounded on him, drawing a scream.

Custom binding our family, courtesy of the integral
Connected through our virtue, virtuous for the sacred life
Strife for serving our land, standing once more as one

Screeching, he thrust a weakened fume at me.

I blocked it with a shield and retaliated with a flare of light.

The Gouge attempted to parry it with a swirl of conjury—but half the light still struck him, burning his gray palm. Matching the paling charcoal of his magic.

I pressed my advantage with another kick, eliciting a yelp, and another cut, drawing both a shout and blood.

He fell back, panting heavily, bulbous eyes widening. A flicker of fear crossed his features.

Yet it was not enough. So many of my attacks were only successful because he was too shocked to respond with all the skill my conversations with his former captives and conferences with Nademan indicated he had. The attack on Arista had drained much of his strength, but his magic still raged, too powerful for him to succumb to a death-blow even should I strike it.

While my strength flagged. The last three weeks had done nothing to improve my declining health. Indeed, my continued steady stance and clear thoughts were the Almighty's miracle.

Still singing, I sprang forward, twisting my torso, and brought my sword down in an overhead cleave.

The Gouge dodged the blow and stumbled backwards.

Rage darkened his eyes.

Moving faster than he had yet, he lashed out with both hands. Seizing my arm, he peeled back the athar cloth of my glove and clawed my palm.

E'Qahre, Aläm avolemasu ru em. The sacred spell echoed in my mind.

The crimson blood coated his fingers, embedded beneath his nails, sprayed his arms and chest.

I invoked the life in those red drops and infused them with yet more.

The ruby glimmered, then flashed and transformed into pure white, more illuminant than anything born of my Quest-gifted magic. A sign of the divine favor upon me.

The Gouge screamed, releasing me, and collapsed, writhing as the radiance sought to abolish all the evil it touched.

Shuffling my sword beneath my arm, I quickly shed the glove and tore open the seams. I tied it around the wound, staunching the flow, and brought up my sword. Then winced as my hilt abraded against the throbbing spot. But my lips still moved in song.

Tossing aside his ruined armor, leaving his chest clothed in only a tunic, the Gouge rose to his feet. With several brutal growls, he burned what remained of the radiance with a concentrated burst of his magic.

"Fine, you're something I haven't seen before," he muttered, grunting. A wicked leer contorted his mouth. "But you're still a bumbling little boy, a—" foul words demeaning men— "to challenge me, and I'll take great pleasure in killing you, then—" foul words about violating corpses— "and finally breaking all of your bones. No honored burial for you, stupid boy." Then, yowling a war cry, he charged.

Belief whisp'ring through the mountains, passion flowing through the trees
Expanses ablaze by reason, reasoned sure of faith
Bathed by sun the motherland, standing once more as one

I dodged his blows and inflicted four of my own in rapid succession. Leaping forward, I struck his head, splitting his skull open, pouring more light into his body.

His magic paled to ash gray.

The Gouge shot more blasts of conjury but avoided my retaliatory bolts.

I swung at his knee, the flat of my blade cracking the bone.

His punch impacted against my collarbone, breaking it despite the layers of steel and athar armor. But my singing did not falter.

Lucian! my family cried, dueling the last three conjurors, who had broken the shields.

The pain rebounded again.

Falling back, I rolled, carefully spreading pressure away from the injuries, and leapt to my feet.

The Gouge fell to one knee and doubled over the damaged limb. A tentacle of smoke snaked around my ankle and yanked.

I stumbled but maintained my balance and nullified it with a blast of light.

He lifted his head and scoffed, a cruel grin pulling at his maw. Foul words slithered from his throat before he sneered, "I always get what I want. What I want more than anything else I've ever wanted is your death. I'll get it."

Wary, I sent a spear of light toward his head.

Slamming his hands against the ground, smoke billowing around him, the Gouge chanted, the words not of either tongue of Icilia. No flinch when the light cut into his chest. Though the color did waver from the magic in my voice.

My usual level of magical perception revealed nothing.

I called forth more magical catalyst, for both my birth-magic and that of my destiny, letting it pool in a crackling mixture, and gave it a portion of my concentration. The magic heightened my keen senses, and I examined the spell he was casting. Nademan eagerly supplied what she knew of his chants.

*Bells tolling marking our reign, chains breaking ending
    our pain
Triumph rising in the dawn, dawned by the age of mastery
Misery healing by our hands, standing once more as one*

Though at first I could not read it, within moments
I understood...

By expelling his magic in this way, he intended to poison
the land herself. My companions, my guardians, my soldiers,
the townsfolk, the animals, the trees—everyone and everything along with her. No shield would contain this.

It is time for my final plan.

Nademan begged me for help as the first noxious plume
of ash formed in her soil.

I completed the final verse, nullifying with it what more
I could. Then intoned, "E'Qahre, hayyëm dinimas u'shifos."

The last of the conjurors fell, and Elian, Arista, Kyros,
and my guardians sprinted toward me.

I poured my life into the plane of my concentration,
emptying all but the foundations of my soul. Summoned
all the magic of the Quest that flowed in my blood.
And catalyzed.

I began to shine, emanating light even through my clothes.
My crown and my ring glittered, the rubies and emeralds
glowing and refracting sparkles of light over the clearing.

"Lucian?" Elian whispered.

"Why are you shining so much?" Kyros begged.

"What is that light, my Lord?" Ilqan demanded.

"Nephew, just what are you attempting?" Da'ana warned.

"My Lord, what is happening?" Eloman exclaimed.

"What are you doing!" Arista screamed.

I smiled at them.

And light exploded from my person.

Pure, white—a glimpse of the Almighty's Light—embracing my companions, suffusing the land, caressing the faces of my people. Balancing where the Gouge unleashed chaos.

The tyrant screamed as the light consumed his magic. Incinerated him where he crouched. Burning away every trace of poison.

The light ascended to the sky and mingled with the first rays of dawn, white and gold and rose on blue.

I collapsed, knees buckling, my back colliding with the ground. Pain scalded my ribs and collarbone. Agony seared my hand. My hilt slipped from my bloody fingers.

The blackness of night shaded the edges of my vision...

Standing once more as one...

"Lucian!"

SEGMENT 5

CONTRIVING ROLES

Perspective: Nadeya Tahira Enarias, citizen of Nademan
Date: Eyyéqan, the nineteenth day of the ninth moon, Alkharre,
of the year 500, C.Q.

U nbothered by the jostling pace of my horse, I opened
another ciphered letter and held it alongside the first.
Some of these combinations of runes are certainly the same...
I moved the papers to one hand and retrieved my quill,
inkwell, and journal from the saddlebag.

A hand rose from its grip on my waist and stretched,
palm up. "I can help, Sister," Kanzeo said timidly, as he had
since we were reunited.

I passed the letters into his fingers and patted the other hand
clutching the fabric of my gown and the trousers I wore beneath.

He sighed contentedly, despite the inadequate show of
affection, and pressed his thin face into my back. "I love you,
Tahira," he said, his voice muffled.

"I love you as well, Kanzeo," I forced through my emotionless mask.

The delight radiating from his thin body was palpable—it was only the third time I had managed to say those words since the day we were freed.

How much our world had changed.

When the Battle of Ehaya began, I had believed it to be my last day and resolved to do what little I could, despite my failure in protecting my missing brother. Ignoring the general's summons, I convinced the staff to hide according to my instructions, shouldered the sack containing all the most relevant papers within my possession, and left to search for one of the Potentates.

I never expected them to actually believe my warning. No, indeed, punishment was what I expected when I approached my Honor Kyros the Exemplar of Strength.

He had given me safe passage, respect, and my brother instead. His own sigil hung from my throat as I sought his sister, the Quest's Second and Icilia's supreme commander. And she herself had not only accepted my paltry attempts at service, my weak attempts at sabotage, but had bestowed upon me a place by her side—a place allowing me to explore my talents to their fullest while also retaining the presence of my brother. She even granted me a title.

Though Kanzeo's absence had terrified me when I learned of it, his choice to search for the Potentates was well made. Not only had he freed us but all of Ehaya and thus Nademan herself. His plea to our Honor Kyros had persuaded the Quest to accelerate their plans; he was almost as much the cause of our salvation as our Rulers themselves.

In return, all he wanted was the affection I no longer knew how to give.

But I was determined to learn, and the Quest and their inner circle were replete with wonderful examples.

Disregarding my discomfort, I raised one of his hands to my lips and kissed it—prompting another contented sigh—before returning to my work.

Although my Grace had originally asked me to help organize her forces, once the marquis of Ehaya exposed my identity, the Quest's troops became decidedly more resistant to following my orders. They obeyed because my Grace had spoken for me, and they did not threaten me... but it was not optimal for operational excellence. Consequently, my Grace commanded me to complete an equally urgent task: decoding the enemy's papers, both the sheafs Prince Eligeo had brought with such risk and the boxes the Quest had recovered during their reconquest.

I had only once enjoyed myself more...

"Inase Enarias," Prince Darian said, slowing his horse to ride alongside me, "how goes your process?"

I considered my notes on the similarities. "I have nearly finished forming an analysis of the patterns. I now look for either an uncoded portion or a match in writing style from among my own papers."

He nodded and offered me a wry smile, an odd expression on a face only slightly less impassive than my own. "I believe you will have invented a new discipline by the time you achieve success."

Knowing the value of any praise from him, I bowed my head. "Gratitude to the Almighty."

"Gratitude indeed," he replied.

The muffled thuds of more hoof-steps on soft earth melded with our horses' as my Grace joined us. *For what are we now grateful?* she asked lightly in Prince Beres' link.

Though an answer was what etiquette demanded, the prince and I remained silent as we examined her face.

She appeared even more miserable than she had yesterday: her cheeks were almost bloodless, pale with apprehension, and the bruises around her bloodshot eyes, formed by a month of near endless tears, seemed more swollen than ever...

My Grace pushed her lips up into something resembling a smile. *Reuniting with Elian, Arista, and Kyros will help. They promised to share even more of my tasks.*

Prince Darian and I exchanged a skeptical glance. My Grace bore the demands of ruling an entire nation with greater ease than most had in wielding simple knives. She was born and blessed for these duties; their weight was not what ruined her health.

My Grace exhaled quietly but said nothing further as, after a thousand miles of journey, our destination finally came within view: the Makirani tree-town of Natrisso, located mere miles from the place where the Gouge had perished and chosen as the new seat of Nademan's crown during my Lord's convalescence. The sight brought little relief to any of us, and least of all to her.

Prince Darian straightened. "My Grace, your orders?"

She gave a list of specifications for the permanent campsite.

The prince bowed from his saddle. Upon the relayed instructions, the third, fourth, and fifth companies left our columns to set up a permanent camp, while the first and second formed a defensive perimeter—my Grace and Prince Darian trusted my information on the possibility of hidden enemy squads still roaming the forest.

The core of the entourage, my Lord's family and specifically chosen vassals, continued directly to Natrisso.

At the base of the first tree (rather short at seventy-five feet), I tucked away my materials, handed my reins to one of the town's loyal folk, and dismounted before helping Kanzeo do the same.

As I steadied him on the ground, my brother yawned and cupped his mouth. His eyes widened at something over my shoulder. Then he ran from my side to a figure in midnight blue hugging my Grace in welcome.

My Honor Kyros the Exemplar of Strength.

Though more careworn than when he had given me his sigil, as marked with misery as our Grace, he was smiling, beige face shining and gray eyes aglow, ash-blond curls tucked beneath his cap and beard neatly combed. Dazzlingly handsome.

At the sound of my brother's footsteps, he turned and, chuckling, held out his arms.

Kanzeo flung himself at him, and my Honor caught him, spun him around, and whispered in his ear.

As beautiful as his face and figure were, far more so were his character, his kindness and compassion, his strength in helping lead a nation in our Lord's absence. He had saved both of us, Kanzeo and me, without a single expectation of gratitude.

Setting my brother on his feet, my Honor Kyros called, "Blessings, Inase Enarias! I am glad to see you! How are you?"

At those words coupled with his actions, my heart, guarded and shriveled though it was, threw itself at his mercy, warming for him as a bolt of pure dedication threaded through my soul.

And, reeling, I stuttered for the first time in my life, "B-blessings, my- my H-Honor. H-how are y-you?" My cheeks glossed, and I ducked my head, having forgotten to answer his question.

His smile remained just as welcoming as it had been when I had first seen him. "I am better now that my Grace has favored our Honors and me with her presence."

I nodded dumbly... and remembered my most urgent task: "I have your pendant, my Honor!" None besides the

Potentates could undo the clasp, and our Grace had asked me to keep it for my own protection until their reunion.

Still smiling, he came a few steps closer and raised his hands for the clasp. When I offered it to him, he opened it—without allowing his fingers to touch even a thread of my gown or a single hair.

How can I not be loyal? I wondered dazedly. No one except that violet-eyed boy from long ago had ever treated me with so much dignity.

A corner of Kanzeo's lips slanted upwards, his expression eerily perceptive as he watched me.

"My gratitude, Inase Enarias," my Honor said as he pocketed his pendant. "I have prayed that it served you well." Then, turning, he dipped a second reverence to our Grace. "Please, my Grace, if it is your will."

A mixture of sorrow, excitement, and anxiety glittered in her blue eyes as she smiled and led the way up the ladder into the town, her entourage walking with her.

My brother and I linked hands as we followed, warding each other against our discomfort.

Despite how my Grace, Prince Darian, the two Asfiyan warriors, and Inase bi- Dekecer (who carried the same title as me but whom my Grace called 'Little Brother') included us, we did not belong amid the ranks of the Quest Leader's family. We had no place coming to see my Lord on his sick-bed.

A pace ahead of us, Crown Prince Eligeo, shoulders hunched and scrawny arms tight around himself, seemed to feel much the same way.

And Natrisso's townsfolk appeared intent on ensuring we did not forget it, casting us glares full of loathing with every step.

Yet I felt safe during the long walk across the bridges and platforms and up the ladders. Despite the enmity surrounding me, I had utter faith in my Grace's promises. Such stark difference from the thousands of times I had walked the castle's corridors.

I wonder how their anger can be addressed...

As I pondered that question, my Grace's entourage climbed onto the final platform, the highest one, usually the mayor's home but here the Quest's quarters.

Bowing my head, I waited as my Grace greeted our Honors Elian and Arista and three more of the Quest Leader's guardians. Inase bi-Dekecer enveloped my Honor Elian in a tight, clinging hug.

My Honor Arista, as Kanzeo and I noted in shared glances, seemed much better than we had feared after hearing of the Gouge's defeat: though the channels between her plates were still an unwholesome gray, but her eyes sparkled a brilliant amber, and overall her appearance, despite the marks of grief, was one of health.

Indeed, healthier than Prince Eligeo, Kanzeo, and I still appeared.

My Grace nodded to their bows and, breathing deeply, walked into the hut. The Asfiyan princes and guardians followed on her heels. Leaving my Honors and Inase bi-Dekecer with Prince Eligeo, Kanzeo, and me outside.

Refreshing his smile, my Honor Kyros introduced us, a distinction that made me lightheaded and unsteady on my feet as I curtsied. Particularly because it came from him.

Grinning, my Honor Arista exclaimed, "Finally we meet, Nademile Enarios! I have heard much about both of you from my Grace and my Honor Kyros of Light."

Kanzeo's and my cheeks glossed.

She turned to Prince Eligeo, who resembled a rabbit ready to bolt. Tilting her head, she inspected his face, his heart, perhaps his very soul. "Hmmm... I admit that I was not as inclined as my Grace and Prince Darian-asfiyi to reinstate you. I was not as understanding because of your history, though that will indeed sound hypocritical when you learn of mine. However, I can see what my Lord likely will. You have my utmost confidence as well, Crown Prince Eligeo-nadem."

The prince fumbled a bow and awkwardly mumbled words of gratitude. Then he raised his gaze to my Honor Elian, a heartbreaking desperation in his eyes.

My Honor Elian smiled kindly and embraced the broken man (prompting such relief that it was painful to behold). "How glad I am to see you, Crown Prince Eligeo-nadem. The confirmation you gave my Lord of his suspicions about the Gouge's whereabouts was invaluable." He nodded to Kanzeo and me. "I am pleased to meet you as well, Nademile Enarios. We have prayed long in gratitude for all of you. Though it was not clear at the time, you are the reason for achieving our first triumph within one year of our meeting. May you soon be blessed with your chance to pledge to my Lord."

Though he spoke cheerfully, his smile had faded by the end of the last sentence, as had his family's.

"How I wish he was awake to celebrate this day," my Honor Kyros whispered.

"Our Grace had dearly looked forward to it," Inase bi-Dekecer said sadly, "while you were chasing the enemy."

Kanzeo and I bowed our heads, for they spoke of the anniversary of my Grace's ascension, which was today. And, instead of celebrating their triumph, all she received was the sight of his unconscious face. It was why no one dared to congratulate her.

How I wished I could ease her pain, all of their pain.

How I wished I could ease the burden on my Honor Kyros' shoulders.

Several minutes later, the Asfiyan guardians exited, and Prince Darian called, "Elacir, come! Bring the Nademani with you."

With a bow to my Honors, Inase bi-Dekecer beckoned us inside the hut.

In the main room, Prince Beres lay sprawled with such grief on his face that I could not bear to witness it. His elder son, however, wore a cold composure that rivaled my own, and masked his pain much like mine.

Crossing that room, we entered the larger of the two bedrooms, the noble couple's sleeping quarters.

There upon a bed, my Grace kneeling by his side, lay the Quest Leader.

Despite the bandages stiffening his torso and coating his hand, he seemed peaceful, calm and confident even in repose, a faint smile curving his lips.

His face is familiar...

Kneeling on the Quest Leader's other side, Prince Darian said, "My Lord, I introduce to you Crown Prince Eligeo tej-Shehennadem, Inase Tahira Enarias, and Nadeyi Kanzeo Enaries. You wanted to meet all of them..." His cool voice broke, and he pressed a hand to his lips.

My Grace blinked back tears as she adjusted the pendant centered above our Lord's heart.

A pendant, an emerald one, that... yes, it was a twin to my Honor Kyros', but did it not also resemble...

I grasped the emerald that hung beneath my dress at my navel. As I stroked the round, polished surface, the realization was all too clear.

My Lord possessed that silver-cream skin and sunlight hair and beard I remembered so very well... when he opened his eyes, they would be gold-flecked violet.

Those violet eyes.

The kind eyes that had sustained me for five long years.

The respectful eyes I loved as much as my brother's.

The powerful eyes of the Quest Leader, brighter than the clearing blue sky.

Those closed eyes, the day they would reopen unknown even to my Honor Kyros' foresight.

Stifling a sob, I fell to my knees.

Even as I served my Grace and cared for my brother, my dearest wish had been to find that boy whose brotherly affection had saved me so many times.

I had found him. As he lay on his sick-bed.

How I prayed his eyes would open again.

CHAPTER 53

HEAL THE VOICELESS

Perspective: Graced Malika the Exemplar of Wisdom
Date: Eyyéfaz, the thirtieth day of the ninth moon, Alkharre,
of the year 500, C.Q.

In curling, elegant script, I completed the letter and signed my name.

How far I have come, I thought. *Only a year prior, I had forgotten what runes even looked like... all this is because of Lucian. And it has been forty days since he spoke to me but an hour before the battle...*

Blinking back tears, I passed the athar-laced paper to Prince Beres, who folded and sealed it with a drop of athar magic. Once a minuscule glowing version of the Quests' insignia appeared over the flap, I handed the letter of commission to Triona Ekesarie, who bowed as she received it.

Show that letter to the mayors, I ordered. *As long as you are the only one who opens it, the seal will appear with each folding. The instructions within it for the necessity and process of allegiance should be clear.*

Elian, seated on my other side, repeated my words aloud.

"And if they cannot read, my Grace?" Triona's husband, one of Elian's sergeants, asked. His cheeks glossed, most likely remembering his admission mere moments ago of his own inability.

If even the nobles have forgotten how, I commented, *when reading and writing are so crucial to our civilization, then our plan for the nation's education is even more urgent. Say this, Elian...*

Tilting his head, Elian relayed, "Nademile Ekesarios, that is precisely why we explained the letter's contents to you. We trust in your expression of our will. So says my Grace."

The couple's cheeks glossed again as they bowed yet another time. Triona slipped the silver beryl necklace I had provided over her head. Then, promising weekly reports via the jewel's communication spell, the couple retreated to the door.

"Sergeant Ekesarie, remember," Elian called out, "request two horses from the army stables. We have recovered enough from the garrisons for both of you. So says my Grace."

Though terrified, despite the riding lessons our messengers had been given, the couple offered determined smiles. With my permission, they left.

Rubbing his back beneath his cloak and wings, Elian grimaced. "Were the Ekesarios the last today?"

The last messengers at all, I responded, massaging my temples. *The staff of Arkaiso reported this morning that they finalized the assignments in western Zaiqan and Adeban, and Ciro said he finished the ones for eastern Zaiqan and Gairan from Ehaya. We completed those for Makiran, and Kyros himself will deal with Buzuran. All of Nademan has been considered.*

"Gratitude to the Almighty," Elian whispered, sighing in relief.

Gratitude, indeed, I said. *I realized yesterday that even the plan for rebuilding the old roads depends on securing the remaining towns' pledges.*

"That is all of them!" Elian exclaimed. "Law, education, economy, defense, travel—not only rulership. Is there not a better way?"

One that does not require waiting for allegiance? I asked, a bit wry. *I have learned much, but neither history nor experience can provide those answers. Only* he *can.*

Elian winced, gaze drawn to the chamber in which Lucian slept. "I cannot do any more," he said quietly, scales dimming, to both Prince Beres and me. "I feed him sips of water, milk, and broth, I pour my own energy into his body, I care for his needs, I repeatedly adjust his limbs and blankets so that no sores develop, I read to him for hours... but I cannot heal him. Not his physical injuries, not his deeper illness." A whimper escaped his lips. "I am happy to serve him in the smallest ways, but my magic is not useful beyond his nourishment."

I offered my best attempt at a comforting smile. *You know you do not receive censure from any of us.*

Elian nodded, but his eyes flicked to Prince Beres over my shoulder.

The prince stirred from his grief-stricken apathy enough to say, "I hold no blame for you, my Honor. Even Ezam and Amalna, despite their access to the original texts, cannot discern what more we might do." Then he relapsed into desolate silence.

Elian and I exchanged glances, limiting our concern to a medium that did not require the prince's links. Though our entire family dealt poorly with Lucian's illness, though much of the nation lamented, Prince Beres' suffering was unrivaled. Barely functioning, he cared for himself only upon my direct orders. But as worried as we were, drawing attention to his condition would only shame him.

The only true answer to our misery was Lucian's recovery.

Tears glimmered in Elian's dulled green eyes.

I winced, not liking to see him cry—though the sight was so common now—and offered my handkerchief. Since I was unable to touch his shoulder, I impressed my comfort and affection into the link.

Though he rarely liked such attention, Elian accepted the cloth and wiped his face before curling his lips into a small wan smile. "Let me fetch you some water, Malika?"

I nodded, returning that faint smile as he rose and left. Although six months had passed since the last of my years of dehydration had faded, Elian still personally brought me flasks when he was with me and asked with every communication about my supply when he was not. As solicitous as Arista and Kyros were, Elian far exceeded them in his preoccupation with my health.

I deeply adored his care. Every such question reminded me that I was no longer alone, even if the fall of Koroma haunted every shadow...

Though my attempts were unequal to his, I returned his consideration, accounting for his wings in our battle plans and reminding Elacir to clean them. My friend tended to forget to care for his own limbs...

There has always been something odd about that, I thought, *and I am quite sure Lucian knows, because he often insists on cleaning them, even when there is much to do...*

The thought of Lucian again reminded me of his supine form... like my parents on that day...

I exhaled, trying to focus my mind away from the comparison. The wandering of my thoughts inevitably returned me to the fall of Koroma, and I had too many tasks to wallow.

Consulting my list, I continued a proposal for Nademan's defense. During the march to Ehaya, Darian and I had assigned five companies to guard the borders and key garrisons, as well as to perform what patrols they could. Now that the majority of the enemy forces were decimated, we needed to give more consideration to such watches.

Since Arkaiso is noting an increasing trickle of new recruits, perhaps we could assign most of our existent eighteen veteran companies to the same task as those five... Tahira did mention the need for patrols...

I truly ought to involve Eligeo, since it is his crown, but he seems terrified of military matters and rather more adept in grasping Arista's lessons on history and culture. That is something that must be soon addressed... I would think of his siblings, but none of them are ready for such responsibility. So who then...

Occupied by these musings and plans, I flinched when a voice asked, "My Grace?" Darian's voice.

Lifting my head, I beckoned him inside. *Please enter, Prince Darian.*

He actually smiled at me.

My mouth almost dropped open.

After the Gouge's death and Lucian's collapse, the guardians had discovered that the wounds that Arista had sustained were not as dire as we feared—Lucian's magic had not only eradicated the Gouge and cleared the sky but also burned away the conjury she had absorbed from her blood. But the damage that lingered... it could not be healed. The guardians had been entirely at a loss on what to do.

They argued about methods of treatment for days via communication spell... until Darian had solved their dilemma with a simple declaration: athar counteracted conjury, so daily massive infusions of athar magic, as a replacement for pure athar, would be sufficient.

Ilqan, Da'ana, and Eloman had tried his solution and realized it worked. But even after his arrival, they refused to let him participate in the effort, instead relegating him to mere observation.

Hurt had lingered in his expression alongside his misery over Lucian's health...

Now, suddenly, after two weeks of cold composure, he seemed uncharacteristically excited, lavender eyes shining so brightly they almost appeared violet. Nearly bouncing, he swept a bow and then paused. "Where is our Honor?"

At the stream, I answered. *He should return soon. Please, sit in the meanwhile.*

Darian plopped down on one of the stools, foregoing his usual studied elegance. He pulled the seat closer to the desk and the set of three chairs behind it (the town's gifts). Then he simply stared at me.

I squirmed, though faintly amused. *What is it, Prince Darian?*

Beside me, Prince Beres emitted a faint snore, finally asleep after his watch last night by Lucian's bedside. Thankfully, he had remembered to endow enough power into the links so that I could still use them.

Darian's cheeks silvered. "My apologies. I..."

He hesitated so long that I assured, *Please do not feel obligated to speak.*

Darian shook his head, a drop of anxiety souring his enthusiasm. "I do want to tell you, my Grace. I only... it is as Lucian told me: I am afraid to raise your hopes when I cannot guarantee success."

Before I could decide whether to ask, Arista knocked on the doorframe. "Malika, may I enter?"

Please, I replied as I examined her face for any changes. The gray lines marring her lovely olive-bronze skin had not entirely faded, but they were certainly fainter than they were yesterday. Improvement, and I was dearly thankful. Her agony, followed minutes later by the pain of Lucian's collapse, which had prompted the worst sorts of thoughts until Elian contacted me more than an hour later... They counted among some of the most harrowing moments of my life.

Rendering a bow, Arista took another stool and winced as the movement jostled the ever-present aches and sores riddling her limbs.

Though I watched anxiously, I said nothing. She would not accept what she deemed to be Elian's seat.

Settled, she asked, "Why did you call me, Prince Darian?"

The prince, as anxious as I, assessed her face before answering, "I am rather hoping our Honor might return first."

"Well..." Arista snickered. "I raced him back!"

I rubbed my forehead. *Arista, you have been suspended from training for a reason.*

"And that suspension will only increase if you delay your recovery," Darian warned.

She only chuckled.

I gave her a rueful look, both amused and exasperated by her mischievous streak. But such lightheartedness was how she remained functional amid Lucian's illness and her grief for her family, so I did not attempt chastisement. Even if I found smiles and laughter too difficult to produce.

Heavy footsteps thumped across the platform, and Elian called, panting, "Leave, Malika?"

Of course, I said.

He entered, dipped a bow, and placed a pair of flasks on the edge of my desk. Taking his seat, he cast Arista a reproachful look. But, knowing what I did, he did not scold and instead turned his attention to Darian.

The prince stared at his fidgeting fingers for a long moment before he seemed to steel himself. Lifting his head, he declared, "I think I have found the cure for the curse on our Grace's voice."

What? I whispered, unable to grasp what he had said.

Eyes wide and lips parted, Elian and Arista stared at him with equal shock. A shock that quickly melted into effervescent joy, their faces shining like stars, a wonder I had not thought I would see so soon.

"How?" Elian breathed.

"How soon can we perform it?" Arista demanded.

Darian ducked his head, cheeks a bright silver. "Today, perhaps."

"Then tell us what to do!" Elian exclaimed.

Darian blinked, as though he had not expected such a reaction. Then, slipping into the tones of the daily lessons we had resumed only last week, he said, "I theorize that the Blood used three types of magic in crafting the curse: the fear spells of conjury, certainly, to damage our Grace's will to speak, as Ezam and Amalna postulated. But fear spells alone would not be sufficient, even with repeated exposure. Conjury, as you well know, is much like wizardry or mindlinking in that its spells do not last long beyond their casting without a jewel to contain them. Thus, I believe he mixed the fear with his sorcery and so anchored the magic in our Grace's mind.

"Yet that still does not explain all the evidence: our Grace is not only unable to speak but also unable to mouth words. Her mouth does not form the right shapes for speech, though her vocal cords are intact. Consequently, I think he used the second lesser-known type of conjury, alchemy, the ability to change the textures of things, which is evil and harmful only in accordance with its use. Not healing, as wish magic requires convictions about the Almighty, so, even if the Blood's subordinates had the magic, it would not manifest to such degree as to have the power to permanently change natural functions. But this form of conjury could be skillfully applied to thicken and shift the delicate muscles of the throat and mouth. Thereby rendering useless any attempt with athar magic to break the curse."

"So a cure would require healing as well as athar magic," Arista whispered.

Darian nodded. "Healing for the muscle damage, athar magic to absorb the sorcery, and, if you could manage it, a drop of Quest-magic to eradicate the conjury." An oddly sarcastic smile curled his lips. "The Blood has the rare skill to mix forms of magic. We must possess the same, matching him in this one area though nowhere else."

Elian and Arista considered his words for a moment.

Then Arista leapt up and ran to Elian. Shaking his shoulders, she exclaimed, "You must try! Today! Malika needs to be able to speak!"

While Elian assured her that he would, I shrank in my chair and stared at my callused fingers. Although I had understood Darian's theory as well as they had, I had lived so long without a voice that the thought of regaining it frightened me.

Did I truly deserve to speak?

But could I even justify avoiding an attempt to break the curse? I was all too aware that Lucian had switched our responsibilities as Leader and Second, letting me lead our campaign while he spoke publicly and championed our cause.

As loving and kind as his intentions were, without my voice I would never become a true Second to him.

How I wished Kyros were here to comfort me...

"Malika," Elian stated, drawing my attention, "I truly will try. Every day, if necessary, until I can break this aspect."

The words brought a tiny smile to my lips. *Thank you.*

He returned that attempt and glanced at Darian. "May we try now?"

The prince pressed his lips together and removed a sheet of paper from his pocket. Holding it so both Elian and Arista could read, he said, "This healing spell should suffice. I will insert athar magic once your magic takes effect. Once mine does, my Honor, insert the Quest-gifted magic—that, I hope, with its purpose of unifying the Quest, will be enough to bind the forms together."

Arista rubbed her plates as she read. "If only we had received the lessons on this magic's full use..."

"Prince Darian," Elian said, suddenly frowning, "how do we know that an attempt will not prompt some sort of retaliation? Or that the curse is not irreversible?"

I flinched, remembering the duel.

"Because in actuality our Grace has been speaking for a year," Darian answered calmly. "The curse is designed to destroy your dignity as incé, my Grace. If breaking it would cause such consequence, it would have occurred the first time Lucian cast a link for you, or soon after. As for permanence, I believe that you have overcome the degradation of voice-lessness so thoroughly that, if magic were not involved, you would already have regained your physical voice."

My face heated at the rare praise even as my shoulders relaxed.

Grinning again, Arista proclaimed, "Then let us try. Let me form the connection." Stepping between Elian and me, Arista held my hand and one of his.

Elian examined the paper, his scales and fingers beginning to glow green, and intoned, "Patile qatos ne sableh, sireneros latabeseru, zukrerim ke ore radu chanemizu, parenalerim idiesere, dinimas ó Fidaanem u'qalit taseru."

Light blazed through Arista's linked hands to mine, then up to my neck. Settling to a delicate warmth, the light caressed the muscles, stroking each nerve and vein, as it rose up my throat to my mouth and coated my tongue.

It tasted like honey and sunshine, like the undimmed light of the sun revealed by Lucian's own sunlight.

As the taste trickled back down my throat, Darian tapped my forehead with a single glowing finger. Light dazzled my vision. Its cool touch invoked an answering hum in my body...

Fear burst forth in my mind, exploding from a dark corner to devour me so completely that my heart stopped.

Then, just as quickly, it was consumed by another light, one so pure and familiar that my heart soared to perceive it. A drop of Lucian's presence, warm with love and hope, mingled with Arista's bold competence...

I reveled in the light, the sweetness of my family's determination to restore my dignity.

Slowly the magic faded, seeping throughout my person, until only a faint shiver itched the muscles of my neck.

My eyes opened to Elian, Arista, Darian, Elacir, and even Prince Beres expectantly watching me.

"Well?" Arista prompted.

"Please try," Elian urged.

Smiling uneasily, I parted my lips.

Chose the words I wanted to be my first.

And spoke, "The Almighty's blessings upon you, my family."

CHAPTER 54

ADMIT THE TRUSTLESS

Perspective: Honored Kyros the Exemplar of Strength
Date: Eyyéfaz, the thirtieth day of the ninth moon, Alkharre,
of the year 500, C.Q.

I fell on my bottom, so shocked that my knees had buckled. "What?"

A giggle emitted from my pendant. "Blessings, Kyros,"
repeated the rich, musical voice, a twin to Lucian's in all but
pitch, contralto instead of baritone.

"Malika?" I gasped. "Is it truly you?"

"Yes! Oh Kyros, how much the Almighty has blessed me!"
Wondering laughter filled that warm, kind, assertive voice I
had heard so often in the links. "Kyros! How honored I am
to speak your sacred name in my own voice!"

Cool tears spilled down my cheeks. "Malika! Malika, you
can speak! Gratitude to the Almighty!" A thought arrested my
attention, and I exclaimed, "Is your throat hoarse? You should
not tax it so quickly. Has Elian thought to give you anything
for relief? Where is Da'ana? Surely she would know—"

Chuckling, she interrupted my fretting, "My dearest brother Kyros, Elian pushed me to swallow several spoonsful of honey and two cups of chamomile tea before he let me contact you."

I sighed. "Excellent." A wistful smile curved my lips. "How excited Lucian will be to hear you speak when he wakes."

"His happiness would be a blessing..." Malika blew out a breath, her brief instance of mirth vanished. "There is no change, Kyros."

"Or you would have told me." I wrung my hands together. "How I wish Ezam and Amalna had discovered more than passing references to the Quest-gifted magic in the Quest of Light's books."

Malika exhaled another sigh. "I suspect that there is something missing from their searches, something that only opens at our touch. For I cannot imagine Lucian did not know what he was doing. But we are too many miles from either Arkaiso or the refuge to retrieve the books."

"And we cannot ask someone to carry this treasure," I agreed, "without Lucian's permission. Which is impossible to obtain for the same reason why we need the books."

"Indeed," she said. "I will send Ilqan and Eloman tomorrow, now that Arista is nearly recovered and unlikely to relapse."

"Has her health truly improved so much?" I asked, faintly delighted despite the mention of Lucian's illness. The depth of Arista's heartbreak would not lessen for months to come, but greater health would at least alleviate her suffering...

"It has," Malika replied, a tinge of a smile again in her voice. "Elian's magic helped her as well as me when he cast the cure. She certainly seems less burdened."

"Gratitude to the Almighty for his magic," I whispered. "Already its power has saved us four times. Now, please, if it is your will, tell me about the cure."

Indulging me, Malika described Darian's theory and the steps he had taken alongside Elian and Arista.

I leaned back on my hands as I listened, savoring the strong sound of her voice alongside the shockingly intense sunlight and the bright blue sky. If not for Lucian's illness and my absence from my family's side, this would be utter contentment...

Something wet landed on my cheek.

Opening my eyes, I watched as wisps of pale gray cloud drifted across the sky and gathered overhead. Was it really...

"Rain," I breathed without thinking.

"Rain?" Malika interrupted herself. "There is rain? Actual rain? You must describe it to me!"

"I will, Sister," I assured her, slightly amused, as I stood at Taza's approach.

"Are your troops ready to continue after luncheon?" Malika asked, perhaps noting some change in my voice.

"Yes, Malika." I nodded in acknowledgment to the guardian's bow

"Then please report to me as scheduled in five days," she ordered, "and tell me about the rain!"

"As you will," I murmured in obedience, and the connection ended.

"Who was that speaking?" Taza inquired as we rejoined the main force of my contingent.

Attempting a grin (though my mouth was again unable to manage the expression), I glanced around my company, which caught their attention. "My Honors and Prince Darian-asfiyi today broke the curse on our Grace's voice!"

The soldiers cheered, and Taza bowed her head and whispered prayers of gratitude. Then she questioned, tone sharp, "His Highness helped?"

I nodded, retaining a calm expression as we mounted our horses. "Prince Darian designed the solution, as he did for my Honor."

Taza discreetly rolled her eyes but thankfully did not comment. If she had, I would have tossed away my composure. As much as I respected her, indeed loved her as I would a treasured aunt, I could no longer abide her contemptuous dismissal of Lucian's older brother—a man she had *raised*. None of the Potentates could, but I was especially angered, for her behavior reminded me too much of Aunt Cyanna's caustic words. How cruelly she and the other guardians had dismissed his devisal of Arista's treatment...

But, as my mother had once said, no matter how angry I was, if I was not ready to destroy a relationship, it was better to react calmly, revealing my displeasure only in controlled actions.

Once my forces were organized, I set a fast pace north. As excited as I was about the rain, I had heard enough stories from my parents to know that even untainted rain could cause illness with prolonged exposure.

Still, hurrying under the rapidly clouding sky held none of the terror of fleeing storms polluted by the smog. Indeed, my soldiers often stopped to catch droplets with their mouths, so childlike was their delight, until I pushed them onward.

We reached the boundary of Faneresso but moments before the rain intensified.

My soldiers shouted in joy as the downpour drenched their armor and the crisp scent of wet earth filled the air.

Within the town's trees (only fifty feet tall in this region of Buzuran), the townsfolk emerged from their houses and stared at the sky in wonder.

Chuckling a little at their reactions, I sent a messenger to seek the mayor, who returned within minutes with the noble couple, Countess Prozeria and her husband.

The couple's faces revealed not the least bit of surprise as they bowed. With a few quiet words, they arranged shelter for my company inside their town's central hall and invited Taza and me to their own home. Two soldiers took charge of our horses.

Pleased at the welcome, warmer than I had expected, I followed the couple to their home, Taza alongside me.

The hut was no larger than the many others I had seen across Nademan, though different in that it was built on the ground and not on a platform. A thick tree had been incorporated, however, into its construction, through its use as a wall of the main room.

Taza and I shed the water from our robes and, settling on several low cushions, accepted the nobles' refreshments of mint tea and biscuits. A young man, the future mayor, and his wife bowed and joined us with my permission.

Once I had sipped enough to satisfy this province's strictures on hospitality, I placed my cup down and stated, "Countess Prozeria, Count Prozeriet, Nademile, I presume you know why I am here. You were not surprised to see me. And I know it was not because either farsight or foresight warned you of my coming."

The noble couple and their heirs bowed their heads. "We suspected we would receive a messenger," the countess responded, "and that there was a chance one of the exalted Potentates her- or himself would come."

"Why would you suspect that?" I inquired, curious. "My Grace has sent messengers to the rest of the nation; I am the only Potentate away from our Lord's current seat."

The two couples exchanged glances. Then Nadeyi Prozerie said, bowing his head again, "My Honor, Buzuran has wronged you. We were blessed with my Honor the Exemplar of Bravery's own presence, but we were too sure of our own judgment and too arrogant to pledge. We were fools."

I blinked, surprised by such a direct admission. "The Quest does not censure you... but why do you speak so?" I had expected more difficulty, as this was my first visit to a Buzurani town.

"My Honor," Count Prozeriet replied, tone wry, "one only needs to look outside to see how great your favor is. When the sky cleared... we had forgotten how bright the world could be."

Sharing that sentiment as all of Nademan did, I inclined my head. "My Lord's favor is truly great. He is the only reason the Almighty deigns to bless us."

"Of course, my Honor," the countess quickly assented, "and so we beg that he might extend it to us."

I paused for a moment and examined their expressions. "I would be glad to accept your pledge in my Lord's name," I said, speaking in a more measured tone, "provided you proffer so without reservation."

Taza seemed just a bit startled, a barely noticeable flash of shock crossing her face, and then gave a nearly imperceptible nod, discerning what I did: the hint of guile and the tinge of obsequie to these nobles' words. Unusual traits for those of the Nasimih, particularly for the Nademani, but Arista, Da'ana, and Eloman had informed us that Buzuran's folk did not quite fit the rest of the nation's patterns. Just as their trees did not. Such variety was welcome, but it did require a greater degree of caution than I would have needed with the normally open, guileless Nasimih.

The nobles exchanged glances again before Nadeyi Prozerie answered, "We do not have reservations, my Honor. Only questions."

"Ask," I encouraged.

They exchanged a third set of glances. Then Nadea Prozeriat requested, "If it pleases you, would you come with us? We beg leave to show you our granary and coop. There is an umbrella we can offer for shelter from the rain."

Though wary, I nodded and rose to my feet. "I would be glad to see them, and I do not mind the rain." My robes were sufficiently dry now, and the walkways were covered.

"Thank you, my Honor," Countess Prozeria muttered, wearing a tight smile, as she and her family stood, following Taza's example.

"For your happiness," I answered and led the way outside, easily finding the route to the town's food stores. Though Lucian had not actually taught us this, I had learned from his example to never allow myself to be guided. It was *my* duty to guide, and my knowledge of each physical place gave proof of my ability to shoulder the greater task of holy and political leadership.

As I walked on the winding paths, the nobles and the townsfolk murmured quietly to each other, seeming impressed.

Though usually my cheeks would have glossed, my heart only grew heavier, the bleak sight of Lucian's crumpled form flashing before my eyes...

Inhaling a quiet breath, I reminded myself that I represented his promise here and suppressed the memory. Halting in front of the granary, I leaned inside to examine the sacks stored within.

The shed was not even a third full, and most of the contents were pickled vegetables and fruit. Very few of the bags contained flour or meat.

This is the town's entire reserve for the winter?

Pressing my lips together, I entered the chicken coop. The few hens and the rooster present ran toward me and, crowding my feet, squawked loudly, the shrill tones quite resembling complaints.

"The townsfolk are doing their best," I soothed as I crouched and ran my hands through their brown feathers, inspecting their keels and ribs. "They do not intend to starve you—they are thinner than you are." I did not know whether they really understood me, but I prayed the Almighty would grant me the strength to comfort them.

The rooster closed his beak over a finger but did not bite before he released it. The hens shrieked, but none stopped me when I straightened and left the little building.

The nobles were waiting outside. Immediately upon my emergence, Countess Prozeria bluntly stated, "So you see how dire our circumstance is."

"Indeed," I responded, guarding my words, "it is as fraught as most of what I have seen since leaving Ehaya in the moon of Narsaffe."

From the faint twist to her mouth, it was not the answer she had wanted. But still she continued, "We will not survive the winter, my Honor. Even the smallest child knows it. We *need* aid. We need this favor from the Quest. Our allegiance to you will mean little without it."

The implication was subtle but clear: aid was the condition for their pledge. Despite all of her family's earlier words of gratitude and regret, their loyalty was only a tool in bargaining for sufficient supplies.

As much as I understood the horror of hunger... the taste of starvation still too fresh on my tongue from those long, dry winters in which I struggled to feed my sister... I could not accept the blemish on the Quest's majesty that such a negotiation would bring.

So I offered only what Malika had already planned: "The Quest will provide assistance regardless of allegiance."

All four nobles blinked rapidly but were too well trained to show any more emotion. The townsfolk, however, staggered back, eyes bulging and lips parting on soft cries of shock.

"Do you not demand our pledge first?" Nadeyi Prozerie cautiously asked.

I shook my head. "Our receipt of your fealty and yours of our support are unrelated. We only ask for your pledge because it will enhance your kind magic and facilitate our ability to care for the needs of your town and your nation. We would have arranged for the provisions you need even if you had not asked. But we will not accept a pledge unless it is unconditionally given, without reservation or doubt."

Beside me, Taza's eyes glinted with pride. I truly had come very far since my ascension.

The nobles glanced at the people who had gathered under the awning to watch us deliberate. Noting the light in their expressions, Countess Prozeria quickly sought permission for a private conferral and whispered something to her heir, her husband, and her daughter-by-marriage. Each nodded, and, coming to a decision, the countess said, curtsying a little, "We seek the salvation of your promise. We beg the acceptance of our pledge."

Some of the townsfolk cheered in quiet tones.

Giving that acceptance, I prepared for the ceremony, and she and her family lowered themselves to their knees.

As the light of the binding flashed around our hands, something... not right... caught my attention. In each pledge I had received so far, a hopeful trust animated the hearts of the pledging. Yet these hearts did not all possess that sweetness, that kindling fervor of devotion. Desperation, yes, and the spark of loyalty, but not the intensity the Quest had seen in so many places across Nademan.

The discrepancy was not present in every one of the townsfolk's hearts, or even in every noble's. More than half were genuinely excited at the flashes of binding magic—most of the youths, and a few of the most elderly. Nadeyi Prozerie's composure concealed a burning enthusiasm, and his wife, although more wary, seemed willing to let her spark blossom. The rest, however... the countess and her husband, the parents of the youths, the elders... they regarded the light with suspicion even as they accepted it.

I still affirmed all of their pledges. Lucian had counseled us before we had left on our campaigns that a lack of fervency was not a reason for rejection. Even without heartfelt devotion, binding them to us would allow them a chance to witness the fruition of our promises and benefit from the pledge's enhancement of their kind magic. Additionally, as a prosaic consideration, we would have a greater awareness of disloyalty.

Yet even as I sealed their pledges, foreboding tingled down my spine. Their reluctance would not remain so benign, and theirs would not be the only town wavering at the brink of famine.

I was a seer—such prickles of premonition had the weight of true prediction. So, upon leaving the town, I delayed the contact I had promised Kalyca and instead immediately reported to Malika.

Even the lingering fresh scent of the once-more nurturing rain and the awesome sight of rainbows did not relieve my dread.

CHAPTER 55

HEARTEN THE JOYLESS

Perspective: Honored Elian the Exemplar of Esteem
Date: Eyyélab, the ninth day of the tenth moon, Thekharre, of
the year 500, C.Q.

Lightning crackled across half the sky, visible through the linen covering the window. Thunder boomed, loud enough to shake the tree. Raindrops pattered against the wood roof and branches.

Familiar sounds but soothing for the first time since my childhood. For this storm carried healing, the Almighty's mercy, not disease and pain. The first rainstorm Nademan had tasted in fifteen years.

Even the flow of the air through and above the trees was different. It blew and shook, swirled and spun, but the currents were not inclined to form tornadoes in every mass of cloud. Uplifting and inspiring for any wizard or sorcerer of the wind to witness.

That beauty lay beyond my reach.

For even as the rain soaked the earth and the wind called through the trees, my attention was fixed on Lucian's reposed face.

Forty-nine days. Even if he looks as he always does—none of his muscles have withered—except for those injuries which still have not healed—how much longer can he survive in this state? Everything Da'ana has studied about healing indicates that even this is too much time. What if...

No, I cannot consider such a thing. Surely the Almighty intends for him to live many years! We cannot lose him...

The rain poured from the clouds, far exceeding in magnitude the brief, isolated showers the nation had seen since the Gouge's defeat. Many of Natrisso's townsfolk were outside, adults and children alike playing and celebrating.

Though loyal and attentive, sharing something of our sorrow, the townsfolk had eagerly asked this morning if they might celebrate the rain and the possibility of future healthier harvests. Witnessing their enthusiasm and unwilling to dampen it after so many years of precious little happiness, Malika had given permission. But neither she nor our family joined them, unable to share that joy, and instead clung to their tasks.

Their voices a faint hum through the ajar door, Malika, Arista, Kyros, Da'ana, and Tahira discussed the circumstances behind Kyros' hastened return from Buzuran. Elacir and Taza studied his farsight. Darian taught lessons to Eligeo and Kanzeo. Hasima ladled stew into bowls and arranged loaves of bread on plates. Prince Beres was immersed in his grief. I tended Lucian. But no matter the specific task, all of my family refused to leave the hut, preferring to be as close as possible to Lucian. Foregoing the festival, Tahira, Eligeo, and Kanzeo, who were quite attached to Malika, Kyros, and me, seemed determined to keep us company. Though there was not enough space, save in Lucian's own room.

That room, in spite of the pleasant scent of lavender from fragrant bunches in the corners and the bright illumination from enchanted quartz crystals hung on the walls, increasingly resembled a tomb with every passing day. Soon I feared it would become one in reality.

I adjusted the bandages around Lucian's torso and then the ones on his hand. No blood spotted the cream linen for once—which, rather than comfort me, seemed a poor omen. Corpses did not bleed.

A knock sounded on the doorframe, and I rose to accept two bowls of stew, a loaf of sliced bread, and two flasks from Hasima and Elacir. I set all the dishes down on a tiny bedside table and quickly ate the hearty stew designated for me.

Then, kneeling by the bed, I lifted Lucian's torso, slid the opening of the flask between his lips, and tipped a few sips into his mouth. I positioned the bowl with the thinner stew atop the bed, and, again holding him upright, fed him spoonful after spoonful, until none remained. I finished with the remainder of the flask and affirmed with my magic that the food had not choked him in its travel to his stomach. I raised the blanket up to his chin, tucking it beneath his gleaming beard, and cleaned his pale lips. Finally, touching his mouth and throat, I forged a channel of healing magic between us and trickled a thin stream of my own energy into his body.

Each movement was methodical, efficient, smooth—after more than a month dedicated exclusively to his needs, I was too skilled at such care.

Does the Quest end like this? Does he end like this?

The thought knocked all the breath from my lungs more effectively than any blow.

Slumping at his side, wings ablaze and scales black, I cried. My tears mirrored the rain outside, my sobs the thunder, showering the blanket with countless tiny drops.

My family did not stir, save for a few sympathetic glances, too used to such heartbroken tears and well aware of my desire for privacy.

Please, Lucian... You cannot leave me... You promised you would put me back together...

Desperate for his comfort, I slipped my hand beneath his and tried to imagine those smooth fingertips rubbing my palm...

Please, oh Almighty, I beg of You a miracle. You bestowed upon me a miracle when I did not dare to ask, so I know You do listen. Will You not listen now, for Your own savior's sake? Will You not protect Your own servant?

Lost amid such prayers, several moments passed before I noticed the way my palm was being squeezed. The delicate pressure was barely perceptible, but...

I tossed back the blanket and gasped.

It cannot be!

But it was—Lucian's hand squeezed my own. And his eyelids twitched and lifted, revealing halves of violet irises.

Unable to look away, I screamed in the collective link, *Lucian is waking!*

Books, papers, and plates crashed to the floor as my family scrambled to their feet and rushed inside the chamber. Falling to their knees, they clustered around the bed, Malika, Arista, Prince Beres, and Darian kneeling on either side of his torso and the rest leaning over his legs. Only Tahira, Eligeo, and Kanzeo did not enter, instead quietly closing the door.

The lids flickered, closing and opening.

We waited breathlessly.

A few more flickers and a tensing of his hand over mine. Then Lucian opened his eyes and smiled. "Blessings, my family."

His voice was a hoarse whisper, and his smile a fraction of its usual dazzle, but we cheered, wheezing laughs, falling over ourselves to press kisses to his cheeks and hands, and exclaiming our own greetings. Savoring the animation of his shining face, unchanged save for a fainter silver glow to his cream skin.

"I must contact the others!" Da'ana exclaimed and tapped the tiny emerald of her pendant. Soon, the rest of the guardians, scattered across northern Icilia, cried their happiness at his waking.

Laughter rasping in his throat, Lucian addressed each of us by name, caressing the faces that hovered over his limp fingers and kissing the cheeks that came within reach of his lips. The silver glow of his features seemed to strengthen with every whisper of affection.

My never-ending gratitude to You, oh Almighty. You truly do listen to prayers. Yes, usually not soon after we make them. But to answer at all is Your mercy, and Your judgment of when to answer is never suspect. For did You not give us the Quest Leader precisely when we would most cherish him?

My scales shone a pure golden, my beaming grin equally bright, as I dipped my head to kiss his fingers a second time.

With my ears so close to his chest, I heard the faint rumble of his stomach.

His cheeks were silvered. "Apologies," he rasped. "I am afraid that neither Nademan's sustenance nor yours replace a substantial meal."

Chuckling for the first time in weeks, Prince Beres and I helped him sit up while Arista and Darian padded the headboard with the stack of linens with which I was due to switch his sheets. Lowering him gently, we settled him against the soft cloth.

From his upright position, Lucian surveyed all of us, appearing as though he relaxed on a throne rather than a bed with extra sheets as cushions, despite the limpness of his arms and the presence of bandages. His gaze alit upon each of us, meriting a bow in answer—particularly scrutinizing Arista's healthful face and grieving heart—until it reached Malika, who stood beside him.

Sun and sky, I thought. *And finally I know how accurate the description is.*

Lucian lifted an eyebrow. "Something has changed."

Malika bowed, a faint crimson glow emphasizing the delicate curves of her beautiful face. "My Lord," she said shyly.

Lucian's eyes widened. "Your voice," he breathed, the dazzling smile I so loved curling his lips. "How?"

"Elian, Arista, and Darian," Malika mumbled, threading her fingers together. "Prince Darian designed a theory, and Elian and Arista helped him implement it."

Lucian directed that beautiful smile at us. "My gratitude, Brothers and Sister."

All three of us, even Arista, were too bashful to properly meet his eyes.

Lucian returned his attention to Malika. "Speak of something, anything," he urged. "Your voice is the music I have most longed to hear."

"Ummm... I can describe everything that has, umm, happened?" she offered.

"That would be perfect," he said. "Tell me, Sister."

As Malika began the report in her lovely voice, I picked apart the slices of the loaf I had not eaten and put the plate on Lucian's lap, along with my flask of water. Arista tapped the pieces of bread, lightly toasting them with a whispered spell. Murmuring his gratitude, Lucian prayed and chewed his first solid meal in nearly two months.

Our entire family settled to watch, unable to look away. Thankfully, he seemed delighted, not discomforted, by the attention.

Once he had finished the bread, Hasima slipped outside for another meal. The door swung shut on Tahira, who stood just beyond with an expression of desperate yearning, a break from her usual inscrutable composure.

Lucian, who had raised the flask, choked on his mouthful of water.

Malika steadied his hand, and Darian thumped his back.

"What happened? Are you all right?" I exclaimed, frantically examining his body with my healing.

"Yes, I am well," he assured us, coughing and wiping his mouth with Arista's offered handkerchief. Clearing his throat, he gave a piercing look to Malika. "Who is that woman?"

"Tahira Enarias," Malika said hesitantly. "The sister of the boy Kyros met, the Gouge's former strategist who sabotaged him in your name. For that... I... well, I gave her the title of Inase."

"We thought her capable of true freedom," Kyros said anxiously, "when we assessed her heart as you taught us."

"She is dedicated and respectful," Darian offered—surprising all of us with his defense. "Her strategic mind exceeds my own." Further surprise at such public praise.

"And her brother could be one of your warriors," Elacir begged, "if you train him as you did me. Please do not send them away!"

The slow wry curl of Lucian's mouth forestalled the next plea. "Please do not presume my anger, my family—I do trust your judgment. I merely wish for an introduction. To both Inase Enarias and her brother."

My family sighed in relief, as Taza opened the door and summoned them.

Immediately all of us began to fidget, and Kyros' lips trembled in what were most likely prayers.

Tahira and Kanzeo stepped into view and dipped their reverences. Clasping their hands, they stood, heads lowered, as Malika honored them with the introduction.

Lucian's keen violet eyes pierced through to their souls as he examined them. Then his lips began to curl in a slow, pleased smile, breath-taking in its grandeur. He leaned back into his cushion, emanating obvious satisfaction, as though a plan long-laid had come to fruition. Once Malika had finished with his name, he spoke, "Blessings, Sister. The Almighty has finally reunited us."

"What!" my friends and I exclaimed.

"Sister?" Malika added, shocked.

Taza and Da'ana, however, exchanged awed glances. "Is this her?" Da'ana whispered. Hasima, who was slipping past the siblings with a bowl of preserved meat, startled before that same amazement spread across her features.

"No wonder she seems so familiar..." Darian whispered, astounded, realizing what they had.

Tahira herself seemed overwhelmed as she fell to her knees. "So... I truly did meet you?"

Lucian chuckled as Hasima placed the bowl on his lap. "Indeed, yes." His eyes twinkled as he cast an amused look in his companions' direction. "Nearly seven years prior, I was traveling for a mission in eastern Gairan with Da'ana and Eloman. While scouting a town we believed would soon be attacked, I noticed a girl climbing to a high tree branch with a stack of books, each of which were thicker than her own arm. Though I had immediately prepared a spell to catch her should she fall, she adeptly swung herself onto her chosen branch and settled to read. The sparkle of brilliance in her eyes drew my attention.

"Taking abrupt—and entirely uncharacteristic—leave of my guardians, I joined her. Once she had calmed from the shock of my approach, for even then my face revealed something of who I would become, I remarked on the contents of the book open on her lap and asked her opinion of the same. Her face glowed with joy, and, wearing an almost unconscious smile, she responded.

"We did not speak our names, and I could not discover hers of my own accord, for I was only sixteen, far from maturity. Yet I felt the stirrings of brotherly devotion to her regardless as we chattered about strategy, politics, and history. She had read several of the books I had, and she was fascinated by my greater knowledge and natural brilliance, as I was by her unique perspective and profound opinions. I loved the conversation, as I had few others, and so had she, I thought.

"Hours passed, and I refused to leave her company. Da'ana and Eloman paced below the tree, repeatedly calling me to return, but I would not leave. Indeed, only when night fell did we part. Carrying her books, I escorted her down the tree and to her house—a risk, yes, for she was the mayor's daughter and so lived on the highest platform of the town, but I wished to prolong the meeting for as much time as possible. On her doorstep, in parting I gave her a single emerald, my promise that we would meet again. Then, calling her 'Sister,' I bid her farewell and left."

His smile dimmed, tinged by sorrow. "How I wish you had not suffered such tragedy between that meeting and this one, my Sister."

A pained grief flashed across Tahira's face. "I wish I had not betrayed your confidence, and all the ethics we discussed."

His own grief mingling with his awe, Kanzeo shuffled closer to her and wrapped his arms around her shoulders.

Lucian shook his head. "Tahira, you did not betray me. Indeed, as Malika said, you have my gratitude for what you have done for us." Amusement sparked on his shining face. "I promised you that someday I would come for you. But, rather, it is you who came for me. And, as I did then, I welcome you to my family."

Eyes wide with awe, she beamed, her smile truer and brighter than any I had yet seen from her, and her shoulders relaxed as though years of pain and anguish were melting away. Drawing a similar smile from her brother.

My friends and I exchanged excited glances—since the battle, all of us had slowly begun to see her as family. His validation sweetened an already exultant moment.

"So, Malika, Elian, Kyros, we have a new sis—" Arista began.

"No," Lucian said sharply. "Not your sister, my companions. Only mine."

"What?" we exclaimed, shocked by the uncharacteristic vehemence.

"What do you mean?" Kyros added, confused.

"Inase Enarias has our names, as does her younger brother," Lucian stated, "but only I will call her Sister, should it please her."

An odd relief was visible in Tahira's eyes as she bowed her head. "There is no greater blessing." At a nudge from her, Kanzeo bowed and repeated the words.

"Excellent," Lucian said, placing aside his empty bowl. "Now, come, tell me of these strategies you have designed."

At the invitation, Tahira rose and knelt beside Darian, opposite me over the bed, and Kanzeo plopped down between Kyros and me.

On my other side, Elacir leaned his head against my shoulder, one plum wing curling around me. "Happy now, Brother? Prayers answered?"

"Yes," I replied, smiling. "The sun shines again."

And indeed, when I raised the linen covering on the window, sunlight glittered through the raindrops showering from the sky.

CHAPTER 56

ANSWER THE DOUBTLESS

Perspective: Honored Arista the Exemplar of Bravery
Date: Eyyélab, the sixteenth day of the tenth moon, Thekharre,
of the year 500, C.Q.

The rubies and emeralds glinted against the white athar of my crown. Though the jewels were the highest quality I had ever seen, clear and flawless, their colors were oddly muted, somber shades of carmine and pine.

But they shone during the battle with the Gouge... the light actually refracted rainbows onto my sword and my robes as I fought... and that was from only my crown. Lucian's were as vibrant as stars...

Lips tightened in a thin line, I stepped out of my room, my crown gripped in one hand, and knocked on Lucian's door.

No answer.

"My Honor," a quiet voice called.

I pivoted. "Yes, Tahira?"

She immediately dipped a curtsy before rising at my nod. "My Honor, our Lord asked me to inform you that he is waiting outside on the platform. Our Honors also await our Grace and you there."

Despite my kindling temper (which quite nicely dulled the edge of my heartache), I cracked a smile. "Tahira, Lucian already gave you our names. Surely you would listen to him, if not to Malika."

Though she was a full foot taller, she seemed to shrink to a height less than my own, cowering beneath my gaze. "I-I—" she stuttered.

"Please," I entreated, pouring all my compassion into my voice, "do not take these requests as chastisement for impoliteness or attempts to discomfort you. It is merely that the Quest enjoys the sound of our names on our family's lips."

Even amid her discomfiture, Tahira raised a single wry eyebrow.

"The guardians just do not listen," I said ruefully, "not even to Lucian in this matter. They seem to believe that, without the reverences, we would forget our offices. As for Prince Beres... I think they might be his version of endearments. But, then again, Lucian's caretakers can do what they please. You, on the other hand, should copy Elacir."

Tahira snorted at the jest, covered her mouth, and then finally chuckled. "My brother would do better to copy him," she muttered.

"And he is doing wonderfully well," I declared.

With Lucian's waking, Elian and Da'ana had finally relented and ended their opposition to my resumption of training. Ecstatic, I had quickly returned to my favorite duty: drilling my brothers and the soldiers. Though in the beginning of the Quest, I had helped Lucian plan, I was more than happy now to leave that work to Malika, Darian, and Tahira (all of whom had talent I could not rival in matters of strategy).

Tahira gave a quick smile, then curtsied again. "Our Lord awaits you."

I returned the smile, reached up to tousle Kanzeo's hair as he tried to creep past me, and walked outside.

Before I could resume my scowl, Lucian turned and beamed. "How beautiful you are, Arista!"

My cheek-plates vibrated at the acclaim—though he had given it all those months prior as well, when I had dressed in these formal athar robes for the market.

Elian and Kyros, regal in the same intricately embroidered clothes, added their own compliments.

Prompting more vibrations.

Malika emerged from behind me and immediately blushed as the extolments shifted to her. But, unlike such moments in the past, she was more delighted than embarrassed, having truly come into her confidence as a ruler and commander. Her disqualification from maturity was no hindrance. Indeed, she was the image of a queen—or, rather, lady, for she possessed much the same bearing as my Lady Aalia of Light did in the portrait Lucian had once shown us.

Grinning, I twined my arm with hers and whispered my own admiration. The elegant chignon beneath her crown truly suited the bold lines of her face.

"Your austere bun suits you just as much," she whispered back.

I savored her voice as I jested, "Even if it is the only style I allow?" It was a way to honor my mother's and my sisters' memories, so my friends' praise felt like recognition and love for them.

"No, because of it, Hanny," she replied, amused but sincere and earnest.

Those vibrations spread still further across my face.

Lucian quirked an eyebrow as he stepped closer to us. "Do you intend for me to crown you as well?" he asked, a kind humor shining in his beloved eyes as they touched upon the crown in my hand.

I am going to hate ruining that glow. But these questions cannot go unanswered.

Bracing myself, I said, "Lucian, there is something I must ask you."

He nodded, his smile slowly fading.

Although anger had sparked when I decided to ask these questions, now that the moment was here, only a whisper slipped from my lips: "Lucian, what are you not telling us about the magic of the Quest? And, if drops of life bind towns and cities, what bound the Quest?"

Malika, Elian, and Kyros startled. While Lucian briefly closed his eyes, pain tinting his expression.

I was about to press further when Darian exclaimed from the hut's entrance, "I have questions, too!"

Lucian dipped his head as he folded his hands over his waist. "Ask, Sisters and Brothers."

Approaching my side, Darian wrung his fingers, unusually nervous. He quailed, despite Lucian's gentle gaze, and mumbled, "In my leisure since I arrived, I have been scrutinizing your ailments... from this spring as well as after the battle..." He swallowed and fidgeted with his thumbs.

"Ask," Lucian encouraged.

Yet Darian seemed unable to continue, a child unable to confront his elder, nothing like his usual composed self.

In his stead, I spoke, "I have not spoken with Prince Darian, but I believe our questions are similar: how does the magic of the Quest work? What is its cost? And how often have you used it? If my analysis is correct, your recent illness is but an intensification of the exhaustion and lessened glow you suffered in the spring and summer."

"When you left for the Quest," Darian added quietly, shifting closer to me, "you were in better health than you were when you arrived at Arkaiso. And certainly more than in the subsequent months. The decline of your health raised the fear that..." He wetted his lips but again could not finish his sentence.

The terror that I had felt for months bubbled to the surface, and I cried, "We were afraid you were going to leave us!"

Malika, Elian, and Kyros flinched, a quiet horror filling their eyes.

For a moment, Lucian was silent—and I dreaded that he would never answer.

Please, oh Almighty... I prayed.

A grimace creased his lips, then shifted into a wan smile. "Let me first explain to you the foundation of our magic. Though I taught you enough to battle conjury, I have intentionally not fully explained it."

We jolted, shocked as though by a shard of lightning.

It was one matter to *suspect* that he had omitted certain lessons; it was quite another to hear him *actually* confirm it.

"The magic of the Quest," Lucian stated, "is like no other magic in Icilia. It is utter authority, absolute discretion, complete permission, granted with the requirement of stellar character. With it we may do whatever we wish whenever, wherever, and to whomever we please, our faith itself hymn and conviction. No magic is outside our grasp, not even the impossibilities of using wish or arms magic we do not have or transferring magic among each other. We may command great gatherings, control the very land herself, revive the dying, know in entirety the hearts of those who pledge to us—such manner of wonders. Limited only by the boundaries of the Almighty's laws and the dictates of ethics. And the cost."

"What cost?" my words fell from numb lips.

"Life," he answered.

Though I had known that, though I had myself used this magic against conjury on several occasions, I staggered backwards, tumbling onto my bottom. "Life? The energy of our souls? That life?"

My sisters and brothers fell to their knees, eyes wide and mouths agape.

Questions poured from their lips:

"Is this what you spent to save me from the curse?" Malika pleaded.

"Is that what you used to save Elacir?" Elian begged.

"Is that how you have negated residue and rebound all these months?" Kyros implored.

"Is that what you spent to kill the Gouge?" Darian demanded.

Lucian flexed his thumbs. "Yes. To all of those questions."

Silence.

We stared at him in horror.

Darian surged to his feet and gripped Lucian's collar. Lavender eyes ablaze, he screamed, "You child! You imprudent *child! That is your life!*"

Hurt, then resignation, flashed in Lucian's eyes. Though Darian's grip pulled his collar taut around his throat, he did nothing to release it.

Leaping upright, Malika, Kyros, and I seized the prince's robes and hauled him away. Elian unhooked his fingers and held them tightly.

Seething, Darian demanded, as terrifying as Lucian himself when furious, "What could possibly motivate such recklessness?"

We struggled to restrain him, though he ordinarily possessed a fraction of our combined strength and skill.

"My love for you," Lucian answered, calm despite that anguished resignation.

Darian froze. As did the rest of us.

"What do you mean?" I asked.

"I made the sacrifices I found necessary for your sakes," he said, still calm. "Without negating residue and rebound, you would not have remained safe on our journey, much less enabled to study your magic as I commanded. I saved Elacir with it because, even apart from my own care, his death would have again broken your heart, Elian. I dispelled your curse, Malika, because without it you would have lost your sanity. I defeated the Gouge in the manner that I did because he threatened your lives and the lives of all our people by brewing an explosion of conjury. On many occasions, I provided healing or added to your spells because that is what you needed. To bind the Quest, in sealing your pledges, I gave nearly all of my life several times over.

"And in every such instance, I have gladly paid the cost. You are worth all the sacrifice I can offer, my Sisters and Brothers, the Almighty's blessing upon me. There is nothing I would not do to protect you."

As he had spoken, tears welled in my eyes, both cooled by the wonder of his love and heated by the agony of his suffering. Those tears now soaked my cheeks, flowing between my plates, and drenched my collar.

My family was equally overcome. Sobs tore from Malika's throat as she flung herself into Lucian's arms, as did Kyros, while Elian wrapped his around me. Though one hand still held my crown, with the other I clutched his elbow. Darian collapsed again to his knees.

"I beg your forgiveness," Darian whispered. "Brother..."

"Yes, Brother," Lucian spoke over Malika's and Kyros' shoulders, "I would give such sacrifice for you as well. Time, distance, and power have not decreased my love and respect for you. You have committed no wrong for me to forgive."

And that buried flicker of resentment that had so often marred the prince's handsome face vanished...

"Why did you keep this secret from us!" Kyros cried.

Lucian gently drew him and Malika back from his chest. Meeting each of our gazes, he raised both brows and said, "You have so many times refused to accept the depth of my love. How many times have I told you of your value in my eyes? How many times, Darian, have I told you that our relationship has not changed? How often have you doubted my devotion?

"If I had even described the basics of the magic, you would discern most of the circumstances in which I had used it—as you did today. While you doubted me, the knowledge would have exacerbated your fears and uncertainties, forming guilt and not gratitude. You would have believed that these were sacrifices you could have borne in my place, and so believed my actions were further proof of your unworthiness—and unlike any other circumstance, proof taken from my own hands.

"By the Almighty's name, I will not allow such deepening of your torment. I would prefer your displeasure with me over your pain."

Those words provoked more tears, yet entirely cool now, unmixed with ones of sorrow. For his determination to protect us... *How often have each of us dreamed of being so well known? So well protected?*

"I do not think I could be upset with you," Elian whispered shyly, scales a sweet golden.

"I would have doubted myself exactly as you say," I murmured, plates vibrating.

"Unquestionably," Kyros agreed.

"Indeed," Malika said fervently. "But why would you risk telling us now?"

Darian coughed and muttered something that sounded like, "Only you would tell him to keep the secret longer."

Lucian chuckled, and a dazzling smile spread across his lips. "Because you have come into your own, Sisters and Brothers. All five of you, and Elacir. You accept my love."

We exchanged delighted looks, for he was correct, and threw ourselves at him in a collective embrace.

Laughing, Lucian returned the hugs.

"Wait! What about me?" Elacir demanded, landing with a thump and a thud of his wings (from the immediacy of his arrival, I wondered if he had heard Lucian's answers).

Kyros extended an arm and pulled him into our circle.

Grinning, I tilted my head back as I relished the warmth of my family...

"Lucian," Malika asked, shyly curious, "do you possess any more secrets?"

Elian's arm around my waist tensed.

"Yes," Lucian answered. "Some are about each of you: things you do not yet wish to share or do not know—matters it is not yet time to discuss. Some are about the Quest and myself, which both time and a completed study of the lore will uncover. And others... others are about the Shining Guide and Icilia that I perhaps will never share. Knowledge that is entrusted to the Quest Leader alone."

Silence.

I stated, eyes on his, "I am certain I speak for all of us when I say that we trust you entirely."

Our family exclaimed their vehement agreement.

A small, sweet smile curved Lucian's lips, and tears trickled from his eyes.

And... in that moment, he transformed from mortal incé into... something too holy to name. Such light radiated from his person, even as he stood in our arms, that he was too much to behold.

The moment flashed by too quickly to comprehend.

Then, his usual aura of power returning amid a swirl of incense, he chuckled and responded, "My gratitude for your love and loyalty."

Malika, Elian, Kyros, Darian, Elacir, and I could only stare at him, entranced by this man whom we so dearly loved but could not fully understand.

"Now," he said, revealing his white teeth in a rare grin, "Arista deserves her own coronation."

My family laughed and stepped back into a circle around Lucian and me as he gently unfolded my fingers from the crown's circlet-base.

"Kneel, Sister," he encouraged.

My plates actually buzzed as I obeyed and removed my cap. "This is not necessary," I muttered, too embarrassed to properly object.

"It is," Lucian declared, "for the hero of the battle against the Gouge."

"Your aid helped preserve Lucian's life," Malika insisted.

"Also," Kyros said firmly, "we missed even a brief celebration via communication spell on your birthday."

"And today is the anniversary of your ascension!" Elian exclaimed.

"Your second birthday!" Elacir shouted (at which Elian grimaced, for Elacir had trilled the same words all day on his own anniversary).

Though they spoke such happy words, alongside the joy existed a deep awareness in their eyes, a quiet partaking in my grief though I had eschewed every attempt to discuss it, the emotions still too raw.

How did I deserve such a considerate family, oh Almighty? I wondered as happy tears again splashed onto my plates. *After the deaths of my first...*

From what the Gouge had said, I had most likely already lost my first family, without even the chance to protect them. Lucian's family, formed by diving blessing and his favor, were all I had, my world. I would do anything to protect them. Heart, soul, life—anything. Indeed, what I had done to hold the Gouge was a paltry sacrifice.

Oh Almighty, I beg of You that strength...

As radiant as the sunlight, Lucian lowered the Quest of Light's crown onto my bowed head.

CHAPTER 57

PROMISE TO
THE HOPELESS

Perspective: Lord Lucian the Ideal of Freedom
Date: Eyyélab, the sixteenth day of the tenth moon, Thekharre,
of the year 500, C.Q.

The moment the crown touched Arista's mahogany hair,
life pulsed through me. New life, pouring into the well
of my soul, regenerating a little more of what I had spent. As
every instance of my companions' affection had prompted
since my waking.

Oh Almighty, Liege of my soul, I prayed, *how magnificent
are Your blessings. What I begged of You, on Your sacred day,
You have granted: Your favored ones are finally in harmony
with me.*

For months on end, I had spent my life without respite,
relying entirely upon my own soul's resilience to restore
what I sacrificed. My companions' doubt and uncertain
confidence impeded their attunement with me, so I was

without the support my Lady Aalia of Light had urged me to seek.

Only Nademan's insistence on sustaining my life ensured I woke before the end of the year. Yet, because she also needed to use the residue of my magic to cleanse her skies and rivers, seven weeks passed before enough of my life had replenished.

Seven weeks of restlessly listening to my family's pain while merged with Nademan's awareness. Though I learned much from her about the intricacies of the forest, the spread of roots and the growth of fruits and harvests, I had longed to return. My body was in pain, for my injuries could not heal while my life itself ebbed, but I had prayed for my return.

Seven weeks passed as the Almighty ordained before I awoke.

The moment I had awoken, I had sensed something was different: in my absence, my companions had begun to believe in themselves. They had upheld my duties and chosen those responsibilities for themselves. And so they had fully accepted my love and reached harmony with me.

No maturity mattered so much as that.

With that harmony, my life was regenerating faster than ever before. My injuries from the battle finally accepted Elian's healing, and my awareness and my dreams were restored, allowing me to resume those duties. And still greater remedy came from the knowledge that Arista was already recovered from the conjury that had been poured directly into her soul, and that the curse on Malika's voice, which had pained her so, was broken.

Amid such blessing, my heart, mind, body, and soul were in greater health than I had ever known, and the Quest's victory in Nademan was complete, save for one final act.

An act necessarily preceded by what distinction I could offer Arista, with the prayer that it might console her amid her laments.

She refused our family's every attempt at solace and every one of my own to give hope. Compliments, jests, and this gift of distinction were among the only ways we had to show that we stood with her.

How I prayed that she would confide in us.

Caressing her cheek, I bent and kissed her forehead. Then I offered my hand to her.

Arista gasped. "Lucian?"

"My support is forever yours," I answered. My version of mischief slanted my smile, and I added, "My hero." How much she deserved my veneration, having suffered so in protecting me despite what he had told her...

Plates quivering, Arista searched my eyes. Finding what she sought, she accepted my hand and took my support to rise.

Our family cheered.

"You honor me," I murmured, knowing well that she accepted no other's hand.

Every trace of misery cleared from her features as she chuckled and reached up to leave a kiss on my cheek. "I believe I should say that first."

"Perhaps, darling Sister," I replied and kissed her forehead again. Turning, I gave a smile to Taza and Da'ana, who had just reached the top rungs of the ladder.

Both guardians scanned my form, as perennially worried as I could recall my mother being, and Da'ana's fingers twitched, as though anxious to adjust my collar.

I smoothed it for her.

Satisfied, she and Taza bowed, and Taza reported, "Your troops are waiting, my Rulers, and your father has readied the crown prince."

"We follow in moments," I responded, glancing at my family. *How the Almighty has blessed me*, I thought, my heart welling with love, *in empowering their rise to the rank of purity necessary to both ask those questions and accept those answers...*

At the unspoken command in my gaze, Malika and Kyros linked arms, and Arista offered me a bow before doing the same with Elian. Darian and Elacir formed a file behind them.

"Are you sure you do not wish to come?" I said to Tahira, who watched from the hut's doorway.

She shook her head. "I do not want to unnecessarily cause trouble for you, my Lord."

"You are both my sister and my vassal, Tahira," I stated, arching a brow. "I would be happy to bear that trouble for both you and Kanzeo."

"What sort of sister would I be to ask that of you?" she replied, bold but desolate.

Appearing behind her from inside the hut, Kanzeo added, "We can listen from here."

Though I dearly wished to absolve her and include him, I knew well that such change would not come so quickly. "If that pleases you." I acknowledged their reverences with a smile.

Taza and Da'ana hurried to the next platform and whispered to the choir. Below, twined through the bases of the trees, Natrisso's folk and my soldiers fell silent and strained their gazes toward the lowest platform on the central tree—the place where the nobles addressed their neighbors.

A pair of feet scampered up the steps, and Father and Prince Eligeo joined my procession, between my companions and Darian, just as the choir began to hum the song I had used to defeat the Gouge.

May my choice please You, oh Almighty, Liege of my soul.

"Freedom by the Almighty, light of the shining sun..." began the choristers.

Remembering how those words had tasted during the battle, I chuckled quietly. Considering the significance of this ritual for Nademan, the song was *quite* appropriate, and Arista had done well to suggest its recitation.

I led the way down the ladder, following its spiral around the tree in time with the melody, descending toward that platform, my family and vassal on my heels.

As we came within view, my people cried, their voices shrill and quavering with emotion, "Praised be the Almighty! Beloved is the Shining Guide! Glorious is the Quest of Freedom!"

They mean the ceremonial words, Arista commented, pleased, in my collective link.

They truly are amazing, Elian said fondly.

The choir trilled the final lines and then fell silent as we arrived at our places: I stood near the front of the platform, my companions on either side, and the others behind us.

My lordly smile curved my lips, and my people cheered.

Catalyzing several drops of life, I asked, *Mother Nademan, if you would deign to grant my plea?*

Her grass-green form embraced me for a moment, and she bestowed the impression of a nurturing smile before accepting my magic.

A wind shook the branches, and orange and gold leaves showered the gathering.

Then the sounds of towns and cities across Nademan reached my ears. Whispers of conversations trailed into silence, and rustles of clothes stilled. Children quietened, and chickens were shushed.

My voice reverberated throughout the land as I spoke, "Praised be the Almighty, and beloved is the Shining Guide!"

Malika then announced, her voice carried also by the nation's magic, "Listen well, Nademile, for the Leader of the Quest, Lord Lucian the Ideal of Freedom, favors us with his address."

Excited squeaks and shrieks echoed before being quelled by chastising hushes.

I spoke, "People of Nademan, the Quest prays in deepest gratitude for your loyalty and allegiance. You kneeled to us when prophecy and promise were all the recommendation we had; you followed us in battle after battle when you did not yet know the worth of our command; you entrusted your homes and your children to us though your spirits were crushed by the uncertainties of the age. The Quest will not forget your faith, no matter the trials that are still to come. Your land has been my home since my birthplace was razed seventeen years prior, and you answered our call when others turned us away. Thus, we claim you as our neighbors, my people, and so will we always be.

"My neighbors, I understand that dread and mistrust plague your hearts, echoes of the agony inflicted by your last monarch. I understand that you fear the Quest's departure and the next monarch's reign, that your uncertainty casts a bleak shadow upon the future. The wretched Gouge is dead, but other monsters stalk the shadows. The Gouge was the extreme of tyranny, yes, but other sources of tyranny abound. Some of you plead for our reassurance, but many do not know how to ask. Yet, remember, my people, to your voices the Quest is always willing to listen. None are voiceless before us, least of all you.

"To these troubles, we give two answers: the Quest will reconstitute the laws of Icilia as promulgated in Nademan. The laws of the Quest of Light, the laws of our civilization, are the only laws we seek to establish, with their rewards and penalties both. However, before these laws are considered binding, we will embark on a second campaign, one of education. We seek to teach the Quests' laws to each of you and to your children so that none are asked to obey that which they do not understand. All the ruin and distortion the Gouge wrought will be erased in the dawn of an age of good rule under the Quest's auspices.

"As part of such reconstitution, we have also chosen a ruler to act in our stead after our departure. We choose Eligeo, the firstborn prince of the old royal house." I paused and waited for the gasps to subside. "The Quest understands that many dislike this man, even loathe him for the actions of his father. We understand the origin of such sentiments and do not chastise you for them. Yet, as her Grace declared after the Battle of Ehaya, we also believe Eligeo to be the right choice.

"Eligeo understands Nademan's suffering because he suffered himself, directly at the wretched Gouge's own hand. My people, all of us know what sorts of abuses the Gouge wreaked on anyone within his reach. And yet, despite broken bones, bruises, and terrible health, Eligeo chose to serve the Quest from the moment he heard my name. During the Battle of Ehaya, he collected crucial information from the Gouge's own quarters, before the enemy's servants could burn it, and brought us the warning of the Gouge's escape that allowed us to pursue the enemy in a timely manner. Instead of wasting precious moments searching, the Quest was able to depart immediately in pursuit. Such service and heroism certainly earn the Quest's pleasure, but far greater is this certainty: with our divine-blessed magic, we have judged his heart to be capable of true freedom, true dedication to the Almighty's laws. He rejects his father's sins as you do.

"So the Quest chooses and with it declares to both you and him our promise to train him, in all the arts of civilization in which we ourselves are trained. From Nademan's history to the battle-skills necessary to defend her, he will learn all that a monarch is meant to know and attain the magical maturity that all monarchs must have. Before granting his coronation, we will ensure his transformation into the image of the first king of Nademan, favored by the Quest of Light and revered even generations later by you. Thus is our promise, Nademile."

While those words still resonated with the people's hearts, I nodded to Malika, who beckoned Eligeo forward.

The prince kneeled before me, Kyros' athar robes softening the gaunt lines of his person into elegance as they swept around him, and raised his hands.

Drawing from my Lady Aalia of Light's example, I declared, "In the name of the Almighty and the Shining Guide sent unto us, I am Lord Lucian the Ideal of Freedom, rightful liege to all the rulers of Icilia. By what merit do you claim the throne of Nademan?"

Eligeo inhaled deeply, visibly steeling his resolve, and spoke, his raspy voice clear and carried by the magic, "By the Light of the Almighty and the Shining Guide sent unto us, I do not claim but beg for the right to serve my people with all the virtue, magic, and skill of which I am capable. If the throne is granted to this shameful servant, I vow to forever devote myself to understanding the weight of my actions, to know and act upon my shame when I err and to speak of gratitude when I do not. Always will I proffer respect to the Almighty, to the Quest, and to the People of Nademan. Whatever your wishes, my Liege, I will obey. Praised be the Almighty."

Nademan kissed his forehead and blew a wind through the trees, tossing leaves in graceful spirals in approval of his vow.

Well written, I praised in our collective link. *Your time with my father was fruitful.*

The prince's tawny cheeks glossed. *Does it please you?*

I answered, "For freedom by the Almighty, I accept your vow on behalf of Nademan and her people. I grant your plea for the Throne of Conscience, upon the condition of your achievement of magical maturity. Pledge your loyalty, Crown Prince Eligeo tej-Shehennadem."

Joy brightened Eligeo's gaunt face before he composed himself and pledged loyalty in the words of a citizen, the ruler's pledge pending for his coronation.

Catalyzing life, I sealed the connection. Then I invoked Elian's and Kyros' sacred bonds to me, tapped the bonds they had made with their own magic, and confirmed them with the magic of the Quest. Light flashed in towns across Nademan as it did around Eligeo's hands and mine. More life welled within my soul, ignited by my companions' presence.

At a nod from me, Malika held out a thin gold circlet on a velvet cushion. I lifted it so that the sunlight gleamed on the surface of its five jewels, each a different shade of grass green jade, and then lowered it over Eligeo's cap onto his head. The heir's circlet sparkled amid his golden-blond curls.

"Rise," I commanded, and the prince stood with Kyros' support. Immediately he dipped another bow to me, and I proclaimed, "People of Nademan! Hail your future king!"

Silence.

Far away in Ehaya, Ciro shouted his jubilation. So did the staff in Arkaiso. Ten feet below, her eyes on mine, Mayor Evalarias of Natrisso exclaimed, "Long live the Quest of Freedom! Long live the Crown Prince!"

Nademan relayed those words and sounds to every part of her domain.

Silence.

Mayors in other towns repeated the cheers.

And slowly the tribute spread, until the people of Nademan hailed us with near perfect unity.

They actually celebrate... Eligeo whispered in wonder.

Genuinely, Kyros assured him, before adding, *though that does not mean there will not be any future challenges.*

Tears dropped from Eligeo's eyes to the floor of the platform. *Even this much is enough...*

I clasped his shoulder, lifting him from his reverence. *You asked me yesterday why I would choose you if I anticipated so much future struggle. Those words are why.*

You will not regret this, my Lord, he whispered.

I will not, I agreed and raised my hand for silence.

The nation quieted.

I spoke, "People of Nademan, know that the Quest will never abandon you, even as we travel to other nations in the coming months. We will always listen to your pleas, day or night, in war or in peace. We will always answer, for we know each of your names and care for each of your hearts. You will never be unheeded in our court.

"Receive, then, with the certainty of faith the Quest's guarantee of freedom, our promise of a nation whose laws will nurture the virtue of your soul so that you may one day know eternal prosperity. May the Almighty fulfill our pledge. Praised be the Almighty."

My words reverberated across Nademan...

Then seven thousand voices bellowed, "For the Lord of Freedom! Hail the Crown Prince!"

As those cries rippled across the land, the people fell to their knees. A wave of energy reached me, thrumming through the soles of my boots up my person to my crown.

Sunlight reached from the sky to the forest floor, beams of white-gold sheathing whole towns and cities in warm embraces.

My companions, my family, and my vassal knelt, faces bright with wonder. Trilling her joy in the songs of birds, Nademan swept her reverence.

Thousands of hearts beat in time with mine.

I laughed, voice soaring in the musical tolling of bells, and declared, "So we stand together once more as one, in the Almighty's blessing." Then I, too, knelt, toward Mount Atharras.

And across the land, the bells tolled in the celebration of the second Quest.

SEGMENT 6

DEATH-KNELL

Perspective: The Blood-soaked Sorcerer
Date: Eyyélab, the sixteenth day of the tenth moon, Thekharre,
of the year 500, C.Q.

The Blood-soaked Sorcerer laughed so heartily he began to cough. "What- what kind of non-nonsense is that?" he gasped. "The Quest Leader is dead!"

The messenger squirmed but did not dare move his gaze from the Blood's feet. "Your Viciousness, the reports were clear."

The black laughter stopped abruptly. "You dare contradict me?"

"N-no," the man said, barely keeping his voice even, "of course not, your Viciousness."

The Blood raised a sharp brow. "Hmm, no, I think you did." He casually withdrew a dagger from his belt. "I think you also delivered a false report. There is no Quest Leader—I killed or enslaved every last one of the heirs of Asfiya and matched the bodies with their *records* and *portraits*."

The Blood spat out the references to those ridiculous civilized arts, then continued in his nonchalant tone, "This supposed Quest Leader is an upstart rebel, pathetic and weak, and clearly Gouge failed to keep his territory out of his own weakness. He always *was* weak, placing too much trust in that—" he sneered a foul term for a woman. Then thrust lethally sharp nails beneath the messenger's chin and ripped the man's head from his neck, the dagger gleaming unbloodied in his other hand.

The surrounding guards flinched.

Chuckling, the Blood tossed the head over his shoulder and turned to his latest captive. "Gouge always had a thing for that woman. So blinded was he by his obsession that he probably didn't notice when she tricked him and helped this rebel. With a tumble or two under the sheets as her price. Don't you think so, little flower?"

The woman whimpered, fear pouring off her unclothed form in waves.

The Blood relished that chaos as he mused aloud, "The greater problem is the escape of that Zahacit princess... the second princess to escape my clutches, like that one of Koroma. Though, really, it's unlikely to ever be free, just like that Koromic one—who still hasn't realized that I know exactly where it is." He laughed cruelly. "Women are so fragile, so weak, particularly these law-restrained princesses... wouldn't you agree, little flower? You're certainly not one to be restrained, are you?"

Only sobs in answer.

"Though you know what became of its family, don't you?" the Blood whispered, drawing near to his prize. "Don't you know what happened, little princess of Zahacim?"

The woman, who had arrived as docilely as his best slaves, struggled to escape her bindings.

The Blood laughed and had his fill of rape. Slicing her throat, he drenched his armor in the red liquid and engaged in yet more violence.

When little remained of the corpse, he lit the last bits on fire.

His guards scrambled to quench the blaze.

Leaving them to handle it, the Blood strode to the head of his army.

All thirty-five companies shrank away from him and the thick coppery fragrance that wreathed his form.

Savoring their fear, the Blood surveyed the vast expanse of soldiers, enough to blacken the plains of southern Koroma—thousands. Yet not enough.

No matter, he thought. *Clawed, Choker, and Slicer will give me more. None of them want to go the way of Gouge. And Manic is getting more ready. Even if I can't recover Gouge's bit, it should be ready by the time I arrive.*

Satisfied, he turned northwest, towards Asfiya.

His lipless mouth peeled back in a sneer as malevolence gleamed in the eyes that were the abyss itself. Blood-soaked fingers dipped into a pocket and withdrew a tiny red fruit.

A gruesome smile spread across his blood-stained maw, cruelty without mercy.

Seven months. Seven months and five thousand miles until my empire is endless. Free of law. Eternal unrestrained pleasure. The Quest too broken to ever rise again.

The Blood laughed in the voice that was the death-knell of his enemies and crushed the athar tear.

PRONUNCIATION SUPPORT

This guide is for selected names.

THE QUESTS

Aalia—Aaah-lee-ah

Manara—Muh-naa-ruh

Naret—Naa-ret

Lucian—Loo-see-uhn

Malika—Maa-lih-kah

Elian—Eh-lee-uhn

Arista—Uh-ris-tuh ('ris' rhymes with miss)

Kyros—Kai-ros ('Kai' has the same sound as the 'i' in fine; 'ros' has the same sound as 'most' without the 't')

Izzetís—Izz-eh-tees ('Iz' rhymes with fizz, 'tees' is said with extra emphasis) [Elian's former surname]

FAMILY, GUARDIANS, AND VASSALS
(IN ORDER OF APPEARANCE)

Kalyca—Kah-lih-kah ('Ka' has the same sound as 'cast')

Beres—Beh-rez

Darian—Deh-ree-uhn

Elacir—Eh-laa-seer ('seer' has the same sound as 'seer')

Taza Palanéze—Taa-zuh Pah-luh-neh-zehs ('neh' is said with extra emphasis)

Ilqan—Il-qaan ('Il' rhymes with 'fill')

Ciro Tolmarie—Cee-roh Toll-maa-ree

Belona Tolmariat—Beh-loh-nah Toll-maa-ree-uht

Tahira Enarias—Tuh-hee-rah Eh-naa-ree-uhs

Kanzeo Enaries—Kan-zee-oh Eh-naa-ree-uhs ('Kan' rhymes with 'can')

Eligeo tej-Shehenkorom—Eh-lee-hee-oh tehj-Sheh-hen-nah-dem

THE WORLD (IN ROUGH ORDER OF APPEARANCE)

Athar—ut-hur ('ut' has the same sound as 'but', 'hur' sounds similar to 'her')

Icilia—Ih-sill-lee-ah ('sill' has the same sound as sill)

Koroma—Koh-roh-mah

Samaha—Suh-mah-hah

Zahacim—Zah-haa-sim

Rushada—Roo-shah-dah

Bhalasa—Bhuh-lah-sah

Etheqa—Eh-theh-kah

Khuduren—Khoo-doo-rehn

Asfiya—As-fee-yah ('As' rhymes with 'mass')

Azsefer—Az-seh-fer ('Az' rhymes with the last syllable in 'topaz', 'fer' sounds similar to 'fur')

Nademan—Naa-deh-muhn (the accent is on 'deh')

NADEMAN'S PROVINCES AND CITIES, WEST TO EAST

Adeban—Ah-deh-baan

Zaiqan—Zai-kaan ('Zai' has the same sound as the 'i' in fine)

Arkaiso—Ar-kai-soh ('Ar' has the same sound as 'are', 'kai' has the same sound as the 'i' in fine)

Pethama—Peh-thah-muh (the accent is on 'thah')

Gairan—Gai-raan ('Gai' has the same sound as the 'i' in fine)

Ehaya—Eh-haa-yuh

Makiran—Maa-kih-raan

Tadama—Tuh-dah-muh (the accent is on 'dah')

Buzuran—Boo-zoo-raan

Nadeya—Naa-deh-yah [the address for Nademani women; equivalent to Miss or Misses]

Nadeyi—Naa-deh-yee [the address for Nademani men; equivalent to Mister]

THE GLOSSARY OF
THE SACRED TONGUE

CHAPTER 7:
Honored Arista the Exemplar of Bravery:

> Sholit ai sholeh, ashoneret é enerel, sholorim, shosholi-
> torim, shosholehrim! Treperim zidilëm!

> Fire and flame, flicker of energy, burn, blaze, flare!
> Distract my enemies!

CHAPTER 17:
Honored Arista the Exemplar of Bravery:

> Pisterim.

> Shield. (command to turn athar cloth robes into armor)

CHAPTER 38:

Honored Elian the Exemplar of Esteem:

> Simit pe saneru u'wurqet ai teku u'nabtet, taz simirim zidilëm, kaferim ó saneh Dalaanem-ik.

> Wind that rustles leaves and bends trees, blow away my enemies, toss them to my Lord's mercy.

CHAPTER 42:

Lord Lucian the Ideal of Freedom:

> *Hayàsimimas hayye ó rohilele, e'Kairie, ru a'hayàsimeh en zatelem.*

> *Breathe life to their souls, Oh Liege, through the breath in my person.*

CHAPTER 43:

Honored Arista the Exemplar of Bravery:

> Sholit ai sholeh, ashoneret é enerel, nazneremas sasholeh ó sasholeh, i'silih wes abile ai nazhanlile.

> Fire and flame, flicker of energy, let warmth attract warmth, a bond between children and cousins.

CHAPTER 44:
Prince Beres sej-sehasfiyi, father of the Quest Leader and auxiliary heir to the throne of Asfiya:

> Hayàretet ai saretet, ramireh é silérohile, chilerim an lanerelum.

> Soil and clay, foundation of nations, loosen from your repose.

Honored Elian the Exemplar of Esteem:

> Simit pe saneru u'wurqet ai teku u'nabtet, sasirenerrim a'hayàretet, sanerrim a'saretet, zulàsimirim a'simih sir zidilëm.

> Wind that rustles leaves and bends trees, stir the soil, muss the clay, mist the air around my enemies.

CHAPTER 49:
Honored Kyros the Exemplar of Strength:

> Alaëh alasir ai hasnir, daileh é a'ezahram, pisterim u'onem!

> Light bright and true, symbol of the holy, shield me!

CHAPTER 50:

Honored Elian the Exemplar of Esteem:

> Hayàsimile é a'hayitos, sasholos ne zazatet, enisi-
> mirim ai unisimirim, kasirenerrim zulluh kasholir
> ai akasholir.

> Breath of the living, warmed by flesh, whirl and twirl,
> churn water hot and boiling.

Honored Elian the Exemplar of Esteem:

> Kazaqer lamile ai akakaser hadile, damile unuzuler ai
> lananareh ider, paresilerim, pariderim, parobanerim,
> parejiderim, pareneru be ore anemizu kanne.

> Mangled flesh and shattered bone, blood spilled and
> chaos formed, rejoin, reform, remake, renew, refreshed
> as you were meant to be.

CHAPTER 51:

Safiri Eloman ben-Hassem Birretís, guardian of the
Quest Leader:

> Alarim.

> Light. (command)

CHAPTER 52:

Lord Lucian the Ideal of Freedom:

E'Qahre, Aläm avolemasu ru em.

Oh Almighty, let your Light be revealed through me.

Lord Lucian the Ideal of Freedom:

E'Qahre, hayyëm dinimas u'shifos.

Oh Almighty, let my life give healing.

CHAPTER 53:

Honored Elian the Exemplar of Esteem:

Patile qatos ne sableh, sireneros latabeseru, zukrerim
ke ore radu chanemizu, parenalerim idiesere, dinimas
ó Fidaanem u'qalit taseru.

Muscles ruined by magic, twisted unnaturally, remember what you have lost, regain your shape, allow my
Grace speech fully.

ACKNOWLEDGMENTS

At the fulfillment of the first volume of a'Silómizze é a'Raah-é-Fazze, the Archivist proffers gratitude to the Almighty, to the Lady of Icilia, and to the Guardian of Names for the blessing of this chance to behold the glory of the Quest of Freedom. May the Lord of Freedom be pleased with this praise of his name.

***

My first and greatest thanks are to the Almighty, Who is the true Source of my muse. Faith and prayer are what have created *The Bell Tolling*, from its initial conception to its final revisions, and are what have ensured writing this story was entirely a transformative experience. Thus, I proffer all my gratitude to the Almighty and, under divine auspice, the Lord who transforms dust into gold.

My second offering of gratitude is to the Prince of my community, who has supported my endeavors at every footstep. I have no less appreciation for my mother and my father, who spend uncounted hours discussing characters, plot, and setting on numerous occasions and give all sorts of ideas for the theoretical underpinnings of my story.

Third is my praise for Lee Contreras, who designed *The Bell Tolling*'s beautiful cover (from the clouds to the character image), and for Mustafa Pishori, who drew the intricate frame that adorns the edges along with his friend, Murtaza Shakir. No less is my sense of indebtedness to my grandfather, whose kindness is reflected in Elian's face.

Fourth is my tribute to my friends—Lee, Keenan, Elisa, Patrick, Dr. Post, Mrs. Battles, Mary R., Misaki, Hussaina, Mary B., Jasmine, Lydia, and C'Sherica—who helped me develop various elements of my story and writing through their thoughtful answers and eager interest.

Fifth is the depth of my regard to the University of Dallas and her professors and students, who, throughout my five years there and in every interaction thereafter, deepen my understanding of the Divine, ethics, politics, and human nature as a whole.

Sixth comes my credit to the Creators Institute and New Degree Press—particularly Professor Koester, Lyn S., Brian B., Leila S., Michael B., Emma C., Mozelle J., Amanda B., Debra C., Zoran M., Kristy C., Sherman M., Gjorgji P., Bojana G., Nikola T., and Mila G., as well as the author community there—for aid and support on this journey toward the publication of my first book.

Seventh is my appreciation for all of the backers of my IndieGoGo fundraising campaign (ordered as in my 'Thank you' posts on social media):

My mother, Lee Contreras, Rashida Rasheed, Bob Sheaks, Shabbir Hamid, Mr. Cody Dollar, Prof. Eric Koester, Malia Mason, Dr. Abbas Asgharali, Huzaifa Lakkadshah, Ella

Sullivan, my aunt Fatema Turabi, my great-aunt Sakina
Bengali, my uncle Ebrahim Bengali, Mohammed Khurrum,
Abdeali Khurrum, Ruqaiyah Palanpurwala, Mansur Bharmal,
James Mobus, Celeste Gomez, Amena Hussain, Madeleine
Snow, Tasneem Sardharwala, Hatim Patanwala, Rizwana
Hussain, Elizabeth Naughton, Andrew JP Babb, my aunt
Waheeda Qaiyumi, my uncle Mustafa Biviji, my uncle Hozefa
Dhruv, my uncle Yahya Attari, my cousin Insiyah Attari,
my cousins Nooresha & Shayan Vasi, Joseph Scholz, Miss
Stephanie Strike, Farida Shipchandler, Odalys Vargas, Maria
Vargas, Dr. Farida Ali, Mrs. Dawn Bizzell, Maria Akbari, Mr.
Carey Christenberry, Khozaim Khairullah, Juan Ramos, my
cousin Arwa Hasan-Debusschere, Manzoor Mir, Ammar
Gangardiwala, Quresh Tyebji, John Newman, Kauser Ayaz,
my uncle Shabbir & my aunt Lubaina Kapadia, my great-aunt
Fatema Dhruv, my cousin Sameera Rangwala, my cousin
Mufaddal Amin, my aunt Tasneem Bengali (Aurangabadi),
Ramoj Paruchuri, Munira Adenwalla, Jennifer Smith, Siv-
aguru Selvam, Hasanain Rangwalla, Husseina Sulemanji,
fellow NDP author Maxine Smith, Mustafa Hamid, Zainab
Hussain, Fawzia Safdari, Sabhiya Javed, C'Sherica Shaw,
Tasneem Gangardiwala, Abdul Munis, Srini Reddy, Hima-
bindu Moram, Sakina Ismaelbay-Asgerally, Dr. Tasneem
Dohadwala, my cousin Dr. Mariyum Shakir, Mukerram
Hakimuddin, Kaizer Taherali, Alefia Tapia, Shinesa Cambric,
Munir Esmail, Marya Kapadvanjwala, Ted Morin, Meeta
Bhat, Patrick Callahan, Shanthi Patel, Durriya Dawoodbhoy,
Rukaiya Jamali, Michael Fazi, Ruby Elbazri, Nanda Kishore,
Carol Pieri, Rizanne Luis, Dr. Charles South, Mrs. Jenni-
fer Duggins, Liane Barretto, Mariam Macatangay, Santhi
Jayaraman, McKenna Yeakey, Bilqies Ali, Dustin Mayfield,
LTC Terrance Wallace (ret.), LTC Vincent Freeman, Jr. (ret.),

Felicity Samaniego, Mary Reid, Olawale Salaudeen, Insiyah Lokhandwala, Rechelle Villareal, Mufaddal Abbas, Mustafa A. Biviji, Dr. Sakina Poonawala, Fatema Zakir Hussain, Drs. Asgar & Munira Dudhbhai (2), Zahra Adamji, Sakina Jamali, Johratulmajd M., my aunt Sajida Qayumi, my cousin Dr. Aziz Kothawala, my cousins Mohammed & Zainab Manasawala, my aunt Shehrbano Hussain, Mufaddal Sodawater, Mohammed Taskeen, Farida Bandukwala, Fatema & Aliasger Kapasi, Abbas Kurawarwala, Behlul Poonawalla, Fakhruddin Nagarwala, Insiyah Bharmal, Shabbir Degani, Samina Sohel Sabir, Lorraine Mascarenhas, Mustafa Pachisa, Murtaza & Fatema Daruger, K Rangwala, Hussain Malji, Akeel Halai, Yusuf & Zahabiya Unwala, Khalil Alsabag, LadyKevviona Howard, Maryam V., my cousin Aliakber Turabi, Mustali M., Quresh Badri, Muneera Patherya, Hozefa Burhani, Vivi Hoang, Tasneem Shaikh, Umaima Koita, Tahera Ezzi, Salma Mushir, Dr. Jonathan Sanford, Edith Pawlicki, Mufaddal Hussain, Sakina Dalal, Ameer Gomberawalla, Jumana Moosajee, Naahid Kajiji, Huzeifa Rajabali, Gina LaRosa, Dilawer Abbas, Hatim Poonawalla, Zoher Bharmal, Misaki Collins, Elijah Montes, fellow NDP author Nifemi Aluko, Zahra Lokhandwala, Hunaiza Lookmanjee, Huzefa Taher, Ummal B Mahuwala, Fakhruddin Sabir, Saif Arif, Mariam Mogri, Munawar Bootwalla, Shaukat Goderya, Mrs. Janice Battles, Benedict Parks, Keenan Flynn, Fatema Vohra, Farida Iqbal, Taiyebali Zakir, Noshir Chinwalla, Huzefa Khairullah, Taizoon Khokhar, Zainab Anaswala, Zeenat Kheraluwala, Mustafa Sunelwala, my cousin Sameena Sabir, my cousin Abrar Kothawala, Shabbir & Mubaraka Saifee, Daniel LaBarre, Mohammed Mogri, Ali Hazari, Rehana Arastu, Mustansir Shafiq, world-impressions, Sunil Singhal, Munira Hussain, Khuzema Arsiwala, Huzaifa Arsiwala, Maimoon Sales, Sakina

U21, Dr. Matthew Post, Dr. Rob H, Francis Cavanna, Joseph Trujillo Falcón, Dominic Del Curto, Dominique West, David Savitsky, Husaina Rangoonwala, Landon Collins, Rasheeda Jafferji, Tasneem Nurbhai, Ummeaiman Doctor, Estela Delgado, Mansi Thakar, and Abdulla & Tasneem Kagalwalla.

Eighth is my recognition for all my followers on social media, who have done much to bolster my confidence in the public success of my writing endeavors.

If I have forgotten a name in these lists, I ask that you forgive me. My thanks remain true, regardless of mention.

Ninth, I thank you, dear reader, for deigning to peruse this book. I pray that this story meant something to you, that you gained both adventure and inspiration from the writing, and that you felt hope sparking in your heart as you witnessed the rise of the Quest. May that hope help shield you amid these difficult times.

Lastly, I voice my gratitude for the Quest of Freedom, who have been my pillar since the day they revealed themselves. A story is nothing without its characters, and this story most of all, for it is they who suffered and strove in order to show us the freedom that can come from nothing more than faith, love, and determination. Thus, in many ways, it is for Lucian, Malika, Elian, Arista, and Kyros that this book was written. May the second Quest be pleased with the praise of their name.

And above all, may the Almighty bless all of us.

Made in the USA
Las Vegas, NV
08 January 2022

40778825R00376